Alive and Wells

WELLS RANCH SERIES BOOK 1

BAILEY HANNAH

Print ISBN 978-1-7381076-0-5

eBook ISBN 978-1-7381076-1-2

For the city girls in their cowboy romance era. And for the country girls who know a fictional cowboy is always better than the real thing.

Author's Note

This story is set on a working cattle ranch, and that's not something I wanted to shy away from. Because of that, there is mention of slaughter and castration, as well as on-page calf branding. Ranchers do these things with good reason, and it's never intended to be cruel (nor did I set out to write it as such—my cattle ranching family would *not* be happy if I did).

Wells Ranch uses hot branding, which is a traditional way of marking/identifying livestock. In some areas of the world, freeze-branding has become the more popular approach. And, in other places, neither is considered humane. Hot/fire branding is typically done with a steel branding iron that's heated by a wood or propane heat source. It burns a brand into the hair follicles, preventing future hair growth. With freeze branding, the cold iron kills the colour follicles, causing them to turn white permanently. Both methods have pros and cons.

Though Wells Ranch is fictional, it's based on real cattle ranches in British Columbia. Hot branding is still the most common method here, so it felt like the more appropriate choice for the story.

If you ever attend a day of branding, don't eat the Rocky Mountain Oysters.

This book ends with a pregnancy announcement – if that's not your jam, feel free to skip the bonus epilogue & know that you aren't missing anything <3 Taking care of yourself is more important.

Content/Trigger Warnings:

- Domestic violence - mental, emotional, and physical (on page)

- Gun (present but not used)

- Physical violence (on page)

- Death of a parent due to cancer (discussed, not shown)

- Death of a grandparent (discussed, not shown)

- Troubled parent-child relationships (discussed, not shown)

- Alcohol consumption

- Pregnancy (side-character)

- Ranching activities - roping, branding, castration, vaccination (on page), animal slaughter (discussed, not shown)

- Explicit sex scenes including spit play, cockwarming (mild), praise

Welcome to Wells Ranch!

1

Cecily

I've spent the better half of the day listing all the ways I could kill him on the back of my grocery receipt. Now, glancing up from the tiny scrawlings to the microwave clock, I light a match and burn the evidence. Perfectly on cue, KJ's headlights beam through the small window over the kitchen sink. I rush to wash charcoal dust down the drain.

"How was work?" My fake smile comes naturally when he walks through the door.

Practice makes perfect.

"Let's just say I'm glad to be home." He plants a rough kiss on my forehead, and I'm pulled into an unpleasant embrace. I suck in the strong cologne as my cheek smashes against his chest, every muscle in my body rigid in his arms. He sniffs the air and I pray the vanilla bean candle's enough to cover up the smoke.

Clearly not noticing anything off, he focuses instead on the brown paper bags from his favourite restaurant. "You're so good to me, babe. Seriously, how did I get this lucky?"

It's the same song and dance. His pathetic attempt at grovelling because we argued before he left for work this morning. Rather, he yelled, and I stood like a statue until he gave up. A similar pose to the one I'm in now, clutching the marble countertop, waiting for an inevitable critique of something. My appearance, the dinner order, the state of the house... there's *always* something.

KJ waltzes toward the restaurant containers and lifts a lid to peek inside at the hundred-dollar sushi order. It's not even the best sushi restaurant in town—he likes it because it's the most expensive.

Running a hand through his short, black hair, he turns to me. "You must've been really busy today if you couldn't even cook." *There's the comment.* "Pour yourself some wine and sit down, babe. I'll dish us up."

After a brief hesitation, and no further comments from my husband, I open the cupboard. My perpetually shaky fingers wrap around a teal mug. Not the classiest way to drink a two-hundred-dollar bottle of wine, but my last wine glass shattered against the dining room wall on Sunday. Nerve endings buzzing with the memory, I fill the mug and tiptoe out of the room. The moment I enter the dining room, I'm drawn to the burgundy stain splashed across the greige wall above the table. Noticeable scrub marks linger where I spent an hour crying and cleaning.

I'll have to swing by the hardware store for some more paint before our Friday night dinner plans with our friends, Sara and Mike. God forbid anybody asks why our dining room now has a port-wine stain feature wall.

"Fuck!" His booming voice reverberates through the walls, and I swear the house shudders as hard as I do. My breathing falters in the slow seconds that tick between his shout and my mouth opening.

"Are y-you okay?" It comes out meek and screechy.

"I fucking cut myself. Get the first aid kit."

Springing to action, I hurry past the kitchen and down the hallway to our ensuite bathroom. Once there, I leisurely poke around in the medicine cabinet. Rearranging pill bottles and making a mental list of what needs restocking. Pretending I don't know where the bandages are. Staring right at them.

What a tragic accident it would be if he bled out.

"Cecily!" he screams. "What the *fuck* is taking you so long?"

I finally grab the box and stroll back to the kitchen to find his woeful face waiting for me. He holds his hand outstretched, a pained expression furrowing his brows. It's the tiniest slice in his flesh; no deeper than a paper cut.

Good god.

So much for hoping I'd find him missing a finger or two. He probably cut himself on a plastic take out lid or something equally stupid.

"Sorry, I couldn't,"—I fidget with the wrapper, and gently place the bandage over the minor cut—"find the bandages. But, there, you're good as new. What happened?"

"Why are our chopsticks in the same drawer as the kitchen knives? We have a big enough fucking kitchen. I shouldn't have to stick my hand in a knife drawer for motherfucking chopsticks," he snarls before storming away.

I stare down at the opened drawer—specifically, at the large, freshly sharpened chef knife—then at his back.

Better not—too much cleanup.

Taking my place back at the dining table, the burned receipt list consumes my every thought and the weight of a potential first-degree murder charge diminishes my appetite. I lazily push a piece of ginger around. Half-listening to him complain about how hard it is to be CFO at his father's company. Despite how apathetic I feel, I must nod, *hrmm*, and gasp in all the right spots. Dinner goes off without a hitch. After three years, I suppose I'm finally learning how to keep the peace.

"Great dinner, babe." Dropping his napkin on his empty plate, he pushes away from the table.

Once the TV surround sound blares from the next room, I take a relieved breath. It's the beginning of the end—another day nearing completion. In trained silence, I clear the table and, for the next hour, take my time cleaning the already spotless kitchen. With any luck, he'll be asleep on the couch by the time I'm finished.

With any luck.

The drop in his respiration signalling sleep is one of my favourite sounds, second only to his car tires leaving our driveway each morning. Confident he's out for the night, I slip from under the covers, unplug my cell phone, and pad to the bathroom. Sinking to the cold tile floor, I text one of two phone numbers I've committed to memory—adding it to a proper contact profile simply isn't an option. For weeks, I kept it taped to the underside of the bathroom counter, and faced agonizing fear each time KJ bent to grab something from the lower drawers.

Cecily: Is that job still available?

Time ticks on, and I wonder if I waited too long. It's nearly one in the morning, after all. KJ found *John Wick* on cable, which ruined my routine. Rather than falling asleep before the nine o'clock news, he drank four whiskey neats and stayed awake until midnight. When I half-heartedly suggested he get some sleep, he accused me of trying to force him to bed so I could sneak around behind his back. *Like a whore.*

He's not entirely wrong. For six months, I've been secretly talking to a woman named Beryl. We met on a forum I definitely shouldn't be on. I can't bear to imagine what might happen if KJ ever finds out. A support group for women in abusive relationships; I honestly don't belong there, though.

KJ doesn't hit me like the spouses of the women in that group do. He calls me names when he's angry, but he doesn't hit me. He screams in my face, but he doesn't hit me. He smashes wine glasses, plates, and the drywall directly next to my head, but he doesn't hit me. And maybe he's threatened it a few times or grabbed me with enough force to leave a mark, but he still hasn't *actually* hit me.

I've been daydreaming about murdering my husband for days—surely that makes me the violent one. Right?

(555) 276-9899: It's yours whenever you're ready, honey.
Cecily: OK. Thanks.
(555) 276-9899: Are you ready?
Cecily: I mean, I was planning how I'd kill him today. I should probably leave, shouldn't I?
(555) 276-9899: You say the word and you'll have help. You're a strong woman and you can do this, Cecily.

Heavy footsteps move toward the bathroom, and my fingers tap hard on the screen. *Delete, delete, fucking delete.* The text thread disappears in an instant, without a moment to spare. As the doorknob turns, I silently pray Beryl doesn't text me again. She doesn't message unless I've reached out first but, given we're in the middle of a conversation, I can't be certain she won't send another reply.

With any luck.

"The fuck are you doing?" KJ blinks rapidly, adjusting to the bright bathroom lights.

"Period cramps. I couldn't sleep." I clutch my stomach for believability. We rarely have sex, and he's definitely not interested in my bathroom habits. Despite being married, I doubt he has any idea when my cycle should be. Hell, I have an IUD and can't remember the last time I had a real period, but he doesn't even know I'm on birth control.

His dark eyes cut to the phone sitting on the tile next to me. In a flash, he moves to grab it. "Oh yeah? So the fuck is your phone doing here with you? I knew you'd been sneaking around behind my back. Do you think I'm a moron or are you such a whore you don't care about getting caught? In *my fucking house*, too!" His words cover my face in spit as he crouches down, clenching my phone tight in his fist.

I struggle to breathe, waiting for his next move. His eyes bore into me from mere inches away. Pupils blown out with rage. Hot, stale whiskey breath hits me as he grows impatient, waiting for an answer. I have no idea how to respond. It doesn't seem wise to say, *"I'm leaving before I end up murdering you in your sleep."* Telling him I've been cheating might actually go over better than the truth. Maybe then he'd throw me out.

My bottom lip trembles out of control, and he grins maniacally at my fear.

"Nothing to say then? Nothing to say because it's fucking true," he scoffs. The phone screen fractures as his fingers tighten, sending out spiderwebbing cracks at every angle. "Good luck talking to your boyfriend now, whore."

I wince. It's not the first time he's broken my phone. He'll have a brand new one delivered to the house tomorrow, likely alongside another nice apology gift. It's just a shame because, for the first time in a long time, I thought I might actually leave. Or, at least, I thought I would try. Not that my attempts have worked in the past.

Without the ability to contact Beryl, I have no way of getting directions to where she lives. Like it or not, I'm imprisoned for at least another twenty-four hours.

His face draws even closer. Close enough to kiss—not that we would. In fact, the thought of his lips on mine makes me want to vomit directly into his mouth. "Say something, *bitch*."

I scramble on the slick tile, trying to get to my feet. Desperate to put some distance between us. As much as he's trying to get me to defend myself, I know it's stupid to open my mouth. It's asking for a fight, and I don't want to fight with him tonight. Not when we were having a good night. *Good-ish*, anyway.

A sharp pain radiates from my shoulder as his open palm blows against it, knocking me from my squatted position flat onto my ass.

Did he just? I think he just hit me.

No, that's not fair. It was a light push, if anything.

A second blow confirms my fear.

He hit me. He finally did it—he hit me.

He screams directly into my gaping mouth, "Say something!"

I can't help the tears welling. Even though I despise how weak their presence makes me feel.

"I'm done," I whisper. It's a small miracle I'm able to hear myself over the raucous ringing in my skull.

I *am* done. I need to get out.

"What's that now?"

"Nothing. Sorry." I shake my head violently. It was a stupid, *stupid* thing to say. Apparently, I haven't learned quite enough over the last three years to fully keep the peace.

"You're done? After everything I've done for you? This house, the car, all your fancy shit—ungrateful bitch," he snarls. "*Fine.* Go. You don't think I can't get another girl like you? Fuckin' prettier, probably. If you think you can find better, be my fucking guest. You'll be back—you've always been a gold-digging whore. Other guys are going to see right through you, babe."

To my surprise, he stands and sulks out of the bathroom. The door slams, followed by what sounds like the closet door being ripped from the frame. I stare ahead, trying to find the strength to get up and lock him out. But my body may as well be glued to the cold, hard ground. Glass shatters and I'm melting into the floor.

This. This is why I should've kept my mouth shut. Then the room becomes silent. Too silent. After a few minutes, I work up the nerve to peel myself from the floor, and crack open the bathroom door.

KJ's sitting in the middle of what looks to be a tornado disaster zone. A horrific tornado with pretty eyes and a terrifyingly wicked heart. The closet door hangs lopsided, my dresser drawers lie in a heap on the ground, and water trickles down the wall above the bed from where I assume he threw my bedtime glass. And he's crying. Not plain crying—full-on sobbing. Heaving.

I move quickly and silently, filling a duffle bag and laundry basket with clothes scooped from the plush carpet. Ignoring his wails. I've tried to leave multiple times, and he's never let me get this far. Usually, he's barricading us in the room, ripping my clothes from my hands, and keeping a firm grip on my wrists until I agree to stay.

This isn't how I was supposed to leave. I was supposed to plot every-thing out meticulously. I've watched countless girls share their plans on the forum, and I know the drill: have a go-bag packed, siphon money from our joint account, and have somewhere to go. At least I have a place to go and a job lined up. I just have no fucking idea how to get there.

He hit me. Three small words repeat like a mantra, driving me forward despite the pit in my stomach over how unprepared I am to leave.

Everything's too easy as I float down the staircase and out the front door. The driveway's dark and, for once, I'm grateful that my crappy Honda Civic doesn't "deserve" a spot in the garage. One less obstacle in my way. The laundry basket in my arms plunks onto the car's silver hood.

This is easy. I can do this. Piece of cake.

I'm sifting through my oversized purse, searching for keys, when I hear his heavy, ragged breathing behind me.

"Touch that fucking car door. I swear to God, I will kill you."

For some reason, I'm compelled to look at him, and I nearly collapse when I do. I wasn't aware he owned a gun. How long has there been a fucking gun in our house?

My heart stops as I watch the man I once thought I loved...

Pointing a gun at me.

Rage-filled eyes, corded neck, and he's not even shaking. All the emo-tion he had moments ago in the bedroom is gone. Replaced by the face of a cold psychopath with nothing to lose.

Has he been planning on killing me like I've been planning on killing him?

"Kyson. Please, don't do this. Don't do something you'll re-gret—please. I'm sorry. I'm fucking sorry. Please." Each word stabs. Each inhalation is painful. Regardless, when it comes to fight-or-flight mode, my natural inclination is to fawn—at least, that's what my previous therapist called my defence mechanism. The seconds drag on as my eyes cut between the gun and his face. "I love you. You know that, right? We have issues, but so does everyone, right? Please, baby. I love you and you love me. *We can fix this.*"

His hardened face is almost invisible in the darkness, cloaked in the moonlight. His voice low. "Cecily, just tell me if you're fucking somebody else."

"No. God, no. I would never—please believe me, KJ. Please. You know I love you so much. I'm sorry for upsetting you."

"You're lying."

"I swear. I'm sorry for making you think I would do that. I would never. I'm sorry. *Please.*" My voice crumbles at the last word. There's nothing more I can do to convince him not to kill me now.

I should've left years ago. I'm not stupid. I knew, statistically, I was likely to die by his hand. Still, I stayed.

"I didn't mean to scare you. I just couldn't stand the thought of losing you." The gun lowers to his side and he exhales. "Come on—it's late. Let's go to bed."

I palm the car keys and give him a thin-lipped smile. "I'm sorry."

Chucking the duffle bag in ahead of me, I scramble into the car and slam my fist down on the door lock button before he has time to react. The car fires to life just in time for KJ to lunge forward, smacking his fists down on the hood in fury. I shift into reverse and fly backward with my hands in a death grip on the wheel. The laundry basket tumbles to the ground, scattering my belongings across the asphalt driveway. His face is contorted by a horror-movie-like scream that I can't hear over the blasting radio. Glancing in the rearview as I careen down our sleepy suburban street, I see him drop to his knees.

No gunfire.

2

Cecily

My hands slam into the steering wheel with a banshee scream, and I spin it to make an illegal U-turn in the middle of a dead intersection an hour from home. I'll go back and try again another day. I'm confident KJ will be a doting husband for at least a week after tonight. I can last another week. And then I'll have a new phone again. It'll be easier next time. I'll actually do it next time.

Fuck no.

My knuckles grip the wheel so heatedly they turn white. I slow and wait for an oncoming vehicle to pass. He had a gun. *A gun.* Substituting a scream, I emit a horrendous, deranged laugh and make another U-turn less than a block from the initial intersection. Whether or not he would actually kill me is anyone's guess, but I don't want to risk calling his bluff.

Without direction, I'll drive North because a place named Wells Canyon has to be North, right? It certainly sounds like it would be a Northern British Columbia town. Anyway, I'm not far from Vancouver now. Heading South would bring me to the United States border, West would land me in the ocean.

North, it is.

The *whoop whoop* of a police car siren sounds directly behind me, pulling me away from my spiralling thoughts. I drift to the roadside and tears, which haven't so much as pricked at my eyes since I left, finally make an appearance.

"Evening, miss. Do you know why I pulled you over?"

I nod, gasping for air. "Yeah—yes, I know. I did a U-turn and I'm just lost and..."

"*Two* U-turns. Are you aware they're illegal?"

"I am." With a sniffle, I wipe the tear hanging from the tip of my nose.

"You said you're lost? Where are you trying to go and where did you come from?"

"I'm supposed to be going to see a friend in Wells Canyon, but I broke my phone and, without it, I don't know which direction to head."

A deep crease folds between his eyebrows as he watches me suspiciously. "*Right.* You're going to visit your friend at two o'clock in the morning? In a town five hours away. I need to see some ID, please. Where do you live?"

As I dig out my wallet, he shines his flashlight into my backseat, where the few items I managed to throw in the car are strewn.

"6207 Mountainview Terrace. Just...um... back in Kerrisdale. I'm not actually going to visit—I'm staying there. Sorry. My husband and I got into a fight, and I left."

There's a explicit shift in his demeanour. *Am I that transparent?*

"To be clear, are you visiting or are you staying there?"

"Staying... yeah, I'm staying there." I gnaw the inside of my cheek.

"That highway can be a bit tricky to drive at night. Are you safe to go home and head to your friend's house tomorrow?"

Fuck. Either I lie and pray he doesn't insist on following me home, or I tell the truth and pray he doesn't push it further.

I let out a shaky breath. "No, I'm not."

"Are you injured?" he asks, and I shake my head. "What kind of danger are you in? There are a lot of resources available. I can give you some numbers to—"

I interrupt. "Officer, I'll be fine as soon as I can get to my friend's house. Thank you for the offer, though."

He hesitates for a moment. "Okay. I'm going to give you a verbal warning not to make any more illegal maneuvers—it doesn't matter how quiet the roads are, got it? Wells Canyon is North." *I knew it.* Pulling out a notepad from his chest pocket, he begins furiously scribbling. "I'm writing the directions down for you. Once you get to the highway it should be pretty straightforward. Drive safe."

He hands over my ID and the torn note paper, then saunters back to his car. Afraid he might change his mind, I pull away without looking back and follow his directions, searching for the highway. My route is interrupted by the angelic glow of 7-11, stopping me in my tracks. Under the fluorescent buzz, I withdraw five-hundred dollars from our bank account because, honestly, it's the bare minimum KJ owes me. Armed with a Red Bull, an Oh Henry! bar, and a packet of ketchup chips, I feel adequately prepared for a road trip into the unknown. Brimming with confidence I haven't had in years, I'm en route to my fresh start.

One hundred and twenty. Eighty-five. Sixty. My gas light illuminates the dark car, mocking me. All my self-assurance seems to have disappeared alongside the last chip crumbs, which I dumped haphazardly into my mouth thirty kilometres ago. Evidently, I should've filled up with more than junk food at the 7-11. Forty. Twenty. A vibrant orange and green gas station sign breaks up the dismal night sky, and I pull up to a pump in the nick of time. Relief courses through my veins at not needing to add hitch-hiking to the list of dangerous acts I'm involved in tonight.

An old phone booth with broken-out glass sits on the property's border. I'm doubtful it works—*who even uses pay phones anymore?* But I'd rather not show up in Wells Canyon without at least attempting to let

Beryl know I'm coming, so I sift through my car, gathering all the loose change I can.

Trying to touch the grimy phone the least amount possible, I lift it to my ear with two fingers. *A dial tone.* Sucking in a breath through my teeth, I punch in her number. Beryl answers on the third ring with a sleepy voice.

"Beryl? Hi, sorry to wake you up. It's Cecily."

"Morning, honey. Are you safe?" We've spoken every day for nearly six months and somehow I've never heard her before. She's soothing and upbeat, despite the drowsy rasp.

"I am. Um, I wanted to check if it's okay for me to come before I show up at your house. I'm calling you from a pay phone on the side of the highway... I think I'm about two hours away from Wells Canyon. I don't have a phone to map it, but that's what the cop told me."

I wait with bated breath for her answer.

"Oh, Cecily, I'm so proud. If there's one thing you'll learn about me, it's that I don't go back on my word. Get on up here, honey."

She gives me the directions to get from Wells Canyon to Wells Ranch and I repeat them back twice, ensuring they're committed to my memory before I hang up. Somebody in the world knows I left. Now I need to follow through. That might have been the problem in the past. I didn't have anybody to judge me for going back home to my abusive husband. Not that I think Beryl would judge me.

But how embarrassing would it be to turn around and go back after this?

I remember exactly one other phone number. Mostly because I gave it out freely as a pre-teen, hoping my friends calling often enough would make my parents cave and get me my own landline. I don't take a single breath, punching in the digits with a trembling finger.

"Dad?" I croak upon hearing a wheezy, old man grunt into the phone. "It's Cecily. Sorry for waking you up."

We're both aware it's weird that I'm calling. Even weirder that I'm calling at five a.m., considering I haven't spoken to my parents in over a year. Better now than never, right?

"Cece? What's wrong? You're calling from a strange number. Are you okay?"

My rapid heart rate returning to normal, I smile into the phone. Part of me expected him to get mad at me for calling this early in the morning.

"I'm okay. At least, I will be. I left KJ, Dad. And I thought somebody should know where I'm going, so if he reports me as a missing person, you can tell the cops to stand down. I broke my phone. Actually, no, *he* broke my phone." If I'm not going back to him, I need to stop defending him. "But I found a pay phone on my drive and—"

"A pay phone on your drive? Where are you going?"

In the background, my mother's nasally voice says, "Just tell her to come here, Clark."

"Your mother says you should come here."

I sigh. "I have a friend up in Wells Canyon who offered me a job and a place to stay. I already told her I was coming. I'm fine though, honest. I'll call you guys when I get a new phone."

"Do you need money? Where the hell is—Margie, get on the Google and look up Wells Canyon. What do you need from us, Cece?"

"Please don't tell KJ where I am. That's all I ask."

"I wouldn't have told him, even if you didn't ask me not to. Your secret's safe with us, sweetheart."

"I'm sorry for not calling sooner, Dad. I—" Saliva builds in the back of my throat. "I'm sorry for not listening to you guys earlier."

They expressed concern about our relationship over a year ago and have offered to help me in multiple ways. To repay my loving parents, I metaphorically slapped them in the face, gaslit them, and then cut them from my life. I don't deserve for them to still care about me like this.

"Cece, we love you. *Always.* Your mom and I are always here for you. And I'm so glad you called now, sweetheart."

Suddenly, my mom's voice fills my ear. She must've picked up the office phone on the same line. "Cecily? It's mom. I'm so glad you left that jerkoff. You're a smart girl—too good for him—I've always said that. I'm going to talk to your Aunt Harriet—remember she's a big time attorney over in Calgary. We'll get this all sorted. Come here if you need a place to go, okay?"

"Okay, mom. I'm running on borrowed time with this payphone, but thank you. I love you both."

I walk back to the car, feeling weightless. The kind of relief you get when you finally drop your grocery bags on the kitchen floor, after climbing three flights of stairs to your shitty college apartment. Sure, red and purple indents remain in your skin, but the heaviness is gone. Or, like when you take your bra off at the end of a shitty day.

Speaking of which...

Thank God for the duffle bag, so I don't have to show up wearing pink pajamas with cartoon dogs. I rummage through and find a cute, ruffled top and black trousers to change into. Professional, put together... probably not suitable for a ranch, but it'll do.

The peachy orange paint on the "Welcome To Wells Canyon" sign is peeling, and the hand-painted lettering faded. Yet, there's something cute and charming about it—or I could simply be overtired. The rising sun peers over a dramatic mountain range, which makes the canyon part of the name very fitting. It's hard to determine if the town's sleepy vibe is due to a lack of residents or if everybody is still in bed. Either way, it feels like somewhere I can relax into like a cozy, oversized T-shirt.

My car lurches around a corner, the paved road turning to dirt at the far end of town. Am I actually ready to start over? *With strangers?* Thirty more kilometres may as well be thirty thousand, with the anxiety churning in my stomach. Something makes me think my sleep deprivation, and diet of Red Bull and chocolate, aren't helping either.

The dirt road's littered with potholes and hemmed by towering, sun-kissed pines. Tall grasses line the roadside, beckoning me onward with a gentle breeze. I roll down a window, allowing crisp mountain air to fill the car, and take a deep inhale. The pure oxygen pumped directly into my bloodstream wakes me back up like a caffeine injection. To set the mood, I switch from catchy pop music to a nineties country playlist; the music my grandparents always had blasting at their cabin. Maybe country life won't be too bad. After all, I loved my summers spent at their cabin in the woods. Surrounded by nothing but crickets, the lake, and glorious thunderstorms. Plus, KJ will never think to look for me—a tried-and-true city girl—on a cattle ranch in the middle of nowhere.

Pow. Whooooosh.

Two sounds I don't want to hear, and they make my heart skip a beat. A 'low tire pressure' warning flashes in bold, red lettering across my dash display. My eyes burn and I blink up at the grey upholstered ceiling to stop tears from falling. For half a second, sitting on a rural dirt road, I stupidly wish KJ was with me. Not that he would have the faintest clue about how to change a tire, but I'd have somebody with a functional cell phone to call for help.

Preparing myself to cry, I lean against the headrest and shut my eyes. A sudden burst of laughter makes me jump, and I'm even more alarmed when I look in the rearview mirror to see it's me. I'm the one laughing. A deranged hyena with smeared mascara, puffy under-eyes, and... chocolate. I have chocolate smeared on my cheek. Scrubbing it off with my thumb makes me more hysterical. I'm so deep into my laughter it's become practically silent, save for the occasional wheeze or snort, when a massive black truck pulls to a stop behind me. My face drops. It would be just my luck—I leave my abusive husband, and end up murdered on a country road, anyway.

A handsome man in fitted jeans, a thick canvas jacket, and a cowboy hat raps his knuckles against my window. His other hand motions at me to roll it down. I suppose he looks honourable enough, despite the scruffy facial hair and dirty clothes. *Even still.* Evil people look honourable sometimes. KJ's a prime example of how deceiving appearances can be.

I discreetly reach for the lock button, mouthing the words *no, thank you.* The sound of all four doors locking simultaneously is deafening in the otherwise silent environment. Even the cowboy notices, his lip turning up at the noise.

"Gonna have to unlock the trunk if you want me to change your tire, darlin'." The man's deep, gritty voice nearly rattles my window. I look up cautiously to see his chin gesture toward my trunk. This may be my only option for help...

Anxiously nibbling on my bottom lip, I reach and pop open the trunk.

With a minor side-mirror adjustment—thank God for power mirrors—I discreetly watch him haul a tire from the back of my car and get right to work. KJ would be angrily dialing for roadside assistance in this situation. This is much hotter.

Deciding it's unlikely a murderer would fix my flat before killing me, I bravely step out into the warm sunshine.

"How much do I owe you?" My pitch hits a higher octave than normal as it dawns on me how attractive the man towering in front of me is. Definitely better up close than he was in the small, dust-covered mirror. He jacks the car into the air and roped muscle along his arms tightens as he works to replace the flat tire. I gulp, thankful for the distance between us, because I'm sure he'd be able to hear my heart thundering in my chest if I moved closer.

The puffy brown jacket he was wearing when he showed up is draped over the hood of his pickup truck. It was cute on him, in a country-chic way, but the tight grey T-shirt is a definite step up. His biceps bulge when he lifts the old tire off the ground, and the thin fabric displays his muscular shoulders perfectly when he turns to place it in my trunk.

You'd have to be dead not to take notice of him. And I will be dead if my husband finds out I'm noticing a handsome cowboy.

Keenly watching him, I ponder when I'll be able to officially call KJ my ex-husband. After all, I'm not going back... I don't think? *No.* I'm not going back.

I spin the simple gold band on my ring finger, abruptly aware of its presence, and shove my hand into my pocket. Shame trickles through me when I realize I've hidden it because a small part is hoping this cowboy thinks I'm single.

Perhaps KJ's right, and I am a whore. I'm sure no normal married person would be so eager to throw away their ring after seeing one cute guy.

Granted, it's not like we have a happy marriage, nor am I a normal married person. We have sex on special occasions, and give small pecks on the lips when he's trying to make something up to me. I can't remember the last time I truly wanted either of those things. And now I'm five hours away on a dirt road because he hit me. But I suppose it's still wrong to gawk at another man. *Maybe?*

No, it's simple biology. I'm a straight thirty-year-old woman. He's an attractive, and presumably hard-working, man. I'm evolutionarily wired to be interested. It's perfectly natural to assess somebody of the opposite sex—especially when they're basically saving you from being left for dead on the roadside. Anyway, there's no wedding vow about *looking*, is there?

"How much? Fifty bucks?" I ask again, giving the ring a tug. It's pleasantly surprising how easily the band slips off. Almost like it wants to be removed.

The trunk closes with a thud.

"One hundred?" I gulp. I should have taken more than $500 from the bank account, if I'm going to blow through my cash this fast.

"Use the money to get some proper tires. These city slicks,"—he lightly kicks my tire with a big, chestnut-brown cowboy boot—"aren't cut out for the rough dirt roads around here. You're going to keep getting flats from every sharp rock you come across."

"Oh, okay. Well, thank you then." I smile at him, knowing I shouldn't, feeling the damn weight of my wedding ring in my pocket.

With a stolid nod, he strides to his truck, grabs his jacket, and jumps in. It doesn't occur to me that I failed to catch my hero's name, until the only thing left of him is a distant dust cloud settling back onto the gravel road. It's probably for the best. I'm a married woman, after all. Even if my *husband* threatened me with a gun a few hours ago.

3

Cecily

I hunch over the steering wheel to look up at the carved wood Wells Ranch entrance sign looming over the driveway. It's the length of my Honda Civic and flanked by the largest logs I've ever seen. Beryl didn't exaggerate when she said it was impossible to miss Wells Ranch.

The sickly sweet stench of lilacs attacks from every direction, sending a tingling shiver down my spine that has my hair standing at attention. Hundred-year-old lilac bushes lining the backyard were the top-selling feature when KJ and I bought our home; after being together for a year, and married for four months. In retrospect, I should have listened to my friends, who told me things were moving too fast. I was incredibly quick to become defensive, and even quicker to cut those friends from my life for him.

You don't understand. Kyson's my dream man and we're deeply in love. Why wait? Life is short.

Less than three years ago, I thought that was true.

Oh, how the mighty have fallen.

Lilac blooms never last. Even with the high elevation and late last frost here, I give these a month before they're done and dusted. Hatred burns my lungs as I make a pact with myself. I'll grieve whatever I need to, but only for as long as these lilacs stay in bloom. Afterward, I won't let KJ take up a single sliver of real estate in my mind. Not a single fuck will be given. For all intents and purposes, he will be my *ex-husband*. Even if he ends up making it next to impossible to divorce him.

My car rattles across the bumpy cattle guard and over a small knoll, bringing the farm into view. At the base of a distant hill, there's a smattering of varied-size log cabins with red metal roofs. A massive barn-like building is further left, surrounded by rusty farm equipment and tall grass. Vibrant green hay fields stretch as far as I can see, with fences cutting across seemingly at random.

My gaze snags on an older woman frantically waving her arms in the air, backdropped by a stunning white farmhouse. *Beryl*. I know her without having ever seen her. Her brown, spindly body sucks me into a hug the moment my feet touch the ground. My cheek presses into her shoulder, inhaling freshly baked bread that's permeated through her linen button-up shirt. Though we've never met, everything about her feels perfectly familiar and comfortable. And those cozy feelings replace the doubts that began sprouting in my mind on the long drive.

"I was getting worried you'd changed your mind!" She hugs me tighter.

"Sorry, I got a flat tire and was stuck on the side of the road for a while. Some cowboy stopped and helped me."

"Am I ever glad you're here, honey. Come inside. Leave your stuff in the car. I'll show you to your cabin later. I have coffee cake, biscuits—oh, you need to try my homemade black currant jam. Or I can cook you up some eggs and back bacon."

"Just coffee would be wonderful." I follow her onto the sprawling porch that's wrapped around either side of the white farmhouse like a hug. Tintinnabulation of a dozen or more wind chimes announces a swirling breeze. There's no way a picture-perfect place like this actually exists. Maybe KJ did kill me and this is heaven.

The creaking screen door slams shut behind us. I move to take off my sneakers, but Beryl stops me. "Don't bother unless you want to get cow crap on your socks, honey. The men around here may as well be wild animals. It's a lost cause getting them to take their boots off indoors."

My gaze drifts along the intricate woodwork to the crown mouldings and stair banister in the foyer. Then spans across vintage floral wallpaper and down to the faded pine floorboards. They're battered in the most stunning way: dents from cowboy boots, scrapes from furniture moved between rooms, and wear marks from the generations who have walked over this floor.

"Is this your house? It's beautiful." I'm not saying it to adulate. This is easily the most gorgeous home I've ever seen.

"No, no. Jackson Wells and his wife, Kate, live in the big house with their daughter, Odessa. She's a real spitfire, that one. And she has the biggest doe eyes—always turning up when there's fresh baking to be eaten. We use the kitchen here as a gathering spot, of sorts, and it's where we prepare lunches for the employees. Seems there's always *somebody* in the kitchen. You can make yourself at home here, help yourself to anything except the chocolate milk... It's Kate's biggest pregnancy craving." She winks.

She leads me down a dimly lit hallway, and I steal a glance into the living room on my left. My soul momentarily leaves my body when the first thing I notice is a massive deer's head staring back at me with beady, gleaming black eyes. I'm guessing the people around here won't find my story about leaving baby carrots for the deer by my grandparents' cabin very endearing. Still, the rest of the room looks charming enough with its oversized chairs and sofa, brick fireplace, and filled bookshelves. I can picture myself thumbing the spines with a hot coffee in my hand.

Thankfully, there's nary a dead animal in sight when I follow Beryl into the sunny kitchen. At her demand, I perch on a stool at the big marble island and study the woman I consider my best friend, despite today being the first time I've heard her voice or seen her face. Yes, it feels extremely pathetic not to have more friends in my real life. But at least I have Beryl. And right now, I'm thankful my best friend is a talker, because the last thing I want to do is speak.

"So, you take today to settle in properly. I'll introduce you to Kate later—she usually helps me out in the kitchen. We don't feed the ranch hands breakfast or dinner except on special occasions. We do pack them lunches, though. I hope you're good at making sandwiches because, *heavens*, do those boys eat. We also clean their bunkhouses, do grocery runs, and keep this ship running. Essentially, we're the farm wives. Jackson's the one man around here who's had his head screwed on tight enough to find a good one, and nail her down."

A white mug slides across the counter into my anxious hands, and I take a long, calming sip. Beryl's grey hair hangs in plaits down her back, except for a few baby hairs that stand like a crown on the top of her head. Her face doesn't hide the long hours spent in the sun, or the hard life she had before coming to Wells Ranch, but her eyes and smile radiate pure joy.

What I would give to look peaceful and happy like her.

"Now, when you're ready to tell me about what finally got you here, I'm all ears. But let's keep it light today, if you don't mind?"

I'm about to thank her when my ears perk to the screen door, creaking and slamming, causing a visceral reaction. The crash tries to stop my heart. I steady myself on the wooden stool and take a controlled, conscious breath.

"More time around here, and you won't be so jumpy, honey." She rests her work-worn hand on mine and gives it a soft squeeze. "One thing about a cattle ranch—there's noise all the darn time. But nowhere safer you could be."

She releases her grasp as a man strides into the kitchen with a scowl. "Fucking Tate didn't bring in the vaccines. I drove to town and back for nothing, and it means we can't start branding until—" He stops in his tracks upon spotting me.

The handsome, flat-tire-fixing country hero. His eyes rake across me in a way that leaves me feeling naked and vulnerable. Shifting in my seat, I tuck my arms tight around myself, desperate to be smaller and less noticeable under his glowering gaze.

"Language," Beryl scolds before gesturing to me. "Austin, meet Cecily. The new help I told you I was hiring."

With a nod, I say, "We sort of met already. This is the cowboy I told you about—the one who fixed my tire."

He lets out a scoff, his eyes narrowing as they lock onto mine. "I'm not a cowboy, darlin'."

The combination of his mocking tone and the fake flattery of the word "darling" alters something in my attitude. It sparks a flame. "No? Sorry. I guess the cowboy hat, boots, too-tight Wranglers, and compensator truck gave me that impression, for some reason."

Despite Beryl's giggle, I regret my reply as a wildfire spreads through my arteries. God help me. KJ always says my mouth gets me into too much trouble. I resist the urge to bring my hands up to cover my cheeks, which I'm confident are bright red. The corner of his lip twitches as his eyes continue to drill holes through my weak armour.

"Rancher—not cowboy. I own the land, the cattle, the horses. I keep the cowboys employed." He scratches at the thick, dark stubble lining his jaw. "You'll learn the difference if you stick 'round here long enough."

Not that you will. He doesn't have to say it. I can tell what he's thinking, based on his tone and the dark gleam in his amber-coloured eyes.

"Tate didn't get the vaccines in?" Beryl's sing-song voice snaps his laser focus away from my blushing face. "Was the shipment delayed or something?"

"No, the motherfu—the godda—*that man* hasn't even ordered them yet." His annoyance grows with each attempt at a cuss word, which Beryl stops with a single look. "So now I guess we're not branding for at least another two weeks."

Releasing an angry breath, he slams a stack of what appears to be junk mail down on the counter, causing my heart to beat erratically. I guess fawning isn't my only instinct because right now I freeze. Unable to apologize or calm this strange man down when I don't have the faintest clue what he's mad about.

With a final head shake, he leaves. I remain stiff with anxiety until his cowboy boots no longer thud down the hallway, and the screen door closes with a bang.

"Austin Wells," Beryl says with an exasperated exhale. "He might be the one signing the pay cheques, but we all know I'm in charge of the kitchen. He can be a bit prickly, but you don't need to worry about him. He's a good one."

I give her a small, understanding nod as my pulse returns to normal. We both know what she means.

Beryl leaves me, and my assorted belongings, in a small cabin about a hundred yards from the main farmhouse—one of approximately half a dozen cabins just like it. In its entirety, my new place is smaller than the bedroom and ensuite back home... or, I should say, back at my *old home*. I suppose this is my home now. The log walls, small log-framed bed, and 1970s floral couch give it a nostalgic summer camp feel. It's nothing like anywhere I've lived before and it lacks the big house's beautiful antique touches, but it'll do.

And it's all mine.

Without the adrenaline rush to keep me moving, every muscle in my body has the heaviness of water-logged driftwood. After dropping my stuff in a heap on the floor, I fall backward onto the bed. My eyelids struggle to stay open, turning the room into a cloudy haze before I even feel my body hit the mattress.

I'm jarred awake by a braying horse. Evidently, leaving KJ and moving to a cattle ranch wasn't a fever dream; I really am at Wells Ranch. The old-school alarm clock next to the bed reads 9:04. Based on the absence of light streaming in around the thin curtains, it has to be nine o'clock at night.

Good God, I slept the entire day away.

Loud chatter rumbles through the single-paned cabin window. Every tendon aches as I drag my still-weary body to peer from behind the curtain. Seeing a dozen or more happily chatting men on horseback, I duck down and crawl toward the door to check that it's still locked.

A thunderous rumbling tears through me. *Not now, stomach.* I curse myself for not eating more than a handful of snacks in the last twenty-four hours, as my body begs for food. Beryl said to go to the big house for dinner or snacks anytime. But it's long past dinnertime, and I'm not stepping foot outside with all of those strange men out there.

Not wanting to draw attention, I move in complete darkness and rummage through cupboards. Innately aware there could be mouse traps, insects, or Lord knows what else in them. It's a chance I'm willing to take to avoid interaction with any strange men tonight. Luckily, that's not the case, and I manage to find dishes, a hot plate, cookware, and more in my exploration. So I won't need to use my remaining $435 on kitchen supplies. Unluckily, there's not a single scrap of food anywhere in this room. Despite the pangs in my empty stomach, I curl back up on the soft covers.

I've gone to bed feeling worse things than hunger.

4

Austin

As luck would have it, the blonde girl crying over a flat tire turned up at my ranch. I stopped to help her because that's what I was raised to do—I can't leave a woman stranded on the road. If my mom were still alive, she would slap me upside the head for ignoring a woman in need of help. But if I had known she was on her way here, I might not have been so damn friendly about it.

As if there aren't a half-dozen or more women in town who would jump at the opportunity to work here, Beryl went and hired a city girl she found online.

Of all the people to hire and places to hire them from.

She showed up in a car unfit for rural roads, wearing a frilly outfit, and she apparently wasn't interested in actually working on her first day here. Instead, she spent the entire day in her cabin doing God knows what. Couldn't be bothered to show her face.

Speaking of her face. There's the other issue I don't dare mention to Beryl or Kate because, admittedly, it would make me sound like a misogynistic pig. And maybe I am—*fuck it.*

She's hot.

The way she tucked her long, blonde hair behind her ears, looking me over with those piercing blue eyes, made my mouth go dry. All of it—all of her—was downright biteable. Down to the light blush across her creamy cheeks, when her own brazen remark seemingly caught her off guard. A flouncy top showcased perky, full tits. Tight pants hugged her round ass; an ass that would fit perfectly in my hands. Every part of the girl who showed up here yesterday filled my head with inappropriate thoughts.

And there are plenty of men here who don't get to spend nearly enough time around women to get it out of their systems. *Including myself.* Except I don't have the time or desire to chase after women like my ranch hands do. And I've been involved with enough city girls to know they only show up for long enough to cause pain. Which means if even I can't stop myself from picturing the things I want to do to her, the other guys stand no chance at staying away.

There's also the wedding band indent still on her finger, which has me asking quite a few questions I doubt I want to hear the answers to.

The bottom line is everything about her spells out trouble, raising alarms in my head that I can't shake. No doubt about it, her presence around here will be an issue. That is, unless I can convince Beryl to change her mind—which is entirely unlikely. I have a better shot at scaring away the city girl.

I'm leaning back in my chair at the kitchen table, sipping a hot coffee, when I spot her sneaking down the hallway. *Cecily.* Moving through the house like a mouse. She stops outside the curved archway into the kitchen, wide-eyed as she takes in the number of people moving about, and tugs at her dark green hoodie sleeves. Yet another indication she's entirely out-of-touch. Somehow, it seems she wasn't expecting to find a soul around at four-thirty a.m. on a cattle ranch.

She continues her stealthy movements as she steps toward the table, which is heaped with breakfast foods and brown bag lunches for the guys.

"The food's for those who earn their keep here. You gonna work today, darlin'?" I stare at her over my navy tin mug, a little part of me enjoying the way my comment makes her squirm.

"Oh, um... yeah. Sorry, yesterday was just—"

Beryl cuts off Cecily, placing a hand on her shoulder. "She didn't need to start until today, so lay off. Now, honey, take a seat and fill your boots. You must be starved."

Cecily sinks into the chair opposite me, and the way her shoulders slump makes it clear she's feeling everybody's stare. Her blue eyes drop to study the knots and dents in our family heirloom table. For half a second, I feel bad for drawing attention to her when she clearly doesn't want it.

"Wait, who's this?" My youngest brother, Denny, yells from the other side of the island as he crams a blueberry muffin into his mouth. Within seconds, he's turning on the charm. "Why did nobody tell me we had a pretty girl on the property?"

Beryl shoots him a look, rubbing her hand over the city girl's shoulder. "Everyone, this is Cecily. She's my new help. Cecily... well, I don't know where to begin, but this is a good chunk of the gang. You all be nice to her, alright?"

"But not too nice", I'm tempted to add, as the men seem to take notice of her good looks faster than a grass fire. Even in leggings, a baggy hoodie, and hair in a ponytail. I knew I should've told Beryl I thought this was a bad idea. Even if it meant having to suffer a lecture about women being treated equally. It's not that I think Cecily is *less than* because she's a woman. I just don't need my ranch hands getting distracted. Simple as that.

"Hi, Cecily," Colt, Sundial, and Jacky say in unison.

Like that. Distracted like that.

"Grab your lunches and get." I stare down the men until they leave, although each ignores me for long enough to ensure they give Cecily a proper introduction, complete with a handshake. As if they're fucking gentlemen.

She sits up straighter, ensuring each ranch hand has a moment of undivided attention. A smile, a cheery hello. I shake off the desire for a second chance at introducing myself—or third, I suppose, since I technically had two yesterday and fumbled both.

As quickly as the first boys are gone, a second group files in for their lunches. And probably to take a peek at the hot new piece of ass at Wells Ranch. Good news travels fast around here. Red goes so far as to kiss her on the back of the hand during his introduction, earning a blushing smile from her. My stomach drops. She needs to leave. *Yesterday.*

"Well, I've already forgotten half their names." Cecily shakes her head with a honey-sweet laugh. I ignore the weird somersaulting in my guts—clearly I drank too much coffee on an empty stomach. "If I had known everybody would be here so early this morning, I might've brought a notepad with me to write it all down."

"Not everybody gets to laze about in the morning. This is a working ranch." I drop my empty mug into the sink, motioning for Beryl to follow me into the hallway.

"Austin, what has gotten into you?" she scolds, rapping the backs of her fingers against my chest. Even though I was a grown adult when she came here, she's the closest thing I have to a mother now. She definitely has no problem treating my brothers and me like her sons.

I shake my head and thrust my pointer finger toward the kitchen. "She needs to go. Hire a girl from town. She has no idea what it's like to be on a ranch. Also, say what you want about me, but I don't think we need an attractive young woman working here with all these horny ranch hands. You saw how they acted."

"The boys were all perfect gentlemen. You, on the other hand?" She crosses her arms. "You told me I was free to hire anybody I wanted if I needed help. I can't keep up with you lot the way I used to. And Kate's a wonderful help, but she's busy trying to raise a family here, too. I hired Cecily, and I'm going to give her an opportunity to prove she's capable of the job. You don't have to like it, but that's what's happening." She tilts her head with a self-satisfied look, pushing me to spar with her.

"Don't forget, I'm the boss. I could fire her whenever I wanted to...
And you." There's an instant guilty pang when I say it. Though it's
the truth, Beryl's family. There's no way I would ever fire her. *Could
ever fire her.* My brothers have equal say in things around here, and
they'd never let it happen.

"Love to see you try, honey." She winks. Turning on her heel, the
old woman struts back into the kitchen, her long grey braid slapping
against her back.

Though I have nowhere to be right now, I can't go back to the
kitchen. Not after I made a comment about not having the time to
sit around and do nothing. I'm sure the guys heading out to pound
fence posts this morning would appreciate the extra hands. Building
and repairing fences on over 100,000 acres is damn near a full-time
job. Not a fun one, either. But I'm happy to bust my ass in the hot
May sun if it'll take my mind off Beryl's new hire for a few hours.

Normally, we work from sun up to sun down this time of the year.
But today's unseasonably warm, and I can't afford to lose workers
from heat stroke, so we call it quits shortly after lunch.

It's a pleasant surprise to find Beryl and Kate sitting on the front
porch, with my four-year-old niece, Odessa, plucking daylily blooms
from the garden below.

"Does your mom know you're picking her flowers?" I tease as I
walk past, causing her spine to stiffen and the bouquet in her arms
to drop in a whirlwind to the ground. Kate stands up and peers over
the railing, shooting her daughter a scolding look.

I lower my tired body onto the steps and kick my legs straight out
in front of me. "See you took my advice about firing the new girl
then."

Beryl cackles. "Austin Wells. You know me better than that."

My chest cramps. I can't tell if the feeling is annoyance or anticipation about seeing Cecily again. Running my family's 20,000-head
operation, managing twenty-two employees—twenty-three with her
included—would be infinitely easier without a beautiful woman
distracting my men. *Distracting me.* Her presence has already sent
me out to pound fence posts, on a day when I should have been
catching up on paperwork left over from the calving season.

"Heard you've got a problem with Cecily?" Kate stops repri-
manding her kid to start in on me. "And you were apparently a
real D-bag this morning? We need the help here and she's already
proven her worth today. She helped me clean bunkhouses and weed
the flower bed. Now she had to run some errands, so she's grabbing
groceries and Odessa's prescription."

My eyes cut to her cabin. Her car's gone. *Goddamn it.* "In her car?"

Kate and Beryl exchange a glance, both shrugging. "Assume so,"
Kate says.

"Tell her to take a ranch vehicle next time. If she ends up with
another flat tire, she's gone. I don't give a shit what either of you
say." I brush the powdery dirt from my pants and head to my office.

We haven't used the hayloft above the quarter horse stable for hay
storage in over thirty years. Not since the ranch's remuda expanded
well beyond what 200 square bales can feed. Then my grandfather
switched exclusively to rounds, making this space unnecessary and
unused. After spending most of my childhood using the loft as a
secret spot to read the entire *Goosebumps* series, it was a no-brainer to
make some alterations to change it into an office. Especially because
putting a workspace in my small home would mean giving up either
the couch or my bed.

Breathing in the comforting smell of horses, old wood, and alfalfa, I
swing open the hay door next to my desk. Partially for sunlight and fresh
air, but primarily for the view. Grabbing a stack of papers, I plunk into
the well-worn, burgundy armchair pointed toward the open door. My
handmade oak desk may be a more logical place to get work done, but it

overlooks the stables below the loft. And right now, I need the driveway in my sight line.

I've never noticed how many vehicles come and go from the ranch before every set of tires crunching on the compact gravel made me look up. In the middle of making a mental note to have another meeting with the crew about biosecurity, I glance up to see a silver Honda Civic turn the corner. First, there's a reflexive sigh, knowing she made it to town and back safely. Then, a grating inhale when I catch Red and Jacky elbowing each other, as Cecily clambers out of her car with her arms full. Always the damn gentleman, Denny appears from nowhere, and carries her groceries into the big house. Smiling his "lady-killer" smile and shaking out his shaggy brown hair.

Fucking distraction. I shut the heavy hay door.

I swear she's everywhere. Which means I am nothing except sidetracked, day in and day out.

Strolling out onto the back porch with a midday coffee and peanut butter cookie, it should come as no surprise she's in the garden below. If she's not in the kitchen, she's almost always out here. After two weeks, she has the plants flourishing like my mom used to. Yammering on for the last three days about some vegetable that's almost ready to harvest.

I close the door gently and sink onto the porch swing, careful not to draw attention to myself. Sipping my coffee, I listen to her raspy, soft voice sing in a barely audible pitch. The melody's familiar, but I have to strain my ears to hear the words. *Strawberry Wine.* I wouldn't have expected a girl from the big city to know so many classic country songs, but anytime she's focused on her work, she's humming or singing one. Normally, I tune out her voice because I hate the way it scatters goosebumps across my arms, and fills my chest with an uncomfortable fluttering.

Closing my eyes, it's easy to forget I'm supposed to feel nothing but annoyance toward her. I'm too lost in a daydream about her voice—her lips—to remind myself that I don't enjoy having her here. I definitely shouldn't be finding comfort in listening to her singing in the garden. That's the sure-fire path to future heartache.

There's been other girls like her here before. Out-of-towners that I've gotten too close to, just for them to inevitably leave. After being tossed aside for the last time a few years ago, I swore to myself I would never let it happen again. Instead, I've sunk every ounce of energy into the one thing I have control over—this ranch.

I don't even notice the song's finished until she starts up again. Closer this time. I peer between the railings and there she is, crouched down in the afternoon sun, letting her blonde hair blow in the subtle breeze. Pulling weeds, and completely unaware I'm less than ten feet away.

She's too quiet for me to hear the first few words rolling off her lips. That's why her voice becoming deep and manly, belting some Conway Twitty, sends me over the edge. A short laugh bursts out and I clamp my free hand over my mouth to stop it.

"How long have you been out here?" Cecily jumps to her feet, and places a dirty hand over her brow to shield the sun as she looks at me. A soft pink glow inches across her cheeks as her eyebrows narrow in my direction. She's embarrassed and mad and undeniably adorable.

"Just got here, Conway. So, are you a Louisiana Woman or a Mississippi Man?" I'm as taken aback by my response as she appears to be.

"Was that... a joke? From Austin Wells?" Walking onto the porch, she leans on the railing, popping a hip. "You know, it's rude to make fun of me while you're eating cookies I made. They're good though, aren't they?"

Because I can't seem to stop myself from being a habitual asshole when it comes to her, I set the half-eaten cookie down on the swing's armrest, and leave without another word. She's not winning me over with pretty looks, cute singing, and incredible baking.

5

Cecily

None of the muscles in my body have ever ached the way they do after three weeks at Wells Ranch. I can't help but wonder if I'll ever get used to manual labour or waking up early. Although, I truly can't complain when my work doesn't start until six. Unlike the cowboys, who head out at four or five in the morning to spend a full day on the range in the blazing heat, eating hot sandwiches and peeing... Well, I imagine they pee wherever they want to. When that thought crosses my mind as I roll my neck under the hot water, I giggle. No, I get to enjoy modern amenities like running water and air conditioning during the day. If only KJ could see me now. I would've never imagined a life where those things felt like something worth being happy about.

After such a short time, it might be too early to say, but I think I like it here. And, except for Austin Wells, it would seem everybody enjoys having me here. Beryl and Kate have been singing my praises daily, especially as the rising temperatures are making Kate too uncomfortable to do much past noon. I put off Beryl's job offer for ages, thinking it was a pity offer and doubting I was capable of holding my own here. But, despite my only work experience being in an office setting, years of waiting on KJ seem to have given me enough necessary skills to get by.

Slicking my damp hair back into a bun, I slather my face with sunscreen and head to the big house to start my day. The wet, crisp tingle in the air is already dissipating with the dawn and a group of men on horseback ride toward me, bringing the aroma of leather and horsehair in a wave alongside them.

"Morning." The tattooed cowboy, aptly nicknamed Red, smiles down at me.

"Come on down to the river later, Cecily," a large voice belonging to a large man, Colt, calls from the back.

Dust scatters under the clomping of hooves as they continue to work their way past me. I remain frozen in place, unable to help but be intimidated. Not by the cowboys, though my past indicates that perhaps I should be wary of men. As hard as I've tried to prove I'm not a city girl since arriving here, I can't help how my eyes dart from horse to horse. I *think* I can read men. I *know* I can't read these thousand-pound creatures with their heavy exhales, roped muscles, and shifting ears.

"Sorry, guys. Maybe next time," I say. Swimming and lounging in the shade sounds like a perfect way to spend some time, and it would be fun to go relax with those rowdy boys, but the idea carries a small prick of betrayal along with it. Even though, theoretically, it's acceptable for a married woman to have male friends. Knowing that doesn't make the choice to hang out with them any less of a struggle.

Once the men carry on past, it's a clear shot to the big house. Or, it should be, except the resident "Not-A-Cowboy" grump is sitting on the porch steps with a coffee in hand. His cowboy hat balances precariously on his knee, and he runs a free hand through his dark brown hair, keenly watching me. Despite the knitted brows and obvious disdain, there's something about the way he looks at me that always leaves me feeling stripped bare. And he looks frequently. I can't help but wonder what he sees.

Austin's said no more than a handful of words to me since my first morning here. Mostly, he communicates in grunts, scoffs, and huffs. The few times he's spoken to me, his words were sharp and his tone surly. When I can, I give him a wide berth.

Part of me yearns to impress him—possibly because I have a problem with seeking male approval. The other part of me just has nowhere else to go. The last thing I need is to provide him with a legitimate reason to fire me, because he clearly wouldn't hesitate. Either way, this needs to work. Imagining returning to live with my parents or KJ makes me more nauseous with each passing day. If I'm honest with myself, I should have listened to Beryl and come here months ago.

"Morning. It's a beautiful day." I give Austin a tight smile, solely acknowledging his existence because it goes against everything in my soul to ignore somebody who's clearly looking directly into my eyes. Call it being a stereotypically polite Canadian, I suppose.

He grunts. *God, he's such a jerk.*

"Good morning, City Girl. You look beautiful, by the way." I do a terrible impression of his gruff voice, eliciting a nostril flare and the slimmest smile, which he's quick to hide away behind his coffee mug. "I know you spend most of your time around cattle. But humans generally communicate using words."

"Mornin'," he says.

"You forgot the compliment. We'll work on it." I brush past him on the stairs and quietly close the screen door behind me.

"Morning, honey!" Beryl sings while kneading a massive mound of bread dough on the flour-coated counter. "Jalapeño cheddar buns. Whaddya think?"

"Sounds delicious. It'll go great with the chilli we're making for branding tomorrow, too." I slip an apron over my head, as she cuts the dough and plunks half down for me to work.

A few moments later, Austin strolls in like he owns the place. *Because he does, obviously.* But that's no excuse to act like a cocky prick. With Beryl and me working on opposite countertops, he has to squeeze between us to access the coffee maker. As he walks in our direction, my skin involuntarily tingles in anticipation. Despite this being a distinctly non-sexy moment, my body fails to receive the memo. He may be a grumpy asshole sometimes... okay, most of the time. But he's also attractive. I can't help the primal desire or the way my mind sometimes runs rampant, picturing what it would feel like to be close to Austin. What his rough hands might feel like on my skin, whether his truck really is compensating for something, and what his lips taste like.

When was the last time I wanted *a man to touch me?*

His belt buckle drags across my lower back as he passes, making every muscle along my spine contract in concert. He may as well slice me open with the way my skin stings. It isn't even an actual touch. No skin to skin. His exclusive intention is to reach the coffee—not to get close to me. Even still, the sharp breath held captive in my chest doesn't release until he's long gone. This is easily the most pathetic I've ever felt—married and pining for my boss.

Great, Cecily. You really are a whore.

The following morning is warm, but overcast. According to Beryl, it's the perfect weather for branding. When my feet hit the compact dirt, I don't think any amount of eavesdropping or research into calf branding could have prepared me. Wood fire and horse sweat, mixed with burning flesh and hair, nearly knocks me off my feet. I swallow the saliva pooling in my mouth and try not to take in the noxious air. It's no use. There's no escaping it, and I'll be here all day.

"Oh, my God." I gag.

"You get used to it." Beryl winks. I can't imagine how anybody could ever get used to this stench.

"Yeah, I'm sure," I reply, doing my best not to inhale too deeply through my nose.

I stand by the truck like a statue. Holding cookies, which suddenly feel like an inappropriate snack choice, and watching as the men on horseback work in organized chaos. They don't bother trying to speak to each other over the loud moos and braying horses. Instead, they silently gesture as they move methodically through the herd, separating calves, stringing them by their back legs with a quick toss of a rope, and pulling them into the branding area. It's impressive to see the men in their element, moving amongst the cattle and each other like they're performing a choreographed dance.

A hard lump forms in my throat when I see Jackson Wells pull a long metal rod from the bonfire. The end, featuring a prominent W, has a slight red tinge from sitting in the hot embers. I blindly feel for the metal water bottle strapped to my side and take a slow sip, silently reminding myself not to show any emotion. This is definitely not the time to be a pathetic, crybaby city girl. Even if—*Jesus Christ*—Jackson places the hot steel against the calf's right hip. Searing the hide, and filling the air with more sickening smoke.

I look away, swallowing hard, perfectly timed to catch Austin watching me from under his hat. A smug look gives away every cruel thought behind his eyes. Somehow, one moment of weakness as I watch a sweet baby cow being branded seems enough to undo all the hard work I've put in thus far. When the smoke clears, the calf's released and sent happily back to find its mom—seemingly no worse for wear. Relief flows across me and, within another couple calves, my guts are no longer churning with each brand placed.

My eyes flicker back over to Austin. Thank God for the scorching sunshine, so I don't have to make up an excuse for the way looking at him makes me sweat. Worn leather chaps—a cowboy clothing staple I didn't know I needed in my life, before coming here—sit overtop perfectly snug Wranglers. I may have referred to them as being too tight in the past, but that was a defence mechanism. They're incredible—hugging his ass and muscular thighs.

Turning his attention away from the branding action, he casually spits on the ground and an aching takes up residence in the spot behind my hip bones. Clearly, it's been too long since I've craved a man if this kind of thing turns me on. My fingers touch the spot where my ring once was. No longer having an indent there almost feels like I'm single again. And that's all the validation I need to continue staring. *Daydreaming.*

"So, what exactly is the point of all this?" I ask Beryl as we prepare the stockpot filled with chilli to hang over the fire.

"Branding for identification, ear tags for transport regulations, vaccinations to keep 'em healthy, and the boys get castrated because we already have darn near enough cattle around this place." Beryl laughs.

I grimace. "Isn't it painful, though?"

"It's not too bad." I didn't notice Austin moving from the other side of the expansive corral, and his voice makes me jump. I'd almost forgotten what he sounds like; he's been *that* cold to me lately. My breath hitches when I feel how close he is behind me. Close enough, I could spin around and be in his arms—not that I'd be dumb enough to try.

"Oh, yeah? You've been castrated then?"

"No." He pulls a face. Even under the shade from his wide-brim hat, there's no denying his face has a fuchsia hue. "I thought you meant branding."

"I did. And I forgot you speak cow. Did they tell you it doesn't hurt in a series of moos?" I quip.

"First-hand experience, actually."

My smile falters as I blink up at him. *Say what now?*

Placing a brown-work-gloved hand on my shoulder, he shuffles my shocked body slightly to the right and picks up the heavy chilli pot with ease. My muscles react subconsciously, shuddering under his hand. The cast-iron pot swings as he reaches across the massive fire to hang it from a metal rod, making the branching veins across his tanned forearms pop.

Get it together. He's your boss.

Every muscle's outlined by his sweat-soaked t-shirt, rippling as he lets go of the pot. It dangles over the coals and he steps back, taking one last look at my pathetic self before heading back to his work. My brazen stare as he walks away is broken by someone calling my name.

"Cecily, want to give me a hand?" Kate waves her arms from further into the chaos.

Horses, men, ropes, cows... so many different things that could kill me in a thousand different ways. My heart pounds at the thought of stepping into the mayhem. Every functioning brain cell's screaming *fuck no*. I'm afraid I've used up all my luck when it comes to staying alive in situations where I should've died.

"My mommy's callin' ya." Odessa hangs from the fence with a lollipop dangling from her mouth. I don't know many preschoolers, but I can't imagine most kids her age would be relaxed in this environment. I can be at least as brave as a four-year-old, can't I?

Shaking off the nerves, I duck between fence boards, and I'm in it. Like, really in it. Keeping my head on a swivel, and darting to the side as Red trots past me with a calf strung behind him, tugging it across the soft earth to the branding area.

"Thank God, you're here. My feet are swollen, and my back is killing me. Can you take over vaccines for a bit?" Kate stretches her arms overhead with a groan.

"Of course." I hesitantly nod as I watch her inject a calf laid up on the dusty ground. I'm not actually sure I can take over, or even whether I want to. Saying no to a pregnant woman who's been busting her ass all morning isn't an option, though. Almost more importantly, I don't need anybody—*like Austin*—thinking I'm a useless city girl. "Just show me how and then go rest."

The device looks surprisingly similar to a tattoo gun, and the hardest part of using it is working up the nerve to jab the needle into a wriggling calf's shoulder. The jolting pop reverberates in my hand as the needle presses through the thick hide. It sends a shiver up my spine, and I swallow down my tears. I'm not sure why this isn't a job for a vet but, given the primitive way this ranch seems to do everything, I guess I shouldn't be surprised it's not.

Jackson appears next to me with the hot branding iron, placing it firmly on the calf's side. Thick smoke blurs my vision, making my eyes water, and the smell of burning hair has saliva pooling in my throat as I stagger backward; careful not to get anywhere near the blistering steel. After watching the first two shots I administer, Kate gives me an approving smile and starts toward the fence.

"Doing great, City Girl," Colt teases as he releases the contraption that helps hold the calf in place. He always has a warm, albeit somewhat flirtatious, smile when he talks to me. And he talks to me every chance he gets. He goes in for a high-five and my hand smacks loudly against the soft leather of his glove, creating a dust cloud that glitters in the sunlight.

I can do this. Warmed by pride, I take a step back.

"Hey, no!" A booming voice cuts through the noise, stopping everyone in their tracks. I swear even the cattle are startled enough to quiet down. "She's not helping."

6

Austin

A burning electrical current swoops through my veins as I watch Cecily and Colt interact. It's not a matter of jealousy. Exactly as expected, these damn men are too horny to focus on doing their job. With close to 5,000 calves to brand this week, they can't be distracted. I charge forward, weaving between cattle with the expertise that comes from thirty-seven years around them.

"She doesn't know the first thing about vaccinating and when she fucks it up, we'll be shit out of luck for at least two weeks, until Tate can bring more in."

"I showed her how. She's got this," Kate yells back from the fence.

"She's done a couple without issue. I think it's fine, man. Kate needs a break, so unless you want to come do it yourself, you need to relax and let her try," Jackson says. Naturally, he's going to agree with his wife.

A grumble rattles through my chest.

"You mad she's doing a better job than you can, Aus?" Colt chides, reaching out to poke me in the ribs. I grab his hand, yanking it until his fingers all but break before letting go. He shakes off the pain with a hearty laugh.

"I'm not about to be sued when she breaks her foot because she wore sneakers for branding."

"Damn, girly. He's right about that. You need to get yourself a pair of shitkickers," Colt agrees. "It's no fun having these fuckers step on your toes without 'em. Ask me how I know."

My eyes narrow at him. "Don't you have a job to do?"

"She can borrow mine." Kate struggles to pull the cowboy boots over her swollen ankles.

For the next twenty minutes, I do nothing but watch Cecily work. The irony isn't lost on me—I stormed over here because I was worried she was distracting my employees, only to become sidetracked myself. Within the first five minutes, I knew she had the process figured out and wasn't going to screw it up.

Now I'm watching for purely selfish reasons, ignoring the voice telling me I shouldn't. I'm nothing if not a simple man, no better than the rest. I can't help but notice the tiny sliver of exposed lower back, and the way her ass strains against her jeans when she bends over. Standing up, she wipes beaded sweat from her forehead with the back of her hand, and a smile lights her face. Cecily might be the one person on Earth who finds joy in the most boring part of branding.

Quit staring at her, idiot. I can't. Or maybe I don't want to.

The sun highlights her every movement with an angelic glow. Her jeans and t-shirt are coated in dirt, which clouds around her as her palms skate across her thighs. Her blonde hair's pulled back in a tight bun and covered with a Wells Ranch baseball cap, and her bare arms are already lightly tanned from the hours she's spent in the garden. To an outsider, she might look like she belongs here.

Beryl's lunchtime whistle snaps me from my trance, and I finally get the nerve to look away from Cecily. But not before her eyes meet mine through her thick eyelashes. A smile slips across her face that feels meant for me alone, and it's so contagious, I can't help but return it.

It's no use being annoyed at the boys for acting friendly with her over lunch. I understand that. I can't exactly tell them what to do during their off time, although I'd love to try right about now.

It's also not fair to be annoyed over her wanting to sit with them. I'm not delusional enough to think she'd join me, even if she does typically sit directly across from me at the kitchen table. I've been nothing but an asshole because I'm not sure how *not* to be under the circumstances. City girls love to visit the ranch, pretend they're living an episode of *Yellowstone*, and then take off as soon as things stop being exciting. I've been burned by more than one woman who wasn't really in it for the long haul. And every time I walk away less myself.

The problem is, I can't stop looking at her. And I'm having a real hard time reminding myself that I would be doing everybody a favour by pushing her out of here sooner rather than later. Then my guys won't spend every spare moment trying to get her to look at them, and neither will I.

"Since we're making good time today, I think we should give Cecily a little show in exchange for her hard work," Denny announces between bites. "See, we use Nordforks to help wrangle the calves now, because it's efficient and easier on our bodies when we're doing four hundred or more daily. But the real fun is when we get them to the ground by hand. That's the true cowboy shit."

My baby brother looks to me for approval and I give a sullen nod, despite this being exactly the show-off, horny cowboy shit I'm concerned about. He's right about making good time and the day isn't unbearably hot, so there's no real need to rush. Sometimes it's just easiest for everybody if I let the guys have their fun.

"Hell yeah," Red shouts. "Just you wait, Cecily. Maybe the old boss man here will even show you how he used to do it back in his rodeo days."

"Oh yeah? Here I thought you *definitely* weren't a cowboy?" She smiles over at me.

"I'm not," I shoot a sideways glance at Red, "and I will not."

"Oh, let's do a calf-tying competition. Whoever has the fastest time tying gets a case of beer tomorrow—Austin's buying." Denny's practically jumping in his seat with excitement about a stupid little competition.

"Whatever. You guys do what you want." I shake my head.

My agreement is only slightly influenced by my wanting a certain woman to think I'm not a total stick-in-the-mud asshole. I know I shouldn't care what she thinks. Normally, I'm fine with being the responsible eldest brother, even if it makes me somewhat "boring", according to Denny. After all, that personality trait is the reason the ranch is successful. Even after my father left me to take over this overwhelming operation at the ripe old age of twenty-five. Today, though, I'd love to be one of the guys.

A few ranch hands cheer in response. Chatter starts up about rules, betting, and what beer the potential winner wants.

"Sounds like fun. Can I try? If somebody shows me how to tie." Cecily turns to me with a raised eyebrow. Daring me to say no.

Focusing on keeping my face flat, I stare straight back. "Don't sue me when you get hurt, darlin'."

"Hell yeah. We might finally have somebody to do the ladies' steer scramble at the rodeo this year," Red hollers. As if winning a paltry gift card for nearly being mauled by a steer is something to be stoked about. I've done a lot of stupid shit in my younger days, but that rodeo event is asinine—only someone without a functioning brain would sign up.

With that, the guys finish their lunch in record time, and are eager to display their calf-tying skills for the pretty girl. And, boy, do they ever show off. It almost makes me wonder if the Nordforks were a waste of money—all this time, I could've had an attractive woman on site to keep them working diligently.

Who am I to talk, though?

Knowing her ass is parked on the fence and her eyes are on me is almost enough to make me walk out to the pasture, grab my retired roping horse, and show her how a real cowboy does things. I haven't competed in tie-down roping events in more than a decade, but that doesn't mean the muscle memory isn't still there. Denny hauls a calf to me and the animalistic, sex-driven part of my brain takes over. I lift the one-hundred-pound animal with ease. By the fifth time, I don't even care how sore my muscles will be tomorrow. If I'd agreed to join their absurd competition, I'd win by a long shot.

I'm no better than the other men, busting my ass to keep her gaze firmly on me.

When it's finally Cecily's turn, every nerve-ending sizzles as I watch her step forward with unbridled confidence. Nothing like the city girl I expected. Red moves in to help her, but my longer legs are faster—I'm practically on her and she visibly tenses from head to toe. Her body recoiling seems to be reflexive anytime I get close to her. She reacted similarly when I placed a hand on her shoulder to reach for the chilli pot earlier; entire body freezing, face twisted with disgust as she shrunk away.

I hand her my gloves, and she smiles to herself as she pulls them on. Her small hands make the worn leather look like giant ice-hockey mitts. Pulled by a taut rope, a calf appears. *It's go time.* With one hand on her tail and another on the back legs, Red gears up to get the calf to the ground for branding. With little hesitation, Cecily grabs the front like she's done this a thousand times.

"Get the rope round there... yeah, just like... you got it..." She's following the steps and tying up the legs before I even have the chance to get my words out. Clearly, she's been studying how we all do it. Holding down an animal that weighs almost as much as her, she waits calmly for Colt to bring over the branding iron. Every time I have a shadow of doubt, she makes me feel like an idiot for expecting so little from her.

I hate how easily impressed I am by this woman. She's certainly not the first nor the last to help with branding—hell, Kate's usually in here like a dirty shirt when she isn't pregnant. It's not *that* impressive. Embarrassingly, I hate knowing Cecily didn't need my help even more. Leaving me standing there with my hands in my pockets when all I really wanted was to jump right in next to her.

Panting, covered in dirt and cow shit, and radiating pride, she gets to her feet. Cecily stumbles back until she's close enough she can probably feel my hot breath on her neck. Yet, she remains loose and calm for the first time. Likely because she doesn't realize it's me she's standing next to. So relaxed and joyful, I can't help but smile in response.

"Damn, girl." Denny hands her a cold beer. "You sure you've never done this before?"

"Honest! That was cool, though. I can't believe I did that." She cracks the can open and takes a long gulp. At some point, she lost her hat and her hair's no longer slicked back neatly. Loose blonde strands stick out in every direction, and a few small pieces cling to the sweat along her hairline. There's dirt smudged on her jaw, and I can't help but envision how soft her skin might be under my calloused thumb. It would be so easy to reach over and rub the dirt away.

"Glad you didn't fire me yet?"

Lost in thought about touching her face, her voice catches me off guard and stops me just before I do something stupid. Her face shining at me cracks through my chest. And I... clam up.

Fuck, I do this every damn time.

Something about her voice and her smile and her fucking earth-shattering gaze stops me in my tracks every time. I lose the ability to form words, let alone sentences. Leaving me with two default modes: asshole boss and silent douchebag.

The only sound I manage to make is a gruff snort. I guess it's better than creepily brushing my hand against her jaw, but not by much. Her eyebrow raises playfully. She's constantly studying, dissecting, and analyzing me, as if she can read my thoughts.

"He's mad that a girl can do a better job than half his guys." Kate jabs me in the rib with her sharp elbow. "Careful, Austin, your misogyny is showing."

I roll my eyes. *Seriously?*

"Nah, he had a good point about me needing boots and he lent me gloves. If he wanted me to fail miserably, he could've made it happen. So, thanks, boss."

"Welcome," I mutter.

Once Kate leaves to talk to Jackson, Cecily leans over and lowers her voice. "It's okay to admit you're so impressed by my work ethic you can't think of a good enough apology—or maybe admit you liked watching. No shame in either."

Her eyes meet mine, her knowing smile sending my heart into erratic oblivion. I did like it. Too damn much for somebody not looking to have his heart broken again.

And then she adds five words that send my head swimming, making me question every damn decision I've made since she got here. "I know *I* liked watching."

7

Austin

Apparently, I've grown accustomed to seeing Cecily in her usual seat, directly across from mine at the far end of the twelve-foot dining table. I don't realize how much I expect to see her until I walk into the kitchen and she isn't there. She and I rarely talk or acknowledge each other's presence, but it still feels off. She's always unusually happy for five in the morning and, to my horror, I've grown to enjoy the cheeriness. Today's weird vibe isn't helped by the boys being long gone, driving the cattle out to leased grazing land for the summer. I pour myself a steaming black coffee and slump into my well-worn spot, pretending not to notice how quiet it is in here. Beryl and Kate buzz around the kitchen, while Odessa shovels *Cheerios* into her mouth.

"Where's the city girl?" I finally can't stop myself from asking. She busted her ass during the last eight days of branding, and I have a right to know if my employee's sick or injured. Nothing more.

"She has a name, and you know it, you ass." Kate rolls her eyes at me. "She's going to town this morning."

"If she hasn't left, can one of you go tell her to grab the supplement order from Tate's?"

The pair glare at me with perfectly matching contempt. Beryl lifts flour-coated hands in the air and cocks an eyebrow. "We're up to our elbows in bread dough. Man up and ask her yourself, honey. I haven't seen her leave yet."

Fuck. I swear even Odessa stops mid-bite to give me a look about how pathetic I am. What I would give right now to be kilometres away, on horseback, driving cattle with the crew instead of stuck with these three. With a grunt, I push away from the table and walk to Cecily's cabin.

I'm kicking the spare tire she still hasn't properly replaced, when her voice rings through the humid morning air. "Checking your handi-work?"

"Wondering why you still haven't gotten new tires like I told you to."

"I don't exactly make a killing as a 'farm wife'. I'll do it when I can afford to." An echoing beep sounds as she remotely unlocks the doors and begins down her front stairs. Her blonde hair bounces against her shoulders with each step.

"Unless you're driving directly to the tire shop, you're not taking this car anywhere."

She stops in front of me, and her sweet perfume envelops us. A white sundress swishes against her thighs, highlighting how tan her skin has become. I've never seen her in anything but jeans or leggings, which leaves me wondering when and where she's been privately tanning because that golden hue certainly wasn't achieved during working hours. A question about where her tan lines might be sends a rush to my cock. Is it her upper thigh from wearing shorts? Bikini line? Or... fuck. Maybe there's no tan line at all. The thought of her having a hidden spot somewhere on *my* ranch, where she's suntanning naked, consumes me.

And that's when she catches me staring. It's a miracle I'm not drool-ing.

Christ, get it together.

A smirk creeps onto her lips. "I repeat. Why the hell not?"

Why the hell not... what? I rack my brain, trying to remember what we were talking about, fighting to ignore the scorching heat in my cheeks and ears.

"It's unsafe to drive at high speeds or long distances on this spare. Take a ranch truck. And pick up the horse supplements from Tate's." I do my best to shift back into asshole-boss mode. My eyes trained on hers because, if I risk looking anywhere else, I'll start undressing her in my mind again.

Her foot taps the gravel impatiently. "You're aware it's my day off, right? The least you could do is say please if you want me to run your errands."

"When we live this far out of town, grabbing my order for me would be the nice thing to do." My arms cross against my chest.

"Basic manners would be nice, too. Please. Thank you. Your four-year-old niece even knows how to use her magic words. Also, just because you're my boss doesn't mean you control me—I'm taking my car because I won't drive those trucks. Mock me for being a city girl all you want, but they're too big and intimidating. Needing to park one in town makes me nauseous."

"Then we'll take my truck." I start down the pathway toward my house. Sensing she's not behind me, I spin around. Confusion floods her face. "We haven't got all day, City Girl."

"I feel like this is a trap. Are you going to take me to town and ditch me there? No way you're offering to be nice when I'm pretty sure you detest me." She smiles as if she's joking, but the hitch in her voice says otherwise.

I'm too taken aback to dwell on why I'm willing to drop everything I should be doing today for this. For her. "I don't detest you."

"Well, you definitely don't *like* me."

I can see why she'd think that, but it still sends my stomach turning.

"That's not—I just..." I don't detest her. I don't *not* like her. While everyone else seems to be completely comfortable with her at the ranch, I'm becoming more flustered by her presence with each passing day.

Thanks to her, I'm as off balance as a shoddy carnival ride. "I'm sorry for making you think that. Are you coming?"

I gesture toward the truck, taking a step backward, waiting for her to follow.

Cecily remains steadfast, staring back at me but not moving. Her tongue brushes over her bottom lip like she has something she's holding herself back from saying.

"Please." My voice strains.

Admittedly, I've thought about wanting to do *bad* things to her in a few moments of weakness, but the good things she's making me do are terrifying. No. I'm only obliging her because there's no way my conscience will allow me to send her to town in a tin can with only three decent wheels. At least, that's what I tell myself as I watch her climb into my truck.

My fingers tap on the steering wheel, and she leans her head against the passenger window. Offering her a ride was a stupid idea. Sixty fucking kilometres in a truck together. We're not friends. We don't converse. Driving with her as a distraction is likely as dangerous as driving drunk. Plus, if my sudden change in attitude from pissy to nice is weird and unexpected to me, it must be confusing as hell for her. I thought I wanted to dislike her, wait impatiently for her to get bored with farm life and leave. Then go back to not worrying about seeing her face at the kitchen table. I thought I wanted her to disappear because it would be easier in the long run. But every interaction makes me less sure about what I want.

It's because of the dress. You're being bamboozled by a short summer dress and tanned legs.

She rolls the window down as we pass the lilac bushes at the end of the driveway, sticking her head out to inhale deeply. Once the air no longer smells like sweet perfume, there's contentment in her eyes, and she sinks deeper into the leather seat.

"You like lilacs?" I ask in a cringeworthy attempt at being friendly.

"Used to. Now I hate them. But the blooms are almost gone, so I wanted to smell them while I still could. See if I like them again."

"And?" I cock an eyebrow.

"Nope, still hate 'em. At least they'll be gone soon. I promised myself I wouldn't waste another moment thinking about the shit they represent when they're finally gone."

I wasn't anticipating my initial yes or no type of question to lead to even more questions than answers. Regardless, I bite. "What exactly do they represent?"

"The entire backyard at my old house was overgrown with them. I loved them when we bought the house. My... ex and I." She stumbles over the word ex. "Anyway, when I started to hate both him and the house, I hated the lilacs by association."

"Oh... makes sense." Great. The first time I'm alone with her and it's gone from me fighting not to get an erection at the sight of her to talking about her ex.

She grows quiet, and I see her worrying her bottom lip in my periphery. Even though I may be a tiny bit curious, I shouldn't press for more. From the moment she arrived at the ranch, I assumed she was running from something. Nobody without a sordid past leaves everything behind to work on a cattle ranch in the middle of nowhere. Hell, it's how we've gotten some of our best cowboys—running from the law, jilted lovers, child support, addiction. There's an unspoken rule about minding our own business when it comes to the reasons people are here. But *fuck me*, I'm curious.

"So you left the city for a change of scenery?"

She sighs. "And still ended up with the darn lilacs. I don't know how much Beryl might've told you about why I came here, but I'd rather not talk about it."

I turn to look at Cecily, but she doesn't meet my eyes, keeping her gaze aimed at the glovebox like something could jump out at any moment. Her hands rub against her thighs, shifting the hem of her dress up and down.

My fingers rashly reach toward her, settling on top of her shaky hand to steady it. The scorching burn of our skin touching lasts for less than a second before she pulls away. It's enough to leave a lasting impression, though. I want to touch her again.

"She told me nothing," I reassure her.

"Okay... okay, that's good," she says, turning to look out the passenger window.

8

Cecily

"So, where do you need to go?" he asks in his typical, growly timbre.

"Um, I need to pick up my new cell phone and go to the tack shop."

Austin eyes me curiously, suggesting I have no business requesting to visit the tack shop. And, under any other circumstance, it would be the last place on Earth I would choose to shop on my day off. This is a far cry from the time I spent as a teenage mall rat, hopping between trendy stores while drinking an overpriced smoothie.

"I can't expect to keep wearing Kate's boots, can I? And my boss won't let me help with anything other than kitchen chores without a pair of 'shitkickers'." I'm still entirely unsure what constitutes shitkickers versus regular boots, but I'm fairly confident I'll figure it out once I'm at the store.

"Okay, City Girl."

"Thanks, Not-A-Cowboy."

His dirt-smudged hands flex on the steering wheel as he turns into a parking stall on the main street. Making me think about him briefly holding my hand when we left the ranch. I kicked myself the entire drive for pulling away but, with both hands firmly on the wheel, he never gave me an opportunity to reciprocate.

Kate told me the town of Wells Canyon was used for the setting of a Hallmark Movie a few years back, and I completely believe it. Add some fluffy fake snow and gaudy Christmas decorations; it's the perfect town for a corporate snob to be stuck in over the holidays, so they can fall in love with a Christmas-obsessed, small-town veterinarian.

Brick and wood buildings are dispersed along either side of the street, sun-faded and weathered from long, hot summers and harsh Canadian winters. Every spare wall has a mural, most of which are dedicated to the area's rich agricultural history. More than one seems to be specific to Wells Ranch. I glance over at Austin as we walk along the cobbled sidewalk. I can't imagine what it would be like to have this much familial influence over an entire town. My parents still live in the house I grew up in, not far out of Vancouver proper, and I'm not convinced their immediate neighbours would notice if they left.

"Your family's kind of a big deal, eh?"

He snorts. "Something like that. We've been around here for four generations and I'm related to half the town."

"It must've been fun growing up with so much family nearby. I don't have any siblings, and my extended relatives lived far away, so it was just me and my parents most of the time."

"Yeah, I guess it wasn't so bad. Even though we live near each other, we don't really spend time together anymore. Not since my grandparents passed."

"That's a shame. I love the idea of a big family."

I'm drawn in by the hand-painted, floral window art outside a quaint home goods store. My gait slows, allowing me a few seconds to peer inside as Austin plows ahead. So much for my relaxing day in town; he's going to be rushing me to get back to the ranch. I'm sure even Wells Canyon is too big of a metropolis for his cranky ass. After lengthening my strides to catch up to him, I enter the cell phone shop out of breath. He stands around, hands in his pockets, with his usual annoyed expression as I speak to the employee.

"So, he said it'll be about fifteen minutes to set everything up if you have somewhere you want to go," I say to Austin. "Sorry."

"I'll stay here and wait for your phone. You wanted to go into the girly store down the street, so go."

Excuse me? "Who are you and what have you done with Austin Wells? Are you feeling okay?"

"You need to do your errands, right? Caught me in a rare good mood—don't make me regret it, darlin'."

Enough said. I'll ignore the patronizing tone if it means shopping.

"Okay, thanks. I'll be back in a few." I dart from the store before he has the chance to change his mind, and practically skip my way down the empty sidewalk.

My fingers stroke a luxurious towel display, noticing how my once well-moisturized, manicured hands catch on the fabric—thanks to healing blisters and newly callused skin. The feeling makes me squirm with disgust and I scan the shelves for any cream that might fix my mangled hands. I toss two bath sheets, a large bottle of mango-scented hand lotion, cuticle oil, and a charcoal face mask into my basket.

That should help me feel more like myself.

Bringing a candle to my nose, I'm hit with a familiar, gut-wrenching aroma that causes me to nearly drop the glass jar. Even after it's safely back on the shelf, I can taste the tobacco and vanilla perfume in the air. For a brief moment, it jars memories of walking into the ensuite bathroom while KJ got ready for work. I pick up candle after candle, begging for something to relieve me of his stench and his memory.

Surrounded by a blast of cold, oxygen-sucking energy, Austin walks through the chiming front door with a paper bag from the cell phone shop. His presence brings me rushing back to my KJ-less reality—*thank God*. Austin's entirely out of place, and not only due to his dirty jeans and plaid flannel shirt. Or the permanent scowl embedded in his face. For somebody who moves between live cattle without hesitation, he's incredibly apprehensive lumbering through aisles of fragile merchandise. Seeing him anywhere outside the ranch feels weird, and I struggle to hold back a giggle.

"Sorry, I'm almost done." I quickly set down the candle that his appearance made me forget I was cradling.

"Take as much time as you need." He picks up the small jar and raises it to his nose. His face pinches as he slams it back onto the shelf with such force it's a miracle the glass doesn't shatter. "It smells like a urinal puck. Who would buy that?"

I don't think Austin means to be funny, but I can't contain my laughter anymore, even as the woman working the cash register glares at us over the top of her glasses. His lip twitches upward into the faintest smile, and my breath catches in my throat; warmth trickling down my spine.

With a hushed voice, mindful of the employee keeping a glowering eye over us, I say, "Nobody with any sense. It smells absolutely terrible. This one,"—I hand him a leather-scented candle from my basket, enraptured by the way our fingertips graze—"*actually* smells amazing. Now let's go before the old biddy up front boots us out."

Taking a cautious sniff, he nods thoughtfully before grabbing a duplicate from the shelf and heading to the counter. To be fair, I don't know much about Austin Wells. But owning a candle or any décor—other than dead animals hung on the wall—isn't something I expected.

"I'll pay for her stuff," he says, pulling a worn leather wallet from his back pocket.

"I'm a big girl with my own money."

He shakes his head, encroaching on my space to prevent me from handing my cash over to the employee. "No need. Save it for your tires."

My shoulders fall as I watch him pay for all this crap that's definitely less important than tires for my car.

Just as I'm considering telling him to forget it, and putting everything back, he adds, "Consider it a thank-you gift. You, uh, did really well with branding."

I try to hide the fact that I'm blushing by turning quickly on my heel. Austin Wells just... *complimented me.* Without a hint of sarcasm or any clear motivation. And my cheeks have turned to molten lava because those words *did something* to me. Beryl, Kate, and multiple cowboys have sung my praises for weeks, but Austin giving me a single compliment is making my knees weak and my brain foggy.

We step out into the sunshine, and he grazes my back as he steps to the outside. The road edge. Unlike when he raced ahead before, our feet fall in sync. "You didn't have to do that. Thank you, though. I'll get the tires fixed. I do have the money, so you know. Or most of it, anyway. I'll have it all soon. Um... if there's a guy to change them in town or—"

Austin interrupts my rambling when we get to the truck. "Don't worry 'bout it. Tack store?"

"Yes, please." I dig into the bag containing my new cell phone. Even though I have the number memorized, adding Beryl as a proper contact is exhilarating. My fingers tap on the screen, shocked to find there's already a contact profile there. "D-did you add your number to my phone?"

"Mhm," he murmurs, clearly not seeing what's so strange about this situation.

Austin's hand grips my headrest as he turns to back out of the stall. At first, I inconspicuously weave my head away from his incoming open palm. Then, once my nervous system determines the move isn't threatening, his proximity sets a kaleidoscope of butterflies free in my chest. Imagining his hand slipping off the upholstered seat, and touching my bare shoulder, elicits a shiver down my spine.

"You know you need to actually speak—using words—to talk to somebody on the phone, right?" I know he takes ranch-related phone calls a thousand times per day, but he always steps out of the room. It remains to be seen whether he actually speaks to the person on the other end.

The corner of his lip pulls into a strikingly adorable smile. Considering how hot he is with a scowl, I'd be in serious trouble if he smiled like this all the time. If I wasn't staring directly at him, which is something

I find myself doing a *lot* more than I should lately, I would've missed it altogether. Like a shooting star across his face, gone as quickly as it appeared.

"Not if we text, darlin'."

Am I having a stroke?

"Text?" I croak. "I didn't peg you for a texter."

His nostrils flare as he maintains focus on the road ahead. "I could start if you'd like."

It's official. I'm definitely dead because there's no way this grizzly bear of a man who seems to like looking at me, but isn't interested in talking to me, wants me to *text him*. It's a seriously laughable thought. Though he's not laughing. In fact, he's right back to his natural stoic expression.

"Yeah?" My corpse somehow forms words. "What would we text about?"

"I'm sure you'll think of something."

The pungent smell of leather floods my nostrils the moment we step into the tack shop. A shelved wall filled with cowboy boots would be overwhelming on the best of days. Right now, it's definitely too much to think about. What with Austin's offer to text him hanging in the air and all.

I shop mostly in peace, although I can't stop myself from stealing glances in his direction. I want to understand why he's so hot and cold. He says he doesn't hate me, and got visibly nervous when I suggested that he doesn't like me. Austin doesn't exactly exude Casanova energy, so I don't think he's trying to toy with me.

Anyway, I shouldn't care what his game plan is because surely it's too soon to be interested in a new man.

And yet, I'm more interested than I thought would ever be possible.

Thanks to a slightly condescending but overall helpful employee, I learn I can pretty much wear whatever boots I want for work. Which doesn't make my purchase decision any easier. By the time I've made my selection, Austin's too busy arguing with Tate, the store owner, about horse supplements to potentially intervene and pay for my boots. Although a very small part of me wishes he would when the price tag nearly causes me to pass out. I officially don't have anywhere close to enough money for tires. Who knew cowboys are out here trashing shoes worth hundreds of dollars?

Bag in hand, I pretend to be perusing an assortment of blingy belt buckles while watching the heated debate. Tate's in his mid-fifties, and has been sweet to me anytime I've stopped in to pick up supply orders for the ranch. Today, there's an irritated wrinkling between his brows and his lips are pursed as he listens to whatever Austin's rambling about. Before now, I wasn't sure whether Austin was capable of saying more than half a dozen words in a row. I also didn't know I would find it as attractive as I do. Although, maybe it's not the discussion so much as the ass-hugging Wranglers, cowboy boots, and plaid long-sleeve that's tight across his broad shoulders.

After a few minutes, Austin turns and searches for me. A comforting sensation fills my body when our eyes lock. Apparently, the past few weeks of barely talking have taught us to read each other's minds because I briefly look at the open doorway and he's immediately walking toward it. No questions asked—we're back at the truck in under thirty seconds.

"Do you want to see my boots?" I don't leave time for him to answer in my excitement to show them off. While Kate rocks a plain, camel-brown pair, I couldn't stop myself from grabbing the darker shade, square toe with bright turquoise stitching.

"They're boots. Seen one pair, you've seen 'em all," he says, stealing a quick glance out of the corner of his eye. "Anywhere else you need to go?"

I shake my head no, fingering the detailed stitching on my new "shit-kickers". We pull back onto the road and, a couple of blocks later, into the only gas station in town.

In a single motion, he slides off the seat, pulls his wallet from his pocket, and holds it out to me. "You want anything inside? My treat."

Call it trauma, call it feminism, call it stupidity. His offer forms a knotted ball in my throat, that I'm forced to speak around to politely decline. There's nothing about the way he's acted today that should make this feel like a test—yet it does. He's probably offering because it's the chivalrous thing to do, not because he has malicious intentions. But, like the towels and cuticle oil, it's another thing he could potentially hold over my head. And, even though I *am* thirsty, there's no way I can walk into the store with him and buy my own drink. I can guarantee he wouldn't let me.

I shut my eyes, letting my temple rest against the sunbaked passenger window. As I'm still kicking myself for not taking him up on his offer, he climbs back into the pickup.

His gravelly voice makes my eyes pop open. "Dr. Pepper and cream soda slushies. Take whichever one you like. I'll drink either."

Bizarre. Austin outside of the ranch is simply bizarre.

9

Cecily

For a moment, neither of us seems eager to leave the truck. And then cowboys walk around the side of the barn, and the spell over us is broken.

"Hey, Filly," Red shouts in our direction, using the new nickname the cowboys have given me. His tattooed, thick frame moves toward us, leading five other men. He runs a hand through his thick mop of dark reddish-brown hair as he speaks. "We're heading to the river and you have no excuse not to join today."

Austin's truck door slams shut behind me, and his cowboy boots crunch over the rocky driveway back to his house.

"Just give me a few minutes. I'll meet you down there," I yell in the direction of the men.

"No excuses, Filly. Better see you there," Red says.

They continue walking, still dressed in their riding gear and not looking at all like a group of men heading to the river. Without thinking, I follow in Austin's footsteps, catching up to him as he's walking up his front porch steps. When he spins around, there's a fleeting look of happiness in the way the corners of his eyes crinkle.

"I wanted to thank you for today."

"Okay," he says dryly.

The Earth is spinning on its proper axis again; he's back to normal.

"So, you know... thank you. Do you want to come for a swim?"

"I have a lot of work I should get to." He reaches up to rub his jaw, and a momentary fantasy about what his scratchy beard might feel like on my skin almost has me reaching out to him. His stare falls to my lips, and his Adam's apple bobs in his throat. I don't know if he's thinking about kissing me, but I do know I want him to be thinking about it.

The summer air fills my lungs just as a breeze slaps me with the scent of lilacs. A vicious joke. *Thanks, mother nature.* Fluttery feelings are replaced with heavy, KJ-infused chains wrapping around my chest until each inhale is a struggle. I'm not crying, but my vision is hazy as if I am, with floating clouds blurring the world around me.

I try to tell him in a polite tone that I need to leave, but the blood rushing past my ears muffles everything, so there's a chance my lips are moving without sound. Though it feels like I'm trudging through deep sand, I force my feet to move. Without looking back—without even breathing in the summer air—I walk away from the man I don't want to walk away from. Not even a little bit.

When I turn the corner, safely out of sight, I throw my back against the siding of a random tool shed. Leaning on the coarse wood, I take a few forced breaths until the world's crisp again.

I should curl up in bed and cry over my marriage ending. I shouldn't be thinking about a certain rancher, with a thick beard and strong arms, kissing me. I should be upset about cutting somebody I once loved from my life. I shouldn't be eager to hop into bed with the first cute guy I see. I should be heartbroken, shouldn't I?

There's only one person here who can help me figure out what to do. And, luckily, she can always be found bent over a certain marble island, elbow-deep in dough. So I run.

"Beryl!" I blow through the screen door, letting it slam shut.

Her head pops out from the walk-in pantry off the kitchen. "Everything okay, honey?"

"I'm ready to talk. About him. About why I came here."

She forces me to wait until we both have a coffee cup in our hands, and we're seated on the porch swing overlooking the flourishing hay fields. For the first time, I tell somebody the whole truth. How he made everything seem perfect until he had me and then, like Jekyll and Hyde, he flipped. How quick I was to side with him when friends or family expressed concern. And all the events of the night I drove here. Beryl nods along as if nothing I tell her is new or shocking information. By the time I finish, my full cup has grown cold and my throat is hoarse.

"So, are you telling me all this because you're finally committed to not going back?"

"God, I've long been committed to not going back." *Haven't I?* I mean, I've started making friends. I've thought long and hard about kissing somebody new. I bought new towels for the cabin. For *my* cabin. Isn't that enough to prove I'm done with him? "I won't survive him next time."

My revelation is enough to make Beryl feel the need to place a small hand on my shoulder as water brims my eyes. I hadn't said the words out loud before, but it's true. I know it's true.

"I just..." My fingernails tap the ceramic mug. "I want to move on... But every time I get a glimpse of my old self, something comes back to haunt me and steal the moment away."

"Honey, you came in from a heck of a storm. You can't expect to immediately be warm and dry. All you can do is strip the wet clothing, wrap yourself in a blanket, and allow yourself the time it takes to weather it. And it's completely understandable to miss him, or miss what once was, even after everything."

I stare down at the creamy swirl left unstirred in my coffee. "The thing is... I don't miss him. I'm not sad to be without him. I keep feeling haunted by the thought that I *should* be feeling those things. Like I should miss him or still love him or whatever. Instead, I feel guilty because I don't think I'm hurting the way I should be."

"Y'know, you keep saying 'should'. I think that word does nothing except lead to regrets. Whether you're talking about something you *should* be doing now or something you *should've* done in the past, it'll only bog you down. Forgetting about that silly word, what are you actually feeling? Focus on that."

We swing in silence for a long while, letting the chickadees do the talking.

What am I actually feeling?

As I start to check off an imaginary grid of emotions, I get BINGO more than once. *Is it humanly possible to feel every emotion at the same time?* Even with all the feelings circling in my mind, relief about being at Wells Ranch and regret for not coming sooner are the two carrying the most impact.

I need to give up caring about anything to do with KJ, even if the damn lilacs never stop blooming. I'm never going back, so fuck whatever he would think or say about what I'm doing. Fuck being controlled.

"I want to focus on being here. And getting back to who I was before this. I'm going down to the river with the guys. Want to come?"

"Oh, honey, none of those boys are prepared to see me in a bathing suit. Best I stay here, I think." She laughs, patting my thigh as she stands up to head back inside.

With my chest no longer constricted, I drop my cup into the sink and jog to the cabin to slip into my bathing suit. On the days when the guys will be out late, I've been going down to the rocky riverbank to read and relax alone. But having company, especially after such a strange day, will be a welcome change of pace. And I really do enjoy being around the cowboys. It's what I imagine having twenty brothers might be like. Without all the horror that would come with having *that many* brothers.

"Wow, she made it," Red calls out from the boulder he's spread out on, raising a beer in the air in salute. "Thought you hated us, Filly."

"Quit calling me Filly." I roll my eyes, setting out a towel on the least rocky section of the bank, and plopping down. "I don't hate you guys—although, the nickname isn't my favourite. Who would want to be named after a horse? Oh, right.... Sorry, Colt." I smile over at him.

"Rude." Colt shoots me a joking stink eye and I silently mouth him an apology.

"A *young* horse though, Filly. Could be worse." Denny snickers, sinking deeper into the water. I have no idea how he can be so vastly different from his oldest brother. Vibrant, loud, and carefree. Their middle brother, Jackson, is somewhere in between the two. More responsible than Denny, as a soon-to-be father of two, but more easygoing than tightly wound Austin.

Standing next to me, Colt strips his shirt to reveal harsh tan lines that make it appear as though he never took it off at all. His tall frame steps gingerly along uneven rocks to the centre of the flowing water before hopping into the sunlit wading pool. At some point in time, someone built a swimming hole out of rocks. The makeshift wall slows the current down enough that a sunny, hot day makes the water tolerable—compared to the cold, glacier-fed river, at least.

Red nods his auburn hair in agreement. "Exactly. We could go with a cow nickname, though. Do you prefer heifer?"

The other guys giggle as if heifer's a naughty word. Honestly, I may as well be spending time around thirteen-year-olds, not men between the ages of twenty-five and forty-five. And rugged cowboys, no less.

"I prefer my name, to be quite honest."

"No way, Filly. You helped brand 5,000 head. You're a cowgirl now and you need a nickname if you want to be part of the crew," Denny yells over the rushing water.

My heart swells at the notion that I could ever be part of this crew. I suppose I prefer being called Filly over City Girl, which is what they've been referring to me as up until now. *Thanks to Austin.*

"Bullshit. Only, like, half of you guys even have nicknames. But I guess if I *have* to have one, I'd rather Filly over Sundial."

"God, she's ruthless. Maybe she should be called heifer, after all. Coming after a man who's trying to mind my own business over here," Beau Campbell, aka Sundial, shouts from further down the bank as he tosses a rock into the water. Colt's skinnier, shaggier, younger brother. He apparently earned his nickname by "doing so much standing around on the job, you can tell the time by the shadow he casts".

"Sorry, Sundial." I laugh.

I lean back on my elbows, feeling the sun sizzling my bare legs. The smell of hot, tanned skin permeates the air, filling me with imaginings about childhood summers spent at my grandparents' cabin. I've been yearning for slow, relaxed lake days ever since my last visit there at sixteen. At this moment, it feels like I've finally found it.

There's that emotion again. Relief.

I regret getting a cell phone the moment I finish setting it up. *Four hundred* emails clog my inbox—ninety percent coming directly from KJ. I read the first two, which are filled with vague threats that make my heart plummet into my stomach, nearly erasing the respite I've spent weeks working hard for.

Don't make me have to come looking for you. Enough is enough, Cecily. Don't think you can leave me that easily.

Amongst the inbox trash, another familiar name sticks out. Sara Lyons. In the midst of everything happening, I practically forgot about the closest thing I had to a friend in Kerrisdale. We've never hung out without our husbands present—I haven't been allowed any friendships not involving KJ in years. Still, it's enough for me to feel bad about leaving her entirely in the dark for a full month.

Cecily: Hi, I wanted to reach out and let you know I'm okay. I got a new cell phone if you ever want to chat: (555) 259-8228. Please don't give my number to KJ. I need my space. Thanks for being such a good friend to me.

I need my space. Barf.

My fingers linger on the keyboard, debating whether I should give her my phone number at all. Whether I should even bother contacting her. I'm tempted to write an email outlining the shit he put me through, so she can understand why I left. But old habits keep me taking on the blame myself. And I suppose it would be nice to hear a familiar voice. *Screw it.* I hit send and move on.

With my stomach already churning, there's no time like the present to make a promised phone call. I wouldn't have thought twice about calling a few years ago, but now it's foreign and uncomfortable. Like cold-calling a stranger.

My mom picks up just before my call's sent to voicemail. "Hello?"

"Hey, Mom."

"Oh, my God! Do you know how close your dad was to driving to whatever godforsaken small town you said you were going to? It's been a month, Cecily. *A month!*"

"Sorry—I wasn't trying to worry you guys. I'm safe. I've just been working hard."

"When are you coming home?"

I take a deep breath filled with dread, knowing that what I'm about to say isn't the answer she's hoping to hear. "I'm getting my bearings and figuring out what I want to do. I don't know if I want to come back to the city."

"I recognize you've gone through a lot, but running off into the wilderness is not the answer. You are not Reese Witherspoon in *Wild.*

Come home. I spoke with your aunt and she said we can't file for divorce until you've been separated for a year. But we can try to get you a protection order, so KJ can't bother you."

I already know I can't get divorced right away. I managed to at least look that up before leaving him.

"Mom. Thank you for talking to her, but I'm honestly great where I am right now. I was only calling to let you know I'm okay."

"Cecily—"

"Mom, please. I swear you'll be the first to know if I'm not happy here. I'm thirty, not three. I can make my own choices."

I hear her fingernails drumming on a hard surface—likely the living room end table where they keep the house phone. "You've kept us in the dark long enough. If you're staying there, I want frequent updates. Even if it's a darn thumbs up via email. *Please*. I'm tired of worrying about you, Cecily."

Fuck. That makes me feel like the world's worst daughter... and I suppose I probably am. "I'm sorry. Promise I'll keep you guys in the loop from here on. I really am doing great, though. I'm happier here than I've been in a long time. I have friends, I'm gardening... *I helped brand cattle.*"

She laughs. "You *what*? Cecily, I think your dad—"

"Mom. Seriously. I'm happy here."

"Okay, well... as long as you're happy. We love you."

"Love you."

Twenty minutes of family gossip pass before I convince her that I need to get some sleep. After hanging up, I find myself staring at Austin Wells's contact profile with a fluttery feeling. I examine the number until I lose focus and, when I blink to bring my vision back, I'm left staring at my own reflection on the black screen. It seems immature to text him when I can look out my window and see his house. This isn't middle school. I could just walk over there and talk to him—although that would probably only get me a series of grumbles and grunts back. I don't even know what I want to say to him, in person or via text. *Jesus, I'm pathetic.* The last thing I need a month after leaving my asshole husband is to develop a crush on my asshole boss. *Right?*

10

Austin

Beryl plunks down in the chair next to my desk, tossing a stack of mail down and sliding a mug over to me. "Just made a fresh pot and thought you'd like some."

I eye the cup suspiciously. She rarely hand delivers the mail after grabbing it from our post office box in town. And Beryl *never* delivers coffee. If I had a dollar for every time she's told me "you have two feet and a heartbeat" when asked to bring me something I need, I'd be able to hire somebody to bring me coffee daily. Which means she's up to something.

"Ready to apologize?" She tosses her long, grey braid over her shoulder with a smile.

There it is. "For?"

"You were wrong about Cecily."

I huff. "What makes you think that?"

"You would've fired her if it weren't the case. Instead, I heard you took her to town, and bought her some pretty things."

"She refuses to drive a truck, and I needed supplements, so I let her ride along. I paid because she needs to keep her money to fix her tires. Once she gets those, she can drive her own damn self around."

"Oh, honey." She leans over to rub my forearm. "Either you're blind or you're a fool."

"That so?"

"You know she's nothin' like Savannah, don't you? They're different people."

Savannah came here because she needed away from her controlling, hateful parents. She wanted to do things her own way, rather than follow the path they set out for her. She ditched her fancy English riding for Western, taught me how to organize the ranch's finances, and made me fall in love. She inserted herself into so many aspects of the ranch; I assumed she planned to stay. The moment I decided to make things official, she spooked. Never looked back.

There were other girls before her that blew through here on a summer breeze. Losing them hurt, but Sav killed. She felt different from the others. Cecily feels different, too. And I don't have the energy to go through losing someone again. I'd rather run before I have the chance to fall.

I avoid the question. "You and Kate need something better to do with your time."

She chuckles. "Probably true. Am I often wrong, though?"

"Wrong or not, I'm not interested."

I'm a pathetic liar. I'm so interested it's pissing me off, to be honest. A smile deepens the wrinkles around her eyes as she clearly sees through my bullshit.

"How many times have you fallen off a horse?" Beryl asks.

I scoff. I know where this is going. *Get back on the horse.* I decide to humour her because she's never turned off by my silent glares. If anything, a lack of response makes her think she's onto something, so she continues to pester.

"I don't know. A lot," I say.

"And the pain of falling is worth it because riding makes you feel alive."

"Or because it's my livelihood and I have no choice."

Beryl smacks my hand. "Don't be facetious. I'm sure you were falling off horses, cows, sheep, and whatever other critters you boys could try to ride as kids. Long before you were putting any thought into it being your job. Am I right?"

"Yeah."

"Love can give you the same rush, Austin. You fell in love with somebody who didn't stick around, but it doesn't mean that'll happen again. You're too young to be jaded and unwilling to try because a little pain scares you."

"I'm thirty-seven. Not that young."

"Oh, honey. If you truly believe that, you're definitely a fool."

A fool for noticing a pattern and making a conscious choice not to let it continue? I don't think so. Everyone I've loved has either left or died—my brothers being the exception by obligation. I know they stayed because they didn't think there was another option. They're here for the ranch. Not me. Never me.

"And when she leaves?"

"From what I gather, she's taking things one day at a time. Figuring out what she wants. Maybe she can be persuaded to stay. Won't know unless you try, though."

She rubs her hand across my arm with a melancholic smile. This is awfully reminiscent of my mom comforting me when my high school girlfriend dumped me. I was heartbroken for a couple weeks and then eager to get back into the dating game. Not a single concern about potential future breakups. Funny how twenty years worth of adult heartache can screw you up, and make the idea of being alone by choice so much easier to stomach than the alternative of trying to develop a relationship with somebody.

I must have come down with heat stroke. It's the only logical reason why I agreed to have a beer at the river. Denny asked while I was hosing down my mare, Jubilee, after a long morning checking heifers, and I was simply too hot and tired to argue. The rare times I say yes—like today—are enough to keep Denny always inviting me. You'd think I agreed to give him $1,000 by the smile on his face. Almost makes me wish I said yes more often.

Following behind the pack, I listen to talk about the past weekend's rodeo. Sundial, appropriately nicknamed because he's basically useless—always standing around casting a damn shadow—is bouncing with excitement as he rambles on about Denny's winning saddle bronc ride. His voice is so chipper and annoying, I consider turning around. Then we crest the bank down to the swimming hole, and I spot her.

Tan line questions answered.

Goddamn, now I'm really regretting all the invites I've turned down. I'm aware she's been down here with the guys a few times. Honestly, it hasn't bothered me. At least, it didn't before now. My brain hadn't considered the fact she'd be wearing a tiny bikini around them.

But she is. On top of a flat boulder, Cecily's lying stomach-down, reading a book. She doesn't even look up at the guys stampeding toward the river like water buffalo. A thin string tied in a dainty bow on her upper back and bottoms that are nearly a thong, exposing most of her ass. Her white bikini leaves little to the imagination, but I'm definitely fucking imagining. She looks up from the book to accept a beer from Denny, and her feet giddily kick behind her.

Fuck. Why haven't I been coming here?

I can't keep staring without looking like a pervert, so I walk down the hill and sit next to the water. There's not much cleared space down here, and she's in the middle of everything. I'm left with no choice but to be within ten feet of her, regardless of where I sit.

"Hey, Aus—beer," Denny calls out before tossing me a cold can.

It's a miracle I catch it because, once again, I'm looking at Cecily. Except this time, she's looking right back.

"Finally a hot enough day for you to come down and socialize?" she asks.

Say something, dipshit. I take a sip and nod.

"Except not socialize, because it might ruin your grumpy act, wouldn't it?" She closes her book and takes to reading me instead, sitting up and bringing her knees to her chest. "How was your day cowboying, Not-A-Cowboy?"

"Fine." I clear my throat. "Whatcha reading?"

She excitedly holds the book in the air, twisting it to show off the dark blue cover. "Oh, it's non-fiction. About the Essex whaling ship... Um, it's a pretty wild story. Sperm whales, sinking ships, cannibalism. It was part of the inspiration for *Moby Dick*."

Not the answer I was expecting. I assumed she'd be reading a cutesy rom-com or something light. "You're into history?"

"Sort of. Not as much as my dad is. But what's not to like about a whale attack and cannibalism?"

I snort. "Fair point. Is that from the bookshelves in the big house?" I don't remember seeing it there, and a good chunk of the books on those shelves were purchased by me.

"Nah, I've read just about everything in there, so I got a library card."

"Maybe I'll check it out when you're done."

"I didn't know you read." Her face lights up. "I'll totally let you take it when I'm done." Now we share something. Finally, there's a topic I can talk to her about. She's held and read and loved—*hopefully*—the same books I have. If only I could fucking *talk,* or simply *act* like a normal human around her.

Her hair falls around her shoulders, wavy and shining in the sun. Apparently, I *am* a total pervert because I can't help myself from looking when her knees spread slightly apart. "Gonna come swimming? The water's actually not too cold today," she says.

"I'm not much for swimming. Also, not dressed for it."

"That's too bad." She smiles and stands in front of me, running her thumbs under the waist of her bottoms to adjust the fit. Sharing a little peek at the deep tan line running across her hip bones. My cock begins to harden and I'm thankful my jeans are thick and fitted enough to hide it.

Cecily walks gingerly toward the water and I can't fathom why the guys aren't as enthralled as I am. I suppose they've become desensitized—although I don't think it would matter how many times I watch her walk by in a bikini; I'm always going to fucking look.

Submerged up to her collarbones, she looks toward the blue sky and shuts her eyes. Letting the sun warm her face like she doesn't have a care in the world. I might be wearing denim, but I'm strongly considering going in there. Except I wouldn't know what to say or do once I was next to her. Because I'm overwhelmed with the urge to hold her in my arms and kiss her, but neither is possible.

The fuck is wrong with me?

That's not what I'm trying to do here. At best, she could only ever be a short-term fling, and I'm not built to handle casual or short-term. I have an annoying habit of becoming too invested, which is why I shirk off starting an online dating profile every time Denny and Red try. Still, though, I act like a numbskull around Cecily because every muscle in my chest, and every tendon in my body, are aching to have her. And my brain is screaming at me to stay away.

Then she steps onto shore, and all my nerve endings are set on fire.

She said the water wasn't too cold, but the rock-hard nipples visible through her triangle bikini top say differently. As do the goosebumps scattered across her body, which water droplets use like a slalom skiing course. When she walks back from the water, she's close enough I could reach out and touch her. Not that I would, because I know she'd be instantly repelled by the motion.

She adjusts her bathing suit again and rings the water from her hair. "It's refreshing. You should really try it."

That comment alone is enough to make my dick pulse in my pants. Then she bends over to grab her towel, and I catch a glimpse of damn near every fucking thing. The white fabric pulls taut against her ass and...

I swallow as I take in how little there is covering her pussy. A thin slice of material begging to be shifted slightly. One wrong move and it might end up wedged between her pussy lips, and I would be a complete goner.

Okay, that's my cue to leave before I have to walk away from here with a raging hard-on instead of the semi I'm already needing to tuck away before I go. If I didn't know any better, I'd think she bent over and lingered as long as she did on purpose.

I let the cool shower water ease my muscles, relishing the hard stream as it hits my shoulders. I had hoped it would calm my frayed nerves, but a small stream runs down my chest and I'm back to thinking about Cecily emerging from the river. The way the water beaded on her tanned skin, running along the curve of her breast, and trailing down her stomach. The thin bikini top barely contained the swell of her stunning tits, and those hard nipples needed my warm hands. Or mouth.

My cock firms at the thought, and I grip it with my right hand, tugging with frustration. I picture what it would feel like to have her smooth palm gripping me instead. Or her mouth—those plump lips would look good around my cock. My rough hands catching in her hair, or running along her soft body, while she sucks me.

"Fuck," I mumble. Both in anger at myself, and ecstasy as I imagine Cecily.

My mind wanders to the sounds she might make if I pulled the bikini bottoms to the side, and ran my fingers between her wet lips. Her honey-eyed voice would become breathy and needy as I touched her. A groan escapes my mouth at the thought. I close my eyes and lean against the shower wall, desperately trying to replace my own hand with hers.

Would she let me have my way with her right there in the open? I imagine her kneeling down and taking me in her mouth, deep enough she'd start to choke on it. Her tongue would slide up my shaft, and her cheeks would hollow out while she sucked me off. Those pretty, painted nails would dig into my thighs as I held her hair, shoving my cock deeper down her throat.

Arousal drips from the tip, and I spread it down my shaft, unashamedly pretending it's her wet pussy I'm fucking instead of my hand. My grip becomes vise-like, tugging aggressively as I picture teasing her clit until Cecily begs me to take her right there. And I would. I'd bend her over the boulder by the river, sliding that too-small bikini over the curve of her ass. And my cock would fit perfectly inside her wet warmth.

Pleasure licks up my spine, and my balls tighten at the image. My strokes become faster, rougher, and more desperate. Punishing. I already know it wouldn't take much for me to come once I was inside her. It's been too damn long since I fucked anything other than my hand, and she'd feel perfect. Sliding in and out, feeling my balls slap against her damp skin with every thrust. She'd moan my name with the same raspy voice she has while singing, her pussy clenching around my cock when she comes.

Heat travels through my veins and my grip becomes sloppier as I fight the urge to collapse. Squeezing my eyes shut tighter, I thrust my hand one more good time, envisioning her and the way she says my name.

Hot cum shoots out in a rolling wave of orgasm as I jerk myself angrily—the idea that Cecily would ever fuck me becoming instantly shameful. I'm an absolute fool. The illusion's shattered at the same moment my cum hits the shower floor.

11

Cecily

I'm still kicking myself for acting like a cat in heat at the river, as if I thought he was going to jump my bones in front of everybody. Teasing him and revelling in the way his eyes raked over my body, the muscles in his throat with each strained swallow, and the tension in his fingers as he held onto his bent knee for dear life.

He may have looked, but then he left.

Apparently, yesterday's humiliation isn't enough to stop me from subjecting myself to more rejection, though.

I plunk down into my usual seat across from Austin. His black T-shirt, snug across his broad shoulders, makes it hard for me to remember what I came here to ask.

"Hey," I say. We sit here every morning, so you'd think he wouldn't flinch at my presence, yet he does. Granted, I don't usually say anything out loud to acknowledge him. His cheeks turn a deep shade of pink as he looks up at me.

Interesting.

"Jackson told me I have to ask you if... um..." I trip on my words as his studying gaze sends my heart into a panicked rhythm. "Well... I just—"

"Haven't got all day."

"Can I come to the auction with you?"

He scrunches his face in disgust. "No."

While I expected that to be his answer, it doesn't mean I'm any less irritated about it. "Come on. Kate's going and it sounds exciting."

"Darlin', you're seriously disturbed if you think a livestock auction sounds exciting."

His mouth twists into what could almost be considered a smile, and I use this as my opportunity. Teasing him usually gets me what I want because he shuts down and gives up.

A win is a win.

"But you're smiling because you think my excitement is cute." I bat my eyelashes at him. "Anyway, you don't know what sort of things interest me. Let me come with you."

"We're leaving in ten, and I don't want to hear you complain about the long drive or the boring auction," he says.

I take a proud sip of coffee, relaxing into the rickety wooden chair. But instead of returning to his cattle rancher magazine, he continues looking at me questioningly. "Don't you need to get ready?"

"I guess so." I slam back my coffee and, feeling the weight of his gaze on my body, I turn and wink. "I don't think you want me to go. You just want to watch me leave."

When Kate suggested I tag along yesterday, she failed to mention that I would spend two hours crammed between Austin and Jackson in the front seat of the pickup. With Odessa's bulky carseat, there isn't enough room for both Kate and me to comfortably fit in the back.

Austin's leg brushes against mine when he climbs in, striking a match just below my belly button. The air's instantly thick and hard to swallow with him seated so close. Close enough I can smell his spicy, woody bodywash with every inhale. *And I inhale.* Frequently, shallowly. Just enough to breathe him in and feel the rush through my body without anybody noticing.

"I—uh... need in here." Austin reaches between my legs, sending a pulse of heat through my prickling skin. A small miracle that I'm wearing jeans and a long sleeve to hide the goosebumps littering my body. His large hand smooths over the gear shifter knob, jamming it into first, and I have to fight to keep my thighs from clenching. His grip on the shifter remains solid, despite his forearm loosely bumping against my thigh when he changes gears. Jackson and Kate are chatting incessantly, but I can't focus on anything except the sliver of space between us.

By the time we reach Wells Canyon and pull onto the highway, it's a miracle my lungs have received enough oxygen to keep me alive. When his grip returns to the steering wheel, I allow my knotted hands to unravel and fall to my sides. Praying that the feel of my knuckles against his leg makes his mind reel as much as it does mine.

Exhausted from the adrenaline rush of two hours next to Austin—yet dreading the moment our bodies aren't in contact—when his truck pulls into the livestock auction parking lot. Dozens of trucks, nearly all with trailers, are parked outside a sprawling, cement building.

"I want my piggyback," Odessa demands the moment her feet hit the dirt. Uncle Austin obliges like it's routine, hoisting her up onto his back with one arm, and waiting for her to settle in before he keeps walking.

"Don't choke me out," he warns as her small arms tighten around his neck, "or I'll auction you off."

She giggles, and giddily kicks her feet. Austin's hand shoots out to grab her tiny cowboy boot inches before the heel slams into his side. "No kicking either, little miss. I'm not your barrel horse."

I hide a small smile behind my hand, following them through the heavy double doors. Jackson turns into the front office while Austin, Kate, and I continue toward the sign marked *"Sale Barn"*. Tiered seating reaches from the rafters down to a small, rounded pen with an entrance on either end. Unsurprisingly, the smell of cow crap wafts through the air. As a testament to my time spent at the ranch, I don't even scrunch my nose.

"Get all your jitters, scratches, whatever other insane movements you have in your system out now," Austin says.

"What?"

"Even the slightest move counts as a bid and, if you scratch your nose and make me buy a damn dairy cow, it's coming from your pay. Get it out of your system now."

"What am I supposed to do if I'm not itchy now, but I am in ten minutes?" I rub my nose, in case I can somehow bank scratches to be used as needed.

"You do nothing." *Thanks. Truly helpful.*

An older, grey-haired gentleman approaches us as Austin swings Odessa back down to the ground. "Austin, how are ya? Got you a few good ones today."

Austin nods. "Jackson's out back taking a look. Thanks, Rick."

The man's wrinkled, sun-damaged face shifts to me. "And I see we have a newcomer. First time?"

"I'm Cecily. Excited first timer." I reach out and shake the man's large, calloused hand.

"Treat her like a small child, Rick. None of her accidental bids count," Austin says, eliciting a chuckle from the older man.

"Well, best get yourselves a good spot. And get this little lady,"—he flicks the brim of Odessa's pink cowboy hat—"a milk-shake. Tell 'em it's on me."

Kate and I settle into our seats, and I look around at the unfamiliar faces slowly filtering into the room. Nearly everyone comes over to talk to Austin and, while he's still a man of few words, he's shockingly friendly. Terrifyingly so. I'm captivated by how easily he interacts with other ranchers, although I can't follow most of what they're talking about. It's not until Odessa shouts at him about a milkshake, interrupting my stupor, that I realize how intensely I've been staring.

They return a short while later with a milkshake and Jackson in tow. The room's filling up and Rick, who turns out to be the auctioneer, takes a seat on the opposite side of the sale pen. His presence forces a hush across the room and Austin settles in next to me on the hard bench seating.

As anticipated, it feels like I've contracted fleas within the first five minutes. I swear, not a single part of my body has ever prickled and itched as much as it does now. Trying to take my mind off it, I look around the room, and quietly assess the assortment of men and women sitting here. Just as I question whether Austin might've been exaggerating about tiny movements counting as bids, I watch a man in his seventies touch the side of his nose and purchase five calves.

Shit.

Unrelenting tickles, like tiny bugs crawling under my clothes, refuse to leave me alone. The more I think about how I shouldn't be itchy, the worse it becomes. *Fuck it.* I'm cautiously itching my thigh when I feel Austin's knee knock against mine. Electricity spiders out from the spot where our legs are touching, and my heart skips a beat. I look over to see his annoyed glare.

"Stop scratching," he mouths.

"I can't. I'm so itchy." Talking about it makes the sensation more intense, and I scratch harder. It's not like anybody can see my hand moving when it's down low, right? Surely the large farmer in front of me is blocking most of my body from view.

"Jesus Christ." His hand quickly grabs mine and squeezes my fingers together painfully. I jolt in my seat, but he doesn't ease up.

The buzzing under my skin stops as my focus shifts entirely to his hand on mine. To the contrast between my delicate fingers and his calloused, work-worn hands. Then back to his knee, which is still resting against mine. My eyes drag up the length of his thigh until I get to the spot that makes my cheeks flush and my throat clench. An extremely inappropriate daydream about unbuckling his belt, and seeing what he looks like under those Wranglers, creates an insatiable neediness between my legs. I can't help wondering what his rough fingertips might feel like elsewhere on my body.

His grip loosens ever so slightly, allowing for his fingers to interlace mine, and now he's simply holding my hand. *Austin Wells is holding my hand.* If I wanted to, I could easily slip from his grasp, and continue toeing the line with my covert scratching. But I don't want to.

We sit in silence as Jackson bids on, and wins, a massive black bull. Letting heat build between our palms. Pretending like the only reason we're sitting this way is to prevent me from accidentally purchasing an animal. That doesn't explain why neither of us has moved our knees.

When his thumb starts to draw small shapes on the back of my hand, I'm filled with butterflies. They're travelling from my chest down to the hot space between my legs. My stomach flips at the thought of his thumb making the same movement in a very different place. It's a wanting I haven't felt in years, and I fight hard to repress the image before it turns into a needy whimper.

The instant the final auction ends, he drops my hand like it's red-hot metal. I naïvely thought that he'd been feeling the same sparks I had. But it's never been more clear to me that I'm simply delusional.

The next morning, Odessa stands up on her chair at the dining table, shimmying while Beryl cranks *She's In Love With The Boy* on the Bluetooth speaker. With Kate gone for her doctor's appointment, it's a bit of a free-for-all this morning. Odessa even got chocolate chips and whipped cream on her pancakes, which explains the hyperactive dance moves. "I love this song," she shouts over the music.

"You're gonna hurt yourself, kid," Austin snarks without looking up from his newspaper. "And get better taste in music."

Odessa sticks her tongue out at him, but climbs off the chair and runs over to me, grabbing my hands to spin in a circle. I have to duck in close to keep from letting her hit the counter when she throws her head back with a sweet giggle.

"Excuse me, don't you dare speak ill about Miss Yearwood." Beryl flicks his arm with a tea towel as she wipes the surrounding table.

"It's not his fault that he got the short end of the stick... y'know, when it comes to brains." I twirl Odessa under my arm like she's a princess at a fairy-tale ball. "Hold on, I've got a song he might like better."

I let go of Odessa's hand and grab my phone. Pulling up the song I have in mind, I lean my elbow on the counter. Watching Austin, I slowly turn up the volume dial through the opening chords until he looks up from the paper.

"*Should've Been A Cowboy*? That's the best you could come up with?" he asks, cocking a brow.

"Okay, okay. I'll find something more you. Give me a second." I drum my fingertips on the counter while I think. Odessa's already grown bored and moved on—gone outside to chase after the barn cats, most likely. "Hrm, maybe some Waylon and Willie instead? If you're willing to admit your mama did, in fact, let you grow up to be a cowboy? Something about not being easy to love, always alone... Yeah, those lyrics do fit better."

I'm teasing, but it's clear I've gone too far because a deep trench builds between his eyebrows, and he's gone. Out of the house before I've even had the chance to queue up the song.

"Shit. I struck a nerve, didn't I?" Grimacing, I turn to Beryl.

"Oh, honey. You have no idea."

Well, fuck. I thought we were joking around. How was I supposed to know something as simple as a country song from more than forty years ago would bother him this much? Doesn't stop me from feeling like a complete piece of shit, though.

"Austin!" I yell after him as my feet thud across the front porch. With the amount of wind, I'd be surprised if he can hear me over all the chimes out here.

"Austin!" I yell again, running up to him. "Hey, I'm sorry. I wasn't trying to be a dick back there."

"It's fine."

"Clearly not, or you wouldn't have stormed off."

"I didn't... I have work to do. Not everybody gets to goof off all day." His strides quicken, and I'm nearing Olympic-speed-walking pace to keep up as we approach the barn.

"You didn't even finish your coffee, so I *know* you weren't racing off to go do work. I'm sorry, okay? That's all I wanted to say. I didn't mean to hurt your feelings."

He shakes his head. "Can't hurt feelings when they don't exist."

I laugh. Cackle, really. "*Sure*. I'm sorry. It was supposed to be a joke, but it was mean. For what it's worth, Austin, I don't think those lyrics apply to you."

"Okay."

"You don't have to accept my apology."

We're inside the stables, and climbing a steep set of stairs. I'm not sure why I haven't stopped following him yet, or why he hasn't told me to leave. Suddenly, we're in a place that looks suspiciously like a secret office.

This is where he disappears to every day.

"So, this is where you're always hiding." I take in the small space. His desk is perfectly organized and neat, unsurprisingly. If there's one thing I've learned about Austin, it's that nothing about him is ever the tiniest bit unruly. "It's cute."

"Working, not hiding." He sits down at the desk, spinning the black chair to face me. "If I say I accept your apology, will you leave me to work in peace?"

"I'll leave you to *brood*, yes." I plop down into the plush armchair across from him. "I truly am sorry. I didn't know it would bug you, but that's no excuse. I crossed the line."

"Apology accepted." The swirling fire in his eyes calms almost immediately, and we're left staring at each other in the dimly lit room. With a blink, he surveys my lips, and it becomes wildly noticeable how much privacy we have here. I could walk across the creaky floorboards and straddle his lap. Kiss him the way I told myself I would once the lilac blooms disappeared. And they're *long gone*.

"Okay," I say. The force of his eyes assessing me, with the unwavering attention of a predator, makes it hard to speak.

"Aren't you going to leave now?" he rasps. "I have a lot of work to do."

"Yeah... Yeah, I guess I am." I reluctantly pull myself from the chair. Wishing he'd ask me not to go, smash his lips into mine, wrap his strong arms around me.

If he wanted to, he would. And Austin doesn't.

12

Austin

The big house is still pitch black when I slowly creep through the front door and down the hall just before four o'clock in the morning. Kate's become extra murderous about her sleep since becoming pregnant, and I'm not trying to get myself banished by making too much noise. Given the darkness, a strong aroma of fresh coffee comes as a surprise when I walk into the kitchen.

Two tall figures are sitting at the table, barely lit by the moon streaming in through the picture window and dim under-cabinet lighting. I came here early, seeking the quiet solace of a solitary coffee at my family's heirloom table. Hoping to have my moment and duck out before the rest of the crew show up. Even twelve years after her death, my mom's birthday isn't an easy day to get through.

"What are you morons doing?" I whisper yell at my brothers.

"Apparently, Kate said she can hear the buzzing of the overhead light in here." Denny turns to look at me, his eyes giant and shining. "She does know this is a ranch and we need to be up at ungodly hours for work, right? The least she can do is let us see what we're doing when we make our morning coffee. Austin, please tell our dipshit brother here that this is completely insane."

"I'm not going to be the one to risk it, Den." Thankfully, I've memorized the layout of our generational family home well enough I could do everything here blindfolded. I grab a mug, careful not to let the cabinet door creak, and pour until it sounds full enough.

"I don't see you rushing to flick the light switch," Jackson whispers to Denny.

"I'm not about to risk having my food fucked with," Denny replies. "Especially not when she's making pulled pork tonight."

"You coming?" Jackson's question is clearly directed at me, seeing as I'm the only questionable attendance. Though it shouldn't even be a question—I *never* come to Mom's birthday dinner.

Taking a swig of coffee as I sit down, I shake my head. "You two almost done baling the North creek field? Need help?"

"Should be done by lunch. You still looking to avoid a certain Filly?" Denny asks. Jackson sputters his coffee. And, even in the dark, I can tell they're both staring me down with raised eyebrows and wicked grins.

"Shut up. Maybe a guy wants to do some actual damn work instead of pushing pencils."

"Orrrr a guy has a big ol' crush and doesn't know how to handle it." Denny laughs. "If you don't get after it, maybe I'll shoot my shot."

"Not the time, Denny." Jackson cautiously sets his mug down. Each of us is moving in slow motion, terrified of waking up Kate.

This is the farthest thing from a peaceful, private start to my day.

Mindfully placing my half-full mug in the sink, I barely remember to grab my sack lunch as I race to the door. Eventually, somebody will be brave enough to turn the lights on, and I'll never live it down if they see how flush my cheeks are at the mention of Cecily.

"Get to work, Denver," I say on my way out the door.

"Love you," he whisper-yells after me.

Haying's supposed to take my mind off everything, but I underestimated what fifteen-hour days in a tractor can do to my thoughts. For weeks, I was worried about her distracting the ranch hands, and now I'm the one mowing completely wonky lines in the field. I'm sure Jackson and Denny will have comments to make about my crappy hay job. I can't think straight. Definitely can't drive straight.

I absolutely should not be wasting a minute thinking about her. And yet, I can't find it in me to stop.

Every once in a while, it feels like there's something between us. She makes flirtatious comments, her gaze lingers on mine, and her smile seems reserved for me. Then I go and do something like stand too close to her, consider a kiss, or hold her hand at the livestock auction. Every part of her body tenses like she can't stand the thought of touching me, and I fucking hate it.

She'll be leaving soon, I remind myself over and over. I simply need to control myself for a while longer. They never stay. Even the people who are supposed to. My grandpa, my mom, my dad, Savannah.

Grandpa and Mom had no choice, obviously. But Dad and Sav? They left despite all the reasons I gave them not to. Nothing I did was enough for them to stay, so why would this time be any different?

All of this should stop me from wanting her, but it doesn't. I told myself I'd never end up here again, but the rush of feelings I get with her around makes it all seem worth the risk. If there was ever a chance I could win her over and have her while she's here, I wouldn't hesitate. I'll take a day, week, month over spending the rest of my life kicking myself for not trying. Call me a sucker for punishment. Future heartbreak be damned.

Shit, did I just admit to myself that I want to chase after Cecily?

I'm tired and sore and the last thing I wanted was for my little brother to follow me home after work. But he's like a damn golden retriever. So here we are.

"You're sure you won't come?" Denny takes a swig of beer, propping his feet up on my coffee table.

We finally finished mowing the second cut and, once it's dry, we'll bale it and set it aside for winter. With such a mild, early spring, we should have no problem getting a third cut of hay this year. And that'll mean we can feed every animal on the property for the entire winter without spending money. I should be in a fantastic mood...

"No," I growl. "I have no interest in seeing him."

Our father loved our mom deeply—he stayed at Wells Ranch, not for my grandparents' sake, but for Mom. If it weren't for her love affair with this land, and her desire to raise the fourth generation on his family's ranch, he would have moved away the day he turned eighteen. Which is why, less than a week after she died, he did exactly that. Leaving me in charge of everything at twenty-five years old. His leaving might not be quite as hard to ignore if he didn't make a show of coming back here twice a year: on her birthday, July seventh, and her death date, October second.

"Kate's making pulled pork. I know how much you love that," Denny says.

I shake my head. "Food isn't enough to convince me to spend time with that asshole."

"Grandpa wouldn't like this. He built that giant-ass kitchen table specifically for family dinners."

Now my little brother wants to pull out the big guns. Knowing if there's one way to make me crack, it's dragging our dead grandpa or mom into the conversation. Using the pain I'm still harbouring to guilt me into doing things I don't want to.

"Yeah, and I don't think he would like dad giving up on the ranch either," I say out loud. *Or on us,* I keep to myself.

"You ever think he feels bad for leaving, and that's why he comes back?" *Sweet, gullible Denny Wells.*

"Sure he does." I snort and empty my bottle. "Better get up to the house for dinner with your dearest daddy, Denver."

He punches me hard on the shoulder before chugging the rest of his beer and walking out. For years, I used to leave the ranch entirely, so I didn't have to worry about a chance encounter. But I've earned my right to be on this property, and I'm not going to let him make me feel like I can't be here anymore. Instead, I stock the fridge with beer, watch the television I only turn on twice a year, and wait until morning.

Half an hour later, that's exactly what I'm doing when I feel compelled to try my hand at texting. My big thumbs fumble over the screen, typing out the miniscule letters.

Austin: Hey

Within seconds, my phone chimes. I can't help but wonder what she's doing that she's able to reply so quickly. I'm tempted to go to the window and look over at her cabin, although I've already learned I can't see anything except the front porch from here.

Cecily: Wow. Here I thought you were joking about texting.
Cecily: Aren't you supposed to be in the middle of family dinner?
Austin: Wasn't invited

Sure, it's a lie. But only because Denny can't help himself—Jackson gave up trying to guilt-trip me years ago. In fact, until Odessa was born, he didn't care for these dinners either. But now he has a kid who *apparently* deserves a grandfather. Whether our father deserves a relationship with his grandkid is questionable, but it's not up to me.

Cecily: Oof. That's rough.
Cecily: What are you doing then?

Austin: Watching *Happy Days* and drinking beer

Cecily: Sorry, I think I have the wrong number

Cecily: I thought I was talking to Austin, but it seems I'm texting a 70-year-old right now

Austin: Funny

Cecily: Do you want company? I cannot confirm nor deny whether I stole some dinner from the big house before I left. But I might be convinced to share...

A breathy laugh vibrates through my chest. Everybody—other than Cecily, I guess—knows the only people I talk to on Mom's days are Denny and Jackson. And, frankly, after having to fend off Denny's dinner invite, I'm considering adding them to the 'do not disturb' list going forward.

I don't cry about my mom. Not anymore. But I still need the day. So the instant tug in my chest at her question startles me. At the best of times, I'm terrible at acting like a normal human around her. Today, of all days, I don't stand a chance at constructing a logical thought.

There are plenty of rational reasons why I should say no. *And yet.*

Austin: How did you manage to steal pulled pork?

Cecily: And chocolate cake... I can't share details over text in case we've been compromised.

Austin: Better come tell me about it in person then.

Cecily: Be there in five :) Don't start the next episode without me, old man.

Holy shit. I invited Cecily here. Right now. Sweat forms on my palms and my head spins.

In a panic, I race to pick up the few odds and ends lying around. Thank God this place is small—one bedroom, one bathroom, and the main living space has hardly enough room for a couch, fireplace, and tiny kitchen. I change out of my sweatpants into jeans and a plaid button-up, brush my teeth...

Why am I brushing my teeth? Get it together, man. She's not kissing you.

Just as I'm starting to catch my breath, a knock sounds on the thick wooden front door.

"*You* have a welcome mat? Liar." Her playful tone smashes into me before the door's fully open. "You should have a mat that says, 'fuck off'."

Two plates balance precariously in each hand—one heaped with pulled pork sandwiches and the other with chocolate cake. A smile lilts across her face as I take the food, my fingers brushing against hers. She's dressed in leggings and an oversized hoodie, with her blonde hair pulled into a messy bun. A few wisps stick out haphazardly. From the looks of her, she was planning to have a low-key night, too.

"Were you planning on having dinner with somebody, or do you always steal enough food for an entire family?"

She brushes past me in the doorway. The lightest bump of her arm against mine leaves me with a head rush. A belly flutter. A knock in my chest.

"It was all for me," she says. "But I'm willing to share."

I can't help but smile as she enthusiastically peels the plastic wrap, unveiling the feast on my coffee table. I hand her a cold beer, sitting down as far away as my three-seater couch will allow. Cecily in my house already feels like a tremendous step. I'm not pushing it by getting into her personal space.

"Do I have to worry about the cops knocking on my door looking for the cake thief?" I ask.

"Legally speaking, I'm not sure it's stealing when I helped make the food, right? Especially the cake—it's an entirely separate mini cake."

"So you're a lowly ingredient thief, then? I think that kind of crime might earn you a spot in Martha Stewart's prison cell."

Her laughter engulfs the air like fireworks. "Why aren't you this funny all the time?"

"Somebody has to be the resident asshole, I guess."

"Is that why you weren't invited to family dinner?" She tucks her feet under her on the far end of the couch, looking at me as if the question she just asked isn't such a doozy.

"I was invited, actually. But I didn't want to go."

She blinks up at me. Her look of genuine interest—and a tinge of concern—has me feeling the urge to tell her way too much information about my life. Lay it all out like a picnic. "I didn't want to go because my dad's there, and I don't speak to him."

"Ah—explains why things were tense at the house today. I figured it wasn't an average family dinner. Does he visit often?"

I scrape my palm against my stubbled jaw as I decide how much to tell her. "He only comes here for her birthday and the anniversary of when she died. But... he left pretty quickly after she died and I haven't exactly forgiven him for it. I know that probably sounds dumb because it was a long time ago."

My tongue presses against the inside of my cheek, preparing to hear something which diminishes the situation. I'm expecting her to defend him, as if he had no choice but to leave. It's what Denny, Jackson, Kate, and even Beryl do. *He's grieving, too. He's trying to find a way to show he still cares. You were an adult, so what's the big deal he left when he did?*

"Beryl and Kate mentioned it was your mom's birthday. I'm sorry, Austin. That's hard." She's looking at me the way she always does—like she sees me. And that scares the shit out of me.

"Yeah, not made any easier by having to deal with my dad. So I just choose not to."

"Well, it's pretty fucking selfish of him to only come around on those days, don't you think? Has he ever asked if you guys want him around?" She clamps a hand to her mouth, quieting her voice as it trickles from between her fingers. "Sorry, that was rude. I shouldn't be talking shit about your dad."

I bite back a smile. "Don't be sorry. You're the first person who hasn't immediately defended him."

"I'm not in the habit of defending men anymore."

I assume her comment has something to do with whatever her ex did. The guy's clearly an idiot because he let her run off. *Yup, he was a real idiot, but I'm a bigger one.* I've wasted so much time trying to dislike Cecily—for what?

"You defended me to Kate when we were branding," I remind her. In fact, she's defended me at least twice; Denny told me she stood up for me when the guys were bitching about work. They're employees of the ranch, which means sometimes they have to miss a rodeo to help hay before bad weather. They can hate me all they want for it. That's why I'm the boss.

"Okay, I stand corrected. I'm not defending *assholes* anymore."

My body warms from the inside out, like I'm chugging Fireball on a cold night in the middle of calving season. I can practically feel my face glowing when I look over at Cecily.

"So,"—she takes a swig—"how do you usually spend your mom's birthday, if not at the big house with everybody?"

"Alone."

"Oh." Her face falls. "If you want me to go, I can. You can even keep the food."

"No." I exhale. If I want this girl, I need to stop being a closed-off dick. "Usually I drink beer and watch *Happy Days* because it was her favourite show."

"Obviously, I never met your mom, but I bet she'd like that. When I die, I hope somebody sits around every year and watches reruns of my favourite shows to commemorate my life. If not, I'm coming back here to haunt every friend I've ever had. Better watch it, Aus, or I might be in here flickering your lights to piss you off."

My heart has no business hitting a dead stop like it does. Being referred to as a friend should ease my worries about heartbreak if she leaves. *When* she leaves. It should close the door once and for all—confirming she has no interest in pursuing anything further. I should take my slot in the friend zone, and be thrilled to be there. But, for some ungodly reason, it has the opposite effect. It fills my chest with butterflies. With hope. If I was able to move from asshole boss to friend, I can become more.

Cecily seems oblivious to my inner panic as she giggles about something Potsie said on the TV. I hate to admit it, but I'm genuinely glad I'm not alone tonight.

"Now that you know too much about my family shit, tell me about yours," I say.

"Mmm... be warned that it's very bland in comparison. I'm an only child. My dad's a history teacher and my mom works for a dentist. I was born and raised in the city..."

"Obviously." The edge of my lip picks up and our eyes meet. Holding with a playful gaze.

"Hey, I think I fit in pretty well around here now." Her teasing tone tightens around my chest.

"You do." It's not even a lie. She's managed to fit herself into the ranch somehow. Or maybe the ranch has molded around her. Either way, there's no denying she belongs now. "Why Wells Canyon? Did you just lay out a map of BC, close your eyes, and point?"

"Pretty sure that's exactly what my mom thinks I did, yes. She sent me an email yesterday with tips for surviving Grizzly Bear attacks. That reminds me—I should warn Beryl that there might be bear spray in the mailbox."

"It's definitely illegal to ship bear spray."

"What can I say? We're a family of badass criminals." The golden hue of sunset cascades across her as she relaxes deeper into the couch. "I won't give her too much shit for it, though. We haven't exactly had a close relationship for the last few years. So I'll happily accept any form of care package."

"Oh?" Fuck all my previous rules about staying out of my employee's business. I want to know everything about her.

"I made some questionable choices, and one of them was pushing my parents away. But it would be nice to mend things, y'know?"

I think it's a rhetorical question, but I answer regardless. "Yeah, I guess so."

Would it be nice to fix things with my dad? I'm not sure. I was never as close to him as I was to my mom, but I have no real complaints about the kind of father he was. At least, up until he made the choice to chase his middle-aged dreams because his wife was dead and his kids were grown-ish. I'd argue that boys aged twenty-five, twenty-two, and eighteen are hardly grown enough to take care of themselves... never mind a 20,000 head cattle operation. Especially while grieving the loss of one parent. He didn't need to make us lose both.

After a few more episodes, I can see her attention darting repeatedly toward the cake and then back to the TV. With the sun long gone, and neither of us moved from our respective couch corners, only the cool television glow illuminates her face. She stretches out, her toes pressing into my outer thigh. It's not quite the soft touch of her hand from my dreams, but it's the first time she hasn't acted like any parts of our bodies being in close contact repulses her.

"Let me grab a knife and forks for the cake," I say.

"What kind of fancy place do you have here? We're outlaws eating stolen cake—just grab forks."

"So you admit it's stolen." I shoot her a look. "Send me letters from your prison cell. I want to know what Martha Stewart's like."

Cecily pushes me with her feet. "Shush. Just get the forks before I resort to using my fingers like Odessa. Also, she's been out of prison for years. Your pop culture references need some help." She laughs. The kind of laugh that makes her cheeks rosy and her eyes watery. I didn't think I'd find myself laughing today, but it feels right. Everything with her feels right. She's the sunshine of this ranch, bringing light into the parts of me that I thought I'd always keep hidden in the dark.

My legs take a moment to gain full function after sitting for so long. It must be getting close to midnight. Well past my regular bedtime.

I'm not *that* stupid, though. There's no way I'm letting tonight end until she's ready for it to end.

When I return, I sit on the middle couch cushion. After all, we can't share a small cake if we're not next to each other. Cecily's instant rigidity when I sit down doesn't surprise me, even if it hurts. After a heartbeat, her body relaxes into the couch. I can feel her everywhere, although not a single inch of our skin is touching. I know we aren't touching because I check. *Repeatedly.*

As we eat, Cecily talks. About the book she's reading and silly stories from her childhood. The vegetables almost ready for harvest in her garden and what she plans to do with them. I don't say much, but she's either entirely unbothered or extremely understanding. For a day that I typically spend angry and alone, I can't get enough of being with her. Even in the silent moments, her presence is soothing.

"Should we get back to the episode?" she asks, just as I'm searching for the right words—something that will lead to kissing her. Hopefully, my mom would be understanding about the fact I've spent more time tonight staring at Cecily's perfect lips than I have watching the show. I have every episode memorized, anyway. I can't help but stare at the way her tongue darts out to lick a stray cake crumb from her bottom lip. The soft moan at the back of her throat when she takes a "perfect bite"—which is a piece with enough frosting to give you an instant cavity, according to her. It's impossible not to imagine what those lips would feel like on my lips, my chest, my cock. *God.* Would she make that same moaning noise with my cock filling her mouth? Without a doubt, I'd make sure she did. I'm silently praising my laziness for not getting up and turning on lamps as the sun went down. There's no hiding the quickly hardening bulge in my jeans.

I need to make conversation to stop myself from thinking about her on her knees, right here, looking up at me. Or bent over the back of the couch—*fucking hell, stop.* "Not sure if you noticed, but the lilacs are gone."

"Yeah, I noticed."

"So... Now you don't have to think about what they represent. Like you said."

Her fork drops from her mouth, letting her parted lips fill the space surrounding us with a thick, uncomfortable silence. *I fucked up again. This is why I keep my mouth shut.*

"Yeah. Yeah, um... you're right. Anyway, I should probably go home. It's pretty late." She sets her fork down and moves to stand.

"Cecily." I reflexively grab her arm to stop her, and she flinches. She *fucking flinches*. In one small, powerful movement, a lot about her becomes crystal clear. I'd suspected that she came here for a reason, but now I think I understand what she's running from. I understand why she tenses when I get too close. *That motherfucking asshole.* I drop my grip on her and back away—not like a wounded dog, but more like a spooked horse.

"I didn't mean to—I would never. If you want to talk. *Do you want to talk?*"

She's quick to shake her head no. "I should get to bed. Are you okay... about your mom's birthday and everything? You'll be okay alone here?"

"I'm fine." Is she seriously going to pretend like nothing just happened? Deke me out by switching the conversation back to my mom's birthday? For a brief second, I consider switching my answer and saying no, purely to see if she'll stay.

Instead, I wait until her cabin lights go out before grabbing my last beer, and heading outside. Texting the one person I can count on to go along with my insane plan as I start down the moonlit path. And *it is* a completely deranged plan.

Austin: You up? I need your help with a project.
Denny: A project at 1AM? Is quitting the family ranch an option? If so, consider this my resignation.
Austin: Yes or no? Meet me at the end of the driveway.
Denny: Yeah, yeah, yeah. Let me put my pants on.

My brother shows up seven minutes later with a whisky bottle in hand. He takes a pull and passes it to me.

"What's this for?" I take one, two, then three gulps before wiping my burning lips with the back of my hand.

"I assumed anything we were getting up to at this hour was likely illegal or dangerous—possibly both. Thought liquid courage might be good." He takes another slow sip and nods his head toward the chainsaws sitting at my feet. "So, what are we doing?"

"Cutting down the goddamn lilac bushes."

13

Cecily

T he usual kitchen commotion is heightened at five o'clock this morning. I can practically feel the house buzzing with energy. Raised voices, speaking over one another, slam into me before I even walk through the screen door.

I'm surprised to find everyone huddled around the kitchen island. The cowboys should be filling their travel mugs with black coffee, snagging bagged lunches from the massive industrial fridge in the pantry, and shovelling Beryl's homemade blueberry muffins or bagels into their mouths as they head out. Beryl says we're merely responsible for providing them with lunch, but you can always count on fresh baked goods being available. The scent of rising dough's a constant fixture in the house.

"What's going on?" I ask through a yawn as I saunter toward the coffee pot.

"We've been vandalized," Kate says in a hushed voice. "In the middle of the night."

"Holy crap." My eyes widen and ears prick as I focus on what the men are saying. *Shit, they're talking about revenge.* The typically unserious cowboys are deep in discussion about setting up secret watch stations, what guns to keep on hand, and asking neighbouring ranches if they've been hit. A voice I would expect to be prominent in any discussion about protecting Wells Ranch is surprisingly missing. Two voices, rather. I scan the faces and don't see Austin or Denny anywhere among them.

"Where's Austin?" I throw the question into the air, not directed at anybody in particular.

A series of shrugs and grumbles wave over the group. It would seem this is the first time anyone has noticed his absence. Normally, he's the quiet observer in the room, so it's not entirely surprising they haven't noticed he's not here. Most days, they hardly acknowledge Austin as he sips his coffee at the furthest end of the kitchen table. I'll never *not* notice him because he's a magnet, and my blood may as well be filled with metal filings. When he's in the same room, it's impossible not to feel his pull.

A dull pang in my chest hits as I sit across from his usual spot and take a long, tired sip of coffee. I struggled to sleep last night, wanting to go back to him and explain my overreaction to his making conversation about lilacs. Of course, I noticed the blooms dying off—I've been checking every damn day for the last two weeks. Google was quick to assure me that living separately is enough to be considered separated from your husband. But I foolishly made a deal with myself to wait until the lilacs stopped blooming, and then I waited longer to really be sure. It's the reason why I agreed to go to his house like a booty call last night. But I couldn't come out and say *that* when he mentioned the flowers.

Just as I start to worry he wasn't as okay with being alone last night as I thought, a single sentence severs my thoughts with a sharp knife.

"They cut down all the lilac bushes by the front gate." Kate fills in her husband, Jackson, on the morning drama as he sets Odessa down at the table.

"Wait, they did what?" I spin around so hard my chair almost tips backward. My stomach twists even harder than my body.

Kate shakes her head in disbelief. "The vandals took a chainsaw to the lilacs. What kind of person does that? We've dealt with protesters and trouble-making teens before, but this is weird."

Beryl's dark gaze meets mine. Since our initial porch swing conversation about KJ, I've told her little snippets here and there. I told her about the lilac bushes. About my promise to myself to let thoughts about KJ shrivel up alongside the vibrant purple blossoms. I've been careful not to mention the budding crush on Austin Wells, but her wink as we stare at each other from across the crowded room tells me she knows.

The screen door nearly swings off its hinges with how quickly I tear out of the house. Blood rushing through my ears drowns out the sound of gravel underfoot, and I run down the uneven path. A warm, humid breeze carries the sweet and dusty scent of freshly cut hay across the property; an aroma I've come to love since I stopped worrying about smelling lilac with every inhale.

Austin's walking out his front door just as I'm bounding up the steps, out of breath and shaking. His cowboy hat shades light-brown eyes, doing a subpar job at hiding the redness from lack of sleep.

"You," I blurt out between gasps for air. To be honest, I'm not entirely sure why I came. I have no idea what to say.

"Morning, City Girl." If he has any notion about why I'm here, he has an excellent poker face.

"You cut them down." I grip my ribs, trying to massage out the side-stitch. Austin gives me a quizzical look.

He's gotta be shitting me, he has to know what I'm talking about.

"The lilacs."

"Oh, yeah?" His mouth twitches.

Wait, he *did* cut them down, didn't he? I've only mentioned anything about those bushes to him and Beryl. It seems too strange to be coincidental. "Well, yeah, I'm pretty sure it was you who did it. Everybody else seems to think we've been vandalized. But why did you do it?"

"On the off-chance you stay until next spring, you'll never have to think about *him* again." The way he says the word "him" makes it sound like he has a personal vendetta against KJ. Which can't be true, because nobody's told Austin anything about him.

My vision becomes speckled and the muscles in my legs tremble. Even if I had the ability to form words around the heavy mass pressing on my chest, I'm speechless. Nobody's ever done something like this for me.

"I might not know your whole story, but I figured out enough to decide he isn't worth thinking about for a single second. And I didn't want you to have to worry about the lilacs. Do you want to sit?" he asks, eyeing my body as I shake like a leaf.

I drop to the steps without hesitation, and he sits down next to me, hanging his sand-coloured hat off a bent knee. Up close, and in the bright daylight, his dark hair's threaded with the occasional grey that glistens like tinsel. I can't stomach the way his eyes soften when he looks at me this morning—so unlike the way they turn to molten lava when I'm pretty sure he's checking me out, or the darkened slits they become when he's annoyed with the people around him. This look is new and feels full of pity, which is the last thing I want.

Did Beryl tell him more details? How does he know anything? Why does he care?

"Are you—I can replant them if you want me to. Last night you reacted so strongly after I brought them up, and I got—I needed to do something. You probably aren't even going to stay for long, but I want... well, in case you do. I figured it might be nice not to worry about them coming back. We'll dig up the roots in the daylight." He's stumbling over his words like he has a lot more he wishes he could say, but either isn't able or isn't sure how to. "Can you say something? I'm used to you being the talker here."

"Sorry, I'm a bit taken aback, is all. I didn't think you were capable of stringing so many words together." His eyes flash with something else I can't pinpoint. This conversation has had more emotions come from him than I've ever seen before. Is this hurt or anger? I can't tell. "I'm sorry, that was rude. I have a bad habit of blurting out stupid things when I'm uncomfortable."

"It's okay. I get it... You make me nervous, too." His cheeks turn pastel pink, and he stares down at his dusty cowboy boots.

"Don't plant them again. You have no idea how much you doing this means to me." I could hug him. Or kiss him. Or both. "Those have probably been on your property for, like, a hundred years. What if your great-grandparents planted them on purpose or something?"

"They're both dead." He shrugs. "You're here right now—alive and well on my ranch. I care a heck of a lot more about you being comfortable than their spirits potentially getting riled up over some silly flowers."

"Austin." His name comes out breathy and like a plea. My body intuitively leans into him so our upper arms are grazing. If I tilted my head just the right amount, it would be resting comfortably on his shoulder.

His face moves toward mine and my heart all but stops. *Is he going to kiss me?* I inhale his woodsy scent, tucking it away into my lungs like a keepsake. The lilacs are gone, KJ is gone, and I want this hot mountain man to make me forget he ever existed.

The searing heat from his thumb traces the ridge of my jawline, working its way to my bottom lip. Feeling the desperate need to be kissed for the first time in years, my lips part slightly and my eyelids flutter closed. For every cruelly conjured up KJ memory, I try to think of two images of Austin. As if enough thoughts about one will fully remove the other from my mind.

A deep rumble comes from his chest. "I'd really like to kiss you right now..."

The way his voice trails off tells me there's more to that thought. I whisper, "But?"

"But I won't want to stop there. I'll want to run my hands over your body, and kiss every inch of your skin. And I can't. Not when you constantly shy away from my touch."

"I don't—" I try to argue. Deny reacting with anything other than pure desire at the thought of his hands on me. Coming to grips with the idea that I might be ruined by KJ—never able to stand the touch of another man without flinching—is crippling.

"You do. When the time comes where I can do this,"—his rough hand gently cups my chin and his throat bobs with a hard swallow—"without feeling every muscle in your jaw tense, I'll kiss you until you're unable to breathe. And a whole lot more, if you'll let me."

Heat travels through me, forcing my thighs together and making my head float. If there was a way I could will my body to let it happen right now, I would. I'd love nothing more than to let Austin Wells permanently remove every memory of my shitty ex with his bearded kisses, work-worn hands, and whatever is under those fitted Wranglers.

My voice breaks as I admit my newfound biggest fear. "What if that never happens?"

"Oh, darlin'. I have no doubt it will." His eyes remain fixated on my lips, even as his hand falls away. "Not that it's exactly the same but, when I was a kid, I convinced my grandpa to buy me a horse from the auction. She was unbroken, abused, terrified. Couldn't even get within ten feet without her spooking. We went on to win the high school rodeo championships in tie-down roping two years in a row. It just takes time. Trust."

Trust. Can I trust somebody again?

14

Austin

With sixteen ranch hands working and nothing but fences to mend, I'm relegated to my office. I have work needing to be done and bills to be paid. Still, I'd rather stare out at the view. The hay door, once used for loading this loft with square bales, usually gives me an inspiring glimpse of the Timothy Mountains. I haven't looked at those peaks all damn day because I can't take my eyes off a much more stunning picture. Cecily's working the garden next to the house in a black tank top and denim overalls, blonde hair French-braided down her back. When I'm admiring how hard she's working, she does something like bend over, and I'm no better than an animal eyeing its next meal.

Who knew overalls could look so fucking hot?

Unable to stand another minute of watching from a distance, I chug the last of my coffee, pick myself up, and take a stroll over to the garden. Dangling my empty mug from my fingers, I swing open the white picket garden gate. The hinges squeal and Cecily turns toward the sound with a smile.

"Hey," we say in unison.

"I—uh—I came across this book and thought you might like it. Since you're into history, y'know? It's about the history of Wells Canyon."

I thrust my hand forward, holding out a flimsy paperback. By "came across", I mean I specifically went to the local tourist information centre and purchased it after the day at the river. I should've cracked the spine, dog-eared a few pages... made it look less new. More believable that it's just been lying around somewhere.

Standing up, she brushes soil from her hands and walks over to me. Sparks fly from her skin into my veins when our fingers brush. It's not just in my head. There's no uncertainty; she feels it, too. Looking up at me with a bewitching stare and slightly parted lips.

She repeatedly turns the book over in her hands. "This is really cool—thank you. It's probably ninety percent about your family, hey?"

I grimace. "Shit... probably. I would imagine a lot of the indigenous history, too. If this isn't the type of history you're into, it's fine. I'm sure it's pretty boring stuff, but you said you like history books and, well... Forget it."

"No, Aus. It's really sweet. I'm excited to read it." Her eyes slice through me and her smile softens my cringing face. "Thank you."

Shit. I didn't consider what my next move would be once I gave her the book. I shift on my feet, insisting that blood flow to my limbs instead of my face.

Coffee mug, idiot. I swing my empty mug upward, nearly dropping it in the process. "Anyway, just came for a refill."

"Perfect. My back could use a break. I'll join you."

We saunter together up the stairs, and I'm flooded with disappointment when Beryl and Kate are in the kitchen making tomorrow's lunches. It's not shocking to find them here. But there's a sharp pinprick in my chest when I see them and lose the small shred of hope that I'd be alone with Cecily for a while longer.

"So," Cecily says. I turn expectantly, only to find she's not talking to me. A kicked puppy, I return to filling my mug and silently trudge to my seat. All the while discreetly—keenly—listening to her excitedly talk about the variety of tomatoes ready to pick. Hearing her argue with

Kate about wanting to make salsa, rather than tomato sauce, because it's "harder to zhuzh up store-bought salsa, so it needs to be homemade".

Her presence, sinking into the chair opposite me, forces my eyes up from the weathered table. "Help settle the debate, Aus. Do we make salsa or pasta sauce with the bounty of tomatoes we're about to have?"

"Salsa, obviously."

"Right answer." Her foot taps lightly against mine. I'd assume it was accidental, except it's accompanied by a smile which quickly disappears behind her teal mug. Only her radiant, sparkling eyes are visible above the rim as she takes a sip, and they're locked on mine.

In the six days since admitting I want to kiss her—both to her and to myself—there's been an indescribable shift between us. Although I still get tripped up on words and end up not saying anything at all. Although some things I say come out wrong, making me seem like a dick. Although her body still instinctively retreats into itself when I get too close or move too quickly.

There's a mutual understanding that we will kiss—it's a matter of when, not if. And, for now, I'm happy with the long glances, subtle smiles, and footsies under the kitchen table. All of it is a constant reminder that we both want it to happen. I'm willing to wait to kiss her for as long as I need to.

15

Austin

I stroll into the big house for dinner after the most unproductive day I've ever had. At least, the one task I did get done is worth more than any amount of paperwork. I put new tires on her damn tin-can car. It's pretty clear she's been in no hurry to get it done, and I can't help but hope it's because she's also in no hurry to leave the ranch. However, I'm fully aware my hopes are foolish. I've walked in on her, Kate, and Beryl talking about Vancouver before. Confirming my trepidation and cementing the knot in my stomach.

"We're leaving for the Stampede first thing. Last chance to change your mind, Aus." Denny follows me into the kitchen where Jackson, Kate, and Odessa are already sitting at the massive wooden table. I take my usual spot, feeling the grooves from thousands of hours spent in this exact chair. Hell, there's a perfectly worn circle on the table from where I've set my cup down every day for thirty-some-odd years.

"Somebody has to stay here."

"Jackson can manage the skeleton crew, I'm sure." Denny loads mashed potatoes onto his plate, the steam blurring his face from my view. "Let loose for once. It'll be a good time. Lots of beer, lots of buckle bunnies."

"I love buckle bunnies!" Odessa exclaims between sips from her dinosaur cup.

"You and me both, kiddo." Denny's wide grin and finger guns at our niece make her giggle. He cracks a beer and adds, "If I'm lucky, I'll have quite a few wearing my hat, and taking me for a ride, after the rodeo's over. Come on, Austin. Let your hair down."

Odessa leans into Kate and, with a hilariously loud stage whisper, says, "Mommy, why is a bunny going to ride Uncle Denny?"

Kate smacks Jackson as if it's somehow his fault our younger brother still hasn't learned to watch what he says around the four-year-old. Even though Kate pretends to be angry, we can't stop ourselves from laughing. Poor little girl doesn't stand a chance growing up here—I doubt this is anything close to the worst thing she's heard already.

"If you think that's going to entice me, get your head outta your ass." I feel Kate shooting daggers, and I glance over at Odessa. "I mean butt. Get it out of your butt."

The kid giggles, and continues eating her dinner with her fingers. As I said, she's heard much worse hanging out in this kitchen with the ranch hands. But she's also likely the safest girl in the entire country, so I think Kate's willing to let some questionable language slide.

"You're forgetting something, Den. Why would he go to the Calgary Stampede when the girl he's chasing is gonna be here on the ranch?" Kate lovingly points out.

In reality, Cecily staying at the ranch is hardly affecting my decision not to travel ten hours one way to go to the Calgary Stampede. More importantly, I would rather do practically anything else instead of rodeoing, partying, and sleeping with random women. For the first twenty-five years of my life, I wouldn't pass up a rodeo invite for anything. My childhood was spent watching my grandpa and mom head our local rodeo organization; dreaming of following in their footsteps. In my teens and early twenties, I lived for the thrill of a winning run, the lively atmosphere, and—on occasion—the women. But I haven't been interested in any of those things in a *long* time.

"Thought you weren't going to get yourself tangled up with the city girls again after what happened with Savannah?" Jackson side-eyes me.

Denny chuckles. "That was before he and I cut down all the lilacs 'cause she didn't like 'em. Boy's already tangled."

"Shut the fu—frick up, Denny. I'm not tangled, and I'm not getting tangled. I know better than to think she'll stay here."

"You never know. I stayed." Kate shrugs and rests her folded arms across her stomach. "Listen, I liked Savannah, but she was never cut out to stay here. You were too blinded by love to see it, Aus."

"Mmhm." I pinch the bridge of my nose, and look out at the sunset shadows falling across the mountains. I'm so ready to be done with this conversation.

"It's true, man." Denny points his fork at me. "She always liked hanging out for the summer, riding horses, flirting with the cowboys, and heading south for winter. Like a damn snowbird. I really don't know why you were shocked when she left for good."

"Sometimes I wish you'd head fucking south for the winter, Den. Give me a break." I slam back the remaining liquid in my beer can, and put my napkin on my plate.

"Language." Kate glares.

"Sorry."

Denny's still wrapped up in his last thought. "Filly's not like that, though—from what I can tell. She's not flirting with any of the guys. She busts her ass here. And she's never mentioned any siblings in Florida."

"Great dinner, Kate. Thanks." My chair scrapes across the wood floor as I stand up and walk out.

I hear her half-heartedly call my name as I push through the front door. I'm about to become a full recluse and skip dinners at the big house. It seems those three always find a way to steer the conversation to me... and, lately, to me and Cecily.

W

With my crew halved for the next few days, I'm forced to pull more than my usual chore load. I'm quick to volunteer to wrangle with the ranch hands—moving 1,000-head from one grazing section to another sounds like the perfect way to steer clear of Cecily. I may have talked a big game about waiting to kiss her, but it's a promise I find harder to keep with every smile, every whiff of her sweet perfume, and every glimpse at the sliver of skin on her lower back when she bends down in the garden. If I'm going to stick to my promise of not kissing her until she's ready, it would do me good to get the hell away from here for a while.

Maybe I should've gone to the Stampede.

I'm tacked up and waiting before the sun wakes. Red stumbles into the stables a little after four a.m. with red eyes and a sullen face. "Mornin', bossman."

"No Stampede?"

"Yeah, no. Didn't go well for me last year. Too many fake cowboys looking for a fight, too many mounties looking to arrest the real cowboys for giving 'em what they had coming."

"Can't say I'm mad we won't have to bail you outta jail again."

"Thought you'd appreciate that, Aus. You know you love having me here."

I grunt. "You don't know me at all, do you?"

"Oh, fuck off. You love me like a brother, even if you're too much of a jackass to say it. Least Denny tells me enough for the both of ya." He heaves the saddle pad and saddle onto his red mare, Heathen. It's a fitting name—she gives him a run for his money every chance she gets. To make sure they get adequate rest, our cowboys cycle through ten horses each. For whatever reason, Red seems to have the most intense mounts in the remuda.

The rest of the men slowly trickle in until there's nine of us in total. Some are pissed off about being too low in the pecking order to get to go to the Calgary Stampede, the rest are pissed off because they have to do twice the work while we're shorthanded. All grumble equally while they tack up.

"Quit the bitchin'. We have cattle to move and God's not granting us more daylight 'cause we're shorthanded," I shout as I mount my cowy mare, Jubilee. With a few more gripes, the men follow suit and, for the most part, shut up for our ride over the hill.

Nine men on horseback and four cattle dogs. We spend hours driving the herd of steers from one section of grazing land to another, down a long dirt road and across the crystal clear waters of the Timothy River. I can't help but wonder if Cecily is downstream, tanning in her bikini on the riverbank. *God, would I love to be there.* The afternoon sun bakes my forearms, and I tug my cotton rag further up my neck to prevent a burn.

By the time we're circling back, strawberry-wine-painted sky grants us just enough light to find our way to the stables. With a grunt, I lift the saddle from Jubilee, and she lets out a shudder of relief that runs through every muscle. I let out the same shudder as the heavy leather saddle plunks onto the rack. Horse sweat and dust fill the stable, and I inhale the comforting scent deeply.

"I know, girl. We need to get out more often, don't we? Feels good, doesn't it?" I gently stroke her muzzle, working a brush over her sweat-soaked side.

Once she's ready to bed down, the moon's high in the sky and thousands of mosquitoes create a gentle hum in the air. There's a good chance I'll fall asleep standing if I quit moving long enough. Then I see Cecily sitting on my front porch steps, and I could be persuaded to stay awake all damn night.

She looks up at my boots crunching on the gravel and wipes aggressively at her eyes. They're red from crying, and she's trembling as if it's not still a balmy twenty-five degrees Celsius. Seeing her in this state, the fact I'm dead tired and sore no longer matters.

"What's going on?" I look her up and down. Is she hurt? Was there an accident? My train of thought runs at a thousand kilometres an hour in the seconds it takes for her to respond.

"I'm sorry, I just—I didn't know where else to go. I fucked up. I think I might be in trouble and I—" Her voice breaks and it takes everything in me not to scoop her into my arms. Whatever the trouble is, I want to make it go away. I need her to stop crying. "I can go. Never mind, don't worry about it. I needed somebody, and Beryl's gone visiting her family. Kate's pregnant, and doesn't need to deal with my bullshit. I just... panicked and came here, but then you weren't here and—I'm sorry."

"Hey, no. No. Stay. I'm glad you came here. Come in." I hold out my hand and, to my surprise, she takes it and follows me into the house.

I fill a glass with water and hand it to her as she sits down on the couch. "What's going on?"

Cecily lets out a drawn-out exhale, patting away the dampness on her cheeks. "I fucked up, and he knows I'm here. I gave my phone number to somebody who I thought was my friend and, I mean, she *had* to have been the one to give it to him. *Shit.* I questioned even sending it to her in the first place—she hasn't called—why did I even bother? He got the phone number, googled it, narrowed down my approximate location, and threatened to show up here. I don't think he'll know to look for me on the ranch, but what if he figures it out somehow? What if he shows up here?"

No clarification is needed about who *he* is.

"Okay. It's not your fault—we'll deal with it if he shows up. It's okay, though."

"No, Austin, it's not. It's *not* okay. He's going to come here and,"—her voice drops until it's barely audible, despite the room being dead silent—"I'm scared he's going to kill me."

The blood coursing through me heats to its boiling point in an instant. "Over my dead body."

Cecily blows air from her nostrils like she thinks I'm joking. I'm not. "I just... I don't know. Never mind, my head's a mess," she says.

"Let me into your head. What's going on?" I rip the bandana from around my neck, and kick off my boots, before sinking into the couch next to her.

"I don't want you to feel like you need to be involved if I do."

"Darlin', you live on my property, and we're friends, right? If there's somebody who's a threat to you, I'm already involved."

She nods solemnly. "Okay, I guess I should start by telling you... I'm married."

I drag my fingertips across my forehead as a sharp pain forms in my temple. There was an indent on her ring finger when she showed up here, but after all this time and no mention of it, I started to wonder if I had been seeing things.

Married.

I almost kissed a married woman. I was almost willing to risk getting my heart broken again... by a married woman.

"Well, separated. And, assuming he'll sign the papers, divorced once I'm able to file for it. We have to be separated for a year before I can. I wanted to clarify because of... you and me." The corner of her lip picks up for a brief moment as our eyes meet. "I met Beryl online, but not through a job board like she told everybody. We met in a forum for women escaping domestic violence."

There's that boiling blood again. My fists clench in my lap. When her eyes land on them, I see fear flash through her, causing me to release my fingers. And I flex them open instead. Splayed out across my thighs so I can feel the heated tension in each finger. The last thing I want is to be the source of more fear for her. I'm aware Beryl has a troubled past. She doesn't talk in specifics about it, but I've caught enough vague comments over the years to know things were bad with her ex-husband. I hadn't ever considered she could be talking to strangers online about it, though.

"Beryl and I texted every night for months after KJ—that's his name—went to bed. She offered me a job and a safe place to stay, but I kept putting her off. I knew he wasn't right to treat me like he did, but it's not like he hit me. He could be really sweet, too, so I second-guessed whether I needed to leave when I wasn't in danger. He did a lot of other things, but he didn't ever hit me..."

I can tell what her next words will be by the quiver in her jaw and the slow lick of her bottom lip.

"Until he did, on the night I came here."

Linking my fingers behind my neck, I stare up at the ceiling with a shaky exhale. Thick saliva pools in the back of my throat.

"He *hit* you." The words don't feel real, even though I suspected he was the reason behind her tense muscles.

"It's stupid, but I don't think I would have even made it all the way to Wells Canyon if he had stopped there. I would've gone for a drive, cooled down, and then went home. At least he's always remarkably loving for a while after we fight. But he was eerily calm while I packed up my stuff and, to be honest, that should've been my first clue. No way he'd let me go without a fight normally."

My eyes focus on the knotted wood planks below us, following each groove to stop the angry pricking behind my eyelids.

"But he didn't stop there?" I finally put my trembling hands to good use by grabbing hers. She looks like she needs a hug, and I'd love nothing more than to be the one to comfort her. Every tendon in my arms ache to grab her. If only I was convinced she would want it, too.

"No," she whispers. "When I tried to leave... he had a gun. Threatened to shoot if I got in the car."

Our collective breathing fills the otherwise soundless room for the next few seconds. Everything feels heavy, the air thick, and every bone in my body begs to be closer to her.

Fuck it, she needs a hug.

"I'm going to hug you. Okay?" I watch her intently, waiting for the slow, subtle nod.

Letting go of her hands, my fingertips skim up her arms before wrapping around her shoulders, drawing her to me. I ignore how taut she feels against my chest, holding a tight grasp, and letting her wet eyes soak through my shirt until I can feel her tears on my heart. Silently praying there's a way I can absorb her anguish and take on her pain.

I'm trying to remember the last time I hugged someone. Felt the weight of a body pressed into my chest, the warmth of breath against my neck. She needs to be held and I'm consumed with an endless need to hold her.

She sucks in a ragged sob, and I selfishly hold tighter. Within moments, her muscles melt into mine, and I use the leverage my hand has on her back to pull her closer. So close our hearts beat in unison and our breathing forms a perfect melody. She curls up in the space between my legs, and my chin rests firmly on top of her head.

"I'm sorry for the trauma dump. That was a lot to unload on you, and you didn't come home tonight wanting a crying girl in your lap."

I hate seeing her cry. But I'm definitely okay with her being in my lap.

"Don't be. You shouldn't have to deal with this shit by yourself, and I'm happy to listen. I'm glad you came here instead of being alone."

"I didn't feel safe at home and wasn't sure where else to go. I thought I'd be safe here... with you."

Her head slips tighter under my jaw, settling into me. A sugary coconut smell drifts up from her hair, and with a single thought—*fuck it*—I take my chances by stroking a rough hand over the silky tresses.

Fuck my heart, too, I guess. There's no keeping her at a distance or convincing myself I only want something casual with her. I didn't honestly think I had it in me to do either, anyway. It's going to hurt like a bitch if she leaves, but it'll be worth it.

"You're safe. As long as you're here with me, you're safe. I won't let anything bad happen to you," I whisper into her hair. A mass sits on my chest, and I doubt I'll be able to breathe normally until the day comes when she doesn't need to be scared.

"I know." Two simple words fill my heart. If it weren't for the seething pain in my heart, I'd be floating to the clouds right now.

"Austin?" Her voice is small.

"Mmm?" I'm struggling to stay awake in this position, with my head resting on hers and her body like a warm blanket over me.

"You smell like horses and sweat."

"I bet I do." I laugh. "I'll take a shower, and we'll get you to bed. You're sleeping here tonight. I'll stay up and keep lookout so you can rest easy."

In a testament to how scared she is, she simply nods. Part of me hopes he's stupid enough to come here tonight. I'd love to release the pent-up rage rooted in my stomach from her confession. The other part of me doesn't want her to ever have to see his face again.

I tread to the bathroom and turn on the water. With any luck, a cold shower will help wake me back up enough to sit by the window all night long.

"Austin?" Cecily's voice accompanies a light tapping on the door.

I fling it open in a hurry. "What's wrong?"

"It's silly. Can I sit here while you shower?"

She's asking because she's afraid to be alone, but my cock really seems to think it's for other reasons. And the sudden friction in my pants only contributes to my inappropriate thoughts. *It might be safest if we shower together.* Fucking hell.

I manage to force out an appropriate response instead. "Yeah, of course."

She sinks to the floor just outside the bathroom and I shake my head. "Don't sit on the floor. Just... either I can leave the door open and you go back out there or you can sit right in here."

"Okay." She sits down on the closed toilet seat and places her hand over her eyes. "Okay, go ahead. I promise not to look."

My wobbly fingers take longer to unbutton my shirt than normal, but eventually, I'm down to my boxers in the small bathroom. Less than three feet away from her. As I hook my thumbs on the waistband, the solitary thought crossing my mind is, *fuck, she could choose to open her eyes at any moment.* The idea of her discreetly watching—seeing me completely naked—brings my semi to a full erection before my boxers have even hit the floor.

"You can open your eyes," I say from behind the shower curtain.

Despite the massaging way the water pelts against my sore muscles, this is the least relaxing shower I've ever taken. It's a struggle to focus on anything other than the gorgeous woman on the other side of the curtain, her motherfucking abusive husband, and the poorly timed boner that needs to go away. Especially because I can't do a single thing I want to do about those problems right now.

When the cold water's finally worked well enough that I can get out without sporting a towel tent, I wrap a navy towel around my lower half and step out from behind the curtain. Her eyes drift across my body like a phantom touch before settling on my chest.

"Jesus Christ. Is that... a brand?" She shoots to her feet and her fingers are suddenly on the faded scar. Tracing the "rafter W" mark cautiously, as if handling a fresh wound. Causing a flurry of sparks to shoot across my body. As badly as I've been craving her hands on me, I've been hoping it would be under different circumstances.

"Told you I had first-hand experience."

"I thought you were just messing with me. *Wow*. It's a bit unhinged, but also pretty badass. How much did it actually hurt?" Her eyes flick up to meet mine, but she doesn't remove her hand. My skin feels like it's being seared all over again under her soft, warm touch. If I had known she'd react this way, I would've ditched my shirt weeks ago.

"It wasn't great—humans don't exactly have a thick hide like cattle. The whiskey helped."

"Now that I think about it, Denny and Red have one too, don't they? I never asked, but I assumed they'd lost a bet or thought it was a good idea after too many drinks. Does everybody here have one or are you secretly super wild under your mask of responsibility?"

"Just those who stick around long enough to earn it. Me, my brothers, Red... my dad. And I wasn't always the stick in the mud I am now, by the way. I used to be quite fun."

She shakes her head with a chuckle, blonde hair sweeping over her shoulders. "Saying you were 'quite fun' isn't very convincing, and I didn't say anything about you being a stick in the mud. You have a whole ranch to run and people who depend on you. If you acted half as recklessly as some of the guys around here, this place would crumble. It's admirable the way you take control of everything, even if it makes you a grump sometimes."

Her hand mindlessly continues stroking my chest, the pads of her fingers tracing the brand's "W" over and over. A form of witchcraft—the way she seems to be directly accessing my heart.

"You know," she muses. "I also used to be fun."

Used to be? She's constantly cracking jokes with the guys, hanging out by the river, dancing around the kitchen with the girls, and singing in the garden. "You seem plenty fun now."

"Because I'm making a conscious effort to get back to it. You know, it wouldn't kill you to do something for yourself sometimes. Lose control. Enjoy yourself... be a bit reckless." Her fingertips drag across my chest from shoulder to shoulder, leaving a scattering of goosebumps in their wake.

"Yeah?" My eyes meet hers. The warm overhead lighting has the light blue specks in her eyes shimmering. It doesn't feel like we're talking about an innocent kind of recklessness right now.

The corner of her lip quirks and she seems to be closer to me than she was even a second ago. I don't know if she's moving into me or I'm leaning into her. But there's no denying how narrow the space has become when her hand, still drawing along my brand, barely fits between our chests.

"You're a good man, Aus. But there's no shame in doing things you *want* to do sometimes, not just what you think you should do."

I *want* to kiss her. Rip her jeans from her body and let my towel hit the floor. Wrap those pretty, tanned legs around my waist and carry her off to bed to fuck her until she forgets about the asshole ex. Taste her, kiss every inch of her body, make her come, and then hold her all night long. Fuck her senseless, bring her breakfast in bed, and then spend tomorrow showing her how *good of a man* I can be.

There's no shame in doing things you want to do... sometimes. The same night she received threats from her husband and then cried in my arms? No. It's not the time for doing anything I want to do.

"I'll remember that, darlin'." I smile softly down at her.

She steps back and lets her hand fall to her side, as if she's suddenly aware how far she's encroached on my personal space. Not that I care. In fact, I wish she'd get closer. "I never thought to ask when we were branding, but what does the design mean?"

I clear my throat. "The W is for Wells, of course. This shape above it is called a rafter or half diamond. When my great-grandparents created it, they wanted the rafter to symbolize the home they were building here. I don't think they had any idea they were creating this legacy. They were trying to feed their six children and, back in the day, the government would give you land for free if you were willing to farm it. So they moved here, and that was that."

"That's beautiful."

I've never really thought about it, but I suppose it is.

"Come on, do you want a T-shirt to sleep in? Or I can run over to your place and grab you some stuff?" I follow her out of the bathroom and away from the magical, intimate moment between us.

"A T-shirt's fine. I don't want to be alone at all, and I definitely don't want to go outside tonight."

"Let's get you to sleep, then. It's late and I bet you're tired."

"What about you?" She yawns, taking a light grey ranch t-shirt from my hands. "You've been working all day. Aren't you tired?"

"Darlin', I've spent many nights keeping watch with a gun in my hands during calving season. I'll be perfectly fine. You need rest more than I do."

I'll be chugging coffee straight from the pot all damn night. But I don't care.

16

Cecily

It wasn't a restful night but, if I was going to be awake and anxious, at least I was in a lush king-sized bed that smelled like Austin's spicy, cedar-scented body wash. I might have briefly breathed in his pillow, trying to work up the courage to ask him to join me. If only so I could have the same comfort he gave on the couch. I'm lost in that thought, dreading having to face the day, when I spot the candle he bought with me on his nightstand and can't help but smile.

Slowly opening the bedroom door, I'm somewhat stunned to find him still sitting vigilantly, in an armchair he dragged to a spot by the living room window. True to his word, there's a rather large gun laying across his lap, which momentarily starts up warning bells in my mind.

Not all guns are bad, Cecily. If he wanted to kill me, he could have a hundred times over. I breathe through the panic until my heart rate slows to nearly normal. As normal as it ever is, when Austin's nearby.

The rising sun filters through a large fir tree just outside, casting branching shadows across the wood floor and far wall. Similar to my cabin, Austin's house features log construction and basic amenities. Although he's lucky enough to have a separate bedroom and a slightly larger kitchen.

"Good morning, my valiant defender," I tease—forever trying to downplay situations involving KJ.

"Mornin'. There's coffee in the pot." Austin turns in his seat. Red, weary eyes meet mine, and I'm filled with regret for making him feel like he needed to be involved. Especially when KJ clearly didn't show up last night. Austin was out driving cattle all day; he needed his sleep more than I did.

"I'm sorry for keeping you up."

"You don't need to apologize for things that don't require apologies."

"I'm sor—"

He shakes his head, a sleepy smile spreading across his face. "We'll work on it. Anyway, I already called Jackson, and he's going out with the men today. You and I are going to help Kate with whatever she needs. And then you'll stay at my house until the guys come back from Stampede. When they're back, we'll make sure there's somebody outside your place every night until *he* admits defeat... or shows up here and gets a nice Wells Ranch welcome. Either way, you don't need to worry about him anymore. He's not getting to you."

I want to tell him he doesn't have to do any of this, but I'm not sure that's true.

"That was a lot of words from you, big guy."

"Cecily." His eyes narrow, giving me a look that's almost fatherly in nature.

"Thank you. Um... did you tell Jackson and Kate about what's going on?" I gulp air.

"No. Everybody here has a story, darlin'. It's not my place to tell yours. There's trust between people here, and we'll go to war for each other without any idea why."

If I hadn't ostensibly run out of tears last night, I would cry right now. And I really wish I could force even one single droplet to catch on my waterline so he'd lay me against his warm chest again. I could happily spend the morning feeling his fingers run through my hair, hearing nothing but his heartbeat. If last night was the rainstorm Beryl talked about, then Austin was the thick blanket wrapped around me. By a fire so cozy you can't help but fall asleep. Keeping me warm, comfortable, and *safe*.

"Let's go have some breakfast. If I don't get up and move, I'm going to pass out." He rubs his eyes and yawns.

"Get some sleep. I'm just going over to the house with Kate and Odessa."

"Yeah, no. All the more reason why I need to be there, just in case." He stands up with a stretch that exposes his lower stomach, reminding me how close I was to kissing his bare chest last night. How badly I wanted to inch my hand from the brand above his heart to the dark happy trail. Follow it up with slow kisses down him.

"Austin? Can I hug you?"

"You never need to ask, darlin'." He pulls me into him, laying his cheek on top of my head. Clenching the fabric of his shirt between my fingers, I take a deep breath. His hand rubbing slow circles on my back eases the stress woven into my muscles. *Now* I can face the day.

As we walk to the house, I pull my phone from my pocket and hand it to Austin. At this point, it seems best to lay it all out on the table. He can see the shit I'm dealing with, and I won't fault him if he tells me to leave the ranch. Especially now, since he's reminded me that my presence isn't exclusively a danger to me, or to him. If KJ shows up here, it's putting everybody at risk.

All it took was a few text messages from a blocked number to assure me that—regardless of how close I thought I was to moving on—KJ still has power over me.

Unknown Sender: Last chance, Cecily. Didn't think I'd get your new phone number, did you? Didn't think I'd google the area code? I've got your location pretty much narrowed down. One of a handful of small towns.

Unknown Sender: You know you don't belong there, babe. I doubt
    you're able to have the manicures, massages, and shopping sprees you
    require.

Unknown Sender: Come home and we'll pretend this little psychotic
    break of yours didn't happen.

Unknown Sender: Don't forget we're married, Cecily. If you don't
    come home, I'll come to you. I'll find you in whatever shitty little town
    you ended up in, and you'll be coming home one way or another. Till
    death do we part, babe.

Austin stops in his tracks, his boots stirring up dust as he spins to face
me. "Jesus. That's definitely a threat, if you ask me."

I grimace. "If it's too much, say the word and I'll go. I don't want to
put your family in any danger by being here, and I have no doubt he'll
make good on his word. Maybe not today or tomorrow or next week.
But I'm sure he'll turn up, eventually."

"I'm sure he will, too. I mean... I can see why he'd want you back." He
blushes, and it makes my heart skip a beat. "I can't, in good conscience,
make you leave here right now, though. When you want to go one day,
I'll understand. But it's not going to be until after we've dealt with this
asshole. You got it?"

"Got it."

"You can tell Kate what's going on if you want. But maybe don't
tell her about the gun, okay?" He starts toward the house again, not
waiting to hear my answer. I assume he doesn't want her to hear the
whole story because she's a smart woman with a family to worry about.
Doesn't matter that she and I have become friends. I'll be removed from
the property faster than I can blink if she senses any serious danger.

"What the hell?" Kate's waiting on the front porch, and the way her
hands are holding her lower back makes her belly jut out even farther
than usual. "Why did you send Jackson out first thing this morning? The
phone woke both Odessa and me up, by the way, asshole."

"Sorry," Austin mutters, pushing past and into the house.

Kate shakes her head at me, clearly confused and worried about why her husband was called out of bed before daybreak on his day off. Especially seeing Austin isn't gone with the crew like he should be.

"Kate, I have some shit to tell you." My head tips toward the wicker chairs next to the front door.

I run through a stripped-down version of everything, pausing to answer her million questions about my life before Wells Ranch. All the shit KJ put me through over the last three years. In my periphery, I catch Austin slipping through the door and taking a seat on the front steps with a fresh coffee. A quiet observer. He's only heard a little about the night I left and my current situation, so this other information is new to him, too. Thanks to her pregnancy hormones, Kate cries... *a lot*. Austin sits with his head buried in his hands. His leg bouncing anxiously on the step. All the while, I remain surprisingly apathetic. Numb. Cold. As if I'm rehashing a book I read, rather than telling my own story.

When we get to the present situation, I follow Austin's advice about omitting the involvement of a gun. Kate's sobbing so intensely you'd think this was her trauma, not mine. I don't need to make it any harder for her pregnant emotions to handle, so the omission doesn't make me feel too guilty.

Once her tears have adequately dried, the three of us head inside. The day continues almost as normal, except that Austin does his paperwork at the kitchen table and Kate grills me with question after question. By the time I'm done with my tasks for the day, I'm mentally and emotionally drained. When Austin suggests heading back to his place, I can't even find it in me to respond with words. A simple nod and slow walk to the front door suffice.

For at least twenty minutes, he and I sit in blissful silence before working up the nerve to talk.

"Should we have dinner here?" Austin's eyes are pleading from the opposite end of his couch.

I exhale loudly. "Please. I don't think I can handle any more crying. Does pregnancy make your tear production a hundred times more efficient than normal? I was starting to worry she might become dehydrated."

All day, Kate welled up every time she looked at me. *Every single time.* If I accidentally made eye contact for too long—full-blown tears. I told her I was happy to answer any other questions she thought of, and I regretted that instantly. Not because I was uncomfortable answering them, but because it made her weep. To the point where Austin had to go play with Odessa outside to stop her from worrying. Despite my concern that her being stressed all day wasn't healthy, Kate insisted she hear all the details. I'll admit it felt good to have open, raw conversations, and no longer need to carry the weight of keeping such a burdening secret. After three years with nobody in my corner, dealing with every situation alone, I wasn't even sure I was still capable of letting people know the real me until I came to Wells Ranch.

"Great. Kraft Dinner okay?" he asks. "I don't have much for groceries here."

KJ never would've allowed boxed macaroni and cheese into his house. Only expensive, fancy meals for him—which is nothing like the Lunchables, Kraft Dinner, and Sugar Crisp I grew up on and love. Even if I insisted on having some, he'd *never* cook it for me. Or cook anything, period.

"God, yes, *please.* I haven't had that in years." I sink deeper into the couch cushion with a moan that makes his eyebrows raise. "Ooooh, do you have hot dogs too?"

"You're easy to please. I like it." He smacks his thighs and stands up. "Hot dogs and KD, coming up."

"I can help." I follow behind him, fully aware the kitchen is too small for us to work side-by-side without bumping into one another. My skin warms with nervousness like I'm a preteen girl hoping the cute boy's pinky might brush mine during our chaperoned date. "You get the water boiling and I'll grab the hot dogs."

Watching the pot come to a boil won't fill my grumbling stomach any faster, so I look at him. He's leaning against the oak cupboards, arms crossed over his chest. Veins on his forearm lead an enticing path up to his biceps, under his shirtsleeve, and my mind wanders to how good he looked last night. Chest hair still wet from the shower, the dip in his clavicles, the stretched muscles covering his shoulders. Full-on, rugged eye-candy, and he doesn't even seem to realize it. He's so handsome it's not fair to the other cowboys—and some of them are *definitely* considered conventionally attractive.

Catching me staring, he smirks. "What are you thinking about?"

How badly I want to tear your clothes off. I'm not bold enough to say what I'm thinking. Not when his eyes are ripping me apart like they are.

"Kate asked me approximately one billion personal questions today, and you didn't ask any. Now's your chance."

Austin's tongue presses against the inside of his cheek, his eyes darting to the floor. After a few silent heartbeats, his low voice asks, "Do you still love him?"

"God, no," I impulsively say, caught off guard. It's the truth. "For a long time, when it first started, I did. I thought loving him enough would make him change. Then, even as I started to understand that I didn't still love him, I fought it. Hard. I mean... I feel sad sometimes about the way things turned out. But, to answer your question, no. I haven't loved him in a long, long time. I meant it when I told you I'm filing for divorce as soon as I can."

In typical Austin fashion, he grunts a single time and stares at me.

"Any other questions?"

"Oh, I have questions, but none of them are for you."

"Okay, can I ask you a question?"

He raises an eyebrow, a muscle in his jaw twitching.

"Do you see me differently now?" I swallow hard, awaiting his response. Looking everywhere except at him, for once. The black cupboard knobs, the striped towel hanging from the oven door handle, the singular tree-shaped magnet on his fridge—which looks like it was probably painted by Odessa. I'm unsure whether I want him to say yes or no. Neither feels like the *right* answer.

"I do." Thankfully, he takes a deep enough breath for the both of us because my lungs have seized. "You've had so many things happen to you—things the most resilient people I know wouldn't come back from. Yet somehow, you're still the sunshine of this damn ranch. I would've never guessed you had this much crap going on. Shit, I have no idea how you're as strong as you are."

His words settle over me like a soothing balm. "I don't think I'm half as strong as you give me credit for. I didn't cry about it today because I've run the well dry more times than I can count. I'm not strong so much as numb to it all, and I'm not sure that's something to be admired."

"Trust me, I've been there..." A troubled look flashes across his eyes, here and then gone as he sharply turns away. His messy dark hair tousled the tiniest bit out of place by the movement.

The uncooked macaroni splashes into the pot and Austin circles back to me. "I knew something was up on my mom's birthday when I grabbed your arm and you flinched, but I didn't expect everything you told us. I want you to know I would never have done that—grabbed you—if I'd known. I'm sorry."

"The thing with keeping secrets is you can't blame people for not knowing about them."

His arms fall loosely to his sides and, overwhelmed with an unexpected urge to be closer, I step into him. My chest presses on his, and I'm relaxing into his large, warm body. Austin's firm arms come around my back, gently holding me closer. Every piece touching him is on fire as if I've been dunked in a tub of Icy Hot. Burning so good. His fingertips draw a line down my upper arm and the delicate brush sends a spark dancing, twirling across my skin.

Tilting my head to look up at him, I run my palm along his jaw, pulling his gaze to meet mine. My eyes shutter, leaning in to feel his breath on my skin. On my lips. Wrapped around my waist, his arm tightens and his hand lightly squeezes my hip. The same motion KJ did in public places when he wanted to make it look like we were in love. Without warning, my body jerks like I'm falling. A traitorous reflex that didn't even give me the time to fight it. Ever the observer, Austin pulls away and his eyes flutter open, awash with concern. I'm vulnerable and despondent, unable to wipe away the embarrassed tears that dampen my waterline.

"Cecily, I can't. *We can't.*"

"I'm sor—" His furrowing brows trap the word in my throat. *No apologies.* "I want you to touch me, even if my first instinct might always be to pull away. Because this broken piece might be irreparable. I don't want it to be, but I'm scared it is. And, if that's the case, does it mean I don't deserve to feel a loving touch ever again? Am I too damaged?"

"You deserve nothing but a loving touch. Always. You're not damaged or broken. You're perfect, but your body's scared... for good fucking reason. And I don't want to do anything to make you uncomfortable. Especially when I'm not sure you'd tell me if you were."

He's entirely... *not* wrong, as much as it hurts to admit to myself. I doubt I would ever have the strength, or the desire, to tell him if I wasn't comfortable with something. I want him too damn bad. Knowing whatever I say won't carry enough weight to make him believe me, I hold a hand to his cheek and slowly rub along his jawline. Our chests rise and fall in concert with every wordless breath, letting a hungry kiss linger in the space between us.

"I'll wait as long as I need to for you to trust me," he says.

With a gentle nod, I rest my head down on his chest and bask in his sauna-like heat, easing the day's heaviness, until he gently whispers against my hair, "I think the food's done."

My hands skim his thick torso as I step back and stare up at him to decipher what he's feeling. His eyes are always a dead giveaway for every emotion and, right now, it's clear he didn't want me to leave his embrace any more than I did. I may be starved for affection even more than I am for dinner.

I think he is, too.

"Come to bed," I mumble on the way out of the bathroom, adjusting my pajama shorts. It must be true what they say about a lack of sleep impairing your judgement in the same way as alcohol. "Sorry. Not like that. Just sleep."

Although...

"I'm good here." He pats the worn-in couch with a wary smile.

"Please. I really want you to." *Again, I'm clearly impaired.* "We can be adults and sleep in the same bed, can't we? Nothing more than platonic cuddles. You need to get some decent sleep tonight and I... don't want to sleep alone." It sounds even more pitiful out loud than it did in my head. Friends can share a bed though, right? Even if they're male and female friends? Even if I'm going to be tempted to kiss him the entire time?

Too tired or unable to find a valid argument for my sound reasoning, he follows me into the bedroom. His hands absent-mindedly find their way to his T-shirt hem before pausing.

"Take it off." I crawl under the soft, thick duvet. "Okay, again, not like that. I'm sorry, I lose the ability to act normal when I'm tired. Sorry."

A breathy laugh rumbles up from his chest as he yanks his T-shirt off, then his jeans. "Quit apologizing to me."

When he looks at me, standing in the bedside lamp glow in nothing but boxers, a warm bubbly sensation like the first sip of champagne tingles in my lower stomach. For a split second, I consider asking him to take off even more.

"Sorry. You're just... *a lot.*" I giggle, drunk on emotional exhaustion, unashamedly ogling his body. Tall, broad, and confident. As he moves toward the bed, it's evident in the flex of every muscle how strong he is, and dark blue veins branch across his forearms as he lifts the duvet on his side. But what I loved the most when I touched the faded brand scarred on his chest was the soft layer over top. He's warm and cozy, not chiseled from stone. It's the body of a man who works hard on a farm all day, then goes home to eat good food and cuddle his woman at night.

For tonight, maybe I can be that woman.

"You're overtired." He shakes his head.

"True. But also, you have to know that you're unfairly attractive."

He reaches to turn off the bedside lamp, then squeezes my hand in the dark. "Nothing compared to you, City Girl. You're... *fuck.*"

His body weight shifts the mattress as he gets comfortable. If we were in my cabin, with my double bed, our bodies would have no choice but to touch. That would be perfectly fine by me—preferable even, to a bed so big we could build a pillow wall between us if we wanted. It's not long before his breathing changes, becoming deeper and slower. Unlike every other recent time I've shared a bed with a man, I'm not tempted to sneak away once he's sound asleep. Instead, I scooch back a few inches and reach for his heavy arm. The warm limb drapes across my torso, pinning me to the mattress. I can't remember the last time I willingly sought out comfort like this at night, rather than actively avoiding KJ in bed. Using Austin's arm like a weighted blanket, it's hard to imagine how I survived years without affectionate human touch.

17

Austin

I wake up smelling coconut and assume it means God did me a solid by letting me into heaven. But when my eyes open, it's even better. My face is less than an inch from Cecily's golden-blonde hair, my chest pressed to her back, my arm around her waist, and my... *fuck*. I pull away in time to hear a quiet, sleepy laugh.

"Austin... was that what I think it was pressed against me?"

I clear my throat, attempting to play it cool. "You're in my bed—practically naked—and I'm just a simple man, darlin'. Can't expect me to be unaffected by that."

She reaches for my hand and wraps my arm back around her. I don't bother trying to fight it. Her stomach quivers against my palm with silent laughter, the warmth of her skin seeping through the thin tank top.

She lets out a contented sigh. "That was the best I've slept... possibly ever."

"We should get going. Beat the heat," I say because I feel like I should, although every needy ache in my body is begging to stay right here. I can't remember the last time I slept that well, either. We're spending the day making sure the trail cameras—situated along the road and at every gate—are in working order. While I'm thrilled to have hours to talk with

Cecily uninterrupted, I'd rather be here where I can feel her warm body against mine.

She groans. "Ugh, okay. I still can't believe I'm going to ride a horse today."

"I can't believe it's taken this long to get you on one."

"Not for lack of trying by Colt and Red." Her hips wiggle slightly so she's pressed against me again. "They've been trying to convince me to go horseback riding for weeks."

Lord, give me strength. If we were spooning for any reason other than her *husband*—though thinking of her having a husband makes me gag—scaring the shit out of her, I'd be kissing her bare shoulder right now and insisting we stay right here.

"Honoured you decided to come with me instead. Although—don't tell him—Red might be our best cowboy. So I can't say you wouldn't be in good hands."

"Decided? You told me I had no choice. And are you admitting he's better than you? Maybe I should go with him instead, if that's the case." She's clearly teasing me by the way her fingers thread through mine, still holding tight against her stomach.

"I'm not a cowboy, remember?" I squeeze our hands. "But, if I were, I would be a hell of a lot better than *Red*. I'd be the best around. Come on, you saw us branding."

"Ehhh, I didn't know enough to judge at the time. Who's to say who's better?"

Our bodies are so close to being intertwined, I can feel the way Cecily's pulse races as she turns to face me with a playful smile; the kind that sends my heart into an unsteady rhythm. I'm quickly running out of self-control. It's next to impossible not to throw myself at her when she looks this good at five-thirty in the morning, when there's sunlight filtering through the crack between my curtains, and nobody's waiting for us to be anywhere. It's the perfect set-up for a lazy morning in bed. A morning I won't get to enjoy because I still haven't worked up the nerve to kiss her. Friends who cuddle don't spend all day in the sheets.

Cecily sits up, swinging her legs over the bedside. The skimpy pajama shorts and tank top aren't covering as much as they probably should be, considering we're "friends" sharing a bed. And they're not helping my morning wood in the slightest. It's no wonder I was rock hard pressed up against her ass when we woke up.

"Alright, Not-A-Cowboy." She yawns. "Let's go before I fall back asleep. Your bed's so cozy. How do you manage to get up in the morning?"

"It's usually a hell of a lot easier than it is today, for some reason." I drag myself out behind her.

The horses pick up on Cecily's cautiously optimistic attitude immediately, greeting her with gentle sniffs and quiet whinnies. Normally, the first to the barn is met with a barrage of hungry horses, ready to form a coup if they don't receive grain immediately.

"Ready, darlin'?"

"Not at all, but I said you need to be more reckless, and I guess I should follow my own advice."

Once she's settled in the saddle, I pony her horse behind mine, checking repeatedly to make sure she's okay as we start up the winding trail to the first camera. Jackson and I set up trail cameras four years ago after a poaching problem lost us twenty cattle in one summer. Who would've thought they might come in handy for vindictive ex-husbands one day? I mean, given the history of some of our employees, maybe it wouldn't have seemed completely insane. But I wouldn't have guessed I'd be involved. I had Savannah, and thought she was my forever. Two years and countless rides along this trail together—I didn't know on the day we hung these cameras that I was mere weeks away from losing her. Déjà vu barrels into me. I'm confident I've ridden this same dirt path at least five-hundred times since then, yet this is the first time Sav runs through my mind. Almost as a warning.

Then I think about *her* leaving. And by *her*, I don't mean Savannah.

We check trail cameras while I wrestle with duelling thoughts of Sav and Cecily. Not that I have any feelings about my ex-girlfriend. It's just impossible not to compare them when the scenarios are eerily similar. Granted, Sav was running from her terrible parents, rather than a terrible husband. But, in both cases, they're city girls using Wells Ranch as a hideout. A place to weather the storm until it's safe to go somewhere else.

"God, how do you guys do this all day, every day?" Cecily stretches, gently massaging her thighs when we stop for lunch. "I don't think I'll be able to move by the time we get back. If KJ comes for me tonight, leave me to die. There's no shot I can keep up if we need to run."

"Do you always need to make light of literal life or death situations?"

"I was the dumbass who stayed in an abusive marriage until he was pointing a fucking gun at me. If I don't make some jokes from time to time, I'm going to completely fall to pieces over it. Either way, you'll be uncomfortable, so get used to it."

"He's the dumbass... not you. Never you." I can't argue with the rest. Pulling the lunches from my saddlebag, I point to a shady spot beneath a poplar tree. "Come on."

I spent hours yesterday grappling with everything; taking small comfort in knowing if he had a sliver of decency, she wouldn't be here. I wouldn't be the one next to her. With every fucked-up story, I tried to wrap my head around how somebody could manipulate, belittle, scare, and abuse her. Though my blood pressure skyrocketed, and my heart pounded in my chest with each thing she said about him, I bottled it up for her sake. But, oh Lord, I *cannot wait* to unleash my fury if that motherfucker ever shows his face around here.

"Oh my God, this view's beautiful," she says as she walks toward the cliff's edge.

She isn't wrong about the stunning panorama—there's a reason I chose to stop here. It's one of the best viewpoints on our 100,000 plus-acre ranch, and I knew she'd love it. On a clear day, like today, you can see the entire Timothy Mountain range, with tic-tac-size buildings making up Wells Canyon at the base. Green treetops, winding dirt roads, and smaller rolling hills surround the town. In the foreground, Wells Ranch looks both vast and miniature at the same time. Dollhouse-size, red-roofed buildings seem to spread on forever, surrounded by nothing but farmland for tens of kilometres.

"Mhm." My view certainly is beautiful—though I'm not looking at the valley. My eyes refuse to take in anything other than the wind blowing in her golden hair. Her shirt flutters up with each gust to reveal the small sliver on her lower back that I've become incredibly obsessed with. Denim stretches over her hips and round ass, dirty and begging to be stripped off. And I just know her eyes are wide, exhilarated, and the corners creased thanks to a smile I'm confident is lighting up her face.

"Okay, I'm starting to understand the appeal of this cowboy thing." She sits down next to me and unwraps her sandwich. "I love a mountaintop picnic."

An amused sigh blows from my nose. "Hate to burst your bubble, darlin'. We aren't usually stopping for picnics."

"You should. What's the point in owning all this land if you aren't taking the time to enjoy it?"

"Well, the point is to feed the cattle."

"Mmm—but what a waste of a beautiful view. I bet the cows don't appreciate it enough. Although, for all I know, they do. Actually... I like to think they're up here living their last days with a stunning view, you know?" She pauses for a second before bursting out in laughter, which echoes down the valley. "Wow, that was a *very* 'city girl' thing for me to say, wasn't it?"

I chuckle. "It was."

"Just... I'd eat lunch right here every day if I could. I think this is my new favourite place on Earth."

"My grandpa's, too. Not to ruin the mood, but we spread his ashes up here, actually." When the words spill from my mouth, I realize I hadn't thought much about that before now.

Does that make this an inappropriate place to bring a girl I like for a picnic?

"That doesn't ruin the mood. If anything, it makes it more special. Like we're having lunch with him."

"If he were here, he'd tell us to quit dilly-dallying and check on the cows. 'Only need one hand to ride. Eat your damn lunch while you work.'" I do my best impression of his deep, no-nonsense voice, recalling him yelling those words at a young Denny, who was a big proponent of picnicking. "He was a grumpy old man—sometimes hard to get along with. But he'd give you the shirt off his back."

"Oh, so he was basically you." She nudges me with her shoulder.

"You're not the first to say that." I take a sip from my lukewarm water bottle. "Before you choose this as your favourite spot, let me show you mine."

"It's going to be hard to top this, but let's see what you got."

She jumps to her feet and brushes the dust from her jeans. Watching her palms swipe across her rear, I'm reminded of how incredible it felt being pressed against her this morning. I wish I'd had the nerve to run my hand over her, along the soft skin where her ass meets her thighs. My obsession with her ass isn't aided by me assisting her into the saddle. With her left foot in the stirrup, she bounces on the right and springs upward. I hold tight to her upper thigh, giving enough support to help swing her right leg over. And she no longer needs me as she settles into her seat, but my hand lingers.

"Shall we?" She smiles down at me. The rational part of me knows what she means. But that doesn't stop the flooding of blood in my groin.

The blazing midday sun shines relentlessly, creating visible heat waves on the shale-lined trail. Horse sweat fills my nostrils as the massive animals grunt along the shadeless journey to the lake. But looking back at Cecily, she doesn't seem to mind any of it. Even when I complain about the heat, or apologize for misremembering how long it would take to get there, she affectionately smiles and says she has nowhere better to be today. We dip into a small valley and the air grows instantly cooler as the horses amble toward the thick, deciduous greenery. Though I've seen it more times than I can count, the Caribbean-blue lake still takes my breath away.

"Alright, you might win for the best spot, after all." Cecily jumps down from her horse like she's been doing it her whole life, without ever taking her eyes off the clear, shimmering water. "If we can swim in it, I'll concede that this place is better than the mountaintop."

"You can." I start rolling up my pant legs—assuming I'll only be dipping my feet in—when I look over to see Cecily's shirt flying over her head. Bronzed skin and blonde hair radiant in the afternoon sun, my eyes rake over her.

"It's hotter than hell out here. I know you don't like swimming, but you gotta come with me." The buckle on her belt pings against a rock as her jeans hit the ground, but I dont follow suit. Noticing my hesitation, she adds, "I'm already *extraordinarily* well acquainted with you in your boxers, and my underwear isn't any more revealing than my bathing suit. Quit being a baby."

Okay. Fuck it. I follow her lead and strip down to my boxers, suddenly feeling self-conscious about how pale I am next to her perfect, sun-kissed body. Another reason I should've accepted more invitations to go to the creek with the boys. We delicately step across the hot, rocky lakeshore until the cold rush of glacier-fed water hits us like a truck. She sucks in a small gasp at the coldness, and the sound goes straight to my cock.

"Jesus fuck. I remember it being cold, but not *this* goddamn cold." I swear every part of me is blue and my dick might be inside my body now.

"When was the last time you swam here?" she asks.

"Um... probably ten years ago. Or more? This was my mom's favourite place. We spent lots of summer days here as a kid."

"From what I've heard so far, I would've liked your mom. I too enjoy a beautiful lake and *Happy Days*." She lowers further into the water until it hits mid-chest. Sunbeams reflect off the glassy lake surface, lighting the small divot in the tanned skin above her collarbone.

Mom would've liked Cecily, too.

"Everybody loved her. When we were kids, she made up a 'cowboy's club' for me, my brothers, Red, and his four brothers. Looking back now, I think it was because she needed a way to get us outta her hair. She'd send us on these wild scavenger hunts, and give us chores that would probably have someone calling CPS these days. Like making us collect eggs, but the only way we could get to or from the coop was by riding sheep. I don't think a single egg made it back intact. All the kids at school were jealous of the adventures she sent us on."

"She sounds like an incredible mom. It's no wonder her boys turned out great."

"Yeah, she was the best." I gulp. I'm not going to cry in the lake, in my underwear, with a beautiful girl. *I am not.*

The way she's quick to move the conversation along makes me think she can tell my eyes are burning. "You didn't tell me Red grew up with you. His brothers didn't stick around, though?"

"It's not my story to tell, but they all left after some issues their dad caused. Red came back. He's kind of like a stray cat—just keeps comin' back."

She tips her head, letting her hair radiate out across the glassy water behind her. Pressing her breasts up to the surface. There's no way I'm not going to look when they're perfect and round and right in my sight line.

"Seems to me Wells Ranch has a bit of a stray cat problem. There's a lot of us hanging around. But you know what they say about feeding strays, and Beryl's constantly baking delicious stuff."

"Guess I'll have to give her a raise if that's the only thing keeping people here."

"She definitely deserves one, but I don't think her muffins are the only thing worth sticking around for."

When she lifts her head, a bead of water rolls from her temple down her cheek before clinging to her jaw. Before I have time to consider whether I shouldn't, I reach out and gently catch it on my finger. A slow smirk draws across her lips.

"Hey, Austin, notice anything different?"

My eyes narrow at her as I anxiously try to figure out what she's talking about. She drifts through the chest-deep water. Closer. Closer. Until we're almost touching, and she's still smirking up at me. I have no idea what I'm supposed to be noticing, but that question always feels like a test coming from a woman, so I'm beginning to panic.

"I'll give you a hint." Her hand lifts above her head, and water falls from the ends of her fingertips. Drops land on her hairline before gracefully sliding down her cheek. Her eyes never leave mine. "Aren't you going to wipe them away for me?"

"Yes, ma'am." I raise my hand, nerves burning a hole in my stomach as I prepare for her to pull back.

Not a single twitch, fear flicker, tug of anxiety. There's simply... nothing.

There's no way she can't hear the aggressive pounding in my chest, not with the way the rest of the world seems to have become utterly silent. My palm cupping her face makes her jaw become slack in my hand, and her lips slowly part. With my pinky finger resting on the delicate skin of her neck, the drumming of her heartbeat changes the rhythm of my own. I'm completely at her mercy, and that's exactly where I want to be.

18

Cecily

His eyes—dark, intoxicating, and full of unknown emotions—are locked on mine.

A rough, worn hand catches my face with an unexpectedly tender caress. His touch moves briskly upward to my hair like he's striking a match—igniting a fire in my core. His fingers comb through my wet hair until he reaches the nape of my neck. And a gentle tug sends a tremor down my back, which makes his nostrils flare.

"Please," I whisper, praying my lips might make brief contact with his as I speak. "Please don't pull away."

"Darlin', I told you I—"

"Show me how gentle you can be. Show me I can trust you." My hands slide across his bare chest, feeling the raised skin over his brand, then over his shoulders and down his thick arms. If I'm breathing, it's just barely. "I want you to kiss me."

I'm paralyzed with anticipation as his lips draw closer. Slowly, closer. And closer. Until they're so dangerously close, I can feel his warm breath fanning across my face. His eyes remain transfixed and I can't bring myself to close mine. Instead, I'm swimming in the molasses of his gaze, completely helpless. Thank God for the lake water's buoyancy or I would be a boneless puddle on the ground.

Our lips brush in a touch so faint I'm left wondering if it really happened. Only proving to me how badly I want this. Filled with anticipation and desire, revelling in the ache beneath my pelvic bone.

Then he kisses me. *Unmistakably*. With hot, supple lips and tenderness I've never felt. Slow and explorative. He breathes me in and, on the exhale, obliterates me with a deep, impassioned kiss. I sink into him with a quiet moan. It's the feeling of coming home from a long trip. It's the warmth of the summer sun as you lie in a hammock with a great book. It's the kind of kiss that lasts forever and ends too soon.

When his hands run up my naked back, I have to resist the urge to flinch. I don't want to be this girl. I want my body to know, beyond a shadow of a doubt, I'm safe with him. I want him to see there isn't a single piece of me off-limits anymore. I want to be touched. Be loved. I fight my nervous system and ease back into his warm palms.

His lips brand mine, searing his name across the tender skin. There's an ache in my bones and a tremor in my heart. Piece by piece, Austin's mending me. And I kiss him harder, knowing I'm never going to take this moment for granted.

I've never felt this alive.

I can't help but notice the way his fingers spread as his hands run down my body. As if he's trying to feel as much of my skin as I possibly can. As if he can't get enough. He pulls back momentarily and studies me. Austin's eyes mirror the conflicting and expansive emotions swirling behind my own. From what I see, this kiss is blissful and healing and scary for him, too.

His lips sweep across my cheek until the heat of his voice blows against my ear. "Can I kiss you again?"

Yes. Yes. Goddammit, yes.

"Please."

His lips crash into mine; he's kissing like he's starved for me. I nip at his bottom lip, and he holds my hips, pulling our bodies tight together. His hands slide to the backs of my thighs, sending a lightning bolt straight to my clit. Austin lifts me so my upper half is above the water, and a warm breeze instantly dries my skin. My legs encircle his waist, fitting us together like puzzle pieces.

I'm consumed by the way his hands roam across my body before wrapping in my hair. This isn't enough and it might *never* be enough. I want all of him. More than that, I want him to have all of me. My hips subconsciously gyrate against his, driven by a feeling that's been dormant for years. *Wanting.*

I let out an involuntary sigh, and drag my fingertips across his scalp. I'm kissing him. He's kissing me. Although I've known him for two months, it feels like I've been waiting my whole life for him to kiss me. It's raw and uninhibited and pure fucking bliss.

And I don't know how much time has passed when we stop to catch our breath, but the sun sits lower in the sky. When I lick my lips, it burns the chapped skin. I'm weak and unsteady, intoxicated by him.

"We should head back," he says in a low voice. "I don't want to but..."

For once, I'm the one without words. "Mmhm," I sigh into his neck as I unfurl myself from him.

The air's cooler than it was when we walked into the lake, and the chill sends a shiver across my body. I tug jeans onto my damp legs and slip my shirt over my head, feeling my soaked bra instantly saturate the cotton. For once, Austin makes no effort to hide his staring as he boosts me into the saddle. Something about him looking at me makes me feel sexy in a way I never thought I was before. Like a prize he's vying for.

"You win, by the way. This is *definitely* my new favourite place," I say with a smile I refuse to let go of. I'm going to go to bed like a giddy teenage girl tonight—cheeks aching, a flutter in my chest, kicking my feet in the air, squealing into the pillow.

I wish I'd brought my phone to take a photo of this moment. Specifically, a photo of his lopsided, boyish grin. The undoing of my grumpy, Not-A-Cowboy. Doing what he wants, enjoying himself, being reckless.

In the mountains, it's easy to forget everything except us. Consumed in each other for so long, everything else fades away.

Despite how much I love being at Wells Ranch, my heart plummets into my stomach when our horses round a corner, the farm buildings come into view, and reality sets back in.

Rough wood planking catches on my shirt as Austin presses me against the stable wall. His lips lock onto mine, and I need to tighten my arms around his neck to keep from buckling. Until today, nobody has ever kissed me in a way that melts my bones, and makes my heart feel like it'll leap free from my chest.

My hands wander over him, feeling the way every muscle in his upper back dips and curves. Austin's fingertip outlines my bra through my thin T-shirt, and I kiss him harder. My pulse's steady drumming takes up residence below my navel. We're lost together in the quiet stable, and I no longer understand why I was worried about getting off the mountain. The magic doesn't need to end. My fingers hook his belt loops, drawing our hips together. There's no mistaking his desire for our clothes to be gone, and I roll my hips to feel his hard bulge against the spot that's beginning to throb. It's not enough. I need more friction. A frustrated whimper rattles in the back of my throat as he grinds into me.

I fumble with his belt buckle until his hand covers mine. "Darlin'."

To think, a few weeks ago, it felt condescending when he called me darling. Now I'm turning into a puddle at the sound of that word rolling off his tongue with a deep, wanton rasp.

"Aus," I whine back. I don't want to wait. Having to ride for two hours without feeling his hands on my skin or his lips on mine was more than enough torture.

"Darlin', I'd love to do everything you want me to. I'd be so good to you. But the first time's not gonna be here, in a dirty stable surrounded by horse shit." His reassuring lips close over mine as a promise of what's to come.

Somebody who's neither him nor I clears their throat. There's the stupid reality we had to come back to, staring at us with an amused grin and flaming auburn hair. Rather than stepping back, Austin's hand on my waist holds tighter.

"I'm not usually one to interrupt... Hell, I love a good fuck in the barn as much as the next guy. But you two are right in the way of the tack room."

"Oh, we weren't..." I start to defend, trying to suppress the heat crawling up my neck, but Red puts his hand up to stop me.

"No need to explain, Filly. Just let me by ya real quick, and I'll be outta your hair." He skirts around us and through the door. A small laugh escapes me, and I plant one last, slow kiss on Austin.

"Kate's likely waiting for us for dinner," I say against his hot, blushing cheek. His quiet grumble of dissatisfaction cracks through my chest.

With a smile, I rub away the wrinkle formed between his eyebrows with my thumb. His eyes narrow with confusion and he pulls back slightly.

"Didn't anybody ever tell you if you keep making that face, it'll get stuck? Do you want this handsome face to have permanent frown lines? I certainly don't."

He rolls his eyes, leaning in to kiss me softly. Lips curving into a loose smile as they meet mine.

Kate knows instantly. Jackson probably does, too, although he makes a better effort to restrain his face. Not Kate. A smile reaches up to her eyes, which flit between us eagerly. I suppose there's no hiding the redness on my face from Austin's beard, and the plumpness of our freshly kissed lips.

"So, how was your day?" She cuts bite-size pieces on Odessa's plate.

"Trail cams are good," Austin says, disregarding Kate and looking over at Jackson instead. Jackson nods as he shoves a piece of steak into his mouth.

"But how was your day?" Kate asks again.

"Fine," Austin says. He's done with the conversation before it's begun.

Swallowing a bite, I lick my lips slowly. "It was good. I'm not about to enter any rodeos anytime soon, but I didn't fall off the horse. I'm counting it as a win. And Austin showed me the lake over the other side of the mountain—thank God, because the heat was brutal up there. And we checked the cameras and came home."

I mean, we did a bit more than that, but I'll let them fill in the blanks on their own.

Odessa perks up. "I want to go to a lake and I can ride a horse. Why didn't I get to go?"

"It was a long day, kid. Too long of a ride for four-year-olds." All the gruffness in Austin's voice evaporates the moment his words are focused on her. A flurry of emotion fills my chest watching it. I've seen them interacting plenty of times before, and it's always sweet—Odessa's lucky to have so many uncles and honorary uncles looking out for her—but it's affecting me so much more tonight.

I wonder what he'd be like with his own kids.

She thinks about his answer for a moment. "Maybe next year when I'm five?"

"Definitely next year when you're five," Austin says.

With a little head bob, she seems to accept that as a perfectly reasonable answer, and returns to her dinner.

"Did you take her to the falls, too?" Kate leans back in her chair.

Austin's glass clunks heavily onto the wood table. "No."

I look over at him, trying to figure out the sudden shift from grump to grumpier. "How can I be expected to decide my favourite spot on the ranch when you're holding out on me? I like waterfalls."

"The water's hardly flowing this time of year. You didn't miss much."

"Really? I thought it's usually pretty lovely still?" Kate frowns, looking over to Jackson for backup, but he simply shrugs. Rather than Austin's overall grumpiness, I think Jackson simply doesn't give enough of a shit to get involved in anything Kate's worked up over. That's why he's always quiet.

For the rest of the meal, nobody speaks except for Odessa. She's eager to show off a new song she made up today and tell Uncle Austin all about a family of squirrels she found by the chicken coop. Thank God for her. If this is how tense a regular dinner is for the Wells family, it's no wonder why Austin refused to come around when his dad was here, too. The food's great, but I'd much rather be eating KD and hot dogs on Austin's couch again.

"Are things always that weird?" I ask the moment we're out of the house.

"No."

"Do you want to talk about it?"

"No."

Silly me. Somehow, I thought he might be more open with me after everything that's happened over the past forty-eight hours.

19

Austin

F amily dinners were designed by somebody who wants hell on Earth, I'm sure.

Kate wasn't being malicious in bringing up the falls. She couldn't have been. Unless she had a secret conversation with Savannah in the years since she left, there's no way Kate knows anything about the falls. Or about the proposal. None of it matters, though, because she got into my head. There are damn good reasons I didn't take Cecily to the waterfall, and it has nothing to do with the summer weather running it dry. I don't need yet another reminder that I'm already in too deep with another person who's most likely going to leave me.

Before dinner, I was looking forward to continuing what we started in the stables. After dinner, I'm so far in my own head, I just want to go to sleep.

"Are things always that weird?" Cecily quietly asks as we walk down the front steps.

"No."

"Do you want to talk about it?"

A puff of air forces its way from my nostrils. "No."

As we approach the farmhand cabins, she says, "If you still want me to stay at your place tonight, I need to grab some clean clothes first."

"Okay."

"Oh, and Austin?" She stops in her doorway. "If you want me to stay, you need to cut this shitty attitude. I'm not interested in hanging out with a grumpy asshole. Whatever you're thinking about right now—you either drop it by the time I'm back or we can talk about it."

I'm kicking both her car tire and myself when she reappears a minute later.

"Yeah, yeah. Save the lecture about my tires." She rolls her eyes, tucking folded clothes under her arm. "I swear I'll get around to it."

"No lecture. I changed them for you already." I assumed she noticed but forgot to say anything. The days since have been a bit of a whirlwind, after all. Talking about her car tires hasn't been a priority for either of us.

"Wait, *what*? You didn't need to. You shouldn't have done that. I wish you wouldn't have. I have the money. For real this time. I'll pay you back for it." Her words are rushed and stilted. Panicky.

"You needed the tires, and I know a guy who gives us a good price. Threw 'em on the other day. It's not a big deal."

"I don't expect you to understand, but don't buy me shit anymore. It is a big deal. I'm paying you back for the tires."

Tonight somehow keeps getting worse and worse. By the time we reach my house, she's painfully silent, and I'm tempted to make up an excuse to walk away. She can stay here, and I'll keep watch from a distance. I could always get Red to stay with her instead.

No, that's asking for it.

I trust Red with a lot of things, but a woman I'm interested in isn't one of them.

"Help me understand why you're mad, because I thought I was doing a nice thing here." I tug my boots off and crack a cold beer. "God forbid I help you out so, when you want to leave, you can go safely."

"I don't owe you an explanation."

"You don't. But it would be nice to understand why I'm suddenly in shit for doing something most people would think is a kind gesture." The couch relieves my sore muscles, but it does nothing for the painful cramping everywhere else. This is why I'm better off alone.

We may as well be right back to how we interacted weeks ago. The lake has never felt further away.

"Fine. I don't do well with gifts, okay? They feel like a trap or something."

"A trap? Putting tires on your car, so you can *leave* when you want to, feels like a trap?"

"It's not about the tires. It's..." She tucks her feet under her and takes a deep breath. "KJ comes from money, and spending it is how he wins people over. He would buy me expensive gifts, but he always found a way to throw them back in my face. I already feel like I owe you so much because, like, Beryl offered me this job and a place to stay. That was hard enough to finally say yes to because I didn't want to be a burden. I've busted my ass here to not feel that way—to prove I'm useful. Now there's all this shit with KJ, so you're letting me sleep here, staying up all night to make me feel safer, changing your work around to accommodate me. It's a lot, and the tires are just... it's a nice gesture. *It is.* I know I sound absolutely insane complaining about it because, let's be real, who knows when I was going to get around to changing them. And you're just... *you*. So you figured that out and did it for me. Which is nice—so much nicer than I'm used to. But I don't want to give you a reason to resent me or make me feel like shit later. I don't want to owe you yet another thing if I don't end up staying here."

"He was trying to manipulate you. It was the only way he'd get somebody as incredible as you to stay with a piece of shit like him. I put tires on your car because the last thing I want is for you to feel like you have no choice but to stay. If I give you a gift, it's because I want to see you happy. No ulterior motive."

"For now."

I'd rather be slapped across the face.

"For always, Cecily. A gift is just a fucking gift for me. I'm not plotting out how I can use it against you down the road. I could've bought you a whole new car and, if you left tomorrow, I wouldn't give a shit." The empty beer can tings against the wood of the coffee table.

She's silent, but I understand the look on her face well. Probably because I've seen the same expression in the mirror. Shut down, ready to give up on the conversation... and probably give up on me altogether. Walking away now from whatever's going on between us would be easier in the long run, but I really, *really* can't stand the thought.

"I don't mean—well, I'd give a shit *you* were leaving. Not the car. I'm not rich, but money doesn't mean fuck all to me beyond ensuring the ranch stays afloat, and everybody here's taken care of. And that includes you."

"You don't have to take care of me. I threw you into this situation with KJ threatening me, but I don't need you to take care of me beyond that. I'm perfectly capable."

"I get that. Clearly, you've made it through a hell of a lot without my help. But I want to be here for you because..." My words trail off, even though the ending of my sentence is playing on repeat in my mind.

"Because it's what friends do. I know that but—"

I interrupt, "No. Because I care about you. I like you a hell of a lot. I don't know about you and your friends, but I don't kiss my friends the way I kissed you today."

The way my body reacted to her kiss terrified me. *Nothing about that was friendly.* It wasn't even casual summer fling kissing. I needed her. I craved her. I want her lips to never touch anybody else's for the rest of her life, and I don't want to go a single day without tasting her. The day she showed up on the ranch turned my life upside down, and kissing her seemed to flip everything once again.

"But you *do* kiss your friends, then?" Her tongue darts out to lick her bottom lip as a mischievous smile crops up.

"Good Lord, woman." I shake my head and wait until her eyes meet mine again before continuing. "If you don't want me to buy you things, fine. You aren't paying me back for the tires, though, because you run errands for the ranch in your car, so they're a business expense. If anything, you should be mad at your employer for not paying mileage—tires are a lot less expensive than fifty-cents per kilometre for weekly trips to town."

"Now you mention it," she says.

"Don't go getting any ideas. I can teach you how to drive the ranch trucks to save me some money."

"Maybe you should help me get some practice, anyway. I mean, once the snow falls, I don't think my car will do a good job making it to town and back."

Once the snow falls.

"Even with the trucks, snowstorms can trap us here for days at a time." I watch her reaction intently, preparing for any sign of discomfort. Savannah used to get antsy about winters—in hindsight, that should've been a clue she wasn't cut out for life here. It's not like leaving to spend a month or two with her sister in Florida every year would've been an option if we had gotten married and had kids.

"Well, now I'm sold. Winter here sounds like a dream. Watching it snow outside while I'm curled up by the fire with tea and a good book. Sign me the hell up. Although, we need to get something other than *Happy Days* on DVD to watch because, as much as I love the Fonz, I'm going to need a break at some point. Oooh, and we can make s'mores inside—your fireplace is like the perfect spot for it."

I nearly choke on my spit at Cecily wanting to make plans for the winter. Plans that seemingly involve me.

"Don't let the guys hear you talking fondly about snow and cold. It's a pain in the ass—things freeze up, engines don't start, it's more work to keep the animals fed and safe." All that might be bearable if it means coming back to a warm house with a beautiful girl inside, though.

"I'm sor—I shouldn't have gotten mad about the gift thing when you weren't aware it was an issue for me." She shifts on the couch so our legs are touching. On top of the hot electrical jolt it creates, I'm awash with relief. "You're a good guy, Aus."

"Yeah?"

"You know you are. It's too bad you aren't always this humble, *Mr. Best Cowboy Around.*"

"Nothing cocky about telling the truth, darlin'. If I were a cowboy, I'd be the best."

Her laughter is pure magic.

"Okay, Not-A-Cowboy, let's go to bed. Platonic cuddling?" she asks through a yawn.

Yes, fucking please. It may not be exactly what I had pictured doing to her tonight, but I'll take anything she's willing to give me. Especially since, for a while, it seemed like I might not be welcome in her presence at all.

"I should shower first," I say.

"Good call. I should, too. You can have it first."

"You're good out here?"

"I think I'll be okay tonight, yeah. If my murderous ex-husband shows up. I'll try to give you enough warning to throw some pants on before you have to fight him." She smiles like she's the most hilarious person in the room. I could—maybe even *should*—tell her it's inappropriate to make jokes about somebody trying to kill her. But I'm not ruining another moment with my big mouth.

"Thank you. I'd hate for the first time you see me naked to be while I'm beating the shit out of your *ex*-husband." I emphasize the "ex" part—though it's not legally true yet. I need us both to be on the same page that what's going on between us isn't breaking marital vows.

"Who said it was the first time?" She cups her hands over her eyes, and spreads her fingers to wink at me.

20

Cecily

B y the time I crawled into bed next to him last night, my limbs were aching and my eyes heavy. In the dark room, he looped his arm around my waist. Held tight to him, we breathed the same air. Sleepy, feather-light kisses swapped back and forth under the smooth sheets while his hands roamed my body without urgency. I don't remember falling asleep. But I slipped into a calm, contented dream with my face burrowed in the space between his collarbone and jaw.

In the quiet of morning, I reach behind me and skim over the sheets, searching for his warm body. Expecting to find the slow rise and fall of his thick chest. My heart flip-flops at the unexpected absence on his side of the bed; a small twinge of fear running rampant through my veins.

No, if something happened, I wouldn't have been left asleep in bed. I roll over and confirm what I already knew. He's gone. The panic slows when I look at the clock: *7:04.*

Oh, I'll be hearing all about this today, I'm sure. It's the latest I've slept since I got here, and I'm well aware how Austin feels about late risers. I groan into the pillow. Whatever mattress he has, I need to save up and buy the same for my place, because I swear I've never slept this well in my entire life. Although, maybe it has more to do with who's in the bed with me—might need a few more nights snuggled in his arms to be sure. *Y'know, for science.*

Shuffling out from his room, the aroma of bacon, eggs, and fresh coffee wafting through the air greet me. Austin's sitting comfortably on the couch reading. Well past when he should be working.

Clearly, I'm still asleep.

"Is this a dream?" I ask from the doorway, watching him abruptly set the book down and look over at me. "If so, you have to tell me. I think it's like when you ask a cop if they're a cop."

"Not a dream, darlin'. Also, that's a myth. They don't have to tell you shit." He stands up and walks toward me, placing a barely there kiss on my forehead before striding into the kitchen. Trailing sparks of a firework explode out from the spot his lips just left.

"Then what's all this?" I gesture to the food on the counter. "And why aren't you working?"

"A certain city girl couldn't get outta bed after a long day of cowgirling, and missed regular breakfast. And not for lack of trying. I literally shook you, but it was like waking the dead. I guess this is—what do you call it in the city? Brunch?"

"Relax, funny guy. It's seven a.m. and, to normal people, it's definitely still breakfast time."

He motions toward the couch, and I sit down, tucking my feet underneath me. A full plate magically appears on my lap seconds later. Followed by a coffee, which looks suspiciously like he's been paying attention to how I take mine. I look into the cup and then at him, watching the single nod of his head to indicate he read my mind. Three years of marriage, and I bet KJ wouldn't have the faintest idea how I like my coffee. Which is incredibly embarrassing because it's not even hard—a splash of milk and two sugars. The more time away from him, the more I'm realizing how all these little things stack up to prove he never cared at all.

"So, whatcha reading?" I peer across the couch at the novel balanced on the armrest.

"A mystery from my favourite author. It came out a while ago, but I've been, uhh, a little unable to focus lately. Finally started it this morning."

"Just when you think you know a guy." I chew thoughtfully on a piece of bacon. "Now suddenly you only make one snide comment about my sleeping in, you save me breakfast, *and* you're reading a book instead of working at seven in the morning. Are you feeling okay?"

He runs a hand through his thick, brown hair. "The boys rolled in early this morning, so I went and talked to Denny. They're working today. When they get back in tonight, we'll figure out a plan to make sure somebody's keeping an eye on you for the next few weeks, at least."

"He hasn't shown up here or sent me any more messages. You think he's changed his mind?"

I know he hasn't.

"What do you think?" he asks.

"No. I doubt he ever will. But, shit. I don't want to drag the guys into this thing."

"Come with me when I talk to them. You can decide how much or little you want them to know about what's going on. Protecting the ranch is part of their job. Even if you tell them nothing, they'll sit outside your cabin night after night. Simply because I'm telling them to."

I'm aware that, with the rest of the crew back at the ranch now, I'm going back to my own house tonight. Going back was the plan we made to start with. There's no logical reason to stay here, and a few kisses don't change the fact we aren't *together*.

"Okay, yeah. I'll tag along." My voice echoes in the ceramic mug as I go to take a sip.

Immediately after I finish breakfast, Austin heads to his office to work, and I stroll to the big house to spend the day in the kitchen with Kate. The last couple days he hasn't let me leave his side, and now we're apparently pretending nothing happened. Aside from Beryl's absence—she took the opportunity to visit her sister while most of the cowboys were gone—everything is completely back to normal around the ranch. Except it's not, because I'm stuck oscillating between day-dreaming about kissing Austin, and freaking out about telling the cowboys that my psychopath ex threatened to show up here.

"Now it's just us girls. Tell me everything about your day yester-day. I recognize a beard burn when I see one." Kate meticulously adds blackberry jam to jars, while I'm hard at work chopping pick-ling cucumbers on the other side of the massive kitchen island.

"We stopped for lunch on top of the mountain, and I told him I thought it might be my favourite place ever. Then he suggested we go to his favourite place. By the time we got to the lake, it was pretty much a million degrees outside, so we swam and then somehow swimming led to kissing. A *lot* of kissing. And then more kissing in the stable until Red interrupted us." I shake my head as Kate's subtle smile turns smug. "That's all there is to it. After dinner, he was in a weird mood and we kinda got into it a bit. But we had a good talk, and I thought it was all fine. This morning he let me sleep in and had breakfast waiting for me. But now he's randomly fine with leaving me on my own today after not letting me out of his sight for days. And I guess I'm going back to my place tonight. So if you have any insight into what is going through his brain, feel free to share."

If anybody understands the Wells men, it's most likely Kate. She originally came to the ranch as a care aide for their sick mom, so she's been around for everything.

A single laugh escapes her mouth. "Girl, the fact that you say you had a 'good talk' means you already know more about him than probably anybody else here does. I think he talks to Beryl sometimes, but the boys don't exactly have heart-to-hearts, and he definitely doesn't tell *me* anything. Except I'll say he wasn't nearly as growly before their mom passed. I think it hit him hardest. And then Savannah was the final straw. He fully shut everybody out after that."

Savannah? Austin may not be a big talker, but never mentioning that name definitely makes it feel like she's an ex-girlfriend.

"Savannah?"

"Oh, shit. He hasn't mentioned her. Probably should've guessed he wouldn't. They dated for a couple years, and he was devastated when they broke up. I saw the guy casually date around before that, but I don't think he's so much as *looked* at another girl since Sav left. Well... until you. He looks at you like you painted the night sky."

I stare down at the jars jammed with pickling cucumbers, relishing the heat of a blush across my face and chest.

"This makes me happy." She claps her hands together giddily. "He's a good one, and I was starting to get nervous he would never find somebody. Does this mean you two are, like, together?"

"No, no... I like him. But do you think I'm moving on too fast after being *married*? If you and Jackson broke up today, you wouldn't be looking for a new relationship two months later, right?"

Kate does a quick check to make sure Odessa hasn't wandered in secretly. "If he hit me? *Fuck yes, I would.* I'd sleep with his best friend the next damn day. Except I wouldn't, because Jackson's best friend is Red, and that man is a bundle of trouble. But you better believe I'd be shaking my ass at the local bar the same night."

I raise an eyebrow and glance down at her baby bump.

"Okay, maybe I wouldn't be doing that either." She laughs and rubs her stomach. "If I were in your position, I would. That's my point. As far as I see it, he's the one who broke your vows, and now you're free to do whatever the hell you want."

She makes valid points. Although, shaking my ass at the bar, and potentially falling for a grumpy rancher are two wildly different things.

I trudge reluctantly behind Austin down to the barn where the boys are untacking. My stomach's been in knots for hours over what I'll say. How much I'll share. And Austin, who should've been my practice dummy for whatever speech I'm about to make, was annoyingly scarce all day. Showing up only as I was finishing my work in the garden fifteen minutes ago.

"This feels dramatic. I'm sure I'll be perfectly fine without some-body keeping watch. He's probably not going to turn up on the property in the middle of the night and, if he did, who's to say he'd know I'm here?"

"Pretty sure seeing your car parked here will be a dead giveaway. Unless this is your way of saying you'll let me buy you a truck to drive?"

"No, it's definitely not. I'm just unsure what to tell them."

"Like I said, you don't need to tell 'em anything." He slides open the massive barn door to reveal fourteen of the twenty-man crew.

Denny looks up at us and nods knowingly. "Aus. Filly."

"Hey, guys. Congrats on the big win, Jacky." Austin shakes the short, dark-haired man's hand. "Can I talk to you guys for a minute?"

A few men grumble, which gives added power to the nervous whirlpool in my stomach.

"So, we have a... threat." His eyes drift over to meet mine and the men all follow his gaze.

So much for letting me get away with not saying anything.

"Um, hey." It doesn't matter that I've become decent friends with most of these guys, I'm terrible at speaking in front of a crowd. "Shit, I didn't want to have to say anything, but obviously I didn't turn up at Wells Ranch because I'm a professional cowboy or something."

A couple guys chuckle.

"My, uh, husband..." I watch Red's eyes nearly spring from their sockets as he looks at me and then over at Austin. "We're separated so I should've said ex-husband... Anyway, that's not important. I left and came here because he was abusive and—um, a person I thought was my friend helped him track down my approximate location and, basically, he let me know he *will* be finding me. So, Austin—"

"We're going to make sure that doesn't happen." Austin cuts me off. "During the day there are enough people around, it'll be fine. At night, I need somebody to keep an eye on the place. You see any strange vehicles coming up the driveway? Call me."

"You got it, boss." Red's jaw is stiff and his eyes narrow.

"Nobody messes with Filly," Colt agrees.

"We all good to take turns?" Denny looks around at the other guys, who nod in agreement. A unanimous decision to take turns staying up all night, in a potentially dangerous situation, to look out for me. I could cry, and hug each one of them, and cry some more. But they all casually go back to their tasks like we just asked them if they were okay with ham instead of turkey in their sandwiches tomorrow.

"Denny, you good to handle tonight?" Austin asks.

Even though I knew this was the plan, I can't deny that it hurts to know Austin would prefer to spend tonight alone than be with me. Pawn me off on his brother, like I'm a small child who needs to be babysat. Everything he isn't saying is what I hear the loudest; I can't believe I was dumb enough to think there was a chance he would ask me to go home with him.

"Done deal. Filly, you're coming to town with us." Denny smiles.

"That's not the deal." A muscle in Austin's jaw pops.

"Well then, find somebody else to watch her, 'cause I'm going out tonight."

The two men stare each other down, and I ask, "Wait, go to town for what?"

"Jacky won the cutting competition at Stampede, so he's got a good chunk of change in his pocket to buy beer. Plus, a shiny new belt buckle means he'll be wheeling all the ladies tonight. We're going out to celebrate."

Ignoring the burning of Austin's scowl, I say, "Sounds like fun. I'm in. When are we leaving?"

Denny pulls his phone from his T-shirt front pocket to check the time. "Uh, give us half an hour to shit, shave, and shower. Then meet us over at Red's truck."

Would I rather spend the night with Austin? Yes. But that's apparently not what he's interested in doing, so I'm going to go shake my ass at the bar. *For Kate.*

"Cecily." Austin's voice carries across the grass, chasing me as I skip back to my house. I'm already planning out what I'll wear and looking forward to putting makeup on for the first time in ages. By the time Austin finally catches up to his booming shout, I'm standing on the steps to my cabin.

"Just stay at my place tonight. Then you don't have to go to town."

I take a breath, mulling over my thoughts before I say something stupid. Like, telling him I'm mad at him for not suggesting I stay to begin with. He was perfectly content to let me sleep in my own bed, guarded by his ranch hands, until he heard I'd be going to the bar. If he wants to play it this way, so be it. I'll make sure he regrets not asking sooner.

"Did you ever consider whether I *want* to go? I'm going to get dressed up, have some fun, let loose, give you a night off. Plus, Jacky won, so I obviously need to go celebrate."

I have no idea what kind of competition he won, but that's neither here nor there.

"Just... what if he ends up being in town tonight?"

"Then I'll be with half a dozen or more men who have sworn to protect me. I think I'll be just fine."

"Okay." He sighs. "Go have fun."

Wait. That's it? I was expecting at least a small amount of pushback. Instead, he reaches out, gives my hand a small squeeze, and disappears into the quickly fading daylight. And I could chase after him, but I don't.

Exactly twenty-five minutes later, I'm squished between Red and Denny on the front bench of Red's pickup truck, with Sundial and Colt in the back.

Colt taps me on the shoulder. "You look pretty tonight, Filly."

"Thanks. I've been waiting for a good excuse to wear a pretty dress, and put on some lipstick."

I smooth out the skirt on my ice-blue mini-dress. Not to be cocky, but it looks phenomenal against my tanned summer skin, with its short length, tie straps, and cut-out back. And I'm wearing a push-up bra for the first time since arriving here, giving the girls a perky boost. Compliments from the boys are nice, but all I can think about is whether Austin would think I look pretty.

Considering how small Wells Canyon is, the bar's surprisingly busy. A number of people are milling about outside, smoking and hanging out in the warm night air, and they all congratulate Jacky as we pass by. Apparently, I'm the one person in town who wasn't aware he won something. And clearly, Denny wasn't exaggerating about it being a big deal.

So big, in fact, that the bartender gives us a free round of tequila shots when we walk in. The golden liquid goes down like wildfire, and lingers in my burning stomach until I chase it with a Long Island Iced Tea.

"Filly, this is our trusty bartender, Dave." Denny introduces me to the handsome, jacked, fifty-something man behind the bar. "And this is Cass."

The cute blonde waitress sidles up next to us. "No way you landed yourself a girl this pretty, Denver Wells. She must not know you too well yet."

"You know, Cassidy Bowman, if you wanna ride, you could just ask instead of trying to scare other girls off me." Denny takes a swig of his pint. "This is Cecily, she's working at the ranch. I don't think you're coming home with me tonight, are ya, Filly?"

I roll my eyes. "Not in this lifetime, Denny."

"See, Cass? My heart belongs only to you."

"Oh, I'm sure." She lightly smacks him on the back of the head before leaning in toward me. "Nice to meet you, Cecily. I imagine you have these boys under control but, if not, wave me down."

"Another round, please." Denny bats his eyes at her, to which she responds with a middle finger. "Love you, Cass!"

"So, you two?" I nudge Denny, walking between him and Red to a table filled with the rest of Wells Ranch's cowboys.

"Oh, no. No, we grew up together. Nothing more than friends, but I love to razz her."

Red snorts. "Also, Dave is her dad, so touching her is just asking to not be allowed back in this town's only bar."

Cassidy pops up at our table a few minutes later with more shots, which I regret as soon as the liquid hits my lips. Aside from the odd beer with Austin, I haven't had anything to drink in months. My tongue tingles with TV static and my head feels fuller—sloshier—than normal.

"Wanna dance, Filly?" Colt grabs my hand, dragging me onto the dance floor. *Holy shit, I'm drunk.* Being on my feet makes it all the more obvious.

One classic country song plays after the other as Colt spins us across the wooden floorboards, until I'm dizzy, sweaty, and incredibly thirsty. Arm-in-arm, we stride toward the bar, and my next Long Island goes down like water. Red's leaning against the wooden bartop and I playfully snatch the worn, black cowboy hat from his mess of red hair.

"No way, Filly." He grabs the brim, tugging it out of my drunken grasp. "If you put on my hat, everybody in this place is going to think you're coming home with me tonight. Wear the hat, ride the cowboy."

"Shit. Okay... well, sorry, but no thanks."

"Thought so." He grabs his beer and heads back to our corner table. And Colt drags me back onto the dance floor.

I drink, I shake my ass to country songs, and I flirt with random guys from around town by letting them teach me how to two-step. All of it helps numb the sting of rejection, but nothing is enough to fully remove

Austin from my mind. Accepting drinks from very polite, *sweet* cowboys only serves as a reminder that, apparently, I'm not into nice cowboys. I'm into brooding, grumpy, *not* cowboys. One in particular.

When I step into the quiet, poorly lit bathroom, I'm overwhelmed with a familiar, drunk-girl urge.

Text him.

21

Austin

I'm half asleep, and fully hating myself for not ditching my plan to have the guys help watch her. If I weren't such a coward, I would've asked if she wanted to stay here in the first place. Before getting the ranch hands involved. And maybe, if I had, she would be with me right now, instead of drinking at The Horseshoe with other men. I wouldn't be alone in a bed that smells like her—feels like her—with an aching feeling and nobody to blame but myself.

The repeated ping of my cell phone makes me jump, and forms a pit in my stomach as I pick up the device.

Cecily: I wish you were here
Cecily: or I wish I was there. Either way. Why didn't you make me stay?
Cecily: I don't think you know the things I would've done to you if you'd made me stay with you tonight
Cecily: or you do know, but you're a big baby.

So, she's drunk. Very drunk, by the sounds of it. And possibly horny, which makes my stomach somersault. But she's having fun and, regardless of the number of guys there she could be talking to, she's texting me.

This is all okay, right? It wasn't a bad choice to let her go, right?

Austin: Somebody's having fun, I see. You okay?
Cecily: I can think of something more fun I'd rather be doing
Cecily: *someone

My cock doesn't waste any time figuring out the innuendo. Already pulsing against my thin, cotton boxers. Now I'm *really* pissed off at myself for not asking—begging—her to stay here with me. When it comes to her, my mistakes know no bounds.

Austin: You're saying that because you've had a few too many
Cecily: or because it's the truth
Cecily: I want you
Austin: yeah?

I'm already pulling jeans on and heading out the door as I send the text.

Cecily: But you don't care. guess I'll have to touch myself tonight instead
Cecily: or maybe I'll do it now... nobody else is in the bathroom
Cecily: promise I'll think about you

Jesus fucking Christ. Never in my life have I wished I had gone out to the bar with the ranch hands before now. Envisioning her horny, and surrounded by guys that'll be willing to do anything she asks, has me driving well over the speed limit down the dirt road to town. Praying to God I'll make it there before she falls into somebody else's arms. I thought not making a fuss about her going out was the right call—I'm trying to do everything the exact opposite way I imagine her ex would have. But clearly, this was the wrong call.

I should've made her stay with me.

Austin: hang tight, darling. I'm coming.
Cecily: that makes two of us
Cecily: I'm so wet thinking about you
Cecily: too bad you aren't here to help me

Ain't no fucking way.

I call her and it goes to voicemail; she calls back a minute later, just before my heart palpitations turn deadly. The dull thud of bass resonates in the background of her slightly slurred hello.

"You're lying," I blurt out with an exasperated sigh. My cock's crushed uncomfortably against the zipper of my jeans, and my thumbs drum incessantly on the steering wheel, waiting for her response.

"Wouldn't you like to know?"

Clearly.

"Darlin'—" I'm interrupted by a quiet, breathy moan. *Fuck*. What I would give to hear her make that noise in person.

"Cecily, I swear to God." My pulse races, and it's becoming increasingly difficult to remain focused on the road. "What are you doing to me, City Girl?"

"I'm joking, Austin. You think I'd touch myself in a bar bathroom?" She drunkenly giggles into the phone. "Who knew this is what it would take to finally get your attention, though?"

"Oh, you got my attention."

"Want me to call you when I do it for real later?"

"No need. I'll be there in person."

Moments later, I slam my truck into park before it fully comes to a stop and barge through the bar doors with such intensity it forces everyone to look in my direction. Denny's face sinks upon seeing me. To be fair, the only reason I would normally be in this place is under duress, so he probably thinks there's a major emergency.

"What's going on?" Red and Denny ask in unison as they approach from either side.

"Cecily texted me. I'm here to give her a ride," I shout over the loud country music.

"Is everything okay? She seemed like she was having fun last I saw her," Denny says.

Red replies for me, "Oh, I'm sure everything is *more than fine*. You guys weren't the only ones getting some over the past few days, Den."

"Ahhh, about damn time." Denny's hand comes up to smack me on the shoulder, and I don't even feel its impact because I see her.

In a short, blue, ruffled dress that looks way too beautiful for a small town dive bar. Then again, Cecily's too beautiful for a small town dive bar. Without a single care, she lets Colt twist her around as they dance, and her dress twirls across tanned thighs. There's no way I'm going to interrupt her when she looks so beautiful and carefree. Instead, I sit down on a bar stool and observe. Flashes of her bare upper back, and a small hint of cleavage, catch my eye with every spin. There should probably be an overwhelming jealous feeling watching her dance like this with another man, but the way she looks up at Colt is nothing like the way her eyes shred me to ribbons with a single glance.

Besides, I have the text messages to prove she's all mine tonight.

And when she saunters over, still out of breath and laughing from something Colt said, I place my hat on her head to show it to everybody else.

"Wear the hat, ride the cowboy... right?" Her grin's crooked, her eyes are glazed with alcohol, and her voice is raspy. "Red told me 'bout the rule when I tried to steal his."

"You're pretty drunk." I fix the hat she's already managed to knock lopsided.

"I am. Does that mean I'm in trouble?" She sits down on my lap like it's the most natural thing in the world, looping an arm around my neck.

"You're nothing but trouble, City Girl. Let's get outta here."

"What if I don't want to go?" She leans in close enough I can practically taste the tequila on her breath. Her hips swivel against me, creating heated friction between her perfect ass and my cock. "You gonna really let me have it? Spank me?"

Thank God for the dark bar lighting because I can imagine how red my cheeks are, given how hot they feel. "Now don't go giving me any ideas."

She grabs my hand, placing it on her stomach, while continuing to discreetly draw circles with her hips. I quietly moan in her ear. "You need to stop."

"Stop what?" She bats her eyelashes innocently.

My cock presses firmly against her tight ass, begging to escape the starched denim. I'm desperate to feel it in her soft hands, her warm mouth, or—*God*—her tight pussy. I can't keep thinking about it or I'll come in my damn pants. She's a fucking temptress and I'm damn near ready to give in.

"Stop what, Austin? Stop making your cock hard? Maybe I don't want to."

Lord help me, I'm about to do something extraordinarily dumb. Her inebriation must be affecting me by osmosis.

"If I put my hand up your dress, how wet would I find you, darlin'?"

"Do you want to find out?"

Yes. God, yes. But an unfortunate voice of reason reminds me she's drunk. I should've pounded back a few whiskey shots when I got here, so I wouldn't have such a guilty conscience for being into this. Because I'm *really* into whatever it is we're doing right now.

"Well? Be reckless, *darling*." She looks at me with a daring smile. The bar is dimly lit, obnoxiously loud, and nobody seems to be paying attention to what we're doing. Maybe a light touch will be okay... My heart's racing as she grabs my hand and slides it to her inner thigh, deciding for me. I don't need to go all the way to her panties to feel how badly she wants me. I haven't even touched her yet, and it's running down her thigh. Knowing she's wet for *me* makes me even harder.

This woman is going to be the death of me.

"Fuck," I breathe against her neck. "What's got you so wet, beautiful? Have you been imagining my cock inside you?"

Flexing my hand, my fingertips barely graze her soaked underwear. This is, by far, the hottest, most reckless, moment of my entire life.

"For *fucking weeks*, Austin."

My teeth sink into her shoulder. I only have a limited amount of restraint, and right now she's testing it. If I slipped my fingers a bit further, tucking them under her panties, slipping inside her, seeing the expression on her face as I rub her sensitive clit. If I did all that, I'd be too far gone. I'd have to fuck her right here in the middle of the bar.

She knows exactly what she's doing to me. Smiling sweetly, as if she's not begging to be fucked. "Do you dance, Not-A-Cowboy?"

My hand slowly retreats, and I shift my jeans to hide how hard she's made me. "Best dancer in town, City Girl."

"Best cowboy, best dancer... prove it."

I wrap an arm around her torso, lift her feet off the sticky bar floor, and haul her out to the dance floor to prove a *lot* of things to her. I pull Cecily in close, nestling my hand on the small of her back. Her hair flips around under my hat as she swings, spins, and dips—trusting me entirely to keep her on her feet. A smile that causes her eyes to squint when she looks at me sends my heart fluttering faster than the ruffles on her dress. Admittedly, I'm a bit rusty. It's been more than a couple years since I last two-stepped in a country bar, but Cecily doesn't seem to notice or care.

"You look beautiful." I hold her close between songs, still swaying to the sounds of bar chatter.

"You like the dress?" She looks up at me with a smile. "I was hoping you would."

"I do. You're beautiful in anything." And—I imagine—even more beautiful in *nothing*.

She spins into my chest, and her lips are on mine. My hands tighten around her waist, one running up her back to arch her into me. My tongue parts her lips, tasting the sweet alcohol as I explore her mouth and breathe her in. I lift her off her feet, yearning to carry her away from this crowded bar and truly make her mine. If I thought there was a chance she'd remember it tomorrow, that's exactly what I would be doing.

Song after song, we two-step and line dance with plenty of breaks to make out amidst the crowded dance floor. Everybody in town will be talking about us and honestly, the thought excites me. Probably more than being fodder for small-town gossip should. I want everybody to know she's my girl.

Red gives me a tap on the shoulder. "Hey, boss. I assume Den and I are good to go home?"

"Yeah, Red. I got her tonight." I hold a tighter grip on her waist, foolishly hoping the missing knee-jerk reaction from Cecily is because she trusts me, and not because alcohol has numbed her reflexes. "We should probably head home, too."

Cecily pouts, but we follow Red and Denny out to the parking lot. The bass from the bar music reverberates across the gravel at our feet, and I finally take a deep breath of air that doesn't smell like alcohol, fried foods, and sweat.

She sloppily climbs into my passenger seat and kicks her boots off. Her fingers comb through her blonde hair with a relaxed exhale. "I haven't had that much fun in—*God*—I don't know. Years."

Before I have the chance to reply, she's talking again, with a slur that indicates she's still inebriated to some degree. "Why didn't you fight me going out? Oh, right. You wanted a night to yourself, and this was a convenient way to get rid of me. *Silly me*. I thought there was going to be an us, and then you go radio silent like a *douchebag*."

The truck idles for much longer than necessary at the town's one and only stop sign. I'm unable to take my eyes off her and focus on the road. She doesn't even seem mad despite her words implying I'm in big trouble right now.

What the hell is she talking about?

"I didn't want to get rid of you. You said you wanted to go."

She laughs. "No, no, no. I definitely wanted to be with you tonight, but you let me walk away. I took Kate's advice—she was technically talking about getting over KJ, not you. I don't get it. We kissed, and it was a *good* kiss, and I thought something was there between us. Then you acted like a caring boyfriend, letting me sleep in and feeding me breakfast. Just to ignore me all day, and pawn me off on your brother the first chance you got. I don't think I did anything wrong, but it feels like you don't want me now."

Crap. "That's not true. I want you bad. So *damn* bad. But I don't want you to feel like I'm pressuring you, especially when you're still legally married."

Also, I'm scared shitless. I'm petrified because the last couple days have felt like something real, and that's before having sex with her. I'm already in too deep.

"Austin, I'm only legally married because divorce doesn't happen that quickly. But I'm done with him. I want to fuck you. Okay? Got it? There you go. You aren't pressuring me." She throws her hands up in the air with exasperation. "I want to get it out of our damn systems because it's exhausting pretending like I don't want you to fuck me. So *fuck me*, goddammit. I don't need to trust you in order to have sex with you—*good Lord.*"

Her little speech should turn me on. It should make me rock hard, but instead, it creates a pit in my stomach and a crack in my chest. Hitting my body with bone-breaking, heart-stopping ferocity.

"Is that all?" She's so drunk I doubt she'll remember this conversation tomorrow—I may as well put it all out there. "Do you want a rebound or do you want something else? Because I've been trying my damnedest to take it slow—give you time. I want the real deal with you, even though it scares me. I've been trying not to do anything that might make you uncomfortable. But, damnit, if all you're looking for is to get over your husband by getting under somebody else, let me know. You could've told me you needed a rebound guy, darlin'. If that's all this is to you, I'll fuck you until you can't move a muscle for days without thinking of me, and you don't so much as remember his name."

"No."

"No, what?"

"No, that's not what this is. I'm not using you to get over him. You're not my rebound guy." Despite how dark it is, her hand finds mine on the center console. She threads our fingers and tightens. "You might know me better than anybody at this point and I just—I don't want to be ignored. I've been ignored enough, and I thought you would be diff—"

Her voice breaks and, with a tight grip on the wheel, I veer to the shoulder in the nick of time to reach out and catch the first tear to roll down her cheek. The fracture in my chest splits wide open, knowing I'm responsible for making her upset.

"Don't cry, darlin'. Please. It breaks my heart."

"Sorry," she apologizes, wiping the dampness from her rosy cheeks. God, I hate how often she says sorry for shit that doesn't require apologies. Even more, I hate knowing somebody in her life made her feel like she needed to. "I'm a crier when I drink. It's stupid—forget about it."

She rubs her palms across her eyes, effectively wiping away the tears, while also smearing mascara around. Making her look like an adorable, drunk raccoon.

"I never meant for you to think I was ignoring you, I swear. You're impossible to ignore. Have been since the day you showed up here—believe me, I tried. Any hope of being able to ignore you was lost the moment I saw you on the side of the road. Everything about you makes me flustered in a way I've never been before—my head's all messed up when it comes to you. I know I haven't been handling it as well as I should, and I'm sorry."

Her knuckles rest lightly on my cheek, rubbing across my coarse facial hair. Then her lips find mine in the dark, fitting perfectly together like our mouths were made to be connected as often as possible. Though it's not my liquor of choice, I'd drink tequila from her lips anytime.

"Can I sleep over tonight?" she whispers tentatively. As if she honestly thinks I might say no. She could ask to move in permanently, and I'd clear out half of my dresser for her tonight. I never wanted her back in her own cabin in the first place. I've just been so consumed with doing everything I think I *should* do.

"My bed is your bed, darlin'."

"Mmm. Well, we have a *great* bed." She rests her head on the window as I pull back onto the road. "I know you drove all the way to town because I sent you dirty texts... so I'm trying to rally. But, *fuck*, I'm exhausted."

"I was gearing up to come get you from the first message, and not because I wanted to take advantage of you being drunk. I'm all ears if you want to talk to me like that when you're sober, though."

She's snoring lightly before I've even finished my sentence. Her face against the window, and my hat hung crookedly off the side of her head. I slow down for every turn and curve in the road, dodge potholes as best I can, and when I pull up the driveway, I take the longer route to avoid the bright barn lights. There's no way I'm about to wake her up when she looks this tranquil.

I slowly peel open the passenger door, carefully slipping my hand in to keep her from falling out. With her cradled in my arms, I walk down the dark path. As I fumble with my doorknob, she stirs, mumbling something incoherent and curling in closer, so her head is tucked under my chin. I freeze in place, waiting until she's settled before continuing to my bedroom and slowly lowering her to the bed.

Even though she's drunk, I doubt she'd want to sleep with makeup and a body-hugging dress on. I sneak out to the bathroom and dampen a facecloth, then return to pull a T-shirt from my dresser.

"Darlin', hey." I brush her hair away from her face. She doesn't even budge. On the off chance she's just ignoring me, I add, "I'm gonna help you get ready for bed, okay?"

As expected, she doesn't respond. This girl sleeps like the dead. With the warm cloth, I begin to wipe away the smudged mascara from her eyes.

Her hand comes up once to lazily swat me away before giving up and tucking under her pillow. Once I'm as confident as I can be—given the fact I'm working under the glow from the distant bathroom light—that her makeup is cleaned up, I look at the T-shirt next to me. A million conflicting thoughts race through my mind.

Maybe she'll be fine in the dress.

It doesn't look like it would be too comfortable, though.

Is it creepy to change her while she's asleep?

I've seen her in her bra and underwear before... in fact, she's had her half-naked body pressed against mine before.

Finally, I give in and slip her dress straps over her shoulders, keeping a close eye on her for any signs she's waking up. As I'm wiggling the tight dress down over her body, she mumbles something. When I look up, her eyes are half-open and staring down at me.

"I thought you might be comfier in something other than this dress," I quickly defend myself.

She nods, lifting her hips to help me finish undressing her. I grab the T-shirt to begin searching for the head hole, when she unclasps her bra in a swift motion and flings it to the floor.

Holy shit. I swallow and quickly avert my eyes because, even in the little light, I can see a shitload more than I was planning to tonight. Not that I'm mad about it.

"Here's a T-shirt." I blindly hold the shirt out, waving it slightly to urge her to grab it.

"Don't be a big baby. You can look... or touch." There's a soft tinge of humour in her voice. Drunk Cecily is fucking dangerous. "You promised not to ignore me, remember?"

I close my eyes and take a moment to compose myself. "Darlin', I'm definitely not ignoring you. I'm just trying my damnedest to be the respectful man my mom raised me to be, okay?"

"Boo, no fun." She slips the T-shirt over her head and wriggles down under the covers. "Hey, Aus?"

"Yeah?"

"I have a present." She holds her closed fist out with a sleepy smile on her face, so I reflexively reach my open palm toward her. A small, balled-up pair of lacy underwear falls from Cecily's hand into mine, and she lets out a soft giggle.

Jesus bloody Christ in hell. I wish I had gotten drunk tonight, too. Then we could make bad decisions together.

"Fuck, woman. You're really trying to make me do something terrible tonight, aren't you?" With all the blood rushing to my cock, it's a small miracle I'm capable of making any smart decisions right now. "As beautiful as you are, and as badly as I want to make love to you from now until the sun comes up, the most I can offer is cuddles."

She groans in annoyance.

I kiss her head, her hair tickling my nose. "Can you stay awake for a minute? I'll be right back with some water and ibuprofen."

Of course, she can't. A minute later, she's sleeping peacefully, curled on her side, with her hands tucked under her cheek. Despite the soothing sound of her deep, slow breaths, and the warmth of her body in my bed, I can't fall asleep. I can't fall asleep because it dawns on me as I lie here, staring at her, just how deep I am in this. A familiar emotion I promised myself I wouldn't feel sits there, right on the tip of my tongue, waiting for me to come out and admit it. Apparently, it doesn't matter how many times I tell myself this isn't going to work—she'll be gone as soon as she doesn't feel like she needs to stay here. When I hold her and kiss her, none of my fear matters. Nothing fucking matters.

Deep in a dream, Cecily mumbles something I can't quite make out. Her ass wiggles closer to me, and she murmurs my name into the pillow. *She's dreaming about me.* My eyes grow wide in the pitch black room, and my thundering heartbeat fills the silence. I look over at her long eyelashes splayed above her cheekbones, the soft part of her cheek that dimples when she smiles, and the small freckle just above her brow.

Fuck.

I think I'm in love with her.

22

Cecily

"**I** don't want to know about the potentially embarrassing shit I said or did last night." I clutch my coffee mug like it's the only thing keeping me alive. The lights are too bright, and even the coffee machine is too loud. If there's a pro to platonically sleeping with the boss, it's being off the hook for work today.

"Might want to delete your text messages then, darlin'. And drink some water." He kisses the top of my head. "If you need me, I'll be in my office. Okay?"

"I'll be here dying and, assuming a time comes where I'm able to move from this couch, I'll go see Beryl."

"Please try not to die." He calls on his way out the door.

After another thirty minutes nursing my coffee, regretting the tequila shots, and suffering from a slow return of half-memories from last night, I drag my sorry ass off the couch. By the time I start the shower, I'm already feeling significantly better—thanks to the ibuprofen, two giant glasses of cold water, and three rounds with my toothbrush. I grab my phone from the nightstand, needing a pump-up playlist to get me hyped enough to leave the house, when Austin's voice telling me to delete my texts inspires me to open up my chat history.

Shit. I cringe as I read everything I sent him. There's a vague recollection of coming onto him last night, but *this* is next level.

Although... he seemed into it.

I must still be drunk because, rather than hitting delete, I find myself carrying on last night's conversation. *How long does tequila stay in your system?*

Cecily: Want to help me now?

Turning up the ringer, I step into the shower and run the cool water through my hair. The sensation on my scalp kills off the last of my lingering headache, and I barely hear my phone ping over the stream rushing past my ears. I reach out from behind the shower curtain, dry my hand on the towel, and pick up the phone.

Austin: With what? Are you okay?

I'm definitely still drunk. Have to be. Sober, sane Cecily would never have the balls to send him a photo of the handheld shower head in my hand. But I do.

Cecily: Think I should use this or do you want to help instead?

If anybody says country boys are dumb, I'll present them with Austin Wells. Because he catches on and replies within thirty seconds.

Austin: YES, I want to help
Austin: I swear to God, you better not be joking. Give me five min. I have to get rid of Beryl.

I don't answer him. Instead, relishing the way his typing bubbles appear and disappear four times over the next two minutes.

Austin: Please tell me if this is serious
Cecily: Are you really going to risk not finding out for yourself?
Austin: Don't move a damn muscle

Right on cue, I hear him barge through the front door moments later. I can picture him sprinting across the lawn and down the path. He must've been moving at breakneck speed to get here so fast. His fist bangs on the door twice before it swings open, hitting the wall with a thud.

"Darlin', I don't know if you're having fun messing with me lately, or if you've been drinking again. Please tell me if you're being serious right now."

I peer out from around the shower curtain at him. He's flushed and looks mildly uncomfortable, but also like he's struggling to contain unbridled excitement.

"Get in and find out." My voice wavers, finding it way harder to be sexy and bold in person. But, goddamn, if there's one thing I remember from last night, it's how badly I wanted him. Austin was respectful and nice, of course—always the responsible one. I'm dying to see what happens when he finally lets himself have what he wants.

"Get out here. If you're not bluffing, I'm taking you to bed and doing this right."

Yeah, that sounds better, actually. This shower is hardly big enough for me to comfortably shave my legs. Sex would be difficult, at best. He thrusts a towel past the shower curtain, and I loosely wrap it over my body before stepping out. Austin's hand snakes around my waist, pulling me into him, and resting his forehead against mine. I palm the already-hard bulge in his pants to let him know exactly how serious about this I am.

"*Fuck.*" He sucks in a sharp inhale. "Okay then."

The towel falls in a puddle at our feet, and he takes a small step back, drinking me in from head to toe. I thought he made me feel sexy before, but the way he softly bites his lip, raking his eyes down my body, has me lightheaded.

"I've been trying to picture this for weeks but you're more beautiful than I could've ever imagined."

My chest heaves, desperate for him to quit *looking* and start touching. I need his hands everywhere. Hooking my fingers into his belt loops, I step toward him with my desperate eyes meeting his. His hand holds me by the back of the neck, tugging my naked body to him, and I temporarily freeze up. We both feel it, and time stops. My heart sinks to the pit in my stomach, prepared for this to be the moment he pushes me away like a broken object.

"I need to hear you say this is what you want. That you have no doubts," he murmurs, placing soft kisses on my neck between words. His body presses closer and I'm melting into him, full of desperate wanting. "Tell me to stop, or I'm going to get you into our bed and make love to you. I'm going to take my time savouring you, and drawing out every moment of your pleasure."

Our bed.

Austin strokes my jaw with his knuckles, and I'm putty in his hands. "I'm going to do all the things I picture doing every time I look at you."

"You like to look at me a lot," I muse as he kisses my shoulder. Knowing he's been thinking about this makes a wet heat pool between my legs.

"You're all I want to look at. Only you." His lips press to mine, and my mouth parts with a small sigh. "Tell me what you want."

Already breathless from the tenderness of his lips as they move to my collarbone, I whisper, "I want this. I want you."

Then I'm walking backward with his body against mine, kissing with all the pent-up sexual energy from last night, and from every day leading up to this. When my back crashes into the wall, his thick length presses into me through his pants. Familiar warmth knots up in my stomach, and I fumble frantically with the buttons on his shirt. I need to touch him. My hands drift across his chest and shoulders, pushing the shirt away. He soaks in my touch like a man starved, and drags his lips down the column of my neck. Stopping to nip and suck at my sensitive skin until I'm a whimpering mess in his arms.

"I'm going to be gentle with you"—he flicks a tongue across my nipple, and I tug his hair at the roots, rolling my hips against the hard outline of his cock—"until you don't want me to be. You're in control, darlin'."

I feel anything but in control.

His hands run down my waist as his tongue follows a path to the curve of my breasts, then my stomach, and then the thin skin covering my hip bone. I suck cool air through my teeth, and he freezes in place.

Austin stands up and holds my face in his warm, calloused hands. "Are you okay? Want me to stop?"

"No." I pull him into me. I never thought I would crave a man's touch like I do at this moment, but I'm overwhelmed with a desire to have him everywhere all at once. "I want this. Just ignore the way I tense up sometimes, okay? The last thing I want is to feel broken."

Crouching back down, he kisses the spot on my hip that made me flinch. "You're not broken."

My breath gets caught in my throat as his hardened hand delicately runs along my inner thigh, where arousal and shower water have blended. A low rumble resounds in his chest when his tongue drags across the wet skin.

"Bedroom, now." He stands back up, grabbing my ass and lifting me into the air. In reaction, I cling to him, wrapping my arms around his neck and my legs around his torso. The cold metal on his belt buckle rubs against me as he walks us to the room, making my thighs hold tighter with each jostling movement against my clit.

He smiles when he realizes what has me moaning quietly. "If my buckle's enough to get you off, wait until you feel my tongue."

The moment I'm placed carefully on the bed, his exploration continues. Aggressive kisses, gentle nips, and barely-there licks over practically every inch of my body. The juxtaposition of rough and sweet has me gasping for air, collapsing into the soft bedding like I've been drugged. A steamy haze washes over me.

"Do you trust me?" he asks, returning the attention of his mouth to my lips. It seems like an odd question, given the vulnerable position I'm currently in.

"Y-yes." I rock my hips against him as he leans in to kiss my neck. "Why?"

"I told you last night, I've been taking this slow. I need to be certain you trust me. I don't want this to be a one-time quick fuck for you to get over your ex, and I don't want to do anything that could hurt you."

Good Lord, now is not the time to make me think about KJ. Not unless he wants me to become drier than the Sahara.

"Austin, if you don't shut the hell up about him." I firmly cup his chin between my fingers. "I trust you. I want you."

My free hand drags down his chest to the bulge in his pants, and he lets out a shuddering breath as my touch traces his cock through his jeans. I make quick work of undoing his belt, my kisses becoming feral. Neither of us breathing, I boldly slip my hand into his pants—underneath his boxers. His pickup truck's definitely not compensating for anything. His moan tangles in my mouth as my thumb circles the head, slipping through the beaded arousal on his tip and spreading it down his shaft.

"Are you going to say anything else stupid?" I smile against his lips.

He shakes his head no and kisses his way down my body again. *Smart man.* He drops to his knees at the edge of the bed and, gripping my hips, pulls me to meet him. His eyes pin me to the mattress while his palms skate up my thighs. They tremble under his touch and he firmly parts them, taking in my open, waiting, desperate body. Slowly slipping a finger through the wetness between my legs, his shoulders relax, like he's perfectly content with doing nothing more than touching me. Meanwhile, the way I need him is painful. His face is so close to the spot that's begging for him, my body instinctively rocks toward it. Desperate for pressure, relief, anything. He parts me with his fingers, letting his warm breath blow across my sensitive skin. The hum of electrical currents compels my hips to buck under him as his tongue makes light contact with my clit.

Holy fucking hell.

I realize I must've said it out loud when his laugh vibrates on my pussy. His eyes burn up at me between delicately placed licks and kisses, teasing me. Each slight touch has me growing more restless and hungry and wanton for him. His fingers glide through the wetness, and my back arches sharply in response.

"You're so fucking wet and beautiful." His voice is deeper and needier than usual. Wonder and desire threaded in his words. "Just like I knew you would be."

Austin's tongue plunges into me, and I let out a whimper, which seems to make primal instinct take over in him. His eyes darken, pupils fully dilated, and his gaze roams my body. Two fingers inch inside me, crooking immediately to glide against the spot that turns the sparks into a wildfire. At the same time, his tongue drags quick circles over my clit. My fingers are knotted in his dark hair—pulling and gripping to keep from squirming off the bed. Losing the ability to think about anything, besides the decadent sensation deep in my core.

Just as I'm about to reach my peak, he slows. Going back to sweet kisses and a feather-soft touch. I grab his head, pulling him back to me.

"Please," I whine. "I'm so close."

"I promise the build-up will be worth it. I won't leave you wanting. You're going to come on my fingers and tongue, and then again on my cock."

His firm hands roughly grab my hips. He devours me again, and my exhilarated sigh is met with his thundering groan. The sound alone nearly sends me over the edge. Knowing he's enjoying this as much as I am makes it all so much sweeter. Over and over, he brings me there and then stops just shy of what I can imagine will be an earth-shattering orgasm. Repenting with quiet, apologetic kisses all over my skin before starting up again.

I let out an exasperated sigh. "You're about to make me do it myself."

"So impatient. I'm happy to spend every minute I can here. What's the rush?" His fingers press against my inner wall and drag their way down, forcing my hips up off the bed in a plea. My moan fills the room as I grip the sheets, clinging to anything that'll keep me grounded.

With a cocky smile, Austin withdraws his fingers and slips them into his mouth. A look of desire washes over his darkened eyes. My clit, swollen and hypersensitive, throbs in anticipation. I don't *want* him to touch me. I need it.

"You taste fucking perfect. The sweetest thing I've ever eaten." A tremor rushes through my body as his fingers swipe across my entrance, and he licks the shimmering wetness from them once again. "Are you ready for me to quit being gentle?"

"*That* was you being gentle?" My eyes feel like they're going to pop out of my head. Whatever he has planned, I'm afraid, intrigued, and excited as hell.

Austin's beard scratches against my sensitive inner thighs, and I close them around his head. I know what I want. This time, I'm not letting him go until I have it.

His forearms pry my knees apart, and he looks up at me. "Keep these legs open like a good girl. You need to be able to watch when I make you soak my face with your cum. Drown me, darlin'."

Nobody's ever talked to me this way, but it adds to the wet heat between my shaky thighs. All I can do is whimper out a soft, "Okay."

The soft bedding caresses my body, and I sink deeper with every tender touch. It's everything I never thought I'd experience with a man—I've never felt so taken care of. *Loved.* His eyes flit up to mine, looking through his dark lashes, gauging me to make sure I'm comfortable.

My body shudders immediately upon feeling his tongue crash into my clit again, and his fingers draw against my insides in a way only my favourite vibrator ever has. I thrash against the bed, and his nails dig into my thighs to hold me down, drawing out my orgasm with everything he has. All the muscles in my body contract and, even as I'm coming back down, he doesn't stop. His tongue continues to flit across my tender clit, while aftershocks have my legs shaking violently under his grasp.

"Austin," I cry out. I've never been the type to moan a guy's name in bed, but I've also never had one make me come this hard.

"Mhmm." The rumble of his voice against me sends a new wave of desire coursing through my veins.

"Fuck," I whine. "I don't think I can take any more."

Pulling back to look me in the eye, he says, "One more. Give me just one more, darlin'. I know you can. *God*. The number of times I've jerked off thinking about this—your taste and your body writhing under me as I make you come. Now that I have you, I never want this to end."

His fingers plunge into me once more, and I find myself fiercely wishing it was his cock. I'm not sure I can give him one more, but it doesn't seem as though I have a choice. His thumb strums my clit, and I bite my lip to keep from screaming. As he has me chasing my high again, all I want is to be filled by him. To feel like we're one. To have the same effect on his body he's having on mine right now. A second orgasm hits hard and fast, as he aggressively licks, working in a steady rhythm alongside his hand. My nails rake across his shoulders, my feet cramp, and hot liquid rushes through me as I convulse with a final swipe of his tongue.

"Atta girl," he murmurs between my legs. "What I would give to have you come in my mouth all day long."

I tug his hair by the roots, dragging him up until we're face to face, sending a rush of cold air between my legs. Whatever emotion is in his eyes right now, I want to see it every day for the rest of forever. He ravages my mouth and, as his tongue parts my lips, I can taste how badly I want him. How badly he wants me is evident in the rock-hard cock pressed taut against his jeans, which he grinds into me with a muffled groan. I tug at the waist, needing his clothing to be out of the goddamn way already. Anything, even air, is too much of a barrier. It's been years since any man has made me feel wildly desperate, and I can't hold off a single moment longer.

"I need you," I admit. "And I need these off."

Standing up, he lets his pants fall to the floor and I race to sit up, though my head feels uncomfortably light and dizzy when I do. Focusing straight ahead, I hook my fingers in the waistband of his boxers, and pull until his cock springs free. My heart pounds loudly in my chest, echoing in the still, humid air. My mouth's suddenly watering at the prospect of feeling him deep inside me. He reaches down, stroking himself from end to end with two hard pumps, forcing another drop of pre-cum to collect on the tip.

I don't know what comes over me, exactly, but I look up at him and say, "Can I taste you now?"

He chuckles softly, a pained expression of desire on his face. "You really are trying to kill me, aren't you?"

Gripping his hips, I shimmy forward and lick from the base of his shaft up to the tip, swirling my tongue across the salty substance glistening on his cock. I take him into my mouth, eliciting a low, strangled moan of astonishment from us both. Sucking hard on the tip and then, inch by inch, filling my mouth with as much of him as I can handle. Feeling the heat in my cheeks and dull pain in my jaw as I open wider than I thought possible. His breathless moans and stifled gasps urging me to take even more.

My hand drops to cup his balls, and he reflexively thrusts forward, ramming his cock to the back of my throat. Making me gag. Tears pool in my eyes as I look up at him in awe.

To my surprise, I fucking *love* it.

"Sorry," he mutters, apologetically stroking my hair as he pulls out.

"Don't apologize for things that don't require apologies." I throw his own words back at him with a smirk. "Do it again. *Please.*"

I fill my mouth with him, exhaling hard through my nose. He pushes the hair away from my face and tucks it gently behind my ear. "Jesus, you're so fucking beautiful—always, but especially right now with my cock in your mouth."

He slowly pushes forward, not even coming close to bottoming out.

My tongue slides over him as I free my mouth to speak again. "Quit holding back. I said, do it *again.*"

"I don't want to hurt you."

"You won't, I promise. I'll smack you if I need you to stop. Now, please let go for once, and fuck my mouth the way I know you're dying to. I trust you... Let yourself have it."

Austin lets out a breathy exhale and weaves his fingers into my hair, gripping my head firmly. My hands cup his ass, tugging him to me. Desperate. Needy. I don't know what's come over me. I've given a blowjob but *this?* This isn't anything I've done before, nor anything I expected to do, and I can't get enough. Anything he wants, anything he'll give me. I want all of him and more.

He pushes farther down my throat with a whole-body shiver.

"That's it. Take me all the way—deeper... *fuck.*"

His hips jolt ahead, forcing a choked moan from deep in my chest. He's coming completely unravelled. This is, by far, my favourite side of Austin. I want this wild, untamed, impassioned man to fuck me senseless.

"I wasn't expecting you to love choking on my cock, but I knew your pretty mouth was good for more than talking." For the strong, silent type, he's sure a fan of dirty talk. I'm not mad about it. His words send flutters to my clit every time.

My tongue flicks over the tip and he jumps. Cheeks hollowed, I slowly pull away until my lips break the suction around the head of his cock with a loud *pop.* "Better put it to good use then," I tease. Then I take him back in. Slowly. Breathing and swallowing around the shaft of his cock. I'm massaging his balls as he scoops my hair into his fist, creating a makeshift ponytail and moving it in time with my bobbing head.

"Fucking—Christ." He pulls away abruptly and I lick my lips, savouring the saltiness on my tongue. His chest heaves. "No, I'm not coming yet. I need to feel your perfect pussy wrapped around my cock first."

He walks over to his dresser and pulls out a condom. I stare at him, drooling like a dog, as he rolls it down the length of his shaft and hovers over me on the bed. "Last chance to change your mind. If you don't want this—"

I scoff. "Austin Wells, get that idea out of your head. I want you. How many more ways can I show you that?" I grip his jaw and pull him in for a slow kiss that's reminiscent of our first one in the lake. Hot breath and shared arousal mingle as I explore his mouth with my tongue. Reaching between my legs, I finger myself for a moment before bringing my soaked fingers to his lips. A soft moan rumbles through my hand as he tastes me.

"See?" I ask. "I'm soaked—all for you. I've never craved somebody the way I'm desperate for you, and I swear I want this. Please, Aus. Give it to me."

Without another word, he notches himself at my entrance, brushing the tip across my clit until I whimper. I'm overwhelmed by the need to feel something, *anything*, inside me. I'm convinced he gets off on making me beg for him—there's definitely enough evidence from the past twenty-four hours to back up that theory. My breath catches in my throat as he drives forward, stretching me around him in a slow, delicious motion.

"Holy fuck." His husky moan cuts through the thick air. He withdraws all but the tip of his hard cock, then presses back in with more impact, filling me to the hilt and forcing a soft gasp from my lips.

Oh, my God. The hungry look on his face has me wrapping my ankles around his hips, spurring him like a rank bull. I can't help but watch the pleasure pooling in his eyes with every pump. He grips my ankle, moving it to his shoulder, and his hips slam into me. Plunging deeper, and deeper still, until he's bottoming out. He's ravenous, and his hunger translates to forceful thrusts that knock the wind from my lungs.

"Look how well you fit around me—fucking perfect."

I claw at his thighs, urging him as deep as possible. Give me everything and then some.

Snap me perfectly in half.

The heel of his hand presses against the back of my thigh. He's driving deeper and harder, fucking me like he's lost any semblance of control. He's reckless and finally taking what he wants, and I love it. My entire body sinks further into the pillowy mattress, every fibre in the soft bedspread skimming across my tingling skin. His thumb falls against my clit, rubbing smooth circles in time with his thrusts, until I'm screaming into the comforter I'm evidently biting.

"Austin, I'm going to—" My sentence is cut off by my own guttural moan.

"Let it out, darlin'. I want to feel you let go. You're so beautiful when you come for me."

Hot honey melts me from head to toe as I shatter around him. Austin falls forward, kissing my ear and neck as he pumps in and out. Sweat beads along his hairline and his thrusts become sloppier, frenzied, and desperate. I hold tight to his quivering biceps and, in moments, his release has him falling apart on top of me. His lips press to my forehead while his body stiffens with a pause, then slowly relaxes, melting into me. Our sweat-slicked chests press together, leaving us to pant and fight for life. He buries his face in the crook of my neck. His breath hot and uneven on my skin.

"That was... *you're* fucking incredible." He kisses my shoulder and rolls onto the bed next to me, keeping my body tucked into his. I lazily wrap a leg across his torso, still yearning for skin-to-skin contact.

"I could do that every day for the rest of my life."

"For as long as you're here, I have no problem making that happen."

For as long as I'm here? What more can I do to make him believe I'm not planning on going anywhere? I don't get the feeling Austin *wants* me to go. It's more that he's come to expect it from people. I imagine his dad leaving has something to do with it. Savannah, too.

The feeling of being watched makes my skin tingle and I turn my head to find exactly that: Austin looking at me with an amused expression. "Daydreaming?"

"Something like that." I caress his face and plant a kiss on his soft lips.

"Well, I just said we should go shower you off again."

"I don't know if I can move." I groan. "Might need to leave me here to die."

"The last time I left you somewhere to die, I almost got replaced by a showerhead less than an hour later. I don't know if I should let you out of my sight just yet."

"Now that I've had the real deal, there's zero danger you'll be replaced." I laugh, curling around him more, so my head is comfortable on his chest. His heartbeat pounds in my ear. "Can we stay here all day?"

"Unfortunately, I have to get some work done today or we'll have a couple hundred head without transport in a few weeks."

The silly, city-girl part of me thinks it wouldn't necessarily be a bad thing. Imagine that—having sex with Austin could potentially save hundreds of lives. Except that's not how this works, and the part of me who's been working on this ranch knows that. It's how Wells Ranch makes money. How food gets on people's plates. Hell, it's how I have a roof over my head.

He shifts to look at the clock next to the bed. "And I have a meeting I really can't miss in two hours."

"A meeting? In town?"

"Yeah, it's... uh, just some ranch stuff with the lawyers." Grabbing my hand, he pulls me into a seated position. "Anyway, forget about it. Come get washed up."

I step into the shower after him, and he takes his time lathering my body with soap, massaging and gently washing me from head to toe. I kiss him, running my hands through his hair and holding our bodies together under the warm water. No man has ever cared for me this much in my entire life. And I can't help it when I start to cry.

"What's wrong?" His fingers pull my chin up, forcing my tear-filled gaze to meet his. "It breaks my heart when you cry."

"It's good tears. I just—I've never had a guy do this kind of thing before." My bottom lip trembles and his thumb softly strokes it. "Thank you."

"Darlin', I don't want to hear you thank me for doing the bare minimum any more than I want to hear you apologize for shit. There's no place I'd rather be right now than in this tiny shower with you." The fact he considers all *this* to be the bare minimum is shocking. Although, my history with men is severely disappointing; I suppose showing affection after sex might be normal for other people.

The water stops, and he wraps a towel around me. Correction: he wraps a luxurious, buttery soft, white bath sheet around me. When I look over my shoulder at him, he's wearing a smug smile.

"You went back to the 'girly store' by yourself to buy towels?" I don't bother hiding my delight, rubbing the soft fabric against my cheek with a grin. I love the picture of him I have in my mind; in his dirty ranch clothes, ambling through the aisles looking for the fluffiest bath towels they had.

"Well, you only had the two and, unless we want to be doing laundry all the time, I figured I should get more. So I went yesterday. They're definitely infinitely better than the crappy ones I had before." He thumbs the terry cloth, tucking it tighter around me. "They were out of the grey, so I went with white. Hope that's okay."

Now I'm fully sobbing. *Over towels.* Or maybe over the fact that I am inexplicably falling in love with him.

23

Austin

I have a hard time wrapping my head around Cecily's ex *not* show-ing up yet. With every passing day of no threatening messages, and no word about a stranger turning up in Wells Canyon, she seems more relaxed and carefree. On the other hand, I'm more wary than ever. If he had turned up the same night as those initial texts, I could've easily handled him. Now it's starting to feel like he's taken so long because he's plotting something bigger. There's no chance he's given up.

I definitely wouldn't give up.

"How's it going?" I approach the round pen where Denny and Red are leaning on the fence panel, watching Jackson lunge his new colt. Over the next couple years, he'll join the remuda.

"He's a bit spicy." Red peers over the top rail and spits on the ground. "If anybody can handle it, it's Jackson."

"He never picks the easy ones, does he?" I shake my head.

"Nah, look at his wife," Denny says.

Jackson yells, "Better not be talking shit about my beautiful angel of a wife."

"Beautiful angel who screamed at him this morning for drinking the last of the chocolate milk." Denny laughs quietly. "If I ever get a chick pregnant, I hope she just calls me after it's born."

Red reaches over and swiftly smacks him across the back of the head. "You're a dickhead."

I lean next to them, watching the colt run in wide circles around Jackson, who acts like a ringmaster in the middle. "You guys still good to handle loading cattle without me tonight?"

"As if we ever need you there." Denny adjusts his hat. "All you do is stand around and bark orders we don't need."

"Hey, Jackson, wanna lunge Denny next? I think he needs to work the piss and vinegar out," I yell at my brother, who laughs and nods eagerly.

"Yeah, come on in, Den. I'll whip ya into shape."

"I prefer to only be whipped by busty blondes, thanks. Or the occasional wild redhead." He winks at Red.

"Oh, fuck right off." Red tries to smack Denny again, but he ducks just in time.

Good Lord. Sometimes it's like handling teenagers instead of thirty-something-year-old men. Despite all the goofing off, I know they'll be tacked up and waiting when the cattle liners roll in later. And I'm confident they'll get them loaded up without incident.

Seeing the look on Cecily's face when I mentioned needing to ship this load off for slaughter, I decided she'd be better off being far from the ranch while it happens. Arguably, sending the cattle to slaughter is one of the most important aspects when it comes to operating a cattle ranch... and maybe I should be there. But I can't find it in myself to leave her tonight. In a lot of ways, she's assimilated into the ranch lifestyle so well it's easy to forget she wasn't born and raised in the country. But teary eyes as she thought about how we get meat on the table is a clear reminder Cecily was brought up as a city girl. She can face the hard reality another time.

"What do you and Filly have planned?" Denny gives me an exaggerated wink and an elbow to the ribs.

"The drive-in theatre."

"Oh, I've had some *good* times at that place," Red muses. "Never actually watched a single movie, though."

If I thought the few days alone with her while the guys were gone were amazing, the last couple weeks have easily been the best of my life. Waking up next to her, kissing her every chance I get, listening to her sing in the kitchen, showering in the tiny box together, and falling asleep intertwined. I don't care that I've fallen hard and fast for a woman who's unlikely to be my forever. Or, at least, I'm trying not to care by thinking about the possibility of her leaving as little as possible. I want to soak in the feeling of playing house for as long as she'll have me, daydreaming about a future where she's my wife.

When Cecily walks out of the bedroom in painted-on jeans and a tight black tank top, my jaw drops and I consider saying "fuck it" to our date plans. I have more interest in watching her than a movie, anyway. My mouth instantly finds its way to her cleavage, nestling between her tits with soft kisses.

"I missed you," I mumble against her skin.

"Who are you talking to right now?" She laughs.

"You, them, everything."

"I saw you on your way to the barn—like, half an hour ago."

"Nuh-uh." I shake my head, dropping my hands to their usual spot on her ass. "Seeing each other from afar isn't the same as being able to do *this*."

I drag her into me and kiss her with reckless abandon. My dick begins to firm immediately as I picture how great she's going to look peeling those jeans off later. If we skipped going to town, I could make that happen now. She rolls her hips into me with a soft moan that goes straight to my cock.

She breaks away from the kiss while her hips continue absentmindedly grinding against my dick. "Let's go, I'm starving."

"I am too." I bite her bottom lip.

She grips my erection with a soft smile. "I think you're hungry for something very different."

"You're not wrong." I find myself toying with the hair at the nape of her neck. Her body tenses, but I kiss the rigid muscle running along her jaw despite it. She still spooks when I grab her in certain ways or move too quickly, but I've learned it's best to pretend it's not happening. If I bring attention to it, she retreats into herself. And a few slow, sensual kisses always get her to melt under me again. "I can't help it when you look so good in jeans and boots."

"You mean the same things I wear almost every day?" She laughs, leaning into the kisses I'm trailing down the side of her neck. I stop briefly to suck on the rapidly beating pulse point, stealing her breath. Knowing I have this effect on her isn't doing anything to help the hard bulge in my jeans. "And I thought you didn't care about my boots? 'Seen one, you've seen them all', right?"

"Was trying to pretend like I wasn't picturing you in nothing but those boots."

"Now I know what we're doing later. Come on—we'll be late." She presses her palms to my chest to back me away.

"Let me shower and we'll go. Unless you want to join?" I try my hand at a pouty face, which makes her laugh.

"If only you'd gotten here before I put makeup on. You missed your chance, *darling*."

With a playful slap on my ass, she sends me to shower alone. I grumble loudly the entire ten-pace walk to the bathroom, then take the fastest shower of my life. Holding a towel wrapped around my hips, I enter the bedroom to find Cecily sitting on the edge of the bed. Normally, one or both of us would make a flirty comment right now—except there's clear tension in the air, and the excitement I expected to see in her eyes is absent.

My chin gestures toward the phone in her hand. "What's going on?"

"Take a wild guess." She shoves it in my direction and, with a deep breath, I look at what has her so shaken.

Unknown Sender: Wells Canyon. That's where you are, isn't it, Cecily? Only you would be dumb enough to think you can hide out in a town with 2,000 people. See you soon, wife.

"After not hearing anything for so long, I genuinely thought he gave up," she mutters.

I've never wanted to be wrong so fucking bad.

I squat down in front of her, rubbing my palms across her thighs. "I know you did—and I wish you were right."

"We should go. I don't want to be late for the movie and ruin our night," she says in a monotone voice. I'm waiting for her to cry, scream, throw something... she's so stoic it's making my hair stand on end.

"With all due respect, darlin', fuck the movie. If you don't want to go anymore, I get it. I promise the night won't be ruined."

"No, I want to go. I'm not going to just hide here for the rest of my life. If he finds me tonight, it is what it is. Besides, unless he was already en route when he sent that, he wouldn't get here for hours."

Keeping her here would be so much easier. Safer. I maintain some control over who gets onto the property. There are always at least a dozen ranch hands around to protect her. There are guns and dogs, not to mention, being thirty kilometres from town on a rough dirt road deters most unwelcome guests. But, as important as keeping her safe is, I'm also in the habit of keeping her happy.

"If you want to come home at any point, you'll tell me?"

She nods slowly.

"And if I tell you we have to leave, you'll listen?" I stare into her bright blue eyes. "We'll swing by The Horseshoe on our way. Dave will let me know if anybody comes sniffing around tonight."

"Aus, I'm sorry. This isn't fair to you. You shouldn't constantly have to deal with me and my drama."

Giving her thighs a squeeze, I softly kiss her knee. "I'm not *dealing* with you. I'm here because I want to be. I want to sort this shit out together. Because *this*,"—my finger circles between us—"thing that's happening with us is worth it. You're worth it."

"You're sure?"

"Darlin', I've never been more sure of anything in my life. Now come on, or we won't have time to pick up food before the movie, and I wasn't kidding about being starving."

The local dive bar's already busy with regular patrons when we pull up shortly after eight o'clock. Holding her hand, I can feel Cecily's palm start to sweat as we approach the door. Not that I blame her. There's a real possibility KJ could be in the bar, and I'm about to deliver Cecily right to him.

"He's not here," she breathes out the words as the door swings shut behind us. *Thank God.* It's a good night, and he's not here to ruin it. Not yet anyway.

"Hey, Dave. I need a favour." I lean on the wood bar top, keeping a firm grip on Cecily's hand. I don't think I'll feel okay letting her go until there's zero chance he'll appear.

"Austin. Cecily. What can I do for ya?"

"There's a guy—might show up here asking about Cecily. Pretend you've never met anybody by that name around here. And then text me. Tell Cass the same."

"Can do." He looks at Cecily. "You good?"

"Yeah, I'm fine." She smiles at him reassuringly. "By the way, he's about 6'7" with short, dark hair... um, he drives a black Bentley. I'm sure he'll stand out like a sore thumb if he comes in here."

I'd never put any thought into what Cecily's husband would look like. But the only guy I've ever known who hit his wife was short, chubby, and always looked like he needed to wash his hair. My brain pretty much decided that's what I was up against here. Not somebody who's five inches taller than I am and drives a car worth more than my house. A man who wants Cecily back, and is definitely going to want me dead when he finds out I'm sleeping with her. *Fuck.*

"So, uh, anything else I should know about this ex of yours?" I climb into the truck and turn the key, my thoughts rapidly spinning out of control. "Does he compete in Jiu-Jitsu or have military training? Anything like that? Or is he just a giant, armed dude on a warpath?"

"Are you jealous or scared?"

"A bit of both. I didn't realize I was basically going up against Batman."

She tosses her head back against the headrest with a laugh. "Just because he's tall and comes from a family with money doesn't mean he has anything on the best not-a-cowboy around. Tough men don't need to take out their unchecked aggression on their wives."

"Why is he driving a car that's worth approximately ten times the amount of your tin-can?"

"Oh, he hates me driving it. Maybe even more than you do. It's been a point of contention since the beginning. I bought it before we started dating and held onto it because I needed *something* that was mine. He made me quit my job, and the house is solely in his name... even my phone was technically his. KJ was quick to say things were 'ours', but we both knew they weren't. He bought me a fancy car, too, and I refused to drive it."

I try not to think about the hell she probably went through after refusing to get rid of her car for him, and make a silent promise to never be an asshole about it again. "If he doesn't show up this weekend, I'm going to the cell phone place first thing Monday to get you a different number, all right?"

"Then we won't know his next move."

"So far, he's been nothing but talk, and it's stressing you out." I kiss the soft skin on the back of her hand. "Either way, I'm going to keep you safe."

Cecily loops her arm under mine, and her soft fingertips draw along the inside of my forearm while we make the five-minute journey to the drive-in theatre. Her touch calms my heartbeat and relaxes my muscles. My nerves are still a bit shot, though.

Batman or not, he's the one who fucked up, and I'll be the one who gets the girl in the end. I'll make sure of it.

I open her door and she hops onto the gravel below. "I haven't been to a drive-in since I was a kid. Sometimes my cousins and I would go when we stayed at my grandparents' cabin. Did you come here a lot?"

Arms loaded with blankets from the backseat, I boost her into the truck box and together we set up a makeshift bed. "Almost weekly when we were little. They always played kids' movies on Sundays. And then this was basically the only decent place in town to take a date when I was a teenager… so, yeah."

"You mean to tell me I'm not the first girl you've brought to the movies?" She pulls me down next to her on the blanket pile and settles into the crook of my arm. Then pops a French fry into my mouth. "At least tell me I'll be the first one you've fooled around with at the drive-in?"

"Do you want the truth, or would you prefer I lie?"

She smacks me playfully on the chest, nuzzling her head into the space between my jaw and collarbone. I really thought I would tell her I loved her tonight. But with the threat of her *husband*—the word will forever make me gag when it's associated with that asshole—being in town, it'll have to wait. I'm not risking her thoughts being muddied when I tell her.

We're not even twenty minutes into the movie before we're acting like teenagers. She kisses my neck softly, and our bodies intertwine under the thin blanket. Our lips find each other in the dark and her quiet moan is muffled by a firm kiss as I slip a hand up her shirt. Exploring her mouth with my tongue, I grind on her until my cock is throbbing. Her frenzied kisses and wandering hands make the ache to be inside her unbearably intense.

I swipe across her hard nipple with my thumb, and her whimper travels through my veins. I'm positive she skipped putting a bra on because she knew this would happen, and that only makes me more wild. My girl *wanted* me to fondle her during the drive-in movie. I lean over, kissing her nipple through her shirt before pinching the nub between my teeth. Biting and sucking until the thin fabric of her shirt is wet and her nipples are rock hard. Her fingers thrust into my hair, forcing my face between her tits and eliciting a groan from deep in my throat. She could suffocate me here and I'd die incredibly fucking happy. I'd come back as a ghost just to thank her.

My hands rove from her nipples to her waist and down to her lower stomach. I slide over her jeans, the texture so much rougher than the soft, kissable skin underneath. My palm presses against her pussy, rubbing a slow circle overtop of where I'm sure her clit is. Proving I'm right, she bucks in response to the friction and bites down hard on my earlobe, her raspy breath blowing hot air against my neck.

All the blood from my feet rushes upward, and the blood from my head floods my groin. It's all gathering in the space between my hips. Waiting for the sweet relief when she finally touches me.

"I can feel how bad you want me right through your jeans, darlin'." I smile, pressing my fingers against the damp denim between her legs.

"That makes two of us." She grips my cock through my jeans. "Since you're the expert on drive-in theatre hookups, tell me how we should handle this."

I'm *far* from an expert. I fingered a girl here one time when I was seventeen and, truthfully, I don't think I did a good job. But, the way I see it, this is a great way to get our minds off the shitty ex. The movie's loud enough to drown out *most* of our noise and my cousin's the only cop in town, in case we get caught. I have nothing to lose and a striking, desperate need to be inside her.

"You might not be the first girl I've fooled around with here, but do you want to be the first one I've fucked?" I unbutton her jeans and then mine. Already knowing what her answer will be.

The whites of her eyes grow wide and gleam in the night. "Serious?"

"You need to be quiet though, darlin', and that's not your forte." Slipping my hand into her jeans, I circle her swollen clit with my finger and her entire body shivers. As if to prove my point, a loud moan escapes her. I shove my palm over her mouth, waiting until her lips have relaxed before removing it.

"You're not getting my cock until you can show me you can be a good girl." I flick my finger across her clit again, then slide it into her, struggling to keep my own sounds of desire locked away.

She grabs a handful of the blanket and holds it tight to her gaping mouth, fighting to play by the rules as my hand works over her. Her body writhes against mine, muscles contracting in a symphony as her pussy becomes even wetter under my touch. She's soaked, and it's maddening. I wish I could secretly kneel between her legs and get a good taste.

"You're doing so good, beautiful," I whisper as I stroke her soft pussy, brushing against her clit to elicit a strangled moan. "Stay quiet and I'll give you what I know you want."

I can't believe she's all mine.

I plunge two fingers deep inside her again and use her arousal as lube while I lightly stroke her clit, inching her close to orgasm. Her hand joins mine with hectic, fast movements and, together, we make her legs quiver with an impending orgasm.

Mouth pressed to her ear, I whisper, "That's it. Does this feel good, darlin'? Do you like having to be quiet so nobody catches us here?" I stroke her hair with my free hand and she nods eagerly in response to my questions, biting harder on the blanket.

Except she's not all mine. She's married to somebody else.

I choke back the thought and bite my lip hard enough to produce a metallic taste.

"Look at me," I whisper. "Open those beautiful fucking eyes." They snap open, the bright blues meeting mine just in time for her to come. Her moan's muffled, but still surprisingly loud, as her back arches with a lengthy orgasm. All the while, her gaze never leaves mine.

She's mine. Husband or not.

"That's my girl. I'm so proud of you, beautiful." I lick the sweet taste of her from my fingers and then replace the blanket covering her mouth with my lips, kissing tenderly while she comes down. "Give me a second. I have a condom in the truck."

Awkwardly trying to hide my erection, I shuffle out of the truck bed and walk to the driver's side door. I severely underestimated how close all the other vehicles are to us. To our right are two teenagers, who are so deep down each other's throats it wouldn't surprise me if they're about to do the same thing as us. But to our left is an older couple, who look like they're only here because their therapist ordered them to have a date night. They'll definitely be quick to shut us down if they notice. I slip the condom into my closed fist and stroll back to the tailgate, nodding politely at the woman and praying she doesn't look further south than my face.

I slip in next to Cecily and tug my jeans down around my knees. She rolls to face away from me, her own pants already gone, and wiggles her plump ass at me. Even in the dark, every jiggle and ripple of her body makes my already erect cock even harder. My balls tense as I run my hands down her waist.

Fuck, I'm in love with her.

"You still want it, darlin'?"

"You have no idea," she whispers back. "Get it in. Fill me."

My cock forces its way out from my boxers with the lightest tug and I fist it. The tip drags down her ass as I fumble with the condom wrapper in the dimly lit truck bed. My heart's pounding at the crinkle of the plastic, certain the old biddy the next vehicle over is already on to us. Sensing my nerves, Cecily's hand reaches out and grabs the condom, then rolls it down my length with a shuddering breath.

I press the head against her soaking wet pussy, and she gasps when the tip slips inside. She looks over her shoulder at me and mouths, *please*—unravelling me with a single word. She has me ready to do absolutely anything.

Inch by inch, I fill her, careful not to rock the bed of the truck too much as I slide almost all the way out and slam back in. Forcing the sweetest whimpers from my girl. My cock's filling her to the hilt repeatedly as her nails dig into my forearms, leaving behind deep, purple crescent moons in my flesh. She's doing everything she can to keep from screaming. Normally, the sounds she makes are almost enough to make me come, but there's something sexy about watching her fight it. I can't even be certain if the movie is still playing because all I hear is how wet she is around my cock. Her muffled moans.

"What a very good fucking girl you are," I whisper into her ear. "Being so quiet even though I know you want to scream my name for everyone to hear."

Gripping her thigh, I spread her legs so I can reach between and feel my soaking-wet cock gliding in and out of her. She arches her back, forcing my dick to hit her at a different angle and sending a firework of pleasure up my spine.

"Fuck." I fight not to come from the simple movement. My fingers settle into a steady rhythm on her clit while my other hand holds her belly, not letting her squirm away from my touch.

"God, you fill me so fucking perfectly. So fucking deep." She groans, clutching the blanket to her mouth again.

"Shhh," I breathe against her ear. "Quiet, darlin'. I want to hear how wet you are for me. It's intoxicating."

I drag my cock in and out until the edges of my vision blur. I don't even care anymore that the truck bed is *definitely* rocking side-to-side. Hell, there's even a fucking squeak somewhere, which I'll need to hit with some WD-40 before we do this again.

My hips roll when I push back in, ensuring she feels every damn inch. "Come for me. Come on my cock. Make a fucking mess of me. Make me yours."

"You're already mine and I'm yours," she whispers back. "Yours."

Damn right.

My nose drags up the back of her neck, breathing in the sweet shampoo scent. She closes her eyes, preparing to be hurtled over the edge as I grip her trembling thighs and thrust. A rattling moan escapes, her orgasm squeezing my cock until my own release blows out of me. I can't get enough. She is *everything*. I could stay here, with her, for the rest of my life. I wrap Cecily in my arms and remain buried deep inside her until the final credits are rolling. All the while placing kisses across her shoulders and combing my fingers through her silky hair.

If I can't tell her I love her tonight, I can damn well show her I do.

24

Cecily

"Fuck," I curse under my breath as I flip the grilled cheese sandwich half a second too late. The bit of charcoal isn't that big of a deal. I can make sure it ends up on my plate. Eat with the blackened pieces facing down to keep him from seeing. Or I can try to hide the evidence deep in the garbage can. Maybe I should inhale it quickly now so it doesn't go to waste.

When Austin walks in the door for lunch, the burnt bread suddenly feels like a *frighteningly* big deal. I wipe the bead of sweat away from my hairline before pressing two fingertips to my tear ducts to halt production. *Maybe he somehow won't notice.* It's an absurd thought—Austin notices everything about me. There are times when it's as though he innately knows what I'm feeling before I even do.

"Smells good, darlin'." He comes from behind and kisses my shoulder. His hand reaching my lower back makes my spine straighten. Goosebumps scatter. There's no hiding my anxiety when he's this close. "What's wrong? Did you burn yourself?"

"I'm fine. I wasn't paying attention and I guess I had the pan too hot and I burned the sandwich. But I'll eat this one, don't worry."

"No way. I like them a little extra crispy. This one's mine." His touch glides along my arm until he's pulling the spatula from my hand and spinning me to face him. I don't think I even realize how often I still flinch, but the sadness in his eyes right now is a dead giveaway. "Cecily, I don't give a shit about some burnt bread. You could serve me a hockey puck with cheese and I'd break a tooth eating it with a smile on my face. This is never the kind of thing you need to worry about with me... promise."

He pulls me into his chest, and I breathe in his scent. *He's not him*, I remind myself until my heartbeat steadies and I'm safe. His warm body engulfs mine like a heated blanket, the steady thrum of his heartbeat in my ear, and his palm holding tight to my back.

"Well, now both sides have some good charcoal, so it's definitely mine," he says, still holding me in one arm as he plates the blackened sandwich.

"I'm sorry."

"Hush," he whispers before kissing me. "Let's eat—you have a rodeo to get to."

I reluctantly peel myself away from his calming embrace and grab my plate. "You're sure you can't come with us?"

"I'll find you later. I have work to finish up first. Please promise me you'll stay with one of the guys at all times, okay? I don't like thinking about you being in such a public place, not knowing if he's around."

"You know, you could come with me and keep me safe."

He shuffles the grilled cheese around his plate. "Wish I could, darlin'."

He's been so vague about *why* he can't come and, each time I press for more, he's quick to shut down the conversation. I'm over it. As much as I'd love nothing more than to be there with Austin, I know I'll have fun with everybody else.

"Please get there as soon as you can. I want to be there with you," I say.

"I will. Promise I will."

The bathroom air is humid and full of lingering hairspray as we dance along to a nineties country playlist. It reminds me of getting ready to go to parties in high school, minus the terrible fashion and questionable hairstyles.

"I can't believe you've never been to a rodeo!" Kate's excitement over this entire day has me beginning to wonder how big of a deal this whole thing is. She went so far as to buy matching outfits for her and Odessa. Even though she's thirty-five weeks pregnant and sweating profusely, she's been curling her hair for the last hour to make sure it's perfect.

"Well, it's not exactly the type of event my parents or KJ typically attend." I reluctantly plug in my curling iron as the fear of being underdressed in simple braids finally outweighs comfort. "I'm excited to go check it out."

"Austin still doesn't think you should go?"

"Not at all." I shrug. "I get where he's coming from, but... I don't know. Either KJ shows up in town or he doesn't. At this point, I almost wish he would. Then maybe I'd stand a chance at getting rid of him finally."

Three orange drinks appear from behind the door frame, followed by Beryl's exhilarated face. "Who's ready for the rodeo? I got us drinks—the little umbrella is in the virgin."

"Ugh. I cannot wait for this sucker to be out so I can get drunk at rodeo barn dances again." Kate clinks her glass against mine and Beryl's, and we all take a refreshing sip.

"Although, rodeos seem to be how this"—her hand circles her baby bump—"keeps happening. Sexy cowboys, liquor, country music. Be careful tonight, Cecily."

I grimace as if I've shot back straight tequila. Beryl's bangle-covered arms jingle, her entire body shaking with laughter. If I'd had liquid in my mouth when she made that comment, Kate would be wearing it.

"Yeah, you don't need to worry about me." I pat my stomach. "Old faithful IUD up in here to keep it a baby-free zone."

When I was younger, I assumed I would have kids one day. But, after marrying KJ, I decided straightaway it was absolutely *not* something I wanted to do with him. I secretly got an IUD and, thankfully, he never showed more than casual passing interest in the idea of a baby. Mostly, he expected it would just eventually happen. As far as he was aware, we were "not trying, not preventing". The day of my doctor's appointment, I resigned to never having kids. Despite being around pregnant Kate every day, it hasn't crossed my mind before now that kids could be part of my future again.

I think I want kids... not right away, though. Obviously. I need to at least be properly divorced. And possibly remarried?

God, do I want to marry somebody else one day?

As soon as I silently ask myself the question, it feels insane to me that the answer is an immediate and resounding "yes". And there may or may not be a specific dark-haired, bearded man who comes to mind.

Hold your horses, Cecily.

"Austin's great with Odessa. Always has been. He even changed diapers when she was a baby." Kate bites back a smile as she lets the final hair strand fall from her curling wand. "Just sayin'."

Not only am I aware how great he is with Odessa, but that's part of what made me fall in love with him. It's hot as hell watching a man be a good uncle.

"Neither of you are getting any younger, either," Kate adds.

"First of all—rude. I'm plenty young. Let's not get ahead of ourselves here, please." A distant memory from a similar conversation plays in the background. Except back then my friends were listing the reasons why KJ would be a terrible husband and father, rather than a great one. So, really, it's a polar opposite conversation; Kate's gunning hard for me and Austin to be together and make babies. "Maybe in a few years we can have this conversation again. Assuming this thing between Austin and I even lasts that long."

Beryl contemplates it for a second, then says, "When you know, you know. You deserve all the happiness in the world, honey. If that includes babies—or if it doesn't—we're just saying we support you."

Kate nods her agreement, slathering another coat of mascara on.

Then Beryl adds, "And they'd be *very pretty* babies. I can always use more sweet little ones around here to snuggle."

Kate cheers. "Yes, Beryl! Thank you. My kids need cousins and Denny's a lost cause unless he accidentally knocks somebody up."

"My God, Beryl. How many shots did you put in that drink of yours?" I laugh. "Can we deal with one wildly terrifying thing happening in my life at a time? Or did we all conveniently forget I have a crazy ex-husband who could show up any time?"

Kate looks at me with a mischievous smile, bringing her straw to her lips. "All I'm saying is nobody's gonna be mad about some baby-making going on tonight. Least of all, me."

"Or me," Beryl agrees with a wink.

My head drops into my hands with a defeated exhale and a half-hearted laugh. *Absolutely fucking not.*

"Filly, you gonna do the steer scramble?" Sundial asks from the backseat, barely audible over the wind swirling around as we fly down the road with all the windows open. *So much for my perfect curls.*

"I don't even know what that is," I shout back over my shoulder.

"Austin definitely won't like you doing the steer scramble." Denny elbows me jokingly in the ribs.

"Your point is? I'm a grown-ass woman and can make my own choices."

"Ohhhh, Filly's looking to get into trouble tonight." Red whoops a *yeehaw* out the window, swerving the truck back and forth on the dirt road. "Hell yeah, let's get her in trouble before the boss man shows up."

I laugh, gathering my blowing hair in my hand and tucking it around my neck. When Austin said he was going to meet us later, I'm not sure he fully thought through whether it was a good idea to send me with this crew. Not that I gave him a choice. *I'm going to the rodeo with the guys, whether you come or not,* were my exact words.

"So what happens is they tie a ribbon to a steer and turn it loose in the arena with a buncha women. Whoever gets the ribbon wins the prize," Denny explains.

Colt yells from behind me, "You had no problem with the calves at branding. This is basically the same thing."

"*Ehhhh.*" Red's face scrunches up with disagreement. "Not quite."

"This all sounds incredibly stupid. Does anybody seriously sign up willingly?" My head turns rapidly between Red and Denny.

The boys all exchange glances before Colt says, "Yeah, I think most of the women do, honestly. It's a classic event."

I sigh. *What's the worst that could happen?* It might be a bit dangerous, but it also sounds daring and fun. "Alright, fuck it. Sign me up. But I fully expect you guys to buy all my drinks tonight for doing this."

"You bet your ass we will." Red's palm slams against the steering wheel excitedly. "*Fuck*, I love a rodeo."

The truck veers into a sprawling field lined with endless rows of pickup trucks. Some hauling horse trailers, others loaded with people in the bed. A stampede of cowboy hats make its way toward the metal grandstands. It seems the entire town and then some are here for the Wells Canyon rodeo.

I walk alongside the boys, taking it all in. The hot afternoon air smells like horses, dust, and hot dogs. The sun blazes down on the open area, sizzling my sun-worn skin. We pass by food vendors and booths selling everything from saddles to turquoise jewelry. Finally, we enter the beer gardens—also known as the adults-only section of the rodeo grandstands—designed for drinking, dancing, and general mayhem.

"You boys are buying me drinks all night, don't forget. That includes the liquid courage it's going to take to get me in the arena with a steer."

"Shots?" Denny cocks a tempting eyebrow.

"Should probably take it easy until after I have to try and wrestle an animal that's at least twice my size. Beer's fine."

"Just make sure you have enough so you don't tense up if you get hit," Red says. "Trust me, it hurts a lot less the next day if you're all *loosey-goosey*."

What the hell did I agree to?

25

Austin

*W*hat the hell did I agree to?

My presence at the Wells Canyon rodeo is pretty firm evidence I'll do anything Cecily asks me to. When she asks, I actually find myself *wanting* to do all the things I swore I never would.

A flood of memories hits the moment I step out of the truck, and I nearly hop right back in and drive home, but I can't do that to her. Not when I promised I would come. If I explained why I couldn't be here, I don't doubt she would understand. But I would rather suffer silently than admit I don't want to face memories of the way my family used to be. Back when my grandpa and mom were alive, my dad was around, and I didn't have the weight of a multi-generational ranch on my shoulders.

I stroll through the vendors, taking it all in for the first time in more than a decade. This used to be my stomping grounds. I slept all weekend in my truck, still attached to the horse trailer, and didn't have a care in the world beyond possibly bringing home a shiny buckle and some cash. Before I lost the most important people in my life in a span of less than six months. Then nothing mattered except keeping the ranch running and my brothers taken care of.

A hauntingly recognizable voice carries through the grandstand rafters and out across the field. I blink away the pinpricks in my eyes. George Shaw, Wells Canyon's rodeo announcer for the past three decades, maybe longer. It stops me in my tracks. With a town of 2,000 residents, I see him often. But he uses a lower, authoritative tone over the crackly microphone. That's the voice I haven't heard since he had everybody stand for a moment of silence twelve years ago. Just after both Grandpa and Mom passed. *Two vital members of the Wells Canyon community, both of whom were also past presidents of the rodeo association, lost in the same year.* No mention of my dad in George's heartfelt speech, even though he was gone, too.

I manage to spend enough time saying hellos to people I know to completely avoid watching any roping events. Almost as if I had planned it this way. Just as the steer riding is wrapping up, I enter the grandstands and stare out at the crowd.

"Austin!" A voice yells my name from somewhere to the far left of the arena. *I should've known they'd be in the beer gardens.*

"How's it goin'?" Red slaps my back as I approach the group. "Surprised you showed up this year. It's good to see ya here, boss."

"Where's Cecily?" I look around at the faces in the crowd. Plenty of girls. None are her. The only way I'm going to make it through this fucking rodeo is with her hand in mine. It's not a matter of being a jealous or possessive boyfriend.

I need her.

Colt and Levi exchange a sideways glance and Red shrugs at me with a down-turned smile.

"Where is she?" The friendly tone in my voice is long gone. I'm not playing anymore.

George's announcer voice comes over the speaker, declaring that the steer scramble will be starting in one minute. *Don't tell me.*

"Where the fuck is she?" My words spit at Red as I step into him. "If you assholes put her up to this, I will hang every single one of you by the goddamn testicles."

Colt's face scrunches up. "We didn't put her up to it. She wanted to."

Red smacks him hard on the shoulder. I'll deal with these mother-fuckers later.

Blood whooshes past my ears, drowning out the music and raucous rodeo noise as I shove through the throng of people trying to get into the beer gardens. Once I'm free from the crowd, my feet hit the dusty ground harder, sprinting along the side of the arena.

I trusted her. I trusted them. And I'm a piece of shit for not coming here sooner. If I'd been here, she wouldn't be putting herself at risk like this. Preparing to go toe-to-toe with a massive steer that finds fun in tossing people through the air like ragdolls. Broken bones, puncture wounds, concussions...

Fuck. Thank God I made it here in time. Thank God I didn't turn around and go home. If anything ever happened to her...

She's the love of my life. I know that without a shadow of a doubt now.

Driven by overwhelming fear and anger, I can't even tell whether my feet are still under me, but I guess muscle memory's carrying me to where I need to go. I weave through barrel racers lined up for their event and climb over the fence next to the roping chute. For once, it's a blessing I know the layout like the back of my hand. I storm clear across the arena, ignoring the drunken cheers from Red, Colt, and the rest of them. They'll be lucky if they have jobs—or lives—by the time I'm through.

Denny. Of all motherfucking people, I thought he wouldn't be this stupid.

"Where the fuck is she?" I yell at him, charging full force toward the gate he's leaning on.

"Shit. Relax, Aus." My brother smiles.

"You seriously were going to let her do this?"

"She wants to!" He throws his hands up in surrender.

Yanking open the gate, I shrug his hand from my shoulder just in time to see a group of girls heading in our direction. At least twenty of them. Most are locals who have probably done this event before, which makes them even bigger idiots than the first-timer city girls looking to impress a cowboy. No wonder Denny's hanging around.

The women file past us into the arena, and I frantically scan faces until I see hers.

"Austin?" Cecily's eyes meet mine and confusion washes over her. "What are you—"

"Nope." Without stopping, I bend over and grab her by the hips, tossing her over my shoulder in one swift motion. Then I walk away with her. Away from the arena. Away from everybody. As far away as I can get, short of throwing her in the truck and driving home.

"What the hell? What is your goddamn problem? Fuck you." Her fists hit my back as she flails, trying to break free from my grasp, and my arms grow tighter around her in response.

Finally giving up the fight, she becomes limp. Deadweight slung over my shoulder as I march past pens full of rough stock. She can be pissed off at me. I'm pissed off at her, too.

My feet follow a trail I've walked at least a thousand times. The trail to *our* barn. I continue past the plaque dedicated to my mom and, shockingly, that's not the thing consuming my brain.

Once I determine we're far enough away, I set her down. My hands slam against the barn wall on either side of Cecily, preventing her from running back and joining the herd of girls with death wishes. I'm fucking angry—at her for thinking this was a good idea, at the guys I trusted would look out for her, and at myself for not being here earlier.

"What's your problem?" she taunts.

"What's my *problem*? My problem is that I leave you alone for a few hours and you try to get yourself fucking killed. My problem is that you let those morons talk you into dangerous shit. What the hell, Cecily? Over my dead body will I let you go out there," I yell. No, I *explode*. I'm close enough, I'm sure she can feel every word burning on her cheeks. Her lips pull in and she slowly shakes her head like she's holding herself back from yelling right back at me. "Seriously, that's the stupidest thing you could do. Jesus Christ—what the fuck were you thinking? You know you could've gotten yourself killed. What the hell would have happened if I didn't show up here? I can't fucking believe you."

She stares at me with eyes colder than I thought possible from her, looking me up and down with disdain. "You think you scare me? It's going to take more than yelling in my face to scare me, Austin. You want to be just like him? Is that it? *Hit me then.*"

Is that what she thinks I want to do?

I drop my arms and stumble back, taking in her shaking frame. My heart slams into my sternum and rattles down each rib before landing in my stomach at the sight of her. She might've said she wasn't scared, but everything about her body language screams otherwise. I did the one thing I swore to myself I wouldn't do. I swore to her I wouldn't do. Clasping my hands behind my head, I pull my gaze up to the rafters. Heat cascades over my neck and face. *I can't believe I just...*

"Cecily. I would never... I didn't mean—I wasn't trying to scare you. I would *never* hurt you like that." I scrub my hands vigorously across my face with a sharp exhale. "I'm sorry. So fucking sorry. I fucked this all up. All I wanted was for you to be safe. I was so worried when I found out you were there."

"It's a fun intermission event, Austin. It's not that serious. Not something I deserve to be yelled at over."

Clearly, the guys didn't fill her in on all the details.

"It's considered a dud if nobody ends up in the hospital. They have a habit of picking the rankest steer they have and sending it to kick the shit out of anybody who gets in the way. It's not as much of a crowd pleaser if they send a friendly little calf out and all the ladies hug it, is it?"

Her raised eyebrow and pursed lips mock me. "I'm not dumb enough to stand right in the line of fire when there's a damn cow running at me."

"It's not about being—are you so desperate for a $200 gift card to the fucking tack store that you're willing to risk it? Because I'll give you $300 right now if you are."

"I didn't even know what the prize was, actually."

"Jesus Christ." I drag a hand down my face. "What possessed you to sign up then?"

Her shoulders shrug half-heartedly. "I wanted to feel alive, I guess. I'm not going to apologize for it. You try living your life knowing it could all come crashing down at any second. Maybe then you'll understand."

"Oh, I understand the feeling well, darlin'." I rub my temples, still staring at the floor. I can't bear to look at her after what I just did. "But if you're looking for a ride that'll make you feel alive and possibly cause serious bodily harm, I'm right here."

A sputtering laugh is enough to make me look up at her.

"Austin, I'm still pissed off at you. But, I have to tell you, that's easily the cheesiest thing I've ever heard somebody say."

It was embarrassingly cheesy and didn't exactly have the effect I intended. But, at least I got her to stop being quite so scared, mad, and disappointed in me for a few seconds. I shuffle my boot across loose hay on the ground as we stand in awkward silence.

After a tense few minutes, it feels like I should say something again. "No matter how angry or frustrated I might get, I wouldn't hit you. I'm not him."

"I know."

"I swear, I wasn't trying to scare you and I would rather die than do anything to hurt you. When I found out you were about to go out there something in me snapped. If I didn't stop you and something happened, I would never forgive myself."

She shakes her head, clearly annoyed with me. "I'm an adult capable of making my own choices, though. I don't need you to rush in pretending to be my knight in shining armour."

"That might be true, but I told you I would keep you safe. My protection doesn't only apply when we're on ranch property or when we're talking about *him*. I'm going to protect you from anything I think is dangerous. And you can be as mad as you want about it, but I have no problem throwing you over my shoulder and taking you home if it means keeping you safe."

A huff of air blows from her nose, making her nostrils flare. "Oh, I *will* be mad about it. Don't you worry."

"I'm sure you will, darlin'. I don't mind, though. Mad Cecily is sexy as hell." I cross my arms and lean against the wall. "Now, do you want your $300 in cash or should I give it directly to the girly store?"

"Cash. I'm going to bet on Denny's saddle bronc riding. Unless you're going to go toss him over your shoulder and carry him away, too? In which case, tell me so I can make the strangest bet ever and walk away from here rich."

"No, I'm not."

"Didn't think so." She rolls her eyes. "From what he told me, it sounds a lot more dangerous than what I was trying to do. Why aren't you this worried about him?"

"Because it's a different situation. For one, he's been doing this since we were kids. He didn't move here from the city less than four months ago. For two, I love my brother but not..." I swallow, waiting for her eyes to blink up to meet mine. "But not like the way I love you. That's why I can't let anything bad happen to you. That's why I'm not treating you the same way. I love you."

"Oh... Austin," she exhales my name. I can't fucking breathe with her watching me like this. This is it. The moment when she says this has been a rebound. Nothing serious. And then I go home alone again. Swells of fear and loneliness engulf me from all sides. Her leaving has always been inescapable. Falling in love with her was, too.

"It's okay if you don't feel the same way," I lie through my teeth. It's anything but okay, but I'll learn to live with it, eventually. "I'm the one who went and fell in love knowing damn well you wouldn't feel the same. *You* made it worth the risk of getting hurt, because you're incredible and make me feel things I didn't think I was capable of... whether you're in my life for a few months or fifty years, it'll never be enough for me. So, *fuck it*, I'll love you for as long as you're here. I fell for you, knowing I would most likely lose you one day. And if you don't have the same feelings, or if you want to leave the ranch at the end of the summer, I understand. I'm sure you'll want to go back to the city once KJ's not a threat. I just... needed to try."

Needed to try to give her a reason to stay, even if I've given other people the same reason with poor results. Beryl said it was worth the risk and, although I won't admit it to her, she's rarely wrong.

"You're always so confident I'm leaving." Her arms cross over her chest and she stares at me with narrowed eyes. Though her stance is hostile, those ocean-blue eyes are watery and wistful. "Do you notice how often you make comments about it? You've made it clear since day one that it's not even a question of 'if' for you. It's always 'when' I leave. I get the feeling your dad isn't the only person who's left by choice, but I think you should know I'm not her. Just like you're not KJ. We're talking about me and you, not them."

Her. So somebody told her about Savannah.

"You came to Wells Canyon because you needed to escape and this was a convenient place to do it. That's what makes me think you'll go. You know, once this is all over." Like Sav. I hate comparing them because I've realized they're really nothing alike except both women used the ranch as an escape and I fell in love in the process. And now, in another moment where history repeats itself, I declare my feelings and get trampled on. *Déjà fucking vu.*

"That's why I came here, not why I'm staying. Do you want me to leave?" Cecily steps toward me. Her striking blue eyes searching mine for clues about whatever's going on in my mind. I'm at a loss for what's going through my brain right now, but she always seems to be able to tell, even when I can't. "Because somebody who doesn't want me to leave probably shouldn't constantly talk about it. It's like the night I went to The Horseshoe—I wanted to stay, but then you shut down. You let me go even though it wasn't what you wanted. So... what do you want, Austin? Do you want me to leave?"

"No," I whisper. "No. Stay. *Please.*"

"Then I will."

For some reason, hearing her say that isn't enough to remove the vise grip holding steady on my lungs. It's not enough to ease years' worth of anxiety, and the softness in her eyes makes me think she understands.

She thinks she's the one who's broken, but I'm right there with her.

"You've been so focused on earning my trust, but you need to trust me, too. It's not easy to trust people—I understand that all too well. But I'm here and I'm telling you that I'm not going anywhere. So you gotta trust me. The ranch is my home. *You* are my home. There's nowhere else I would rather be than here with you."

My shaky, pathetic held breath finally lets go and her arms wrap around my torso, pulling my chest into her face. My wide, open palm falls to her lower back like it was made to rest there, and I hold her close. The sweet coconut scent of her shampoo filling my nose. I focus on the aroma, trying my damndest not to cry. And failing so horribly, I have to loosen the grip I have on her to wipe my damp eyes before they ruin her curls.

"I love you, Austin."

"You do?"

As if she's talking directly to my heart, she whispers into my chest, "You've never made me feel broken when I can't handle your touch. Even when I've told you about the most fucked up parts of myself, you don't stop showing me how much you care. And you don't only care about me—you take care of all the people you love. You're such a good man without even trying to be. You're sweet, protective, funny. You read cattle ranching magazines and watch *Happy Days* like a seventy-year-old man. How could I not love you?"

"You're not broken. Not to me. I've never wanted you to feel that way."

"Neither are you, Aus. I don't know how anybody could leave you. You're worthy of having somebody stay, and I want to be that person. I'm not leaving you. Not today, tomorrow, or next year. Not ever. In fifty years, you can die before me so you never need to feel abandoned again."

And then she's kissing me. Hard. Not like somebody who thinks I could ever hit her. Like somebody who's in love and can't get enough—I know, because it's exactly how I'm kissing her back.

I move to kiss the soft skin of her neck, goosebumps appearing as I make my way to her ear. "You're everything. All the time I spent pushing people away was just because I was waiting for you to pull me in. You're it for me, and I've been trying to wait for the right time to tell you how in love with you I am."

"Show me." She grabs me by the belt, slamming our hips together. The friction against my cock sends blood rushing to the area, warming my entire body. Her fingers dip under the waist of my jeans, a light touch against my bare skin.

"Show me I can trust you," she says just like she did when I kissed her for the first time. Right now it hits me so much harder because not fifteen minutes ago I made her question the faith she had in me. "Let me show you how much I love you."

"Darlin', I told you I wasn't going to take you in a dirty barn."

"Nuh-uh," she murmurs, gripping my quickly growing erection through my jeans. "You told me the *first* time wasn't going to be in a barn. This is far from our first time."

Now I'm really kicking myself for dragging her to this barn instead of tossing her in the truck and going home.

"I don't have a condom." I wasn't exactly anticipating this. Later tonight? Sure—I tossed a handful in the truck glove box before I left home. But I didn't put any in my pocket because I didn't think we'd find ourselves in a barn in the middle of the Wells Canyon rodeo grounds.

She lets out a soft laugh. "Fucking Kate. You know, she warned me this would happen."

My eyebrows raise in alarmed interest. I'm a bit worried about what they've been talking about for *this* sort of situation to come up.

"She said something about how rodeos have a way of making people horny and to be careful not to get knocked up tonight."

I choke on air, coughing into a fist and feeling every inch of skin on my face heat up. They were talking about us having a baby? *Us. Cecily and me.* Is that what she wants?

"Relax." She smiles, gripping my forearms. Probably holding me down because she's afraid I might bolt. "You look panicky. I told her it was absolutely *not* happening. I have an IUD, which has yet to fail me. So..."

The relief I feel is smaller than I would've expected—it scares me that I'm not as firmly against getting her pregnant as I should be, but I shove the fear aside and look her in the eyes. She smiles and I can't help but smile right back. "Are we doing what I think we're doing, darlin'?"

Her hot breath in the crook of my neck makes my dick jump to attention. I can't believe I'm actually considering fucking her here. First the drive-in and now in a *very* public barn at a *very* busy rodeo. In broad daylight. Without a condom for the first time in my life. Somehow she has that kind of hold over me.

"Please," she says.

I kiss her softly, holding her like she's the most important thing in the world. With fragility, tenderness, *love.* My hands catch in her hair, holding her still as I pepper kisses across her face, down her jaw, on her neck. I gently trace the curves of each breast overtop her t-shirt, then down her waist, stopping to squeeze her fleshy hips. If it weren't such a long drive home, I'd be taking her to a bed where I could properly ravish her right now. She lets out the softest, sweetest moan I've ever heard and the sound goes straight to my cock.

"Do you trust that I'd never hurt you?"

"Yes," she whimpers as I press the seam of her jeans into the right position for pleasure to rock through her.

"Do you trust that I love you?"

"Y-yes." Her back arches as I unbuckle her belt and slip my hand inside, stroking her lacy panties with my fingertips. I've barely touched her and she's already soaked through them.

"Do you trust that I'll protect you until the day I die?"

She gulps. "Yes."

My fingers plunge inside her wet, warm entrance. "Good, because none of those might seem true for the next few minutes, so you're going to have to trust that they are. We need to be rough, dirty, and fast if you don't want somebody to walk in on us."

"Just the way I like it."

Holy fuck.

26

Cecily

Austin pulls me into an empty stall filled with the dusty smell of alfalfa. His eyes are dark and, if I didn't trust him with everything I have, I'd be alarmed at how intense he is. *I do trust him*, even if things got a bit heated. The announcer's voice blares somewhere in the distance to indicate the end of the steer scramble, leaving thumping music to blast throughout the rodeo grounds for the remainder of intermission.

I'm fully clothed, yet I feel naked with my back against the wall and Austin staring at me with the look of a predator. He carefully rolls the sleeves on his dark blue plaid button-up, exposing his forearms, like he's about to get to work. His palm presses on the wall next to my head and his eyes pin me in place. Just as before, but without the fear and all of the heat. Then he kisses me as if he's starved for oxygen and I'm the only source, stealing my breath. Austin makes quick work of undoing my belt and shimmying my jeans down around my thighs. His fingers slide over my underwear and, discovering how wet I am, a deep groan rumbles from his chest.

"Fuck, you drive me wild. You know that?" His teeth graze my ear. "Knowing you're this wet for me—it's too much."

My hips reflexively roll into his hand, urging him to touch me. Inching closer to him. He hooks my underwear with a finger and slides them down to meet my jeans. I let out an agitated exhale, already struggling not to come undone when all I really want to do is yank his pants down and climb him. The empty ache is overwhelming and we're so perfectly made for each other—his cock is the only thing that will truly satiate me. His fingertip makes hard contact with my sensitive clit, waves of hot electricity pulse through my core, and a loud moan vibrates up my throat.

"Jesus Christ," I whine as I lean into his chest, losing all my senses.

With his free hand, he removes his cowboy hat and places it gently on my head. Claiming me. I smirk up at him. "Wear the hat, ride the 'Not-A-Cowboy'?"

"You're wearing the hat because I can't do *this* with it on, darlin'." Austin drops to his knees, burying his face between my legs, and runs his flattened tongue across my skin.

I suck in a breath as his tongue replaces his fingertips and begins drawing frantic circles on my clit. Warm currents travel my spine with each brush. My hips rock against his mouth in ecstasy, feeling the rough wooden wall scraping my back. Catching on the hem of my shirt and dragging it upward inch by inch until my stomach is exposed and my back's inflamed. And I cling to his head, fingers woven through his thick brown hair in a desperate attempt to stay upright. Every drag of his teeth and tongue over me drives me wild with the need for more of him.

Maybe it's the threat of being caught or knowing the man with his gorgeous, bearded face between my legs loves me, but I'm squirming and begging for release within seconds. My knees buckle and his hands come up to grip my ass, keeping me right where he wants me. His tongue plunges into me, and I press my hips into his face for even more friction—the sensation too much and also never enough. When my needy clit's sucked into his mouth, I explode. *Fucking explode.*

His name leaves my lips in a wail, loud enough I'm sure the entire damn rodeo heard—thanks to the perfectly timed song end.

When he stands up, his chest is heaving and a broad grin sweeps his face. "Good. I want every guy in this place to know you're mine. Let them all hear who's in here making you come."

Our hands fight to undo his pants, letting them fall in a heap around his ankles. I grab hold of his bare cock, pumping along his hard length, every vein throbbing against my palm. He curls into me with a groan when I use my leverage to drag him to me for a kiss. Spreading my legs as far as the rigid denim around my knees will allow, I tremble as I watch the tip of his bare cock tease my clit. Never slipping inside, even as I arch my back to try and coax him into me.

His smirk is obvious against my lips. "I love it when you're so needy for me. So fucking hot."

Austin's eyes meet mine as he notches the tip into me. Almost as if to confirm I still want to do this. I've never wanted anything more than I want him right now. My chest rises and falls in an unsteady pattern as I wait to feel him stretching me, filling the empty space that's yearning for him.

Austin's spit lands on the head of his cock, and his hand smooths it down his shaft, seconds before he powers into me with a deep, gravelly groan.

Okay, damn.

I'm feral. Grabbing the back of his head, I tug his hair by the roots and kiss him. His bottom lip snags between my teeth and the taste of iron fills my mouth but, even still, I don't stop kissing him.

"Aus, do that again," I pant. "Spit on your cock and fuck me."

A lustful smile crosses his lips. "Yes, ma'am."

Moving at a torturously slow pace for somebody who said we needed to make this quick, he withdraws all but the tip. I'm squirming and whimpering in his arms, begging to feel him.

"You like when I use my spit as lube? Moan for me, darlin'. Show me how much you love being my filthy girl."

"Please," I moan against the pulse point on his neck.

Leaning forward, spit falls from his mouth and drips down either side of his shaft. A whimper sneaks out around where I'm biting down on my lip, and his eyes flutter closed for a second in response. Kissing him with desperation, I reach between us and spread the liquid on his cock, feeling his moan travel down my throat.

"Oh, God." My hands fall against his chest, balling up fistfuls of his shirt.

His head drops to my shoulder for a moment before pulling out and spitting again. I'm trembling with anticipation—ready for another forceful, deep thrust to the hilt—when he tears himself away and spins me around. My hands barely come up in time to catch myself on the wall as his slick cock glides into me from behind.

"Holy fuck," he groans.

Every muscle in my body turns to jelly and my cheek hits the barn wall, dragging across the rough wood. Thank God for Austin's arms gripping my waist, or I'd be face-first on the cement floor.

"I got you. Rub your clit for me so I can fuck you into this wall. Play with your perfect pussy."

I reach back and slip my fingers into his mouth. He sucks with a groan and I drop my wet fingers between my legs. Frenzied but feather-light flicks catapult me to the edge until I'm struggling to remain in my own body.

True to his word, he's rough and fast, piling into me over and over again. Forcing my chest into the wall with every thrust. Angling my body just right, he hits the spot that has me gasping for air as he bites my neck and shoulder with low, needy grunts. My skin will be covered with plum-coloured marks tomorrow, but I don't care. Every moan makes him bite and suck harder. Every rough touch brings me closer to a fiery peak.

"That's my good girl. I want to feel you explode on my bare cock while I fill you up until my cum's running down your pretty thighs. Leave you thinking about this all fucking night."

"*Fuck*. Aus—it's so deep." I throw my head back as his hand slaps my bare ass. "Don't... fucking... stop. Give me more."

He pulls me further into the cradle of his hips, filling me with every single inch he has. Caught up in primal momentum, we're fucking away the angry emotions we had earlier. If I didn't know how much he loves me, I'd think he hates me.

My fingers are drenched, working my clit, and I fill the air with a guttural moan. The ravelled burning heat in my core threatens to burst. My lungs lose oxygen with each impassioned thrust.

Pressing his chest to my back, he leans in to whisper in my ear. "Who knew the pretty city girl likes to get dirty and rough in the barn?"

I certainly didn't. "I'll take it anywhere and any way my Not-A-Cowboy is willing to give it to me. I'm yours. Come in me. Fill me up, leave your cum running down my thighs, sign your fucking name inside me."

I turn my head to the side and he kisses me. All teeth and tongue as I collapse, feeling an orgasm rip me from head to toe. A tsunami destroying me for anybody else. As my moan echoes through the barn, his thrusts become sloppier and even more frantic. I hold tight to his forearms to stay steady and his deep, raspy moan drowns in my hair as he spills into me.

He lays his chest against my back, breathing in time with my rapid heart rate as he reaches down to shimmy my jeans back up. When they reach my ass, he pulls out with a shiver, leaving me uncomfortably empty. I'd rather it be like the drive-in, where he stayed inside until long after we had both come down from the sex high. It was the most intimate moment of my entire life. But cuddling with his dick inside of me isn't a possibility after a quickie in the barn.

"Fuck, I'm so lucky." His words slur slightly as he struggles to take a hard-earned breath and button up my jeans. "Do you know how perfect you are? I'm fucking obsessed with you."

I kiss him softly, wiping a bead of sweat from his forehead with my fingers. "I'm the lucky one—whatever this was, I think we need to make it a habit."

"Don't have to twist my arm. That was... *God*, I don't even know. I've never experienced anything like that before." He buckles his belt and reaches to smooth down my hair, which I assume looks as though I've been fucked in a barn.

Taking my hand in his, he walks me back out into the hot summer sun. I squint for a moment, my eyes struggling to adjust.

"You know, this is my family's barn." His head twists to point at the building we just walked out of. "Built it when I was about fifteen. My grandpa was rodeo president then. And, after that, my mom was president until... well... There's photos of us and everything in there."

With a firm grip on his hand, I tug him back inside. "Where? I want to see."

He scrunches his nose in irritation but relents. "In the tack room here." Flipping on the light switch, I'm faced with more than a dozen family photos hung on the walls.

"Ugh, I'm pissed I left my phone with Colt now. I *need* this picture of you." I point at a photo of a smiling little boy who's missing a front tooth. *Mutton Busting Champion '93* is the caption. "That's easily the cutest thing I've ever seen."

I study each photo. His grandfather proudly presenting his grandsons with various rodeo awards, Denny on the back of a bucking horse, the three boys as little kids sitting on a fence. I'm careful not to comment on any photos that include their father—a man that's the spitting image of Jackson. Actually, if it weren't for how insanely alike they look, I wouldn't have assumed he was related to Austin at all. Because Austin looks identical to his mom.

"Your mom's name's Lucy? Really?" I lean in to read a framed news article about her being Wells Canyon's first female rodeo president. "My middle name's Lucille."

"Hmm."

Trying to lighten the mood, I jokingly pat my stomach and add, "At least we have a girl name picked out for this rodeo baby."

As expected, he doesn't audibly laugh, but his nostrils flare and the corner of his mouth perks up at my terrible excuse for a joke. I'll count that as a win.

"She was beautiful. You have her eyes," I say, looking over to see Austin gnawing on his cheek, his stare fixated on the ground.

"Let's go. I decided something just now." I smile and nudge him with my shoulder.

"Oh?" He wastes no time flipping the switch and closing the door behind us.

"Tonight I want you to be—how did you put it? 'Quite fun'? You drink, I'll drive." My fingers weave into his like it's their permanent home and we walk the long way around the arena. The announcer's voice and cheers from the crowd boom through the humid air.

"You don't drive trucks, and I said I *used to* be fun."

"I'm capable of driving them, even if I don't particularly enjoy it. It's not fair that you've seen me incapacitated and I haven't had the pleasure of witnessing you let your hair down outside of sex. And I *really* love it during sex, so I'm dying to see you drunk. Also, I'm going to play the 'your cum will be leaking out of me all night' card. You owe me for dealing with the mess you made."

He laughs, his hand rubbing his brow bone as he weighs his lack of options. "What if KJ shows up?"

"What's he gonna do at a busy rodeo dance? I'll still be right there with you and the other guys all night." I squeeze his hand. "Please?"

"I'll drink, but don't say I didn't warn you when this gets outta hand."

"Oh, I can't wait." I drag him into the beer gardens and, after a brief stop at the bathroom, to the bar. I don't even care about having to remain sober and be responsible for our entire group of drunk cowboys. It'll be worth it just to see him let go.

It's nearly two a.m. and, unsurprisingly, the boys have gone completely off the rails. Beryl, Kate, and Jackson left five hours ago and I've been on my own to wrangle everybody else since. Although there have been times when I feel like I'm herding cats, I have no regrets because Austin's good mood is filling my heart. And, honestly, mending it too. It didn't dawn on me until after he'd consumed multiple drinks that I never questioned whether he could be a mean drunk. Despite my past, I guess I subconsciously knew it wasn't a possibility with him. And looking at him now—no shot. The only way he would potentially hurt somebody tonight is with an out-of-control dance move gone awry.

He grabs my hand for what must be the four-hundredth time tonight and begins to two-step. Anytime a country song comes on—which is a lot, given we're at a rodeo dance—he insists on two-stepping with me. Everything I know about it I learned while drunk dancing with Colt at The Horseshoe, but I'm trying my best to keep up. My aching feet cramp with every step. Austin's relentless, swinging me around and dipping me so low the ends of my hair skim the ground.

"Aus, I need to sit for a while. My feet hurt," I yell over the music as one song ends and another begins.

He sticks out his bottom lip for a few seconds before saying, "Fine, party-pooper. Love you!"

Party-pooper? These guys turn into complete ten-year-olds when they're drunk. Sitting back down, I take a headcount. *Oh, for fuck.* Colt's shirtless on stage with the band, but I'm too tired to give a shit. They'll kick him off if they don't want him there. Denny's making out with a girl on a picnic table. Sundial's dancing with Jacky and Austin. And Red's next to me. Good, everybody who should still be here is accounted for. I let out a relieved sigh.

"Havin' fun, Filly?" Red shouts my way.

"Yeah, my feet hurt and I'm getting tired though. Why aren't you out there?"

"I'm a lot of things, but not a dancer." He swigs from his beer bottle and we both watch the crowd jumping in time with the song's bass. "He loves you, eh?"

How do I respond to that? "Oh... yeah."

"He hasn't been back to this rodeo since the year their mom died. Sav barrel raced and he wouldn't even watch her race here. So I don't know what you said to get him here but it's good. I'm glad he came."

"Yeah, me, too." Truthfully, I said nothing except that I was going to be here. I smile at Red and then go back to watching Austin, acting like a complete idiot as he twirls shirtless Colt around. *God, I love him.*

When the band stops playing to announce last call for alcohol, the crowd groans while I bite my tongue to stop from cheering. It's been fun, but I'm painfully sober and no longer enjoying my babysitting duties. The boys grab their final beers and huddle around my picnic table.

"Heard there's an after party down at the roughies camp," Colt announces as he rushes up to us.

They all look at me intently and I shake my head with a firm no. "Not happening, I'm going home. It's too late and I'm too sober."

Austin comes up behind me, pressing his chest to my back and sloppily wrapping his arms around me tight enough to make me groan. "Might be fun."

"Do I need to remind you about the jizz situation happening in my underwear right now?" No amount of cleanup in a public rodeo bathroom was enough. My lips brush the shell of his ear. "Consider yourself lucky I stayed here this long."

"Fuck, are you trying to get me hard again?"

"Always." I wink.

With a kiss on top of my head, he looks at the guys and says, "Home time, boys. Listen to the lady."

"I'm taking all of you? How?" There are definitely not enough seats in Austin's truck. Or Red's. If I absolutely had to, I suppose I could make two trips, but it's really late and I'm exhausted.

"It's cool, we'll ride in the box." Denny slams his empty beer bottle down on the table. "Let's go."

"That's dangerous. No way."

"We do it all the time, Filly," Denny retorts.

I look to Austin for confirmation and he nods. This is absolutely not something that would be acceptable back in the city. Then again, it's probably not much more dangerous than sitting on your friend's lap in the back of a taxi. I've done that dozens of times to save on fares.

"Ugh, fine." I start toward the gated exit. "If you're not all at the truck in five minutes, I'm going home without you."

Austin's hand holds my waist as we walk through the half-empty parking lot to his truck. We're swaying, hips repeatedly bumping into one another. He laughs more on the five-minute walk than I've ever heard, and I've never been so in love.

Once the guys pile into the back, I start the truck and crawl it out to the main road—anxiously checking the rearview mirror every few seconds to make sure the guys are safe.

For the first ten minutes of the drive, Austin's so quiet I assume he must be asleep. Hearing his voice in the dark cab makes me jump. "I've been thinking."

Holding a hand to my chest until my nerves unscramble, I ask, "Thinking about what?"

"I decided I'm fine with being your second husband because I'll be your last."

I nearly veer off the road as I spin to look at him. *Good God, where did that come from?* My brain's mush. I'm unable to think in words, let alone form a meaningful sentence.

He turns sideways in his seat to continue talking. "You'd be my first and only. But you know what's funny?"

No, I don't because I have no idea where this conversation is heading. He's shared small, happy bits about his mom and his childhood, but the only time we touch on hard topics is when they're about my life. I've been dying for him to fully open up and let me in. Although, I'm not sure doing it while he's wasted is the best way.

"If Sav had said yes, I would be so fucked because you can't have two wives and I still would've wanted you. You're everything."

I hold back a laugh. "Okay, why don't you lie back and get some sleep."

"Like... well." His brain seems to short-circuit for a second. "I guess if she hadn't left then you wouldn't be here, right? So I wouldn't have met you and maybe I would've still been with her. But... nah, probably not—everybody keeps telling me she was never going to stay. News fucking flash for me. Should've told me before I made a fool of myself. Oh well... maybe I'm happy she fucked me over because I *really* like that you're here."

"I like that I'm here too." I reach over and squeeze his hand.

"I know you know about her. I can guess who told you... *Kate*. But, here's the gossip nobody knows." His words slur together slightly and he holds up a finger as if he's about to make an especially important statement. "Well... the day she left, I asked her to marry me. At the stupid fucking waterfall like a stupid fucking chump. Know what she said?"

I don't. I mean... I can make an educated guess, but I'm definitely interested in hearing about it now.

"She didn't think we were serious. *Excuse me?* Two years and living together isn't serious?" He throws his hands in the air with an exasperated sigh. "I don't know. It was probably my fault. I suck at talking about things so, like, I think I didn't make it obvious how serious it was for me."

"Seems pretty serious to me." My fingers tap anxiously on the steering wheel and, for the hundredth time, I flick on the cargo light to make sure all the guys in the back are accounted for. As much as I wanted him to open up, hearing him relive all this pain about a failed proposal makes my stomach churn. It's not fair, because he's never made me feel bad about being *married*, but try telling my heartburn that.

"Fuck it, though. Y'know?" There's a small hint of hurt in his voice even still.

"Maybe it's for the best she said no? Instead of staying and not being happy."

"Oh, yeah, no, for sure. My dad did. He stuck around here for my mom and then when she died, he just said *fuck it*." His hand flicks through the air.

Christ. Okay, we're getting into everything tonight.

"Austin." I look at him. Half of me wants to tell him to stop because this doesn't seem like a good conversation to get into right now. The other half wants to let him finally get this shit off his chest.

He lets out a long exhale. "It's fine. Everybody leaves and figures it's cool because I can handle it. Don't worry, Austin can clean up the mess. Grandpa dies, Mom dies. Not even six months apart, if you can believe it. And then Dad is all, like, 'poor me, I need to find myself and get outta my hometown'. *Fucking eh.* Leave the twenty-five-year-old in charge of everything."

With the exception of his brothers, who were forced into their roles almost as much as he was, everybody he's loved has left. No wonder he's insecure about us. And it's not like I'm helping ease his fear, considering I'm still legally married to somebody else. My nose burns and the corners of my eyes sting when I look at him. If it wouldn't lead to questioning from the boys in the back, I'd pull this damn truck over right now to hug him. He needs it badly.

"I'm sorry. It wasn't fair for you to be put in that position. You deserved better from your dad—regardless of how he needed to grieve, he should've considered you."

"It's... whatever." He rolls the window down slightly, taking a deep breath of the warm night air. "It was a long time ago and I probably shouldn't even still give a shit about any of this. Least now I got you."

"You do." I give him the best smile I can, to hold him over until I can wrap my arms around him. "I'm not going anywhere."

"By the way, this is serious, right? You and me? I don't want there to be any confusion this time."

"It's serious. And I seriously love you."

27

Austin

Stripped down to my boxers, I flop onto the bed with only a trace of a buzz still lingering. Turns out nothing sobers you up as quickly as thinking about your ex-girlfriend and family trauma. Cecily's washing her makeup off in the bathroom, leaving me alone with my thoughts. And that's a dangerous place to be.

After one of the longer waits of my life, she silently slips into the dark bedroom and pads to her side of the bed—probably assuming I'm asleep. The easy thing would be to go along with it and avoid the nagging feeling that I should clarify the shit I overshared.

The mattress compresses as her warm body slides under the sheets next to me. Her ass backs up and I automatically roll to my side to cuddle her. Pulling her into my chest, I cup her breast in my hand and nestle my cock against her ass with a content grumble.

"You awake?" she whispers.

Shit. I can't straight up lie to her.

"Mhm."

"You okay?" She places her hand over mine and rubs her soft palm on my skin.

"Perfect," I murmur against her wet hair. "You showered without me."

"I thought you were sleeping." Her voice is low as if there's somebody else in the room who we need to worry about waking up. "Or needed some alone time."

"I needed you," I admit.

"I'm here."

"About the shit I said on the way home tonight—"

She cuts me off, slowly rubbing the length of my forearm. "We don't need to talk about it, if you don't want to. It's okay you aren't a big sharer. I don't need to know every detail about your past to know you and love you."

"You've shared yours, though. So ask me, I'll tell you." I exhale slowly, immediately beginning to regret offering. Although, if there's ever a time to have this conversation, it's in bed with her at three o'clock in the morning.

"Red told me you haven't gone back to the rodeo since your mom died. Why did you come today?"

My lips press to the nape of her neck to remind myself why I'm willing to have this conversation. I kept Savannah at a distance and I think it's safe to assume it's why she never thought we were serious. I can't repeat that mistake with Cecily.

"You were there." My reason for going was as simple as that. "I did lie, though... I wasn't late because I had work to do. Well... I had work, but I probably could've put it off until tomorrow. I wasn't sure if I could handle the entire rodeo. When my grandpa and mom were alive, the rodeo grounds—and the ranch, obviously—were our entire life. I haven't been back since they died and I was nervous that it would be too much. Seeing people I haven't in years, hearing the announcer, watching the roping. But you made the entire thing a lot easier to deal with—kinda ripped the bandaid off for me."

She rolls over and I open my mouth to protest her changing positions until she kisses me. Her fingers stroke my beard and I can feel her lips smiling on mine. "Thank you for coming today."

"In more ways than one?" I smirk. Just the thought of what we did in the barn makes my cock flick.

"You're an idiot." She swings a leg over me and, fuck, I'm glad she's started wearing my T-shirts to bed because her bare pussy is pressed against my thigh.

"I knew you weren't going to hit me today." Her fingers slowly weave through my chest hair. "You're nothing like him."

"I scared you, though. So not as different as I hoped to be."

"No." She twists herself on top of me. My cock's viscerally aware of her close proximity and the lack of real clothing between us, leaving me struggling to focus on her voice in the dark. "You're a better man than he could ever dream to be. You're thoughtful and caring."

She kisses me on the lips.

"Strong."

Her teeth graze my ear.

"Selfless and loyal."

Her hips grind on mine as she kisses a trail across my chest.

"You make me come harder than anybody ever has. And you look so fucking good doing it."

She kisses me with a rough hunger as her hand slips down to grip my cock.

"And I love you, Austin."

Then she falls forward, wrapping the full weight of her warm body around mine. Clinging to me like a koala. Our chests rise and fall in symphony as we kiss. Leisurely, slow, explorative kisses while my hands traipse across her, slipping underneath her shirt to feel the smooth skin on her back.

She holds tight to me—the warmth from between her legs heating my crotch. It's making me wish I'd come to bed naked because I'm about ready to shred my boxers just to feel her against me. Bare skin on bare skin.

"Tell me about your parents."

"Ugh, do we have to right now?" I lift my hips, hoping my hard cock rubbing on her clit will change her mind.

"You thought you were going to get away with answering one question? Considering how talkative you normally are, I don't exactly trust I'll get another opportunity like this."

I sigh, placing my hands on either side of her hips. Normally being in this position with her is so much more fun.

Her hands tangle in my hair as she brings her lips to my ear. "I know it might be hard to talk about. But it's only me and you here—let me into your head. *Please.*"

I think she's catching on that the word "please" coming from her mouth with a soft, sweet rasp is my kryptonite. There's no request I would deny if she tacked please onto the end.

I groan. "Umm, they were high school sweethearts. Got married at nineteen and had me pretty much immediately after. Mom lived for this ranch and Wells Canyon—I have no clue how she did it all. She took care of things here, volunteered at our school, organized town events, took us to rodeos every weekend." I stop to kiss the bridge of Cecily's nose, thinking about the tiny scattering of freckles that have popped up over the summer. It may be pitch black in this room, but I can picture the location of every single one perfectly. "Anyway, um... She got breast cancer. It was me, Jackson, and Grandpa running the ranch while Dad drove her to the city for chemo all the time. Then Grandpa died, and my mom less than six months later. Afterward, my dad decided there wasn't anything worth sticking around for. Apparently, he never wanted to run the ranch in the first place. Which is funny, because he had no problem forcing the burden on me instead."

Her lips are soft and warm on my cheek. "Do *you* want to run it?"

"Yeah," I say without thinking. "It's too important a place for me to give it up. I wouldn't ever pressure our kid like that though... I mean—I don't mean we're going to have a kid."

"Shh, you're spiralling. I'm happy to hear our rodeo baby, Lucy, won't be forced into running the family farm, though." I hear her hand jokingly pat her stomach and, for a second, I allow myself to think about a sweet baby girl with Cecily's blonde hair. Honestly, it's not something I would even be the slightest bit unhappy about. "You know his leaving wasn't because of you, right?"

"Not because of. But definitely in spite of."

"I wonder if he regrets it. It's not the same thing—*at all*—but I was quick to ditch my parents when my head was a complete mess. And I regret it." Soft fingers create a path back and forth across my chest and I want to tell her that he doesn't regret anything. Except I can't say it with any amount of certainty because, the truth is, I don't know. I don't remember details about the last time we spoke but we definitely didn't talk about grandpa or mom or the ranch or how either of us felt or *anything* that fucking mattered.

"Maybe he does." I lose myself in wondering.

The only sound in the room is the quiet whir of the ceiling fan. Cecily's head rests on my shoulder and, although it's hard to tell from this angle, I think her eyes are closed. Her balled fist rests in the centre of my chest, perfectly still.

"Are you sleeping?" I run a hand over her hair, releasing the intoxicating coconut aroma I love so much.

"Just thinking."

"Whatcha thinking about?"

"How happy I am that every girl who came before me didn't realize how good they had it."

"I'm the lucky one. I don't deserve you for a damn second, darlin'. But, if you let me, I'll work every day to become a man who's worthy of loving you. I'll give you more of myself than I did with any girls from my past, and I'll treat you better than any of the guys from yours."

My finger traces her cheekbone, then down her jawline. Her hand holds my face and her forehead presses into my jaw. One minute turns to two turns to three. Holding each other in a darkened room, in a world made up only of us.

28

Cecily

Dusk settles over the ranch, soaking the kitchen in golden orange light, as I help Kate wash the last of the dinner dishes. With the boys gone late, I came over to the big house to eat with her and Odessa. I sling the drying towel over the oven handle and grab a cold beer from the fridge on my way to the back porch. Kate follows with a glass of ice water. It's the perfect late-summer night. Loud crickets chirp, a warm breeze carries mist from the nearby sprinkler, and the hayfields are a rich emerald hue.

"You know, when I was pregnant with Odessa, I couldn't wait for it to be over because I couldn't wait to hold her. This time 'round, I just want it to end so I can sleep comfortably, drink a beer, and not risk peeing my pants every time I move too fast." She sinks down onto the porch swing with a loud exhale.

"Only a few weeks left now, at least."

She fans herself with her hand. "And with this heat, it cannot come soon enough. Plus, another month and we'll be deep into the busy fall. We got a third hay cut to do, a couple thousand long yearling cattle to ship out, and the entire herd comes home for the winter around mid-October. Once all the fall work starts up, Jackson will be almost entirely useless to me here."

"I know it's not the same, but I'll help with anything you need."

"Honestly, you're probably a better help than Jackson any day." She laughs. "I love my husband, but it's like his brain turns to oatmeal as soon as a baby starts crying. Can break the wildest of horses but panics and freezes with a seven-pound newborn in his arms."

"I'm sure he'll be better this time around. Since he's been through it all once." I take a long sip and watch Odessa run through the sprinkler set up in the garden. Her pink knee-length dress is soaked and her light-brown hair is plastered to her face and neck.

"Damn well better be if he expects me to ever do this shit again."

The sun is sinking below the treetops, and headlights shining over the space where the lilacs used to be alert us to the approaching vehicle before we hear the tires crunching along the road. Kate leans forward for a clearer view of the ranch entrance.

"Huh, never seen that car around." Creases form between her eyebrows as her eyes narrow to a squint, trying to determine who would be showing up here so late in the evening.

I stand up to see past her and my knees immediately buckle at the familiar headlights and grill. My body falls to a heap on the wooden decking and shooting pain skyrockets up the length of my arm when I try to catch myself. The edges of my vision become black. The haze barely allows me to make out the knots in the wood decking an inch from my face. I think I might be sick. Or scream. My mind has to be playing tricks on me. There's no way. He couldn't have found me.

Not here.

Not him.

"Oh my God, are you okay?" Kate's focus shifts to me.

Through sharp breaths and around the hard rock in my throat, I manage to squeak out a single sentence. "Take Odessa and go inside."

She places a hand on my shoulder. "Are you—"

"Go the *fuck* inside, Kate. Now." I try not to scream. The last thing I want to do is draw attention to us back here. With any luck, the twilight kept us hidden from sight well enough.

My skin must be blanched with fear because Kate's eyes grow wide and cut over to where the car was seconds ago. Then back to me.

"Cecily." Kate's voice is barely audible over the blood pooling in my ears. She's a human-shaped blob through the lilac haze clouding my vision. I blink rapidly, trying to clear the blanket over my eyes and determine what I need to do next.

I have zero fucking clue.

Austin. *I need Austin here.* I may have handled KJ a million times on my own in the past, but I don't want to. Not anymore. Not when Austin promised me I wouldn't have to.

"Odessa Wells, get inside!" Kate whisper-yells. Jumping to her feet, she grabs her daughter by the upper arm. "Go up to mommy's room and stay there until I come get you, okay?"

"Can I do a make-over?" Odessa pushes the damp hair from her eyes.

"Sure, baby. Makeup, hair, clothes, even mommy's high heels. Stay up there until I come get you. Do *not* come downstairs."

Odessa's eyes nearly pop out of her head and she sprints inside. Her small feet thud their way loudly up the stairs and a faint slam of Kate's bedroom door signifies she's safe and happy. At least there's a small glimmer of hope that she's not in harm's way, even if I am.

"Kate, you should go inside, too. Go be with Odessa." I work to capture a single breath, pressing myself back to my feet despite the trembling in my legs. "I need to deal with this myself."

"No, we'll both stay put until the boys get back. Should be soon."

How soon will be soon enough, though?

Kate pulls her cell phone from her back pocket and types in a number. "And if they don't get here quick enough, the boys' cop cousin, Nick, should be able to get here in about half an hour."

Austin almost certainly doesn't have cell service—as soon as you get too far from the main buildings, you lose it—but that doesn't stop me from dialling his number over and over.

He's going to figure out I'm here the moment he sees my car. I should've taken Austin up on his multiple offers to get a truck instead of being stubborn. Then I could've hidden in a closet somewhere until he left. I might've stood a chance of him never coming back here if simply hiding was an option.

"The longer it takes him to find me, the more worked up he's going to get." *The more dangerous he's going to get.*

"Nothing the guys can't handle. It's not worth you going out there."

"Stay here."

Whether driven by naivety or insane courage, I will myself to move in his direction. My feet feel like they're encased in cement, but I manage to work up the strength to shuffle like a zombie through the house. From the back porch, down the dark hallway. The metal handle on the front door burns my palm and a hand on my shoulder makes my heart stop.

"Sorry, I didn't want to yell after you in case he's right outside," Kate whispers. Her words are tattered. She's scared. "Nick will be here as soon as he can. If you're going out there, I'm coming with you. If anything, he'll know you're not here alone. Maybe buy you time until the boys are back."

I shake my head but she grabs either side of my face, forcing my eyes to fall upon hers.

"Cecily, quit being stubborn. You're basically my sister now and I'm not letting you go out there alone. So either you stay inside and wait for the guys, or we go out there together. Either way, I'm right with you."

The silence as I deliberate my options is broken when KJ screams my name. Loud enough to nearly shatter glass.

Fuck.

After a long, painful breath, I reach for the handle again and step outside.

He silently scrutinizes me with furrowed eyebrows. I look down at my worn t-shirt and dirt-stained jeans. The soil under my fingernails from gardening. The tanned, freckled skin on my arms, my hair in two messy French braids. And this is the first time he's seeing me without makeup. All of which are things Austin has never made me feel ugly for. In fact, his gaze makes me feel beautiful, sexy, wanted. Despite that, thinking about how KJ sees me right now causes sudden self-consciousness. I look nothing like I did when I left him—obviously I know that, deep down, but it hasn't been something I've put much thought into.

"Wow. When some guy in town told me you'd be here, I honestly thought he was fucking with me." His harsh laugh cuts through my flesh. At least he doesn't seem to have a gun. It very well could be hidden—honestly, it probably is—but it's not currently in his hand. That buys me time. "Look at you, looking like a damn country bumpkin."

"What do you want, Kyson?" His stupid name feels like a razor blade cutting its way up my trachea.

My shoulder leans against the post at the top of the porch stairs. I'm aiming for an uncaring demeanour, actually needing the stability to keep from toppling over again. Kate rests her elbows on the railing next to me, close enough I can feel her seething. There's no melody from the windchimes—the air oddly still with the impending tornado in front of me.

"It's been long enough, Cecily. I hope you had your fun making me search all over the damn countryside for the past few months, but it's time to come home now."

"No."

"No?" He grits his teeth. "I came all this way to get you and that's your response?"

I look past him, at Austin's home—*our home*. This is where I belong. With him, in our comfy bed or on our worn couch watching *Happy Days* and eating KD with hot dogs. I don't want to be anywhere else. "I didn't ask you to look for me. And I'm sure as hell not going back with you. I'm staying here. I'm done, KJ. I'll file for divorce as soon as I can."

His eyes flash from me over to Kate. She was right about needing to stand out here with me. He's always on his best behaviour when other people are present.

Except, I guess, when it comes to the D-word.

"The fuck you will, Cecily." Both the volume of his voice and the anger behind it increase drastically. I guess he's done, too. Done playing nice, that is. "You're my wife and I'm not signing any fucking divorce papers. You're coming home with me right now. Cut the shit."

"I'm not." I bite the inside of my cheek, and Kate's hand slips across my lower back. "I'm staying here. This is my home now."

"*Babe.*" He says the word like it's an insult, and I tense in response. "You're coming with me. One way or the other. Don't make me force you."

He gives Kate a playful eye roll and smirk, as if to say, "*damn wives just never listen to what's best for them, eh?*". I don't need to look at her to know she doesn't return the pleasantries. The drop in his face, from sociopathic grin to murderous scowl, says it all.

"The cops are on their way. I suggest you get off my property," Kate says with a cold tone.

"Cecily, let's go. Enough is enough. Quit being a fucking cunt. Don't make me do anything to embarrass you in front of your little friend here." He takes a step in our direction and my spine stiffens against Kate's hand. Her fingers curl on my shirt, gripping as if she's going to be strong enough to keep him from grabbing me and running.

Thank fuck for Kate.

"I'm not coming with you. You're an abusive, worthless, piece of shit and I wish I had never married you. A few months away have made me realize you never deserved me. You never loved me. You never treated me the way you should have. I'm not yours anymore. Leave me the fuck alone."

Fuck yeah. I'm pleasantly surprised by my boldness. I've spent hours imagining what I might say if he showed up here, but I never thought I would actually have the guts to stand up to him if the time ever came.

"Let's fucking go," he shouts as he starts toward us.

"Leave!" I scream at the top of my lungs. "Leave me alone. Go fucking die and rot in hell."

"Don't make me do something I don't want to do, Cecily."

The steady clomping of fast-paced horses makes the jittery muscles around my heart ease. KJ doesn't have the faintest idea what he's about to be in for, but he stops in his tracks and turns toward the sound.

Austin.

Austin comes around the corner of the stables at a breathtaking pace. On horseback, flying past the bunkhouses with Denny and Jackson flanking his sides. I struggle to stop myself from running toward them. Climb up on his goddamn horse and ask him to take me to the lake. Take me anywhere but here. Not far behind, Red, Jacky, and Colt are hot on their heels.

I look at KJ in time to see his nostrils flare and a single laugh burst from his lungs. "Ah, so this is why you came here, isn't it? Fuck, you always have been such a *fucking whore*, haven't you? Came here to let a bunch of cowboys take turns with you or what?"

Austin's horse, Jubilee, isn't even fully whoa'd up yet and he's leaping to the ground. Dust clouds around where he lands, and he strides toward us with a fire in his eyes.

"You okay, darlin'?" he calls out to me.

I give him a shaky, uncertain nod. I think I'm okay.

Then he turns and says, "You KJ?" And Austin, *my fucking cowboy*, smashes his fist straight into KJ's nose.

29

Austin

After a long day in the blazing heat, all I'm thinking about is a cold shower and Cecily's hands on my tired muscles. The final two-kilometre stretch back to the barn is always the slowest. Once you crest the ridge, there's a clear view of home for the rest of the ride. Knowing she's there, so close yet so far away, makes time drag.

That's never been more true than it is tonight. After more work than I expected fixing irrigation, we stayed out later than normal—well past dusk. Despite having an intimate familiarity with the trails, I prefer not to ride them in the dark. So we take the trip home slow, each man keeping a keen eye for potential dangers. Potholes, stray roots, large rocks.

Jacky's the one who spots the biggest potential danger. One I had accidentally let my guard down about.

"Were we expecting a visitor?" He points toward the big house and my gaze follows.

A dark-coloured car is sitting with headlights on. There's not enough daylight to determine the exact colour or make, and we're too far away to see any people outside. None of that matters.

I know exactly who that is.

The sudden tripping of alarm bells and a sinking feeling deep in my stomach is more than enough for me to no longer give a shit about anything except getting back as soon as physically possible.

"We weren't." My spurs hit the mare's sides, sending her down the hill at breakneck speed. Hell-bent on getting home, I'll run this horse ragged and, assuming we get there safely, apologize to her later. Right now, neither the possibility of my horse breaking her damn legs or flinging me from a cliff is enough to slow me down. Potential dangers be damned, I'm making her run as fast as she can. Never once easing up even on the tightest switchbacks or steepest inclines. When she fights me—tries to whoa up around corners or near obstacles—I kick harder. Yell harder. Push harder.

It doesn't matter if I'm bloodied and crawling to Cecily by the time we reach the house. I *will* get there. I *will* get to her.

I assume I'm tearing down the hillside alone until I hear Denny yelling at his gelding to pick up the pace. He and Jackson are right there, with the rest of the men following suit. They must've figured out why I took off, and they're willing to put themselves and their horses in danger to race through the blackness of night with me.

My heart's pounding and the brutal wind on my face makes my eyes burn. If anything happened while we were gone, I will *never* forgive myself. I got too lax about Cecily. Somebody should've been with her. After so many weeks filled with empty threats over text messages and no word from people in town about a person matching his description, I had started to think KJ would never materialize. Hell, he's known she's in Wells Canyon for a full week and *still* nothing. It doesn't matter now, because he's at the house. And I'm not.

"We runnin' for the reason I think we are?" Jackson pulls up next to me as we reach the flat, wide-open field at the bottom of the hill.

"Think so," I shout.

I glance at my brother and see untethered fear in his eyes. He has as much of a reason to be worried as I do, with Kate and Odessa at the house right now. Even without knowing all of the details, he trusts my fear enough to be scared himself.

Fuck, leaving the girls alone was straight negligence.

Rounding the corner by the stables, I see Cecily and Kate standing on the porch. Backlit by the small light next to the front door. And hovering at the bottom of the stairs is the piece of shit who, based on the expensive car, must be KJ.

Momentary relief flashes across both of the girls' faces when they see us approaching, and my feet are hitting the ground at a run before Jubilee's even stopped. I want to kill this fucking man.

But, first, and most importantly: Cecily.

"You okay, darlin'?" I search her face to be sure the nod she gives is the truth.

We made it. We got here in time.

Now. Him. "You KJ?" I ask, and he gives a single, sneering nod.

No need to introduce myself—my fist does it for me. A hard blow lands square in the centre of his face and, based on the immediate blood pouring from his nostrils, I just broke the fucker's nose.

"I have a gun, asshole," he says. Holding one hand to his profusely bleeding nose, KJ grabs frantically at the car door handle.

Denny and Red are quick to pull him back, but not before his hand catches on the handle, swinging the black passenger door wide open. Sure enough, there's a handgun on the seat. Most likely illegally owned—definitely being illegally transported—given the laws in Canada.

No clue why I was ever concerned about this prick putting up a good fight. He may be taller than I am, but his spindly body and perfectly pressed clothing put me at ease. This guy's never fought a day in his life. And if you're going to bring a gun to a fistfight, don't leave it in the fucking car.

"This gun?" Denny lets Red grab both KJ's arms, so he can look at the gun. "Buddy, the safety's on and it's not even loaded. What did you think you were gonna do with this?"

I hear Jackson's unmistakable howling laugh from somewhere behind me on the porch.

KJ certainly isn't finding this funny. "Cecily, what the fuck is—"

"No." I cut him off, stepping to the side to block his view of *my girl*. All of the laughter stops around us. "You don't talk to her. Me and you are talking now, asshole."

"She's my *wife* and I'll talk to her as much as I please."

I smile, maintaining a hard stare into his dead, evil eyes despite the way the word *wife* rolls off his tongue like a slap to my face. "On paper, maybe. But you can be damn sure I know her better than you do, treat her better than you do, and *fuck her* so much better than you could ever hope to. In every way that matters, she's mine."

"Jesus, you're such a fucking *whore*," he shouts over me.

My fist slams into his jaw, sending bloody spit hurtling from his mouth. All over his fancy, baby-blue dress shirt.

"The fuck did I tell you about not talking to her?" I grab his jaw, pressing my thumb against the tender flesh. He winces. "Unless you want more, I suggest you listen."

The moment I let go, he spits at me. I don't even give a shit when his bloody spit lands on my already-filthy work shirt. It's the principle. I deck him again. And again... for good measure. He keels over, fighting for breath and spitting more blood onto the dusty gravel at his feet.

"Hey, darlin'?" I call over my shoulder, not taking my eyes off the douchebag in front of me, watching him frantically wipe at the blood spilling from his nose. Within seconds, Cecily's standing next to me. My hands fall to her arms and I look into her sad, blue eyes. "You're sure you're okay?"

"Yeah," she whispers. Her focus darts from me to him and the way her lip trembles makes me want to beat the ever-living shit out of him.

"I'm sorry I wasn't here sooner," I whisper, placing soft kisses on her cheeks and nose. "Don't look at him, Cecily. Look at me. You're safe. You trust me, right?"

She answers by kissing me hard on the lips and somehow this feels so much more like a victory than breaking his nose does. She palms either side of my jaw, kissing me as if there's nobody else present. Slow, hard, and like she's trying to prove a point as much as I am.

Fuck you. I win.

"When the cops get here, I'm pressing charges," KJ yells.

"No, you won't." I grab Cecily's hand and stare him down. "You're trespassing, for starters. With a gun I'm quite confident was illegally obtained."

Cecily clears her throat, gripping my hand like it's the only thing keeping her steady on her feet. "If you say anything, I'll tell the police about everything you've done to me. I sent my friend text messages when we were still together. I have proof. You say a word and I won't just go to the cops—I'll tell your family, your coworkers, your friends. I'm sure Nana would like to hear the truth."

Even in the dark, I can see how hard his Adam's apple bobs. He has nothing, and he knows it.

That's fucking right. I knock our conjoined hands lightly against her hip and give her a small smile to show how goddamn proud I am of her.

"Can you please go get your wedding ring for me, darlin'? Colt can go with you." I tuck a strand of hair behind her ear. "And there's a brown envelope in my sock drawer. Grab that too."

Her eyes narrow in confusion but she turns to Colt, who holds out a hand to lead her away.

"You know that saying, right?" KJ has the nerve to speak up again. *Somehow.* "If they do it with you, they'll do it to you. She's cheating on me with you. What makes you confident she won't turn around and cheat on you? Maybe with one of these other cowboys here."

He's trying to get into my head, which might've worked if I didn't know everything I do about their relationship. As it stands, he's just talking for the sake of talking. Throwing shit at the wall, as they say.

"You see, I think she might be inclined to stay with me because I'm not hitting her and threatening her with a gun."

"She's a psycho, lying bit—" His words are cut off by the loud thud from my knuckles hitting his brow bone.

God, I'm starting to actually grow bored of punching him.

"Nothing you say is going to make me doubt her. Like I said, I know Cecily better than you do, pissant. Now—you're going to shut the fuck up and listen. You speak, I hit you. When she gets back here, you're going to act like the proper fucking gentleman that you desperately want the world to think you are. You're going to do exactly as I say, no questions. And *then*, you're going to leave. You're never going to come near Cecily again because, if you do, me and my men here will track you down and kill you."

KJ snorts.

"Don't believe me?" I challenge him. "I own over 100,000 acres of private land and a chunk of ground with so many buried animal carcasses you'd simply get lost in the shuffle. No neighbours to hear you scream for dozens of kilometres and the only cop in town to look into your missing case is my first cousin. Half my guys have been to prison and have no objection to going back for the right cause. I suggest you choose your next actions accordingly."

"Hell, we could run him out a hundred kilometres into the woods and leave him to die 'naturally'," Denny suggests. "Break both legs for good measure. Tragic hiking accident."

The bridge of KJ's red nose wrinkles as he side-eyes Denny.

"So, what'll it be?" I look him up and down, still amazed Cecily could've ever been interested in *this* pathetic excuse for a man.

"Whatever. You can *fucking* have her, you redneck asshole. She's a bit—"

This time it's Denny's fist that lands square in his gut.

"God, he's fucking stupid. Who gets hit that many times and doesn't learn to shut their trap?" Denny shakes his head with a twisted smile as KJ slumps against his car.

The wide-eyed expression on Cecily's face when she returns to see KJ, beaten and filthy on the ground, almost makes me wish we hadn't handled this situation in such a brutal way. Not because he didn't have it coming—he absolutely did. I just didn't stop to consider whether kicking the shit out of him could be traumatic or hurt her until her eyes meet mine with a look I don't recognize.

"Hey." I grab her shaky hands. "Maybe you should go. Colt can sit with you if this is all too much."

"No. I'm okay. Here's the envelope you asked for." She fishes in her pocket and pulls out a thin gold band, scrunching her nose as she hands it to me. "And the ring."

My lips press softly on the top of her head and her shampoo temporarily replaces the stench of blood and dirt embedded in my nostrils. "Thank you, darlin'. I promise this will all be over soon."

Turning back to the piece of filth on the ground, I say, "So, pissant, ready to do what I tell you now?"

Either because he learned his lesson or because he's physically incapable of speaking, KJ merely groans. *Finally.* As much as I'd love to see him dead, I don't think I can hit him again with Cecily watching. Not with that look on her face.

"You're going to sign the post-dated divorce paperwork in this envelope. And Cecily's going to file it exactly one year from the date she left your sorry ass. You won't fight it, you won't say a damn word, or I will hunt you down and end your pathetic life. Lucky for you, she's not going to ask for anything in the divorce... darlin', you don't want anything from him, do you?"

She shakes her head no, covering her mouth with a hand to hide her smile. Finally, it seems I've made the *right* choice for once.

"And then, my guys here are going to make sure you get yourself back to town. And I never want to see you or hear your name again. If I catch wind about your scrawny ass anywhere within a hundred kilometres of this ranch, or if you ever bother *my girl* again, I'll make good on my promise to end you."

I pull the paperwork from the envelope and Jackson clambers down the stairs to hand me a pen. Crouched down in front of him, I growl, "You fuck it up, you're a dead man."

His bloodshot eyes are already so swollen he struggles to look up at me, and he signs his name with a shaky hand. It seems like there are a hundred pages with how painstakingly slowly he scrawls his signature. Blood stains the bottom of each one. I don't take a single breath the entire time, waiting for him to do something that'll give me no choice but to commit murder.

He doesn't.

It's entirely anticlimactic—*thank God*, for Cecily's sake.

Denny and Red pull him to his feet as Colt jumps into the driver's seat of the fancy-ass car. "*Fuck yes*, I can't wait to rally this thing down the dirt road. Denny—*man*—you gotta ride shotgun. How fast you think this thing goes?"

Jacky's already waiting with my truck running to follow them to town. I grab KJ's jaw, forcing it open with a harsh squeeze. His eyes are pleading for mercy, and he's fucking lucky I refuse to do anything that might scare the woman I love.

Instead of finishing him off—even though it's arguably what he deserves—I pull the gold wedding band from my pocket and hold it out behind me. "You want to do the honours, Cecily?"

Her footsteps are slow but steady, and she delicately scoops the ring from the palm of my hand. She tugs at the knot on the sweaty, dirty wild rag around my neck until it comes free. Her long exhale blows warm on my arm, and she tosses the ring into his mouth like she's playing a game at the fair. His jaw tenses with a small gag just before she crams my bandana in.

"Choke," she snarls.

She wins, motherfucker.

I'm not even watching as Denny and Red shove him into the back seat and slam the car door. My body's already firmly wrapped around Cecily, pulling her head into my chest and absorbing loud sobs that ring through the quiet night air. I stroke her hair, rougher than I'm intending, as I fight back my own emotion. My chin rests on her forehead and I hold on so tight she struggles to breathe.

"Shhh, darlin'. He's gone. You're safe," I whisper. "I got you. I'm here. I love you."

Her wrists wrap around my neck and I scoop her into my arms. If only I'd been able to carry her away from here earlier. Before he showed up. Saved her from everything.

My chest tightens as I look down at her. She's too good for the shit she's been dealt. And now it's my job to try and undo the damage KJ has done to her heart.

Her tears roll down my neck, drenching my shirt collar as I cautiously walk through the dark. My deep, hoarse coos slowly calm her cries until she's perfectly silent, save for the occasional sniffle.

"I love that you did all of this for me." Her voice is muffled against my neck as I fumble with the front door handle.

"Told you that you're safe as long as you're here, didn't I?" I softly set her on top of the bed. *Our bed.* "I'm going to shower quickly and then I'll be right here, okay?"

"I'm coming with you." She quickly stands up, her knees nearly buckling as the adrenaline drains from her body. I look at her, prepared to protest, but it's no use. She's already padding barefoot across the floor to the bathroom.

I pull at the hem of her shirt, lifting it overhead, then tug her jeans and panties down to her ankles. Under any other circumstance, I would kiss her from head to toe and take my time indulging her. Instead, I tuck an arm around and bring her into the shower. A low sigh escapes her lips as she leans back against my chest, letting the warm water run over our snuggled bodies. Washing away *his* blood from my hands. Carrying away the dried salt left by her tears. Coating us like a healing ointment.

"Did I scare you tonight?" I squish her soft stomach, pulling until her back is flush against my body.

"That was a side of you I've never seen before." Her words make my heart temporarily seize. She strokes my forearm, telling me she doesn't mean it in a negative way, giving my lungs permission to work again. "It was intense and possessive—or, no. Protective. But I wasn't scared. Not after you got there. All I could think about when I saw his car pull up was how badly I needed you."

"Okay, good. I was worried you'd be upset with me for acting that way. Scared I'm the kind of guy who goes around breaking noses regularly."

"I *know* you aren't that guy. I would've been disappointed if you hadn't punched him. What did you think I'd want you to do?"

"I don't know. Maybe you'd think we should've talked it out like adults."

She laughs under her breath. "I told him to drop dead moments before you showed up. I wasn't interested in watching you try to reason with him..." She's quiet for a moment, holding a damp cloth over her eyes to ease the redness from crying. "Were those divorce papers for real?"

"They're real. You'll need to fill out and sign your parts, of course. But at least you don't need to worry about getting his signature."

She spins around to face me with a hesitant half-smile. "So... wait. I feel like my brain isn't working right. How? Why? I think I blacked out as soon as you said what was in the envelope."

I'm tempted to give the air a quick fist pump. Weeks of feeling like I've made so many awful decisions when it comes to Cecily. *Finally, the right one.*

"They're real, they've been sitting in my drawer for weeks, and they're post-dated for May. You can't legally file for divorce until then, but my lawyer said waiting a year is a lot easier than proving you need an earlier divorce because of abuse. I thought getting him to sign everything would be a lot harder than it was, though. I started making plans to go pay him a visit this fall if he didn't turn up here."

"And then... I'll be done with him?"

"Darlin', you already are. He's gone."

30

Cecily

He's gone. I don't know why, but I thought I would have a stronger emotional reaction to everything. Of course, I had a breakdown right after the boys drove him down the driveway. Now that I've finally weathered the storm, I'm just... okay. *I think, anyway.*

"Okay."

I lick the clean water droplets off my lips and reach up to his jaw. The twist in my wrist reminds me of my earlier fall with startling pain. I suck a harsh breath through my teeth and yank my hand away.

"What's wrong? Did he?" Austin's gaze darkens as he tentatively reaches for my hand.

"No. I just... I fell on the porch earlier and hurt my wrist. I forgot about it until now."

He tenderly inspects my hand and wrist. There doesn't seem to be bruising or swelling; just a sharp pain if I bend it too far. He nods thoughtfully. "I think it's just a minor sprain. I'll get you some ice once you're in bed. Stand here, darlin', and let me help you wash your hair—you shouldn't be using this wrist."

I relax into the warm water, and he delicately massages shampoo onto my scalp. My eyes slowly close, making it difficult not to fall asleep with his gentle, loving touch. Then jets of soothing water rinse my hair, and he follows up with a healthy coat of conditioner.

Austin smothers my skin in both kisses and body wash. Ensuring every inch of me has been adequately covered by both, working his way down my body. Despite the heat and humidity, his lips create a path of goosebumps. Every part of today is worth it for this moment.

I'm floating, soaked in a delicious sleepy haze, when he shuts the water off and wraps a towel around me. My wet hair clings to my neck, releasing a trickle of water down my chest. Standing behind me, Austin attentively runs a comb through my hair, stopping only to wipe the tears clung to my eyelashes.

"What would I do without you?" I whisper. Not only about the shower. Everything. He's done *everything* for me.

"I think you'd manage just fine. But I'm happy to be of service." He tucks my towel tighter around my shoulders. "Ready for bed?"

Oh, God. Yes, I am.

In a familiar scene to our first time, I stand in front of Austin and drop my towel. Overcome with the need to have him touch me. Softly caress my body with the same hands I watched punch my ex-husband in the face earlier. My bare breasts press into his chest and I'm slipping my hands behind his head. The hair at the nape of his neck twirls around my finger. "Aus, thank you. For everything you do. Especially for kicking the absolute shit out of KJ today. *Please*, take me to bed and touch me."

"Here I thought hitting him like that scared you." His hands swipe over me, ignoring the prickling tension in my muscles, and finally land on the small of my back, drawing me into him.

I kiss him. "I was scared when he showed up. And then there you were. Riding in like the cowboy hero from an old western and punching him without hesitation."

"I should've been there sooner. I never should've left you."

"Don't do that." I trail a hand down his stomach. "You were there when it mattered."

"I always will be."

His hands grip the backs of my thighs, lifting me into him, and he takes me to bed. We flop together onto the crisp sheets, and I take my place in the crook of his arm. My place, my home, my love. It all could've been gone in a blink if KJ hadn't been brazenly confident in his ability to wordsmith me into his car. If he'd started the conversation with a gun already in his hands, there might not have been enough time to wait for Austin.

"What did it feel like?" I ask while staring at his right hand under the warm glow of our bedside lamps. Lacing and unlacing our fingers repeatedly. His knuckles are marked up, a bit swollen.

"What?"

"Punching him. I've never punched somebody before, but I wanted to hit him."

"Should've said something, City Girl. Watching you knock the smug look off his face would've given me spank bank material for life." His free hand trails along my thigh. "As far as how it felt... hitting him was good, but kissing you in front of him was so much better."

I roll my eyes with a laugh into his chest. "You just liked marking your territory. Men are animals."

"Who kissed who, darlin'? My little animal."

"Okay, okay. I'll take responsibility." My grip on his chest tightens, the steady drum of his heart banging against my palm. "I don't think I ever kissed him like that. Maybe way back in the beginning... not in a *long* time, though. It felt like a good final 'fuck you'."

"Should've forced him to watch while I made you come then. Really hit him where it hurts."

My laughter shakes the entire bed, leaving tears brimming my eyes as I hold onto Austin. "He wouldn't even recognize what he was looking at because he's definitely never seen me come before."

"Jesus, he missed out. Can't say I'm not a bit happy to hear that though." He kisses my hair before smoothing it down with a gentle stroke. "And now it's my new goal to give you all the orgasms you missed out on over the years."

"Can we start now? You have a lot of making up to do." My lips drag across his neck, smattering kisses and pressing firmly to his pulse point.

"Good thing we have nothing but time," he says, slipping his hand between my legs.

I know I have a bad habit of rushing into things, but I swear I'm going to marry this man.

Waking up, I'm exactly where I belong. In Austin's arms, with my leg strewn across him, listening to his heartbeat's gentle rhythm. And, for the first time in years, I feel completely at ease.

"This is a dream, isn't it?"

Eyes still closed, Austin yawns. "Not a dream, darlin'. Although, I'm not under any obligation to tell you."

"Are you a cop?" I poke his rib and he laughs heartily. The kind of laugh I last heard when he was drunk and walking back to his truck after the rodeo. It's the laugh of somebody who feels as relieved as I do this morning.

My hand trails down his chest, past the slight V tucked into his boxers, and settles along the waistband. My fingers begin grazing the delicate skin underneath. He melts under my soft touch and his eyes flutter open to meet mine.

"Four orgasms down... how many are we shooting for today?" I ask.

"My plan for today is to spend as much time between these gorgeous legs as you'll let me." His lips press against mine and his hand is right back where it belongs. Tucked between my legs, drawing loving circles across my tender clit. "Let me know when you're famished and need a break, beautiful."

With that, he slips out from under me and disappears beneath the thin bedsheet. Creating a path with kisses and beard burn down my stomach, then along the inside of each thigh.

I'm floating. His tongue drifts toward my pussy with slow, affection-ate movement until he's honing in. Small, gentle licks. Sending pleasure washing over my body like a warm blanket. I moan into the pillow and slip my hands under the sheet to grip either side of his head.

"Have I told you how much I love you?" I say as he softly kisses every inch of me. "Because—*fuck*—I'm madly in love with you."

He stops the sleepy kisses for a second. "Keep telling me."

A kaleidoscope of colour coats the backs of my eyelids as his tongue works my hypersensitive clit. It turns out, I'm still recouping from last night. Everything's a thousand times more heightened than normal.

"You're it for me. You're everything." I gasp as he sucks my clit into his mouth. A warmth takes hold at the base of my spine, growing in intensity with each quick flick across my tender skin. He moans, enjoying every second of pleasing me.

"I want to fall asleep tucked in your arms every night for the rest of my life." My back arches as two fingers slide into me. "And wake up exactly like this."

He breaks away for long enough to say, "I can make those things happen."

No mention of *"for as long as you're here"*. Maybe, just maybe, he's finally figuring out that I'm in this for the long haul. His fingers bend, filling me, until I'm fighting for my life. Until his firm hand on my stomach is the only thing keeping me from crawling out of my skin.

"Aus, I love—*oh my God.*" Sweet, flooding relief starts at my scalp and works its way to my toes.

Half an hour passes; two more orgasms send my world spinning and my heart racing. A hum, like TV static, moves across my skin. Austin kisses his way back up my body until his mouth is devouring mine, the sweet taste of my arousal on his tongue. A needy groan rumbles in his throat as I grab hold of his hard cock.

"Fuck me, please. Make me yours," I whisper into him, my body wriggling under his. Straining to feel his cock, praying he'll satiate my need to have him inside me.

"Darlin', you were made for me. You've always been mine and you always will be." The tip of his cock notches at my entrance and I whimper, which makes him smile. "But if my girl needs to be fucked to prove it, who am I to say no?"

He presses into me with a gravelly moan. Austin grabs my ankles, tossing them onto his shoulders. His cock grinds into my body. The grip he has on my thighs should be painful, but it only adds to the tightly coiled warmth deep in my core.

"Fuck, you take me so well." He throws his head back with a forceful thrust that has the headboard smashing into the wall.

Just when I think I can't take another breath without coming, he pulls out and slams back in. The arches of my feet cramp and my legs won't stop vibrating as I writhe under him. I dig my nails into his thighs, looking up at him with weary, bedroom eyes. Every part of my body is delicate and aching—both with desire and exhaustion.

"Aus, I don't know how much more I can take."

"You tappin' out, darlin'?"

"One more," I groan as his pumps slow. "Let me have one more."

He bends down, licking me slowly, and basking in the space between my thighs. Knowing exactly what it'll take to push me over the edge for the final time, he spits directly onto my clit and rubs it with his thumb. My eyes have rolled too far back in my head to watch him spit on his cock, but I hear it just before he plunges back inside me and I come completely fucking unravelled.

My thighs tremble out of control and I'm filled with warmth as his hot cum fills me. My ankles fall from his shoulders and wrap lazily around his waist. Keeping him in place while his chest heaves.

"You okay?" he murmurs against my hair.

"Tired, a bit sore, and the most content I think I've ever been."

Everything feels perfectly in place. The threat of KJ is gone, Austin's still inside me, and his breathy voice is whispering how much he loves me.

"I'm officially famished. But I also don't want to leave here."

"Then let me go get you food." He pushes up and I tighten my legs around him, keeping him exactly where he belongs.

"No, I don't want you to move." I laugh. "I bet Kate would send over a breakfast tray with one of the guys, if we asked."

He smiles and shakes his head. "Do you really want somebody to bring food in here with my cock still inside you? You look stunning, but I'm in a compromising position and would rather my brothers not walk in on this. We have some stuff here. Let me go make you some food."

"Ugh, fine." I let go of my hold on his waist and feel every inch reluctantly pulling away.

"Don't worry, darlin'. We'll get right back to it after I make sure you're fed and taken care of."

As tempting as it is to never leave the confines of Austin's house, it's also not practical. Especially given the lack of real groceries in his fridge. Had I known nearly the entire crew would be waiting at the big house when we showed up for dinner, maybe I would've been okay surviving without food for tonight.

Beryl's the first to pull me into an embrace when we step into the busy kitchen. My eyes shut and I breathe in her comforting scent, taking a second to ignore the weight of everybody staring. "You're okay, honey. Brave, brave girl," she whispers.

The moment her skinny arms begin to ease up, Kate's tugging me into her. I'm a rag doll being torn between the two.

"Okay, let me go, you guys." I laugh and slip out from between them. Only to end up, shockingly, in Denny's arms. Squeezing me so tight, I groan.

"You good, Filly?" Denny asks as he lets go. "That was a bit wild last night."

"Alive and well, thanks to you guys."

"He's a real piece of work. Denny had to give him a couple more smacks on the drive back to town because he wouldn't shut up." Colt strides across the kitchen and wraps an arm around my shoulders in a side hug. "He's long gone, though. Peeled outta town so damn fast. We tried following him down the highway for a while, but he lost us pretty quick."

"Thank you," I say quietly, giving the guys a tight-lipped smile. "I don't know what I would've done if you all hadn't turned up."

"Love ya, Filly," Denny says.

"Always happy to help with giving a guy the whooping he deserves." Red laughs from his seat at the kitchen table. "Since Filly's finally here, can we please eat?"

"Yes, everybody dish up." Beryl gestures to the spread of food I hadn't even noticed set up on the counters. I glance over at Austin, who seems as surprised by the dinner spread and amount of people present as I am.

The guys rush the food like a pack of wild dogs, and I snuggle up next to Beryl. My body relaxes into the circles her palm is rubbing between my shoulder blades.

"Since when does everybody show up here for dinner?" I look at her weathered, peaceful face in my periphery.

"Special occasions. Tonight we're celebrating you. Go get yourself a plate and enjoy, honey. You deserve all the good coming your way now."

Everybody's laughing, joking about Denny's latest buckle bunny conquest, discussing the upcoming rodeo a town over, and teasing Sundial. It's all normal and joyful. And, like every day since I arrived here, I'm wholly consumed by the handsome, grumpy rancher seated across from me. Our feet bump into each other and eyes meet in the golden sunset cast over the table.

The lake's now in second place. Because sitting around this kitchen table, with my family and the love of my life, is easily my favourite place to be.

Epilogue - Austin

I wish I'd gone up the mountain with the crew. It would've been better than pacing my office to the point of leaving wear marks on the antique wood floor. Or I should have cancelled all my work and driven to town with Cecily, since I'm the least productive I've ever been anyway. Every moment of the last two hours has been spent watching the driveway from the open hay door, listening for tires on gravel, and hearing phantom phone notifications.

When the truck finally rounds the bend in the road and starts up the driveway, I sprint down the stairs. Nearly crashing as my boots hit the slick cement at the bottom. I'm waiting in front of the house when she pulls up, my teeth chattering and skin itching with nerves. She's trying, and failing miserably, at keeping a poker face.

"So?" I watch her with bated breath.

"Do I look different? Single?" She twirls around, her yellow floral sundress floating and falling with a swish against her thighs.

"Divorced. *Not single*." I wrap her in my arms, squeezing her warm body and inhaling her sweet hair. "And you're the most gorgeous woman I've ever seen."

"Let's celebrate. I bought champagne—well, I bought the closest sparkling wine Wells Canyon has to champagne." She pulls away to grab the bottle, then skips into the house. By the time I walk in behind her, she's cheerfully filling two wine glasses. And the biggest smile is plastered across her face.

"So, no issues with KJ then? The paperwork was fine?" I sit down on the couch and she joins me, snuggling up under my arm like we do every single night.

"Paperwork was great—the lawyer was a little skeptical about the blood stains. I told him I got a bad papercut signing them. But KJ didn't try to contest it... nothing. Although, I said I didn't want the things I was entitled to in our prenup, so he probably thought he was coming out the winner."

"Good." I take a sip and then lean in to kiss her, overcome with swirling emotions that make my head spin. *It's all finally over.* Her lips smile on mine and we lock eyes. Those baby blues glitter and I swear I've never loved anything as much as her.

She whispers, "Now it's only you and me. Well... for the next half hour. Then we have to go babysit Odessa and Rhett."

"Cockblocked by kids that aren't even mine." Somehow, we've gotten roped into babysitting every other week so Jackson and Kate can have date night. It's a damn good thing they're cute, because I'd rather take Cecily to bed and stay there until this time tomorrow.

"Just gonna have to make it quick." She's straddling my lap and kissing me with reckless abandon. She sinks down into me, rocking her hips to make my cock swirl inside my pants. Unbuckling my belt and shimmying my jeans down my thighs before I even have time to register what's happening. I'm not sure what I did to deserve this. Deserve her.

"You and me," she repeats with a needy whine as her hand grips my quickly hardening shaft. My head crashes back into the couch cushion with a groan. "I think it's about time I repay you for making him sign those papers."

"Darlin', you don't owe—"

She shuts me up with a raw, hungry kiss as her hand pumps my cock aggressively. Sending sharp jolts of intense pleasure through me with each stroke from end to end. My fingertips dig into her thighs and I lift my hips in time with her hand. Her thumb rubs across the tip to catch my dripping precum and, looking me square in the eye, she slips her thumb into her mouth and hollows out her cheeks with a moan.

"Fuck, you're so hot. And you're all mine. Only mine." I kiss her as my hand slides up the inside of her thigh, toward the wet heat between her legs.

Fuck. She's been wearing this damn sundress all over town without any panties underneath?

Her eyes meet mine with a mischievous glimmer. I suck in a breath as my fingers slip across her soaking wet pussy, and she melts into my touch with the sweetest sigh.

"I can't believe I get to be the only one who fucks you like this now." I grab the base of my cock and hold it steady, letting her centre her entrance around my tip.

"It's only ever been you fucking me like this."

Like the filthy, amazing, gorgeous woman she is, she spits in her hand and strokes it along my shaft before sinking down with a loud moan. My chest stutters, missing a beat or two as I revel in the feeling of her.

"So goddamn hot," I groan.

Her hips fit perfectly in my hands. Everything about Cecily seems made for me. We're perfect together. I guide her up and down, providing stability as she rides me until her body's fighting to remain upright. I drop a hand to her clit, working in fast circles. Her moans and shudders become louder and more impatient. The yellow sundress flounces around us, tickling my hypersensitive skin.

Fuck, I love sundress season.

Her pussy squeezes my cock like she never wants to let me go, and I have to bite my lip hard enough to draw blood to keep from coming already. She's riding me like a fucking rodeo queen and, no matter how many times I've been inside her, the feeling is *always* too much for me to handle. One strap on her dress slips from her shoulder and a nudge with my fingers frees her bare breast. Her perky nipple fits perfectly in my mouth. I'm sucking and flicking my tongue across the soft, pink skin until she's gasping for air—her entire body becoming rigid in my arms.

"Oh, fuck. *Yes.*" Her high-pitched voice pierces the air as her head lolls backward, letting her long, blonde hair reach down to her ass. In a drawn-out wave of pleasure, she gushes around my cock.

"Holy fuck, that's my girl. Drench my cock."

I thrust upward, filling her with every inch I have and moving with a new ferocity. My thumb strums across her clit until she's nearing a second release. I could watch her like this all day. She's beautiful and she's all mine. My heart races as I feel the start to her coming undone, contracting to pull my own release out of me.

"Come all over me again. That was so fucking sexy." I barely manage to get the words out and she's gripping my chest, sinking her claws into my flesh, and making a mess on my dick again.

I can't take it anymore. I grab onto her as she wiggles on my cock. Each movement sends stars across my field of vision, and a tingling sensation travels from my balls up through my spine. She's too sensitive to handle another second of this but, like a good girl, she's taking it anyway. When she moans my name, I give in to the building pressure with a hoarse "*fuck*", flooding her with hot cum. Deliriously falling apart while staring up at the best view in the world.

There's a cold blast of air when she lifts up, releasing her firm hold on me, and a slow cum stream trails down her thigh. Without taking a pinch of time to think it through, I drag the tip of my cock across her skin to collect it and raise my hips to push it back inside her. She groans as she falls to my chest, breathing heavily through her nose.

"Did you just—"

"Yeah. Yeah, I did." I have no idea why; an animalistic urge took over. It's not like I'm trying to overthrow her IUD or anything—not yet.

"Okay." The devilish smirk on her face as she remains firmly seated on my cock makes me think she found it as hot as I did.

I'm the luckiest goddamn man alive.

She presses her forehead into mine and takes a slow, hard breath. "I love you, Austin. Thank you for everything."

My name coming from her lips is my favourite sound in the world. Then again, she could probably say anything and the sweetness of her voice would make it my new favourite word. As far as I'm concerned, Cecily is *everything*. She slowly lifts off me once again before curling into my lap.

I shake my head with a smile. "You're never going to learn not to thank me for the bare minimum, are you?"

"You're consistently raising the bar. I have no idea what the bare minimum even is with you anymore."

"Good, that's what I'm going for." It dawns on me; I nearly forgot about the surprise I have for her. She threw me off my game when she hopped on my dick within seconds of getting home. "That reminds me. I have a divorce present for you. Once again, you're proving to be a distraction here."

She sits up straight, the post-sex glow still present on her face. "A what? You didn't have to do that, Aus. You know my feelings about—"

"Relax, I know how you feel about presents. I haven't spent money on you. At least... I haven't *yet*. Wait here a second."

I stroll into the bedroom and fish a large envelope from my sock drawer, returning a brief second later to see her rolling her eyes and laughing.

"I need to start snooping through your drawers, don't I?"

"But think of all the surprises you'd ruin." I plop back down next to her, sliding the manila envelope into her eagerly waiting hands.

As she rips into it, her eyes narrow and she gnaws at the inside of her cheek. "Wait, what is this?"

"Well, I figured if you're still planning to stay." Cecily smacks me on the chest with the thick envelope and I cough as if it knocked the wind out of me. "Okay, okay. I know you're staying. This house was fine for me but... well, for us. And for whatever comes down the road. I thought we'd maybe need something bigger. You know? Something that's ours.

And um, I narrowed it down to a couple different plans I thought you might like so you can pick. There are a few potential building sites we can choose from, too. So..."

Dead silence as she stares down at the mountain of paperwork in her lap. *Damn, I have a bad habit of just gifting this girl paperwork she needs to take care of...*

"Darlin'? Say something, please."

Her eyes bat up to mine, tears brimming her lower lashes. The corner of her lip lifts in the smallest gesture. "A house? You can't be ser—this can't be real. That's—God, I don't know what to say. That's not just a small divorce present. You don't have to do th—"

"I do." I cut her off. "You deserve a nice house, a nice kitchen, a shower big enough to fuck in, and room for babies or dogs or whatever you want."

"Babies or dogs or whatever I want, hey? You gonna make an honest woman out of me before you get ahead of yourself?"

"Jesus, woman. You've only been legally able to marry somebody new for an hour and you're already laying the pressure on me?" I can't help but smile. Marrying her has consumed my every thought since the day I realized I was in love with her. "If I was certain you weren't a bit gun shy about marriage, I'd take you down to the courthouse today."

"If you weren't gun shy about proposing, I'd say yes."

"You'd say yes?" I shift so I can fully see her eyes, the blues looking right into my soul with a playful expression.

"Obviously. Don't tell me you didn't know that."

"So, let me get this straight. *You will. I will.* What are we doing sitting here right now then?"

She laughs and kisses me, swiping her champagne-soaked tongue along my bottom lip, then pressing through to tangle around my tongue.

"Hold your horses, I'm not racing down to the courthouse to get married on the same afternoon they filed my divorce paperwork. Imagine the small town gossip."

I don't give a shit about the busybodies. It's not like everybody in town doesn't already know we're together. Hell, two weeks ago we spent the entire day at the Wells Canyon rodeo. Holding hands, kissing, dancing. Everyone knows she's my girl.

"Okay, fine. You deserve a proper proposal, anyway. With a beautiful ring and a whole prepared speech. And maybe not with my cock still half-hard."

"Or your cum running down my thigh. Really, Aus. I don't need fancy, proper shit. You cut down the family lilacs. You forced my shitty ex-husband to sign divorce papers. You've taken care of me every single day since I got here. Now you're offering to build me a house. I think you've made your fair share of love proclamations."

"Even still." I take a knee in front of her. "Darlin', this isn't the time or place I planned on doing this. But I need you to understand I'm not apprehensive in the least about proposing to you. So I'll ask you here now to prove that. Then we'll go pick out a ring to buy with *our* money. And I'll do this all over again properly."

I clear my throat and grab her hands, resting them on her trembling knees. Though I have no idea why she's nervous.

Oh, never mind. I'm the one shaking.

"When I first met you I didn't think I could ever feel this way about somebody. I didn't think I wanted to—until you. You've been *everything* since the day you turned up here. The first thing on my mind when I wake up, and the dreamy thought that lulls me to sleep. You're in my head, knowing me better than anybody ever has, and you constantly push me to be a better man." My hand lazily strokes the soft skin of her thigh as I talk. "Now here I am, once again doing something I swore to myself I never would. All because of you. I'll do anything you want me to, Cecily. For the rest of my life, I'll do anything to prove I deserve you. I love you and I so badly want to be yours forever, darlin'. Will you *please* marry me?"

She wipes a stray tear the second it falls from her eye, and then another. She blinks up at the ceiling for a second before flitting her eyes back to meet mine.

God, she's perfect.

"You're mine and I'm yours. And I *cannot wait* to be your wife."

Her lips brush mine like they have a million times before, with a hint of something different. *My wife.*

Bonus Epilogue - Cecily

R ain pelts the windows at a ninety-degree angle and I lean against the cold windowpanes in the front door, peering between droplets to see the barn. The lights are on and there appears to be movement, so I release a pent-up exhale and sink into my heels. *The boys made it home safely.* Thankfully, my Not-A-Cowboy husband isn't typically out for long stretches with the ranch hands—I don't know how Kate handles never knowing if Jackson is safe when they're riding in weather like this. Especially when they're gone overnight to move the herd long distances. Sure, they have satellite phones, but that doesn't mean they're great about checking in.

At least this was the final day bringing cattle home for the winter. After a few long weeks barely seeing Austin, I can't wait to curl up with him in bed for the next... two, three, or more days. Considering how crappy I've been feeling recently, I'd love to snuggle under the covers straight through to spring. Warmed by the wood fireplace in our bedroom and his big arms wrapped around me.

I throw open the door and lean against the frame. Despite the rain and wind, it's pleasantly warm out for a mid-October evening. The fresh air eases the near-constant migraine I've had all week. Seeing two shadowy frames walking toward home liberates me from the small kernel of anxiety still in my chest. Austin and his dad. Because somehow having some security in his life over the last three years—combined with seeing me put effort into a relationship with my parents—inspired him to reach out on the anniversary of his mom's death. Rather than beer and *Happy Days*, we actually attended the family dinner. Then Bennett offered to stick around and help bring the cattle home for winter. And, to everyone's amazement, Austin said yes.

They're far from perfect, but watching them walking side-by-side and hearing their muffled voices makes me tear up. Maybe it's the hormones.

I can't find it in me to wait for him to be out of the rain before I'm moving in his direction. My feet barely make contact with the front porch steps, careening toward him. Launching into an embrace on the front lawn.

"Hi, Bennett," I call out over Austin's shoulder, to the man who looks like Jackson but acts exactly like Austin. He wordlessly waves and continues on to the big house.

"I missed you." I kiss my husband, rubbing his scruffy jaw with my palm. "God, I missed you."

He laughs, pressing his lips against mine. "I missed you too, darlin'. I've only been gone two days, though."

The rain's already soaked my shirt through and my hair's clinging to my neck. I might catch a cold out here but I don't care. I kiss him like he's been gone for a year, legs wrapped around his waist, feeling the warmth of his hands on my ass.

"Feels like it was longer," I admit. It has. Normally when he's gone, it's bearable. Not this trip.

"Let's get outta the rain and you can keep telling me how much you missed me." His hands slide along my thighs to my knees and he slowly untangles our bodies. I reluctantly let go, setting my feet on the squishy ground and staring up at him.

When we're in the warm house, he peels his clothes off to take a shower. He's drenched from the rain, smelling like horses and sweat, and flecks of dirt speckling his face and hands. He's the most gorgeous man I've ever personally witnessed, and I sit on the edge of our bed, beaming at him.

"Somebody's in a good mood." He tosses his clothes into the laundry hamper. "I don't think I've seen a grin quite that damn big before."

"I'm happy you're back."

"Well then let me go take a shower and I'll show you how happy I am to be back, okay?"

He leans in to kiss me softly and I run my hands through his grungy, dripping-wet hair. Holding his face close to mine, I take a nervous breath.

"Okay... daddy." I bite my lip, waiting to see if he'll catch on. I can't wait another minute.

He smirks and raises an eyebrow at me. *Damnit.* I'm fairly certain he thinks I'm being kinky, not understanding what I'm trying to hint at.

"Just thought I'd see how the name suited you. Think you'd be more of a *papa*? Nah. *Father*? No, too stuffy. Yeah... you know, Aus, I think daddy's going to suit you best."

"Wait." Kneeling at the edge of the bed so we're eye level, his eyes grow wide as they search mine. "Are you saying what I think you're saying?"

I nod, feeling his hands already grabbing either side of my face to kiss me deeply, the cool metal of his wedding band pressing into my jaw. My lips part under the pressure of his, breathing him in. When he pulls away, my eyes flutter open just in time to catch him quickly rubbing away watery eyes.

"Aus, don't cry." I swipe my thumbs across his cheeks and do my best to blink back my own tears. My hormones are already getting the better of me.

"Get used to it, darlin'. I'm pretty sure this won't be the last time I get emotional about our baby—*holy fuck. Our baby.* That feels surreal to say.

I love you so damn much. Thank you. Thank you, my beautiful girl." He places at least a hundred kisses across my face like he's scattering stars in the sky.

"So you're happy about this?" I tease. There's never been a single doubt in my mind about how he would take this news. Over a year after having my IUD removed, we'd come to terms with the idea that kids might not be in the cards for us. Since the second I found out yesterday morning, I've been counting down the minutes until he got home so I could tell him. And time felt like it was standing still. I've been unable to leave the house or speak to anybody, knowing I'd accidentally let it slip.

He pushes a lock of hair behind my ear. "The happiest I've ever been. You make me the happiest man every day and now *this*. Why wouldn't I be? I'm not exactly a godly man, but I've been praying every single day for the last year for this."

His warm lips, with an uncontrollable smile, press against mine. "It's still what you want, right?"

I kiss him back softly. "It is."

It really, really is. He threads his fingers through mine and, when Austin Wells places a single kiss on my stomach, I'm the most alive I've ever been.

If you enjoyed this story, please consider leaving a review!

Reader reviews are so instrumental in the success of indie authors. An honest review posted wherever you're most comfortable (Amazon, Goodreads, TikTok, Instagram, etc.) means the world to me.

And follow along on social media (@baileyhannahwrites everywhere) to be in the loop for Wells Ranch's next love story.

Acknowledgements

First and foremost, thank you to my incredibly supportive husband. I told you I wanted to publish a book and, while you didn't know you were signing up to listen to me run through every plot point and character trait, you took it all in stride. Including hearing about the multiple completed novels I wrote before finally taking the leap and publishing this one... Sorry! I love you!

Big hugs to my sassy and sweet daughter. You may not know how to read yet (nor will you be allowed to read this for at least fifteen years), but you're my biggest inspiration. In wanting to teach you to take risks and chase your dreams, I realized I need to do the same. Without you, Odessa Wells wouldn't be the feisty four-year-old that she is.

To Brooke, for putting up with my late-night venting, working through plot holes with me, and helping keep my spirits high when imposter syndrome is dragging me down. Girl... how the hell did we meet via our dog's Instagram accounts and realize we're basically the same person?

My incredibly supportive parents—you always gave me so much encouragement when I was a little kid writing my first books. You helped instill a dream that I'm excited to finally be pursuing twenty years after the fact. Mom, I know you're reading this even after I grimaced and said not to multiple times... let's never speak of the content in this book.

My amazing beta readers! Without you, this book would be a shell of what it is. Your feedback, critiques, and swooning helped push me. I'm a better writer because of all of you.

Speaking of which, Naomi and Andrea. Your editing really solidified that this was finally the book I was going to publish. Naomi, you questioned every little detail of this story and that thoroughness really brought the characters to life. Andrea, you're a magician. You managed to catch errors that my hundred self-edits and half-dozen beta readers missed, and *thank Ggod* you did. And thank you for catching/fixing issues about *ahem* blowjob logistics.

To Acacia from Ever After Cover Design. Thank you for making a cover that makes me want to squeal and kick my feet in the air every time I see it. You took my "I don't know what I want, but lilacs and cowboys are nice" and came up with THIS?!?!

And to all the incredible ARC readers—last but definitely not least. I could do the work to write a book, have a million people beta/edit it, and I would be nowhere without the readers. Especially those who care enough to review my book, scream the title from the rooftops, and share all over social media. Thank you for supporting my debut novel. You all mean more to me than you could ever know.

About the Author

Bailey Hannah is a Canadian romance author. She loves to write strong heroines and rugged men who aren't afraid to love their woman hard.

Born and raised in small town British Columbia, she loves to add rural Canadian flair (dirt roads, rodeos, ketchup chips, and a two-four of beer) to her stories.

She lives with her husband, daughter, two dogs, and chickens. A chronic middle-of-the-night writer, during the day Bailey can be found camping, baking sourdough, or being her daughter's chauffeur.

a amazon.com/author/baileyhannah

♪ tiktok.com/@baileyhannahwrites

◎ instagram.com/baileyhannahwrites